SIN
AGAINST
The RACE

SIN AGAINST The RACE

Gar McVey-Russell

To Pam,
Thank you for being wonderful.
Love & hugs,

gamr books
Oakland, California

Oakland
2017

gamr books
gamrbooks@thegarspot.com

First Edition Published 2017 by gamr books

Printed in the United States of America

ISBN: 978-0-9993815-9-2
E-ISBN: 978-0-9993815-1-9

Library of Congress Control Number: 2017914260

Cover design by Teddi Black/teddiblack.com
Interior design by Megan McCullough

In memory of

Louise McVey Russell
(1928 – 1996)

Jefferson D. Russell
(1926 – 2006)

Robert A. Russell
(1955 – 2014)

ACKNOWLEDGEMENTS

I give thanks every day to my wonderful family, who made me who I am today: my parents JD and Louise Russell, and my siblings Tania, Robert, JK, and Louis. Thank you for your warmth, love, guidance, and inspiration.

Special thanks and respect go to my OG readers, Alan Miller and Louise Russell, who both read the original version of this story. It evolved to where it is today thanks to their input. Thanks also to Alexandra Soiseth, who provided professional feedback in the early stages. And I am grateful to Jane Barbarow, Beth Montano, and Matthew Florence for reading the beta draft.

Editor Mark Rhynsburger provided invaluable feedback and whipped the manuscript into proper shape. My thanks, always. Teddi Black produced a beautiful cover that made this labor of love real for me. Megan McCullough brought the book to professional standards with the interior design.

Music guided me throughout the writing process and jazz forms the backbone of the story. Some of the artists whose work inspired me receive a shout out in the story. Buy their music. Much of my knowledge of jazz comes from listening to the amazing folks at KCSM—Jazz 91, San Mateo, California. Whenever I got stuck, someone at the station seemed to play just the right tune to get me back on track again. Thanks for all the wonderful music.

And to the one who means everything to me, who supports and encourages me, who I've often called my "stage mother spouse," my beloved husband Peter, words simply aren't enough. *Du bist für immer in meinem Herzen.*

ONE

S IRENS BROKE ALFONSO'S SLEEP, BUT WHEN HE AWOKE they'd gone. His mind switched on, he again found himself in the desert of another sleepless night. Disasters stirred in the dimly lit alleys of his mind. Sweat sopped his forehead. Closed eyes longed for sleep. Weariness eventually drifted him into what his cousin Carlton described as a halfway to dawn state, neither dark nor light, neither asleep nor awake. He wanted to linger in that state for as long as possible and cocoon himself in its ambiguities.

Halfway to dawn is a Billy Strayhorn expression, Carlton explained.

Alfonso wasn't familiar with the jazz legend. Who is Billy Strayhorn? he asked. His cousin scowled and said, You better get an education, young man! That night, they listened to "Lush Life," "Chelsea Bridge," and other wonders.

Carlton often visited him halfway to dawn. All of their moments—tender, sweet, sublime, catty, silly, confounding, fierce—coalesced into one. None overpowered the other. A blues requiem whose stanzas were a work in progress.

1

When dawn proper began announcing its presence through his bedroom window, Alfonso denied it by placing his pillow over his head. Then his iPhone vibrated on the nightstand. He fought the urge to reach for it. Halfway to dawn needed to last just a little bit longer.

Moments later, a different sound jostled him. He recognized the heavy footsteps as either his father's or his sister Belinda's. Before he could decipher which, he heard his father's voice outside his bedroom door, at the top of the stairs.

"No, no, that's alright. What's going on? ... No! Really? ... Seriously? ... It's burning all the way down? ... Oh, man! ... No, you did not call me too early ... You made my day, my friend! You made my day!"

His father descended the stairs. The words became fainter.

His iPhone buzzed again. He couldn't ignore it a second time, not with his father also up and excited about something. He grabbed it off the nightstand. The time flashed 6 a.m.

Two text messages from the local news station jerked him upright.

"Holy shit!" his dry voice croaked.

Alfonso hurriedly dressed and stuffed what he needed for the day into his backpack, though the first day of classes was the last thing on his mind. He made a point of rushing past his father's study on his way out the front door so that his passage would go unnoticed.

Did my dad really say, "You made my day"?

He descended the hill on Beacon Street where his family lived and wound his way from Peele to 44th to Stevens, until he reached the northeast corner of Huckleberry Park at Stevens and 45th. A brisk walk west down 45th brought him to the park's stone gateway at Carver Street. He paused, then entered. Trees lined the path as the grade descended. It eventually leveled out, emptying into a large, grassy field.

In the not too long ago, he and his father rushed furtively out of the house together and came to this grassy field to play baseball. The early hours of a steamy summer morning required that they do nothing less. They snuck out to avoid his mother's disapproving stare. She hated that they played with a hardball, even if Alfonso wore protective gear. Take the softball, she'd say if she caught them leaving. They did, but only for show. During game time, they always kept the ball small, round, tightly wound, regulation down to the last stitch.

Walking through the middle of the field, he could picture his father's tall, imposing frame clad in black shorts and a gray tank top striking a familiar pose: body in profile, head turned toward his objective, the ball clasped close to his chest. Alfonso, in deep concentration, held his bat at the ready. When his father played in college, they called him the Wizard, because he made balls disappear. No one saw them as they whizzed by. The years had changed nothing. His father still had a mean fastball. Whenever Alfonso connected, they set their eyes skyward, following the ball like Charlie Brown followed his kite, with hope that they'd be able to track and retrieve it so that they could send it soaring again.

What if someone got hurt? Would he say "You made my day" then?

He veered right, trudged across the damp grass toward his destination.

Over the summer, the Huckleberry Community Clinic had become a living memorial, a place of homage. He went by it nightly after it had closed for the day to glimpse at what his cousin had helped to bring into the world. During each visit, he stared at the founders' photo that hung just inside the door, taken on opening day. They stood in front of their new space, faces beaming brighter than the sunlight that struck them. And at the far end of the group, sitting down with a reserved smile on his gaunt face, was Carlton. Alfonso didn't attend the opening ceremony, but his cousin didn't give him grief about it. *I'm still taking your ass down there to get your HIV test!* He told Carlton that he was looking forward to it. Two months later, Carlton was dead.

He went up an embankment and through a thicket of trees, reaching the park's western border at Lincoln Avenue. He hid in the bushes. From there, he witnessed chaos.

Across the street, smoke billowed from the smashed-up front of the clinic. Broken furniture spilled onto the sidewalk. Water sprayed hard into what had been the tastefully appointed reception area. Firefighters rushed everywhere. Broken glass crunched under boots. Flames shot out an apartment window above the clinic. Barely dressed refugees from the building stood on the sidewalk, dazed. Paramedics triaged in the street. A baby howled. Fire engine lights cast the area in red.

Alfonso choked on tears and soot.

Through his teary eyes, he recognized faces from his cousin's world also dealing with the fire. Mrs. Parker, wearing a long black dress, sat in the middle of the street next to an ambulance, helping a young boy with an oxygen tank. She was Carlton's favorite nurse and his cousin hated when they forced her to retire. But retirement clearly had not diminished her sense of duty.

"Fierce!" Alfonso muttered.

Then he saw a familiar bald white dude run up, wearing his trademark jeans, white T, and leather biker jacket. His heart sank. Bingo Cincinnati, sweet bear-hugging Bingo, a cofounder of the clinic. The leatherman hung out frequently at Carlton's apartment. Alfonso loved his handlebar mustache, which Carlton often quipped came mail order from the old *Drummer* leather magazine. *No, dear, this is a Tom of Finland exclusive,* Bingo always retorted. His laugh and smile were infectious.

That morning Alfonso saw neither. "I have to protect our patients' records!" he heard Bingo scream as police restrained him from entering the charred inferno. Then Bingo just stood with his hands over his face.

How he wanted to rush to Bingo so that they could support each other. But thoughts of his father kept him in check. Showing his face now, in this crowd, was impossible.

"You made my day." About this, he fucking said, "You made my day."

His father *never* approved of the Huckleberry Community Clinic's presence in his district and often disparaged it as "that damn needle exchange clinic." Small wonder Councilman Alfonso Rutherford "Ford" Berry, II danced an early morning jig—and he'd expect others, particularly members of his family, particularly his namesake and heir apparent, to dance along with him.

In frustration, Alfonso turned himself away and walked back toward the center field of the park.

Carver Street, 8 a.m.
Sammy Turner's Corner Grocery

Sammy bent over to pick up the Monday papers as he entered his store at 44th and Carver. He threw the stacks on their racks still bound by their tight plastic straps. He resolved to get back to them after a while. Before doing a damned thing, though, he needed his morning cup of blues coffee. He walked to the back room to set himself upon this ritual task.

Making blues coffee was more like invoking an incantation than following a recipe. And that morning he needed his blues old school, so he put on the disc featuring Alberta Hunter, Lucille Hegamin, and Victoria Spivey. Miss Spivey soon rang out with "Black Snake Blues." For authentic blues coffee, he used his old tin drip pot on an electric burner in the storeroom at the back of the store. As soon as he got it going, he returned to his store-opening chores.

Charlotte Hunter arrived right on cue, the usual bag of croissants in hand. She often shared Monday blues coffee with him. He figured she would arrive in short order, given the day's events. She walked straight to the storeroom without pause. Sammy was sitting at the low end of the counter when she returned. He waited for her verdict, since she took it straight.

"It's a keeper," she said.

Sammy nodded and took a sip. She always added just the right amount of cream to his.

"I can't believe this shit, Charlotte. I just can't believe it."

She sat silently.

"Have you been there?"

"Didn't have the heart. Liz and I both couldn't stop crying." Sammy handed her a tissue. She dabbed her eyes and blew her nose. "I hate to think what that man is going to say on the news about it."

Sammy scowled at the Councilman Berry reference.

"'I won',' he said.

Charlotte shook her head and dunked a croissant into her mug.

Alberta Hunter began singing about reaping and sowing when her doppelgänger walked through the door. Mrs. Parker not only shared Alberta's deep seasoned voice, but also had worked as a nurse well past normal retirement age. Ash discolored her coif of straight white hair and her long black dress, but she otherwise looked her usual stately self.

"Got any more of that coffee back there, Sammy?"

"Mrs. Parker!" Charlotte said.

"Great Dizzy!" Sammy said. "What happened to you?"

"You weren't at that fire, were you?"

"Yes, I was there, and what a heartbreaking sight it was. Just heartbreaking. That beautiful, beautiful center destroyed just like that. It's a low-down, dirty shame."

"That it is, Mrs. Parker," Sammy said.

"It makes me so angry I could spit. All that hard work. Poor Bingo was there. He looked like a train hit him."

"But what happened to you?" Charlotte asked.

"Oh, nothing. I guess I look a mess. I was just helping them out some." She sat on the crate next to Sammy behind the counter and told them about the little boy she saw crying and wheezing so loud she could hear it over all the commotion. "Asthma attack. I got some albuterol and an oxygen tank from the paramedics. I cradled him in the middle of the road until he started breathing normal again."

"Let me get you a mug, Mrs. Parker," Charlotte said. "You take cream and sugar, don't you?"

"Yes, Charlotte, just a little of both, please. I told the paramedics that I was a nurse and that the boy was my godson. Heh! At least I was half telling the truth."

Alfonso wandered aimlessly, then Carver Street beckoned. Going to *that street* was a huge taboo growing up. No one had to explain why—the programming was hardwired into the DNA. Carlton, of course, advised him otherwise.

You need an education. Go and meet Sammy, young man! He's the den mother for all the neighborhood children coming out into the life.

Jazz and coffee greeted Alfonso at the door. He recognized the soothing pulse of Duke Ellington's "Happy Reunion" and lingered a moment to soak in Paul Gonsalves as he began his sax solo. Scanning the little store for the first time, he found it quite ordinary looking. Narrow aisles. Produce bins. Freezers in the back. To his right, he saw Charlotte on a stool behind the register at the high end of the counter. She looked the same, her intense brown eyes softened by her button nose, her face framed by her contoured Afro. He saw Mrs. Parker again, sitting at the low end of the counter. And he saw Sammy sitting in between them. Alfonso had never seen Sammy before, but he looked just like he had pictured based on all that Carlton had told him: large build, round face, slightly graying hair, an old school, hepcat goatee under his lower lip. He looked at them looking at him, a skinny black kid with a dull Afro and sullen face.

Sammy called out his name, which startled him. The storekeeper squeezed his girth behind Mrs. Parker and walked out in front of the counter. He gave Alfonso a warm hug. Neither wanted to let go. The embrace had been a long time coming.

"It's so good to see you, baby," Sammy said.

"It feels like I lost him all over again!" Alfonso began sobbing.

Sammy held him tight, rubbing his head and back. Charlotte came around and joined them.

"I'm so sorry, sweetie," she said.

He switched his embrace to Charlotte somewhat self-consciously—mindful of a history not his, yet a part of him—but felt only sympathy from her. Carlton always told him that Charlotte was the real deal, always straight, always fair.

"You want some coffee, baby?" Sammy asked. "We finished the first pot but the next one should be ready now."

"It sure smells good."

Sammy went to the storeroom. Alfonso turned toward Charlotte again.

"I can't wrap my brain around this. It was there, last night. I walked past it. I just can't believe it."

"None of us can, Alfonso. We're all in grief."

Sammy brought up a mug. "Oh, I forgot to ask if you take anything in it."

"Naw, just black."

"Yep, just like Carlton!" Mrs. Parker said. "He always said keep it hot and keep it black!"

"Ooo, this is good," Alfonso said. "This is from a tin drip pot, isn't it?"

"You know it," Sammy replied.

"My aunt has one. I like the way it chars the coffee."

"That's the blues effect. It ain't blues coffee unless it's been bruised a bit, to get some attitude. The trick, though, is not to bruise it too much or it will get bitter."

"Well," Mrs. Parker said, standing, "I think I better get home and wash up. Otherwise I'll smell like soot all day, and I certainly don't want that. Charlotte, do you think you can walk me home?"

"Of course."

"You sure you don't want us to call a cab?" Sammy asked.

"Naw. Better to walk. Need the exercise. Sammy, thank you so much for the coffee. It's still the best in the Huck."

"Anytime, Mrs. Parker."

As she passed Alfonso, she stopped to give him a hug. "Take care, sugar. Come by and see me whenever you want. You know where to find me."

"Thank you, Mrs. Parker."

They exited the store, leaving Sammy and Alfonso alone. It remained an eerie, still morning, as if the fire had sucked the oxygen out of the whole neighborhood.

"Come join me behind the counter, baby," Sammy said. Alfonso obliged, sitting where Mrs. Parker had, dropping his backpack on the ground. He stared forward at nothing in particular while taking slow sips. Even in silence, Sammy provided comfort. Alfonso found him an easy presence to be in, someone who did not force himself on you, but took you at your own pace.

"This summer's been hell," Alfonso finally uttered.

"Yes," Sammy agreed.

"I'm crying for real. But part of me is just so angry. What the hell is going on? First Carlton. Then Eddie."

Carlton lit up brightest when Eddie was in the room. He snapped and clapped loudest when Eddie threw it down, reading this person and that person. The music funked hardest with Eddie in the house dancing his tail off. Alfonso loved it when Eddie dropped by.

Iron bars and alcoholic rage silenced Eddie, barely two months after Carlton died. Four weeks in a coma, still no response. It happened at the cruisy northeast corner of Huckleberry Park.

"Now this fire destroys all that he lived for! His final act on this world, gone! It's like he's being fucking erased!"

He squeezed shut his eyes, not wanting to lose it again. Sammy gave him a tissue, with which he blew his nose.

"In my family, Carlton was invisible," Alfonso continued. "Even at his own funeral. The reverend said his name twice. I counted. Then at the reception, at my aunt and uncle's, no one mentioned him. It was just like any other family get-together, like Thanksgiving or something. Food, drinks, kids playing on the grass. It wasn't a funeral."

Sammy shook his head.

"Aunt Emmy, Carlton's mother, wouldn't even acknowledge me. That was harsh. She's like a grandmother to me, you know, since she's so much older than my mother. And I never knew my grandmothers. But she looked straight through me when I stood in front of her, wouldn't say a word. No one saw how upset I was.

Finally, I was like, fuck this shit. I stormed home, went to my room, slammed the door, and pumped Billie Holiday as loud as I felt like and cried my fucking eyes out."

"Gloomy Sunday" had filled Alfonso's head during the service while the organist played anonymous dirges, dreck that failed to capture the complexities of Carlton's life. His cousin often sought salvation from Billie's bruised singing, "Gloomy Sunday," "Some Other Spring," "Good Morning Heartache," others.

"We played lots of Lady Day at the remembrance we held for Carlton," Sammy said.

"I so wanted to go to that," Alfonso sighed. "When my family got home, my mom came up to the room. You know what she said? She told me it was disrespectful to leave like I did. I screamed at her, 'Disrespectful?' and slammed the door in her face. I had never done that to my mother." He took another sip, looked into his emptying mug. "And then later on, after they all had dinner, my father came. He said I made such a scene, that I made my mother upset, that I was being too emotional, that none of this was gonna bring Carlton back, so that I'd better get over it. By this point, I was like, yeah, whatever. I spent the whole summer locked in my room."

"Mmm, mmm, mmm," Sammy intoned.

"I've become as invisible as Carlton. Maybe I've always been and I'm just now realizing it. You know what I'm saying?"

Sammy patted the young man's hand as it clutched his mug. "Have you ever read *The Souls of Black Folk*, by Du Bois?"

"Yeah. It's like a bible in my family."

"Uh-huh. I read it while hitchhiking to the March on Washington."

Alfonso turned to face Sammy. "Hitchhike? For real?"

"I was young, alright?"

Alfonso giggled.

"It was a different time. The whole atmosphere was charged. You could smell it and taste it. Anyway, as I read it I got more and more excited. I kept saying, 'Yeah, this is my life. It's my life!' And I really wanted to talk to someone about it, but I couldn't. 'Cause I wasn't talking about being black—I was talking about being gay. Everything he said about the masks, the veil, the dual identity, all that, that was how I felt! I'm sitting around a bunch of black folks, reading Du Bois…"

"And you couldn't talk to no one about it."

"And I couldn't talk to no one about it."

They stared at each other.

"And, you know," Sammy continued, "Du Bois died the night before the march. So folks liked that I was reading it. But I couldn't tell them what was really going on for me."

"That's amazing, Sammy."

"It was amazing."

"You should have written about it."

"I did."

"Really? Was it published anywhere?"

"Oh, no, honey, I didn't write no essay. No one wanted to hear stuff like that from some know-nothing sweet pea. If you wanna know how we were treated back then, read Eldridge Cleaver. Naw, I wrote a tune called 'The Lavender Veil Blues.'"

"Now wait," Alfonso said, shifting on his seat. "Carlton never told me that you wrote music."

Sammy smiled. "Didn't he?" He stood up. "You want some more coffee?" He took both of their mugs and walked to the back room.

Alfonso absorbed the music playing. How comforting he found it, a piece of his cousin's soul immune to erasure, beyond invisibility, living, vibrant.

Carlton gave him jazz. *Take all the music before the vultures come.* He had resisted previous offers. But the "vultures" comment got to him, as Carlton no doubt calculated it would. More than anything, his cousin wanted his immediate family to enter an empty apartment after he died, so that they would receive exactly what they had given. Nothing. *Defy the vultures* became his last rallying cry, one Alfonso in the end could not resist, even as he resisted the end.

"Is that Johnny Hodges?" he called out.

"Nope," Sammy said, walking back with the mugs refilled. "It's called 'Checkered Hat.' It's a eulogy for Hodges after he passed."

"Carlton told me he learned jazz from you, but he never said you're a musician. What do you play?"

"I don't play no more. Honey, that was a long-ass time ago." He took a sip of coffee. Alfonso wouldn't stop staring. "Drums," he finally said.

"Bet you still can."

Sammy said nothing, downed more coffee.

The sax sounded eerily like Hodges's distinctive embouchure, as if he were being channeled, obliging his lifelong colleagues with one last performance. Alfonso found himself shifting side to side with the easy swing of the piece.

"I hear you're quite the dancer, like Carlton."

"He tell you that?" Alfonso smirked. His sashaying stilled.

"He said you studied it seriously once."

"Yeah. Once."

He felt Sammy's stare, but would not return it.

"I had my reasons why I stopped drumming. I wonder now, all these years later, if they were good ones."

In their safe space on the field, Alfonso once asked his father if he had ever thought about going pro. A silent smile appeared. After a few more tosses back and forth with the ball, he mentioned that major league scouts once saw him pitch a no-hitter. No, really? Seriously? What happened? The silent smile reappeared, followed by mumbled words about it being a long time ago.

Someone entered.

"Hello, Miss Vera," Sammy said.

"Hi, Sammy." Her clipped diction matched her pace to the refrigerators in the back.

She wore black jeans and boots, a pale-white top, and a light-blue windbreaker jacket. A golden headscarf, matching her light-brown complexion, covered her hair. When she returned with orange juice, her camera came into view, dangling around her neck.

Vera's camera keeps it real, Carlton explained. She's recording our history, our essence.

Sammy stood at the register to ring her out. She reached into her pocket for bills. Their motions were robotic. Neither said anything. Alfonso wondered if they would have spoken more freely if he hadn't been there. As she pocketed some loose change, she looked down at him, an intense stare, like a search beam.

"You're Alfonso, aren't you?" Her voice sounded bourbon-soaked, just as Carlton described.

"Oh, I'm sorry, I thought you two knew each other," Sammy said.

She moved her camera gently to the side, then reached down over the counter to embrace Alfonso. He did not expect it, but reached up and hugged her as well. When she stood up, a small smile softened her face.

"You going to or coming from?" Alfonso asked.

"Going to. Take care, Alfonso."

He nodded.

"Bye, Miss Vera," Sammy said.

"Miss Vera!" Alfonso called out as she opened the door. "I was just wondering if you could maybe make me a copy of that photo, you know, the one that you took of them at the clinic when it opened?"

"Of course, sweetie. Sammy, I'll leave it with you, alright?" He nodded. She flashed another smile before going outside, her clipped pace taking her southbound.

"Sammy, why did Miss Vera give up modeling?"

"She didn't give it up. She just got tired of it. I think ultimately she always wanted to do photography."

Sammy walked behind Alfonso to get to the stereo. Alfonso looked up at the wall behind him and saw photos he hadn't noticed earlier. One was of Charlotte and Carlton, sitting where he sat now, laughing their asses off. Next to that was a photo of a younger, skinnier Sammy standing in front of his store, leaning against the glass, his arms folded, a beret on his head. Above that hung various awards, a business license, other official notices.

Strayhorn's "Day Dream" came on, the composer himself at the piano. Alfonso closed his eyes.

"This is one of my favorites," he said. He loved how blue chords kept the ethereal piece earthbound, a sacred dance performed by fallen angels.

"Carlton lived," he said. "I want to live, too, Sammy."

Mrs. Parker kept her eyes forward, silently noting, as she always did, the further deterioration of the park—the graffiti, the broken pavement, the crumbling band shell surrounded by a dilapidated chain-link fence. She normally eulogized its yesteryears whenever she walked through it with someone, but uttered none of her familiar verses during their long walk. When the 48th Street brownstones came into view, she stopped suddenly and turned to face Charlotte.

"You've got to get rid of that man," she said, referring to Councilman Berry. "This area can't survive four more years of his neglect. It's been eight years since you last ran against him and I know that ain't a whole lotta time, but a lot has changed since then. The demographics have changed. People moving in want to see a real, thriving neighborhood. Not the mess it is now. Besides destroying a beautiful health center, you know what else that fire did? It gave us another boarded-up storefront and that's the last thing this neighborhood needs.

"Anyway, he can't pull the same stunts he pulled eight years ago and get away with it. Attitudes have changed. Folks won't take kindly to that sort of bigotry no more. People respect you. They respect the work you've done. He can't take that away from you."

She paused long enough to catch a breath and register the reaction on Charlotte's face.

"You're worried about Alfonso, aren't you, sugar?"

"He looks so fragile."

"Sugar, we all knew this day would come sooner or later. Alfonso is slowly coming into his own. And that's a fragile time for anyone. But he'll be alright in the end, I know he will. How his father will react, that's for him to decide. There ain't nothing any of us can do about it. Now, I've said my piece. And I'm not gonna talk about it no more, alright? I promise. But I'm asking you, I'm asking with all my heart to at least think about it. Please do that, Charlotte. Talk to Liz and think about it. OK?"

"Alright, Mrs. Parker. I promise. I'll think about it."

"Good. Good. Thank you for walking me through the park, Charlotte. I'll be alright from here."

Charlotte waved as Mrs. Parker crossed 48th Street to her brownstone. Whenever Sammy gave her crap about running again, which he did repeatedly, she usually dismissed him with *Don't start with me, Samuel Turner.* But somehow she didn't mind hearing it from Mrs. Parker. In fact, she was flattered by her breathless appeal.

She slowly turned around, weighted by the events of the day, and headed back to the north side of the park.

Two

A LFONSO BOARDED THE LINE 21 BUS AND FOUND IT already crowded with comatose students heading in for the first day at State University. He slowly migrated toward the back and saw Roy Prince sitting on one of the inward-facing seats south of the back door, his face buried in his cell. He looked taller, still skinny, still dressed sharp. He accented his outfit with a red vest, a silver feather earring on his left lobe, and a smallish black trilby cocked back, revealing his short red hair. Carlton described Roy as coming out of the womb with zero fucks to give, his first word likely a high-flung snap with lips pursed. He began hanging at Sammy's as a precocious 10-year-old, with his mother's blessing. He'd go with her shopping, then just stay there. She died when he was in middle school. With his father often away on long hauls in his truck, the whole village stepped in to raise this child of Carver Street.

During the one year they overlapped in high school, he saw Roy play Romeo in a school production. Damn, he was good. He could more than hold his own at Juilliard or RADA.

Despite the Carlton connection, they only hung out sporadically, a result of Alfonso's insecurities, not their three-year age difference. If he had come out the womb with zero fucks, Alfonso posited, maybe he wouldn't have stopped dancing. Could he have attained Roy's courage and attitude by osmosis from hanging with him regularly? He wished he had tried.

It's a new day, Alfonso thought, as he squeezed to the back to stand in front of him.

"Freshman jitters?"

"Nah, not yet," Roy said. Then he looked up. "Alfonso!"

"How's it going, Roy?"

"How are *you*?" He stood and gave him a quick hug, which took Alfonso by surprise. "I was just reading about the clinic fire and thinking about you, wondering if you heard." He sat down again.

"Thanks, Roy."

"You wanna sit here? I'm about to get off anyway," said the woman sitting next to Roy.

"Thank you." Alfonso took the woman's seat. "I went over to see it for myself. It still doesn't seem real."

"Right?"

"Then I spent the morning at Sammy's"—a slight smirk came to his face—"getting my boo-hoo on. But it felt good to be there."

"Welcome to the tribe, sistah." They fist-bumped with glitter.

Alfonso wanted an immediate crash course: How to be fierce. How to negotiate a difficult parent. How to live in the life with all eyes watching. Instead, he teasingly asked Roy about his future as an Astronomy major. Roy laughed, said he wanted to be a star the size of Betelgeuse.

"I auditioned into a workshop taught by Dee Patrick."

"*The* Mr. Patrick? Four Tonys Mr. Patrick? I'm scared of you!"

"I'm scared of him!"

They chatted freely all the way to the campus bus depot, swapped contact info after disembarking.

"Roy, did you go to the remembrance for Carlton?"

"For sure. He's an OG from Sammy's store. Had to represent."

"I was too scared to go. I'm such a fucking chickenshit."

Roy gave him another hug, and then kissed him on the cheek. "No, you're not. I'll see you at Sammy's, alright?"

Roy dashed off to class. Alfonso's broad smile screamed, Yes, you will!

Leon the football player sat in the middle of the classroom, his large frame stuffed into one of the standalone desks, the usual black beanie cap on his head. Unavoidable, Alfonso sighed. The morning had been like a blues ballad, offering tragedy and heartache but with enough space to allow a full exploration of those feelings, a first step toward purification. Now he had to lockstep with his homies, to keep it real. Like Carlton once told him, a march is a ballad with its swing clipped.

He took a seat next to Leon.

"I didn't know you were taking this class, man," Alfonso said.

"Hey, 'Fonso? What up, dawg?" He got up and gave him a manly, one-arm hug.

"First day," Alfonso said.

"Yeah, here we go again. Summer treated you good?"

Alfonso gave him a noncommittal head nod. "You ever take a class with Euclid before?"

"Naw. But this fits with my Communications major, so you know, whatever."

Professor Euclid entered the classroom. He dressed conservatively in blue slacks, a sport jacket, and a white dress shirt. But his powderpuff Afro, goatee, and even his walk said '70s brother-man. Folks just knew that somewhere in his closet were several dashikis. He stood in front, waiting for the class to settle down.

"I'm sure this is the first class of the day for most of you, so welcome back," he started. "Current Topics in the African American Community. During the semester, I want us to cover all sorts of issues and discuss their sociological implications on the various black communities that exist in this country. I had planned something else for today, but in keeping with my desire that the course stay very current, I thought I would start with something very recent and close to home. Some of you live in the Huck, right?" A few heads nodded, a couple of hands went up. "Did any of you smell the fire this morning?" Alfonso felt his body chill. "Well, that was the Huckleberry Community Clinic. It just burned down."

Folks stirred.

As Professor Euclid described the clinic, Alfonso started to recite in his head the mission statement posted at the entry door, just beneath the founders photo. *To serve those in need, To comfort those in pain, To guide those who are lost, To heal those who are ill, To provide for the health and well-being of all the community: That is our charge.* He repeated it, his lips nearly mouthing the words. He remembered them as if he had written them. They clung tightly to him, as tightly as he held Carlton's hand as he slipped further from his grasp, until he was no longer there to hold.

Meanwhile, the class became engaged in a lively discussion.

"What's the impact of the center's loss?" Professor Euclid asked.

"But didn't the county approve needle exchanges?"

"Yeah, Todd, but the city didn't," Leon countered.

Alfonso kept reciting the mission statement in his head.

"But the county runs the health programs, not the city," Todd countered.

"That doesn't matter, Todd," said another student. "The exchange brought the wrong type of element to the neighborhood."

"Sybil," Todd said, "we're talking about the Huck. The 'element' is already there."

"Naw, see, Sybil's right," Leon said, then launched into a rant about the city's rights and disapproving council members. Alfonso stayed silent, refusing to parrot him like a good hype man. He didn't care how many stared at him expecting otherwise.

"People!" Professor Euclid commanded. "You're not answering the question. How will the center's loss impact the community?"

"It means that more people are going to get HIV," the councilman's son said in a heavy voice.

"Why?" the professor asked.

"'Cause they won't get tested. 'Cause with it gone, folks can just keep on pretending that AIDS doesn't exist. All the treatments we got now don't mean shit if you don't know your status. That fire just made AIDS more invisible."

"He's right. Excellent, Alfonso." The professor paused. "What aspect about AIDS in the community have I emphasized? Alfonso just said it. It's invisible. The Huckleberry Community Clinic represented a visible presence, a reminder that AIDS exists. And now, thanks to this fire, that presence has been taken away."

Alfonso felt side eye coming from Leon. He had gone out of step. And part of him just really didn't care. He could have said a whole lot more, but instead remained silent for the rest of the class.

Folks packed up. Alfonso did so hurriedly. He wanted to catch the professor. Then Leon caught him.

"You still tabling today, right?"

Alfonso turned and looked down at Leon, whose face still bore a look.

"Yeah, I'm tabling, man. I gotta ask Professor Euclid something. I'll catch you later."

"Alright, dawg."

He caught up with the professor as he walked out of the building. Professor Euclid shook his hand.

"Thanks for speaking up on behalf of the clinic," he said.

"Thanks for talking about it."

"Like I said, I want this class to stay current."

"Professor Euclid, could I do my term paper on AIDS in the African American community?"

The professor stopped. "Of course, Alfonso. You can write about whatever you want to write about."

"I'm not sure yet, but I just wanted to know if that would fit the scope of the class."

The professor assured his student that it would, and then invited him to his office to discuss it further. But Alfonso had to go. As Leon reminded him with pointed stares, he had to table for the African Students Association. He thanked Professor Euclid again, then sped off.

He first went to the group's office in the Student Union to collect his wares. Then he skipped downstairs and out to the walkway to one of the built-in tables and benches on the main drag adjacent the Student Union. Alfonso always picked the table that sat in front of a little alcove just off the main walk. Folks liked to mingle among themselves in that space, their own personal grotto shielded from the rest of the world by low-hanging trees. It didn't take long for them to show up. Homeboys and homegirls fist-bumped with Alfonso before slipping into the grotto. They talked and reacquainted against a soundtrack of familiar tracks played on a boombox that someone brought. Alfonso normally went along with them, following the rhythm they set. But this time he preferred sticking to his own beat, the jazz and blues from his early morning at Sammy's store. He sat alone at the table, wondering what Sammy's "Lavender Veil Blues" sounded like. Wondering if it had lyrics. Wondering if he ever recorded it. Wondering if the same force that pushed him out of dancing pushed Sammy out of music. Wondering if anything really could change.

Unconsciously, he had been chain-smoking. Butts littered the ground under the table.

"You sure are puffing a lot today."

Alfonso jumped. Jameel startled him.

"Where'd you come from?" Alfonso asked.

"Down the hill." Jameel sat his tall, lanky frame next to Alfonso on the back of the bench and placed his long feet on the seat. "You tabling alone?"

"No. Cynthia's coming."

"I see." Jameel scanned the grotto crowd. "She ain't here yet?"

"No."

Banality, not Jameel's normal habit. Alfonso looked him in the face. Immediately, the eyes drew him in.

"Didn't see you much this summer," Jameel said.

He confided only to Carlton. And only once. It's always the body language, he explained, especially the eyes and the way they linger. But, he added, Jameel has had girlfriends. Lots of girlfriends.

If he is, Carlton replied, then he's so deep in the closet that he'll never find his way out, even with a flashlight.

Later, his cousin punctuated his remarks by playing the Shirley Horn torch song "All Night Long." Alfonso related to the lyrics instantly: lips never tasted, touches never known, dreams never realized. He bought the track and kept it on every iToy he has ever owned.

Alfonso blinked, then turned away and started puffing hard. He didn't need this.

"Too busy working."

Jameel sucked his teeth. "What, at your father's office?"

Their backstory made it almost impossible for them to bullshit each other. Alfonso knew that. He almost looked at him again. But he just couldn't go there. The clinic fire, Carlton, Carver Street: uh-uh. Not with Jameel. He kept sucking and puffing. Jameel stood up and stretched.

"You off?" Alfonso asked.

"Yeah. Food. Later." He got up and hopped across the walkway to the Student Center.

Though relieved, Alfonso regretted Jameel leaving so abruptly.

Cynthia arrived soon afterward. She wore jeans and a blouse/sweater combination that matched her sorority colors. Her perfect hair sat awkwardly under a baseball cap.

"Hello, Alfonso." She had an even-tempered voice.

"Hi, Cynthia." He got up to give her a hug.

"How was your summer?"

Gurneys. IVs. Monitors. Oxygen pumps.

He fumbled for his pack of cigs. "It was alright, you know. It was OK." A cigarette appeared in his mouth. "Just worked downtown, you know." He fumbled for his lighter. "But how was your summer? That internship in DC must have been dope! How did it go?"

"It was a lot of hard work, but it was a beautiful experience."

"Sweet! You felt you got a lot out of it?"

"Yes, I certainly did. You should try for it next summer. I'm sure your father can help you get it into the program."

"Uh-huh, uh-huh." He lit the cigarette.

"So where did you work this summer? Did you end up in your father's office?"

Pills. Hypos. Bed pans. Puke.

"Oh, no, no. I mean I worked at City Hall, but in the City Clerk's office. It was cool. You know, city policy stuff."

"How interesting."

Slowness. Stillness. Sleep. Silence.

He puffed harder.

"Well, welcome back. Thank you for setting up our table. I see folks have gathered back there, so I'll go say hi. I'll be back."

Alfonso remained at the table and kept smoking.

A young brother with a baby face came and stood at the table. He wore blue jeans and a black hoodie with a green shirt peeking from beneath. Alfonso thought he looked shorter than himself, but he had a stockier build, broader shoulders padded with muscles. The brother seemed particularly interested in the brochure about the tutorial program ASA cosponsored with the Beacon Hill First Baptist Church.

"Are you interested in joining the tutorial program, brother?" Alfonso asked.

"I already did." He had a resonant speaking voice, smooth and mellow. "Reverend Johnson told me I should come by and introduce myself. My name is Bill."

"Welcome, Bill. I'm Alfonso. Are you a freshman?"

"Yeah."

"Excellent! Glad to see you getting so involved already, brother." He began his automated sales pitch, talking up the group's many programs on campus and off. "We try to maintain our ties, you know what I'm saying." Bill nodded. "How did you get involved?"

"My mom," he said with a snarky drawl.

Alfonso liked Bill's response and giggled. He turned off the sales pitch voice. "Parents are like that, aren't they, Bill? My family goes to Reverend Johnson's church, too. How long have you guys been going?"

"Since last summer. We just moved into town."

"Alright, then. So your family lives in the Huck?"

"The Huck? Oh, you mean near Huckleberry Park? Yeah, we do. We live on 48th, right across the street from it."

"Sweet. I know some folks on 48th. You know Mrs. Parker?"

"She's our downstairs neighbor!" Bill smiled.

"Small world, ain't it, Bill."

They chatted with ease, but before they could get too comfortable Cynthia returned from the grotto.

"Hello!" she said in a loud, friendly voice. "Are you Bill Hawk?"

"Yeah."

"Lovely. Reverend Johnson told me to expect you. I'm Cynthia Greenfield, ASA president." She offered her long-fingered hand, which Bill took and shook lightly. "And this is Alfonso, our recruiting secretary."

Alfonso found her insertion into their conversation awkward and odd, but let it pass.

"You need to start coming to our meetings. Did you invite him yet, Alfonso? They're open to everyone. And you're already so involved. It's good to see us helping our own."

Leon appeared suddenly, grabbed Cynthia by the waist and pulled her closer.

"Hey, you!" she said. "I'm on duty!"

"'Fonso, man, you're supposed to be watching out for my lady," he said, looking at Bill. "What's up with that?"

Bill made a weak smile that turned more into a blank stare.

"Leave him alone, Leon," Alfonso said. "He's just here to hook up with the group. Reverend Johnson sent him. He tutors at his church."

"Yes," Cynthia said, "he's one of us now. So stop trying to scare him away."

"I'm just messing with him." He stuck out his hand to Bill. "Leon, man. Welcome." A bone-crushing handshake followed. "When did you start tutoring?"

"Just this past summer. I used to tutor at my old church."

"Where at?"

"In a small town, where I grew up." Bill bent over the table and put his name and info on a list.

"It's on, Leon!" a voice shouted.

Leon broke out his Android phone. "Oh, Alfonso, I think your father is about to come on the midday news and talk about the clinic. Let's see what he has to say."

He placed his cell on the table so folks could see the live stream on the tiny screen. Bill walked behind the table and stood next to Alfonso.

> *"Councilman Berry," the reported started, "you have had disagreements about the Huckleberry Community Clinic since it opened last spring."*
>
> *"Yes."*
>
> *"It offered many health services for the community, so how do you feel about it no longer being here, and would you oppose it reopening in the same spot?"*
>
> *"Look, I know that they offered many programs, but the bottom line for me has always been their insistence in maintaining a needle exchange program. A needle exchange program has its place, I suppose, though I think there isn't enough documentation to support whether such programs are beneficial or not."*

Leon's side eye just got real. Alfonso felt it, avoided looking his way.

> *"But the bottom line for me is, this neighborhood has seen enough blight and negative publicity. It does not need a needle exchange as well. Ours is a residential community, a family community. Children live here. This just isn't the appropriate setting for this sort of activity. After the tragedy of the fire, I hope that they elect to move elsewhere."*

"Straight out!" Leon said, clapping. "He's right! He's right! Your father's keeping it 100, Alfonso."

Others from the grotto started clapping.

Bill looked at Alfonso. All the life had been drained from him.

"Alfonso, your father's on the city council?" Bill asked.

"Uh-huh," he said blankly. "Excuse me."

He quickly left the table and ran across the walkway and up the steps to the Student Union. Bill almost wanted to ask if he was all right, but felt awkward since he just met him and no one else seemed fazed by his rapid exit.

"Well, Bill," Cynthia said. "I hope you can come to our first meeting this Thursday. We'll be talking about next week's Freshman Reception."

"Yeah, I'll be there."

"Cool, man," Leon said, offering another bone-crushing handshake. "Later."

Bill walked across to the Student Union and entered the building in search of food, though part of him wondered about Alfonso. He saw the eateries ahead, but noticed a men's room and felt the need to use it. He darted through the door and found Alfonso leaning heavily on a sink.

"Alfonso? Are you OK, man?"

Alfonso stood up, his eyes reddened.

"Who the hell does he think he is, black-checking me like that?" he spat. "Just 'cause I got his name don't mean I have to think like him. Fucking bullshit!"

Bill looked puzzled, but concerned.

"My cousin started that clinic, Bill. He died last summer. He's gone, and now his clinic's gone, too." Alfonso squeezed his eyes shut.

Bill felt no hesitation giving this man he barely knew a tight embrace in a space normally hostile to such intimacy.

THREE

A LFONSO VISITED SAMMY IN THE STORE AGAIN. A renewed swing in his step matched the Old Testament Count Basie playing over the store's stereo. Sammy smiled when he entered.

"Have you met the lizard queen?" he asked, pointing to a small figure sitting on a stool near the front window.

"Hi, neighbor."

"Hi, Ashley," Alfonso replied. He felt silly. Ashley and Aaron had lived next door since forever, but he barely knew either of them. To his family, they were invisible.

"How's it been at school so far?" Sammy asked.

"About what I expected. But I'm alright. Some folks got my back."

Bill's expression of concern still touched him. It was real, uninhibited, despite the newness of their acquaintance. Alfonso dug that stocky little brother and hoped to see more of him.

"This morning felt almost normal. I was sitting in my room with the door closed when I hear my sister Belinda yelling at Lucy, my youngest sister, to get ready for the bus. I like hearing her yell. Felt like it's been a while."

"You're the oldest, right?"

"Yeah. So anyway, I heard Lucy say that she needed to finish a paper that was due today. Belinda yelled, 'Well, why didn't you finish it last night?'" He smiled. "This is a regular morning melodrama in our house." Sammy nodded. "I knew what came next, my stage entrance. Rather than wait for Belinda to come get me, I get up and open the door. I see her coming toward me with Lucy's paper in hand. I'm the proofer, you see."

"Ah!"

"I take it downstairs, grab some OJ, and sit at the breakfast counter. I mark some corrections."

"Were there a lot?"

"Enough to bring her down a grade. It was good, just full of typos. So I'm reading it and my mother comes by. She says to me, 'thanks for helping your sister, again,' then kisses me as she walks off. That was the first time I felt like we really connected since Carlton's funeral."

"Nice."

"It was nice. But kinda sad, too. I still feel like there's so much we can't talk about. Like Eddie. I can't get him out of my head. Do you think he'll make it?"

"I pray that he does, baby."

"I need to believe that he'll be OK. He's gotta pull through, Sammy."

The old man nodded.

Alfonso talked about Eddie's visits at Carlton's place, how the music flipped on and turned Carlton's little one-bedroom into a dance club, how they made each other laugh hard.

"Eddie and my husband were the only ones who could come close to Carlton on the dance floor," Ashley said, still staring out the window.

"Sweet," Alfonso said. "You know, they both promised to take me out dancing for my 21st in December."

"We'll take you out, baby," Sammy said. "Right, Miss Thing?"

Ashley sat preoccupied in a gaze and didn't say anything.

"What you looking at, Missy?"

"Uh-oh."

"What?"

"Here comes Henny Penny."

"Oh, great Dizzy! Is he coming here?"

"Heading straight this way. Now don't be hiding in the back of the store trying to get away from her, Samuel Turner! That bitch is your friend, not mine!"

"Be nice, will you? Just once?" Sammy stood in the door to the storeroom.

Alfonso switched his head back and forth between the two of them, until Henny Penny slammed in the store.

"Sammy! Sammy! Where's Sammy?" He headed straight for the storeroom.

Of Henny Penny Eddie often quipped, *That girl will find eighty words for every one she needs.* Alfonso sat slack-jawed as Henny clucked about a dreamboat of a man he invited to his place for a home-cooked dinner. "But I can't cook!" he squawked. "I burn pots boiling water! Can't you fix me something, Sammy?" Resigned, Sammy came forward and slumped behind the counter again.

"Why did you invite him? And why is this suddenly my problem?" Sammy asked.

"I couldn't say no to him. He's the one. My searching days are over!"

"That'll be the day," Ashley said. "So, you told this trick of yours—"

"He ain't no trick, Ms. Ashley!" Henny said.

"Like I was saying, before I was interrupted, you told this trick of yours—that and you met only God knows where—that you're gonna make him this great homemade meal. And now, when you actually gotta do it, you're running down the street like the Henny Penny you are, 'cause your little world is falling apart on account of you can't cook your way out of a gunny sack. And you expect Sammy to bail out your sorry tail? Well, honey, you need to let the sky fall right on you and knock some sense in that Henny Penny head of yours."

"Sammy!" Henny screamed. "Why you let him talk to me that way! You know how sensitive I am! And stop smiling, Ashley! I'm not a Henny Penny! I'm not!"

Alfonso bit his lip and recited the alphabet backward in his head. He tried to disguise escaping chortles as coughs, knowing damn well that that trick never worked. But it was all he had.

Sammy tried calming Henny down by suggesting that he buy prepared food at the A&P. Some barbecue chicken, some mash potatoes and gravy, all that, he suggested. Then he made the mistake of suggesting that Henny microwave a bag of string beans. More drama. Alfonso bit his lip harder. Finally, Sammy relented and offered to make the string beans himself, the nice ones with the pearl onions.

"Oh, thank you, Sammy!" Henny said. "Thank you so much! This is going to be great! He's gonna come over, and I'll have dinner on the table, and he'll be so happy!"

"As long as he don't see them A&P labels on his homemade dinner."

"Don't start! Don't start on me again, Lynwood Ashley Taylor!" Henny walked toward Ashley, sliding his head side to side.

Alfonso had tears coming from his eyes.

"Curtis!" Sammy bellowed, using Henny's real name. "Go get the food," he said softly. "Come back this afternoon and I'll have the string beans ready."

"Alright, Sammy. Thank you. At least there's one gentleman on this street." He walked past Ashley as he went through the door. "And I may be a Henny Penny, Missy, but at least I ain't no Loosey Goosey!" And then he huffed out.

"*That* girl shouldn't talk no Loosey Goosey shit," Ashley said.

Alfonso finally let it all out in gasps and spasms. He couldn't remember laughing so hard. He even caused jaded old Ms. Ashley to giggle a bit.

"So that was the famous Miss Henny Penny!"

"Yes," Sammy said, "Miss Curtis 'Henny Penny' Whitfield. You can see how he got the name. Hell, it ain't even noon yet, and he's going on about some damn dinner."

"So what's his story?"

"Oh, just another lost puppy that ended up at my doorstep. If you think he's a mess now, you should have seen him back when. Right, Missy?" Ashley rolled his eyes and stared out the window again. "He had it pretty rough, though. His father literally threw him out of the house when he was still in high school."

"Literally?"

"Uh-huh. Picked him up and tossed his butt out the door and onto the sidewalk."

"Damn."

"Yeah, it was pretty nasty."

Alfonso sat still for a moment. "I wonder if he talks to his father now."

"Doubt it. He turned the page on his family."

FOUR

THE AFRICAN STUDENTS ASSOCIATION'S THIRD-FLOOR office was not a particularly big space and clutter made it feel even tighter. A desk sat on one side of the door, boxes and a short bookcase cramming the corner beside it. Chairs and a couch sat on the opposite side. Its main asset was a patio, the only office with such a luxury, accessed through a glass and wrought iron door.

Alfonso smoked on the patio. Jameel stood nearby. When Jameel first saw him smoke during their freshman year he said, You know, dancers really shouldn't smoke. Turning away from dance after just one performance to focus on his burgeoning life as a Poli-Sci major caused him to dump his healthy living pledge in the first place. He was, in his mind, giving himself the middle finger. Fuck my life. No one else had said anything about his sudden butt-sucking habit, much less connected it with dancing. How had Jameel made the connection? Who said I'm a dancer, he retorted, hoping to hear him say *I do*. How fulfilling that would have been to have heard Jameel affirm his dancing, to have had his two passions united together; even better, for the unrequited

35

passion to have attempted to rescue the passion left behind. But the moment never came.

He extinguished the butt. Jameel walked toward him.

"You're quiet."

Alfonso heard the translation: You're not acting all hyper, typing ASA business at the computer with your headphones on, chain-drinking Red Bulls and bobbing your knee like a freak.

"Just chillin'. You and Victor hooking up for hoops tomorrow?"

"Yeah, I guess." He squared up close to Alfonso. "You coming?"

"Yeah."

They stood, faces inches apart. Such long eyelashes. They cradled his eyes with softness. Soaking in Jameel on the ASA balcony, a place so antithetical to such thoughts and emotions, made it that much more enticing. Only playing footsies under his family's dining room table would be riskier. He wondered why he was allowing himself to stare at Jameel's face. And why was Jameel staring at *him*?

Someone entered the office. Alfonso turned and looked. Bill. A sigh of relief puffed though his nose as he turned to go inside and meet the new arrival.

"Hey, Bill! Glad you could make it."

"Did I miss it?" Bill looked harried, sweaty, and sounded breathy.

"Nah. You're good."

"Oh. I was worried, 'cause I'm late."

"Ain't like that here, man," Jameel said. "We ain't on no timetable."

"This is Jameel. Jameel, Bill."

"Alright, man." Jameel shook his hand.

"Hey, brothers," said a voice entering the room.

"Yo, Victor," Jameel said.

On the couch, feet curled under her butt, sat Tamesha. She looked up from her book, eyebrows arched, her lips and nose puckered like something foul smelling was in her presence.

"We need to get this thing going," she said in a slow, nasally voice. "I've got things to do."

As folks sat down, Jameel mouthed "things to do," voicelessly exaggerating the way Tamesha chewed her words. Alfonso caught sight of him and stifled giggles. Jameel flashed a wry grin in return, a secret history shared between them. Back in high school, at Jameel's instigation, they once loaded Tamesha's locker with Milk of Magnesia bottles. After that prank, half the school called her Lady M.O.M.

Cynthia, sitting at the desk, got off her cell and turned around.

"I apologize, Tamesha," she said. "Let's all get together now so that we can start the meeting."

"Is Leon coming?" Tamesha inquired.

"He's on his way. The team had a meeting."

Bill sat on a small chair in front of the patio door. Jameel sat between him and Alfonso. Reverend Johnson had built up the group as something fantastic, but Bill just couldn't see it. Instead of praising Alfonso for single-handedly organizing their Freshmen Reception next week, Tamesha berated him about how the caterer couldn't use the kitchen last year and that it had better not be a problem again. Cynthia echoed the abuse, but with a condescending smile. They brought the room down, contributed to its dreariness like the dusty walls and faded posters of long-past events.

The discussion moved on to event speakers. Leon crashed in, standing awkwardly as folks talked, eventually lumbering to the couch. Tamesha scooted over. He kept his manspread to a minimum, but still filled the room.

"Did you say Cliff's speaking?" Leon asked.

"We were discussing whether we should invite him to speak," Cynthia said.

"Ain't happening. Cliff is history. Period."

"He's a leader on Exec. Board, man," Victor said. "That's important. And he was part of the group for a long time."

"He's bougie," Jameel said. "He don't fit with our agenda."

Victor sucked his teeth. "Jameel, you're too doctrinaire, like most of the brothers in The Party. He ain't Clarence Thomas. And he's made sure we got the funding we needed."

"Yeah, he's a good guy," Alfonso said.

"Who dropped his name in the first place?" Leon asked, looking around. "You, Victor?"

The room got very still. Bill felt nervous, uncomfortable.

"I did," Alfonso finally said.

Leon rolled his eyes. "Why can't your father come and speak?"

"He has a standing meeting Wednesday nights."

"Well, you all know what I think about Cliff," Tamesha said. "He's not very representative of our group given his domestic situation."

From uncomfortable to outright panic. Bill glanced at Alfonso, who quickly shook his head, like, Uh-uh, not what you think. He still felt unsettled.

"Well, alright, then," Cynthia said. "Given the division in the group, I think it would be best if we not ask Cliff to speak this year. Do we have consensus?" She paused. No one said anything. "Alright. Is there anything else?"

Tamesha looked directly at Bill, eyebrows arched severely. "You're a freshman. You think this'll be a good program for people?"

Suddenly he existed, the spokesman for his class. He felt ridiculous.

"It sounds pretty cool."

"Well, invite all your little friends to come along." She went back to her book.

"Thanks, Tamesha," Cynthia said. "And thank you, Bill, for coming. Welcome to the group."

Bill smiled, but couldn't wait to get out of there. As he tossed his backpack over his shoulder, Alfonso stepped toward him.

"We usually go to dinner down in the Commons after the meeting. You wanna join us?"

"Actually, I think I need to get home to do some reading for tomorrow."

"Oh, OK." Their eyes locked for a second. "You mind if I roll back to the hood with you?"

"Of course not."

"Yo, you don't wanna hang out, 'Fonso?" Jameel asked.

"I'm tired. Long week."

"Man, it's the first week. Why you so tired? It's too soon to be pulling all-nighters."

"You'll have to beat me in the arcade some other time, Jameel. I'll catch you later."

Victor shook Bill's hand. Jameel barely gave a head nod as they departed.

As soon as they got outside, Alfonso took out a cigarette. Then he stopped.

"You mind?"

"Naw, man, go for it."

"It's a shitty habit." He lit up.

"Who's Cliff and what's up with his 'domestic situation'?"

Alfonso shook his head. "The ghost of Cliff-gate." He blew smoke in the air. "Last year we had a big split and Cliff was the center of it. He was ASA president the past couple years. A go-getter. Pre-MBA. Entrepreneur. Real sharp. But some folks have issues with him because his girlfriend is white. And last year they had a kid."

Bill's face crinkled with disgust.

"Uh-huh," Alfonso said. "Cliff broke the rules. In their minds, he ain't black enough."

"Shit. So what does that make us?"

"What, indeed."

They reached the bus depot. A number 21 bus rolled up just as they arrived. The driver got off for a smoke break. They boarded and took a seat in the back.

"Bill, look. I'll confess. I was hoping you'd come to the meetings, 'cause I was tired of being 'the only one,' you know what I'm saying?"

"I hear you."

"So I have selfish reasons for your being part of the group. And I know your mom and Reverend Johnson want you to get involved. They have their reasons, and I'm sure they're good ones. But, you know, you're a freshman. You got a lot more important things to worry about than trying to fit in a group you're not comfortable with. So if you don't show up to any meetings or whatever, you know, it's all good. Believe me, I'll understand."

"Alfonso, can I ask you something?"

"Sure."

"How comfortable do you feel in this group?"

Alfonso stared forward. A smile crept onto his face.

"I mean, you know, you did all the work, but they went after you anyway. That just don't seem right to me."

"Thanks, Bill." He sighed. "It was different before the split. Cliff was cool. But he didn't have time for petty bullshit, so he quit. Victor and I are the only ones left that supported him. I'm in ASA 'cause of my family's legacy." Then he added, with leaden words, "Public service. It's what we do." In his normal voice he continued, "If you take a class in state history, you'll learn about my grandfather, Al Berry, Sr. He was the first black elected to the state legislature."

"Whoa!" Bill said. "Is he still alive?"

"Naw. He died in 2010, couple years after my dad got elected. He was old, though. Almost 89."

"Wow."

"He had my dad kinda late, when he was almost 40. Guess he was too busy building his career to have kids right away. And my dad's an only child."

"Cool he lived long enough to see your father get elected."

The bus started, pulled away from the curb. The driver began down the winding road along the east side of campus. Alfonso took out his cell. Over the internal speaker sang Billie Holiday, "Travelin' Light."

"My new addiction, my cousin's music collection. I like to play it. It keeps him near."

"Nice."

"I miss the space we had together. Are you out with anyone?"

"My friend Suzy back home. Folks thought we were a couple, 'cause we hung out at school a lot. She called herself my beard, so I started calling her Peach-fuzz."

Alfonso giggled.

"And there was this music director at my family's church. Everyone knew about him, but the church matrons used to set him up on dates anyway. He used to let his hair down with me and we sort of laughed it off. Sometimes, though, he'd get pissed about it, be all 'why can't they just leave me alone.'"

"Yeah. I heard that."

"I actually had a boyfriend in high school."

"Seriously? And nobody said anything?"

"I guess you could say that we were discreet. And I discovered that folks don't see what they don't wanna see, or what they don't think exists. We hung out a lot, but no one thought anything by it."

"They probably thought you were with *Peach-fuzz!*" Alfonso said, singing the last word á la Nina Simone.

Bill laughed.

"Besides tonight, how has your first week been?"

Bill copped a goofy, lopsided smile. Alfonso stretched out his legs while putting his hands behind his head.

"Alright, who is he?"

"Don't know, yet. Someone I met in history class. We sort of clicked."

"Alright, then."

"I ended up walking him to his next class. That's why I came running into the room at such a tear. I thought I was real late. I think I pissed off Tamesha. She gave me the stink eye."

"Nah. She always looks like that. So who is this pretty boy in history class?"

"His name is Roy."

Alfonso sat up. "Ferreal? Is he tall and has red hair?"

"Yeah! You know him?"

"Hell yeah, I know him! We were in high school together!"

"Shut up!"

Both lit up, clapping and giggling.

"OK, OK," Bill said, "so tell me all about him. What's he like?"

"Fierce. Roy is fierce. He's like, 'Closet, what's that?'"

"OK. That fits. We're in Professor Quill's class—"

"Benjamin Quill? Oh, lord, you're taking his class?"

"You know about him?"

"Everybody knows about Miss Benjamin Quill, child." Alfonso's whole manner opened up. His voice lightened. Hand gestures danced in the air.

"Yeah, OK. I thought he was a pent-up Miss Thing. We're reading *The Epic of Gilgamesh* and he went off about how Gilgamesh and Enkidu weren't lovers. Wagging his finger and shit."

Bill demonstrated. Alfonso laughed.

"Seriously. I was like, this brother has issues."

"Yeah, he's notorious."

"So that was Monday. Today I had discussion section and that's when I met Roy. He sits next to me and then pulls out this drawing, his interpretation of Gilgamesh and Enkidu. He made them look African, real serious brothers with pierced ears and thick arms and legs, standing side by side holding hands. He captioned it 'When We Were Kings.' It was dope."

"Yeah, that's Roy, alright. Like I said, he don't do closets."

"He was dressed real fine. I felt like a slob next to him."

"Don't even trip. He's stylish, but not haughty. And I'm sure he just loves that deep speaking voice of yours."

"Yeah, whatever, girlfriend! What else? What kinda food he like?"

"He's a vegetarian."

"That's cool. I can roll with that. What are his parents like? Are they cool with him?"

"He lives with his dad. His mom died years ago."

"Oh, wow. That's sad. He mentioned his dad, but I thought, you know, that his folks had divorced, like mine."

"Oh, really? So it's just you and your mom?"

"And my baby brother, Derek."

"Uh-huh. Roy's an only child. His dad's a truck driver, sort of a man's man type. They get on alright, but I think he really misses his mom. Truth is, Bill, I didn't hang with Roy like I should have back in the day. I was too scared to. He was way more real than I was ready to be."

"You're more real than you think, babe. And, you know, if I don't go to meetings, that don't mean we can't hang out together."

"I appreciate that, Bill. And thanks for standing up for me, both today and Monday."

Bill put his arm around Alfonso.

"Jameel looked kinda cross when we left. You guys aren't—"

Alfonso smirked. "Ain't nothing there." He took Bill's hand as it hung over his shoulder.

Belinda walked to her room from the bathroom just as Alfonso climbed the stairs.

"Lucy got a B+ on the paper you helped her with today."

"Sweet. How was your day?"

"Alright. Nothing new under the sun." She walked into her room.

Alfonso entered his. He dropped his backpack on the floor and flicked on the TV, the 10 o'clock news. The camera focused on a white van. When it pulled back, the Huckleberry Community Clinic appeared across the street, boarded and charred. A pan to the left showed a table on the sidewalk next to the van with Bingo and others gathered around. The needle exchange, Alfonso thought, pumping his fist in the air.

A reporter spoke with Reverend Tamera Woodson of All-Huckleberry Community Church. She called the fire an act of terror that also displaced neighbors who lived upstairs, but affirmed that terror will not deter them from their work.

A friend once begged Alfonso to attend one of Reverend Tamera's services with her and he couldn't say no. Everything about it blew him away. Congregants lit the church with rhythm and dance and a rainbow of outfits, from stylized dresses and suits to tie-dyes to purple sweatpants. Instead of a choir or organ, West African talking drums backed Reverend Tamera's sermon about the immorality of globalization and deportation—*Companies are legal, migrants are not*—a street theology connected to the here and now. Although Alfonso's family had always attended Reverend Johnson's church, where the black aristocracy gossiped and rubbed elbows, back in the day his father's spirit fell more in line with Reverend Tamera's. He longed for that Ford Berry, the young firebrand attorney defending the underdog, the people's advocate, the man who vanished after getting elected to the city council.

A slamming noise came from downstairs. Alfonso went to the door, poked his head out. Belinda did the same from her room.

"What was that?" Alfonso asked.

"I think it was Dad, going into his study."

His shouting voice confirmed it. "I want this shut down now!"

"Wonder what he's so mad about," Belinda said.

Alfonso shrugged, went back into his room, leaned against the closed door. He so wanted to go to Belinda's room and give her the lowdown on what was going down. He didn't know if he could go there with her. His insecurity saddened him.

Off went the TV. Headphones came over his ears. He dialed up Erykah Badu. In no time, her ethereal voice freed his mind and levitated his body.

FIVE

BILL AND ROY DIDN'T EVEN KNOW WHAT QUILL WAS talking about. So they decided to go to the café for morning croissants and lattes. They sat at a cozy table in the corner next to a stained-glass window and an unlit fireplace.

Roy took out his iPhone. Bill soaked up the foam from his drink with his croissant.

"Never thought I'd be ditching classes so soon," Bill said. "I thought I'd wait until at least my sophomore year." He noticed Roy's expression. "What's up?"

"Eddie died. This morning. Fuck!"

Bill closed his eyes. He thought about Alfonso. "I'm so sorry."

"One of the sweetest guys you'd ever wanna meet. Damn it!" He let Bill take his hand and caress it. "Life sucks sometimes, you know that? Just fucking sucks."

Their foreheads met over the table.

———✦———

Leon and Jameel stood together in line at the counter across the room.

45

"Look," Leon said.

"What?"

"Over there, in the corner."

Jameel looked at the silhouettes in front of the sunlit stained-glass window. "Is that Bill?"

"Sho' is. And you see who he's with."

"Damn," Jameel said, trailing off into slack-jawed astonishment.

"Uh-huh. You believe this shit?"

"I guess they're studying."

"Heh, yeah. I guess."

"You headed to Euclid's class, man?" Jameel very much wanted to change the subject.

"Uh-huh. Can't wait to tell Alfonso about this shit."

They took their coffees and departed.

Roy scanned tweets. "Looks like there's gonna be a vigil for him tonight at 6."

Bill sighed. "Damn. I'm supposed to be at the ASA Freshmen Reception thing tonight. It starts at 5."

"Is that tonight? The Queer Students Reception is tonight, too."

"Ferreal? Are you going?"

"I was gonna go. But I'd rather go to the vigil."

"I'd like to go, too."

"Really? You would?"

"Of course. It's important to bear witness to this kind of shit. I wonder if Alfonso will go."

"He has to be at the ASA thing, too, doesn't he?"

"I'm sure he does. I haven't seen him all week."

Alfonso sat on the floor outside Professor Euclid's office in Zamudio Hall, his head hanging between his bent legs. He had knocked on the door, but no one answered.

The professor arrived. Alfonso stood up.

"Hey, Alfonso. Missed you in class, brother. Where were you this morning?"

"Can we talk for a minute?"

"Sure. Come on in."

Alfonso sat down in the guest chair while the professor pulled his chair around to sit closer to him.

"I'm sorry I missed class today, Professor Euclid. I'm sorry." Another flood of tears came and he buried his face in his hands.

"Hey, hey, it's alright, Alfonso. What's troubling you, brother?"

"I'm sorry," he said, after a moment. "It just hits me sometimes."

"What is it, Alfonso?"

"Did you hear about Eddie Langford?"

"Isn't that the brother who was attacked in Huckleberry—"

"He died this morning."

"Oh, I'm so sorry, Alfonso." He got up and gave him a hug. "Was he a friend of yours?" He sat down again.

"Yeah. He was my cousin's best friend. They were tight. And now they're both gone. Just like that. One minute, we're at my cousin's laughing and shit. And now—" He banged his fist on the desk. "I can't deal with this fucking shit anymore!" He felt self-conscious, though it felt good to shout. "Sorry," he said softly.

"Don't be sorry, brother. Speak you mind. What happened to your cousin?"

"AIDS."

He connected the dots for the professor—Carlton, Eddie, the clinic fire—and explained how the life he knew had ended. Professor Euclid reached out and took Alfonso's hand and squeezed tightly.

"I'm truly sorry, Alfonso."

"Thank you."

They released hands.

"I actually met your cousin."

"Really?"

"Uh-huh. A couple of times. I'm a friend of Tamera's. We went to college together. I met Carlton at her church when the collective was starting to put the clinic together. I got to meet a few of them, Carlton, Bingo, Lucinda, Harry. They're a good group."

"I'm trying to find a way to explain how all this has affected me. I've been thinking about my term paper. I need to expand it. I need to talk about how homophobia has limited the response to AIDS and gay bashings. I need to talk about homophobia in the black community."

Professor Euclid nodded. "I hear you, my brother. That's a broad topic."

"This is how I see it starting." Though he was still sniffling, his hands began to come alive as he spoke.

> "One of the founders of the Huckleberry Community Clinic is my cousin. His name is Carlton Higgins. He was black and gay and had HIV for many years. He's dead. This is his story.
>
> "I knew the man who was beaten to death in Huckleberry Park because some people thought they had the right to do that. His name is Eddie Langford. He was black and gay. He's dead. This is his story.
>
> "My name is Alfonso Berry. I'm black and gay. And this is my story."

The professor started rubbing his eyes.

"This scares me to death, Professor Euclid. You know who my father is, and you know something about his politics, especially about the clinic. They aren't my politics. And I need to start saying that a lot louder. I'm not interested in attacking my father. I just want to be able to speak my own mind. But I need help doing that."

The professor cleared his throat a couple of times.

"Call me Dan, alright?" Alfonso nodded. "Alfonso, you're already speaking your mind, and that's beautiful, my brother. I can't know what sort of pressure you're under with the legacy you have. But the best advice I can give to you—at the risk of sounding nonacademic—is, listen to your inner voice. Know it. Trust it. Your righteous indignation will ultimately take you to where you need to go. You're writing this paper for me, for the class, but really, you're writing it for yourself. Homophobia is a very important subject, one that we don't talk about often enough. With your own personal story, I'm sure you'll make a great contribution to the class. Your loss can help to educate us all."

Outside, he lit up a cigarette and took several puffs while waiting for his cell to boot up. He turned it off after learning about Eddie. It seemed better that way. Texts from Bill and Roy appeared. That made him smile. Then it began ringing. Leon's name appeared on the screen.

"Yeah, what's up, Leon?"

"Where you been?"

Alfonso took a quick puff. "Uh, I was busy?"

"Yeah. I thought you were busy here in the office. I figured that was why you missed class today. But you ain't here."

No shit, Sherlock.

"You know we got the thing tonight," Leon continued.

"Yeah, of course I know, man." The conversation was too ridiculous to take seriously, so he didn't let it bother him. "Look, I had a meeting with Professor Euclid, and I'm just leaving. I gotta grab some food and I'll be in the office in a bit, alright?"

"Oh. OK. See you when you get here."

Alfonso hung up. Ridiculous. He purposely lingered and enjoyed his smoke before going anywhere.

SIX

A LFONSO THE RECRUITING SECRETARY TALKED ON STAGE
about how to get involved with ASA and its various
projects. He spoke robotically, like a flight attendant
reciting the safety protocols for the millionth time. Bill tried not
to laugh. Neither wanted to be there, their thoughts on Eddie and
the vigil.

While Alfonso kept speechifying, Bill started milling around.
The hall seemed low energy and only half full. More Cliff-gate
fallout? He soon found Reverend Johnson at a table for the church's
programs. As he approached, the reverend's clean-shaven, leathered
face wrinkled into its characteristic toothy smile.

"William! Very nice to see you here."

"How are you, Reverend Johnson?"

"Quite well, thank you. An excellent evening, isn't it?"

Bill nodded, saw no point in contradicting him.

"Stick with this group, William. They will take you far."

Bill lingered for a bit and then politely excused himself to get
some of the barbecue he had been smelling. But he was too late.

"We run out every year," Jameel said.

51

"Sure smelled good."

"Uh-huh. You got a minute?"

"Sure."

Jameel walked onto the patio outside the ballroom. Bill followed. They stopped along a railing that looked over a plaza below and the track field in the distance.

"Is your group here?" Bill asked.

"What group?"

"The Party."

"Oh." He chuckled. "We support ASA, but this isn't our type of scene."

Bill felt Jameel sizing him up, casting the type of shade that parents throw when inspecting the new boyfriend their daughter just brought home.

"I hear you're making lots of friends on campus already," Jameel said.

"Yeah, a few."

He stared for a second. "And you and Alfonso seem pretty tight."

"Yeah."

"You know about his family, don't you?"

"Yeah, he told me."

"Now my politics and his family's don't jibe. I'm a revolutionary. But still, I respect his father's position and the legacy he represents. 'Fonso's family is real powerful. And he'd never do anything to hurt that." He coughed. "Not that he would, *consciously*. You know what I'm saying?" He paused, cleared his throat. "Sometimes people do things that have unintended consequences." He coughed again. Bill wondered if he needed some water. "'Fonso knows that standing by his dad will ultimately benefit him. So, you see, Alfonso is an important brother. He's good for the group. He's solid, man, real solid. And we need him to stay that way."

"Yeah, sure." Nothing Jameel said made any sense.

"You hear me, I'm sure, brother." He stuck his hand out, and Bill took it. They shook and fist-bumped. "Take it slow, now." Then he walked away.

Bill stood by the railing. Before he could head back inside, Leon appeared. Bill didn't even see him coming—Leon just sort of arrived.

"Saw you today with Roy. You know Roy?"

"What? Yeah, we're in history class together."

"What history class?"

"Ancient History."

"Quill's class? You know he ain't exactly 'folk,' don't you?"

Bill didn't say anything.

"Well, Roy ain't exactly 'folk' either," Leon added.

"What does that mean?"

Leon sucked his teeth. His body language said, Don't play me. "Look, I know y'all study together and all, but I'm just saying. Jameel and I were surprised that y'all knew each other and hung out together like that."

Bill felt Leon's height and girth bearing down on him.

"Yeah, you know,"—Leon chuckled slightly—"a lot of us came from the same high school. So we've known each other for a while. Roy never mixed with us. We all thought he was too goofy. He lives on Carver Street, man, you know what I mean?"

Leon dropped code fast and heavy. "Like that." "Goofy." "Carver Street." The nervous chuckle. All of it code for *I don't wanna be talkin' about this shit, but you forced it on me, and don't make me hafta do it again, mothafucka!*

"Yeah, well, just thought you should know. Thanks for coming tonight."

With that, Leon disappeared as quickly as he had appeared.

Alfonso dashed onto the patio, saw Bill against the railing and walked toward him.

"Hey, sorry for the delay. I'm finished with my bullshit. Ready to hit it?"

"Uh-huh."

"What?"

"Let's get Roy and get the fuck."

"Bill, what is it?"

"Let's just get out of here first, OK?"

Alfonso texted Roy at the Queer Students Reception upstairs. Roy texted back real fast that he was more than ready to go. They met on the steps of the Student Union. If they hurried, they could catch the next bus, Alfonso said. So they ran like prisoners making a break for it.

The driver had just turned over the engine when they boarded. They headed to the back. Alfonso and Roy sat on one side, Bill on the other.

"OK," Bill said. "So, this happened." He characterized the encounters as a good cop/bad cop routine. Roy jumped out of his seat and started pacing.

"That fucking, overgrown, bovine, piece of shit motherfucker! This shit is not OK! We're going to a vigil for someone killed by fucking haters like that!"

Alfonso sat very still, in disgust and shame. He wondered why Jameel still carried water for Leon. And why, despite everything, Leon was still a part of *his* life.

"Hell," Roy continued, "that's the same shit—he did me like that in high school, too. Now he's taking up where he left off. What a big, fat, fucking prick!"

"Roy, I've seen Leon in the gym," Alfonso said. He held up his pinky finger and wiggled it. "It ain't that big."

Bill sputtered. Roy started laughing, in spite of himself. He sat down next to Bill.

"The only reason they started tripping was that they saw y'all in the Cuddle Corner," Alfonso said.

"Say what?" Bill exclaimed.

"It's next to the fireplace," Alfonso said in a singsong voice. "And you got the little spotlight on you. And in the mornings, you got little spots of colored light from the stained-glass window hitting you in the face. Get the picture?"

Roy rolled his eyes. Bill smirked, stretched out his legs.

"The legend is that if the green light hits you, then you're a home run."

"What if you get a red light?" Bill asked, snickering.

"Stop light!" Alfonso yelled.

"Neon light!" Roy yelled back.

At that moment, "Flashlight" by Parliament came alive, clapping, singing, shimmying, and strutting down the aisle, transforming the bus into a Sooooooooooooooul Train. Bill beatboxed and Roy sang while Alfonso hoofed some serious moves, echoing Eddie, demonstrating all he learned from that righteous queen.

"That's alright, then!" the bus driver shouted. "You kids know old school!"

They disembarked at Lincoln and 54th, then ducked through an alley to get to Carver Street.

"*That's* what we should have done at that damn event, Bill," Alfonso said. "Give them people an education!"

"Preach it, sistah!" Bill said.

"To Eddie!" Alfonso screamed. "Long live the queen!"

"Long live the queen!" Bill and Roy repeated.

The alley opened into a narrow, one-way street: the Leather Strip. They passed a barbershop where the butch sat patiently waiting to get their flattops smoothed out. A few motorcycles parked in front of the Flexxx, a bar with a large leather drop cloth at its entrance. They paused at Ye Olde Leather Shoppe. Roy pointed at a black leather vest that hung on a mannequin.

"I just got a job at The Other Bookstore. This is so my first paycheck."

"Sick!" Bill said.

The Leather Strip emptied onto Carver Street. They turned right to head down to Sammy's.

Bill asked about The Other Bookstore.

"This old hippie couple owned a bookstore," Alfonso said.

"Called 'The Bookstore,'" Roy added.

"And they refused to create an LGBTQ section."

"So, a lesbian couple opened up a bookstore across the street. They called theirs 'The Other Bookstore'" As they passed, Roy pointed out the sign, with "Other" in italics.

"They drove the first bookstore out of business," Alfonso said.

Sammy was locking up as they arrived. "Ah, good, y'all made it. Here." He gave them each a candle.

"This is Bill," Alfonso said.

"Good to meet you, baby." Sammy gave him a hug.

"I'm sorry about Eddie," Bill said.

"It's been a day at the store, let me tell you."

"I can imagine," Roy said.

"Charlotte let herself go, and she never does that. Folks kept coming and going and coming back. The vigil basically got planned by folks meeting up here."

"Harry coming?" Alfonso asked. Carlton always referred to Sammy's assistant as Ms. Activism. He belonged to the clinic collective with Carlton, Bingo, others.

"He's already there, with Charlotte," Sammy said.

Bingo came from around the corner.

"Sorry I'm late, girls. Oh, Alfonso, honey!" He nearly tripped over himself to give him a big bear hug.

Eventually, they joined the slow march toward the park. Somberness subdued the Soul Train sass. For Alfonso, it became real when Bingo appeared. The tightness of their embrace represented his need to cling to folks from his cousin's vanishing world. Roy retreated to silence. Loss often caused him to relive his mother's passing. Bill reflected on a time not long ago when the trees in his small hometown were said to bear a strange fruit.

A sizable crowd gathered at 45th and Stevens, the northwest corner of the park, the spot where Eddie fell. Some rehung yellow crime scene tape around the trees. Some put duct tape over their mouths, the word "Silenced" scrawled on it. Nearly everyone held a candle, the yellow glow reflecting against their faces of multicolored blue. One person held a sign proclaiming the area Eddie's Grove.

Alfonso flipped the hood over his head. He saw a couple of signs denouncing his father and felt it best to stay incognito. But he absolutely wanted to stay. He owed it to Eddie and Carlton.

Vera approached. The usual yellow headscarf framed her face.

"Hi, Vera," Sammy said. He introduced Bill. She lightly shook his hand.

Alfonso looked up from beneath his hood and gave a half smile. She hugged him close, lips to his right ear.

"Don't worry, sweetie," she whispered. "You won't be in any of the shots."

"Much appreciated," he whispered back.

Then she looked at Roy, whose face remained a blank canvas. She hugged him too, short but sweet.

"You alright, kiddo?"

"I'm hanging, Auntie Vera. Thanks."

"I'm going to move in closer to get some shots of Charlotte. Take care, everyone."

"Bye, Vera," Bingo said.

He looked at Alfonso, who fidgeted quite a bit.

"Wanna join me at the edge of the crowd for a smoke?"

"Thanks, Bingo."

They squeezed past the bodies and spindly tree trunks, positioning themselves at a distance, but still able to see Charlotte and the other speakers. Harry stood with Charlotte, holding the megaphone on his head as she held the corded mic and spoke.

"I wasn't going to tell this story here tonight, but many insisted because we've suffered so much loss recently." She paused a moment. "Not long after this horrific, senseless attack, I met with Councilman Berry."

Loud hissing and booing ensued. Alfonso held on to Bingo with one hand and his cigarette with the other.

"I wanted to talk to him about installing better lighting in and around the park. He said to me, 'Well, Charlotte, we have a process.' And then went on about how the city lighting district worked. Now, you have to understand something. I worked for the city. I worked for his predecessor, Councilman James Larkin. I was Councilman Larkin's chief of staff." Snark, grumbling ran through the crowd. "So I gently tried to remind him that I know how things work in the city. But he went on anyway, explaining to me that it was a process and that process takes time."

Bullshit mansplaining, Alfonso thought. His father's first major accomplishment after getting elected was to beautify their neighborhood. Included in the project were kitschy retro streetlights meant to resemble the city's original gas lamps. They sprouted all over, from St. Augustine to Helmsley to Mayfair to Beacon Street itself. None made their way to the flatlands. Alfonso remembered giving tours after the work was completed. Everyone commented on how amazingly fast the changes came. The Wizard did it again.

"This is the eighth attack and the third fatal attack in this park in two years," Charlotte continued. "And the second attack to happen in this corner. Any reasonable person would call that a crisis. Any reasonable person would do whatever possible to bring the attacks to an end. Councilman Berry, this crisis is happening on your watch and at your doorstep and you are doing absolutely nothing about it. Shame on you! Shame on you!"

So began the chant. SHAME! Carlton said every ACT UP demo seemed to include it, shouted at pharmaceuticals, hospitals, politicians. SHAME!—always increasing in volume with each repetition. SHAME! For many it was therapeutic, a release of the undying scream that dwelled within each infected faggot, their caregivers, and loved ones. SHAME! To air their anguish gave them power. SHAME! And now Alfonso claimed that power— SHAME! SHAME! SHAME! SHAME! SHAME!—unable to contain his own undying scream any longer.

⸺⸗⸻

Others began to speak. Alfonso asked Bingo if they could take a walk together. "Of course, honey!" he replied. Hearing Bingo's campy voice felt like its own type of music, and provided similar comfort.

They walked silently down 45th past Carver and then turned right at Lincoln. Bingo lit a cigarette. He drew hard drags and spat them back in the air with equal force. Alfonso refrained. His stomach bothered him too much.

"I just keep seeing him alone, in the hospital, all alone," Bingo said. "No one should die like that."

He stood and covered his face. Alfonso patted and rubbed his back. Eventually, they began walking again.

"I never visited. Couldn't," Alfonso said.

"I hear you. I only went a couple of times. After the first visit, I swear to God I almost drove to the airport and hopped on the first flight to South America." He took one last drag. The spent butt fell under his boot. Another took its place in his mouth instantly. "That's what I did during the height of the plague in the early '80s, just fucking lived in South America for two years. I couldn't deal with it. This whole damn summer's felt like a rerun."

"Uh-huh. Where in South America did you go?"

"Quito, mostly. But I also spent some time in Lima, Buenos Aires. I hopped around a bit."

"What brought you back?"

"Homesickness. Guilt. Sammy kept sending me articles about how nurses were needed. So I came back. I was amazed how little had changed, not just in the death rate, but in the whole approach to treatment—or the lack of treatment, more like it. I helped develop the AIDS clinic at General—that's how I met Mrs. Parker. She was there at the time. She helped me get settled back in the neighborhood. Eventually, I went back to school, got my MSN, and become a nurse practitioner." He smiled faintly. "Eddie teased me about always having my head in the books. He made sure I got my boogie on regularly."

"Yeah. He was always the same way with Carlton, up to the end. Damn."

Bingo put his arm around him as they walked. Alfonso leaned his head against Bingo's shoulder.

"So, can I tell you something?" Bingo asked.

"Go for it."

"One of the last things Carlton said to me was 'Take care of Alfonso for me.'"

Alfonso stared at the ground and smiled. "Sounds like something he'd do."

"And you know, you *know* you don't break promises made to that girlfriend."

"Yeah, I know."

"So I promise to start doing a better job!"

Alfonso gave him a kiss on the cheek. They stayed in an embrace as they walked for a while. Then Alfonso got the urge for a smoke. His stomach still bothered him a bit, but he couldn't help it. Whiffs of secondhand smoke weren't getting it done. Bingo lit it for him.

"There is something you can maybe help me out with, Bingo."

He talked about his paper for Professor Euclid. A tear crawling on his cheek spoke to its urgency. He wiped his eyes.

"Would it be cool if I visited the needle exchange y'all started doing on Lincoln?"

"Of course. But you sure you wanna do that?"

"Gotta do it, Bingo, for all sorts of reasons. That is, if I won't be in the way."

"No, of course not. We're opening some of the other clinic functions at Tamera's church next week. You can visit that, too. You should talk to Tamera."

"I will. For sure."

Alfonso's cell beeped. He took it out. A text from Roy.

<<Sammy's making dinner Sat. nite. Veggie chicken & dumplings. You in?>>

Alfonso texted back <<ALL IN!>>, stuck his phone back in his pocket.

"My angels to the rescue."

Street life emerged about three blocks north of the park, breaking the stillness of their wandering. They could smell a rapid succession of cultures—Chinese stir fry, Italian spices, and Louisiana gumbo. A lesbian couple with a stroller stopped to chat with a husband and wife carrying twins. Two middle-aged brothers sat on a stoop in deep contemplation over a chessboard. Across the street, a mother brushed her daughter's hair while talking on a cellphone. An elderly white gentleman swept rubbish from the curb. A fuzzy gray-and-white cat kept watch on a garbage lid in an alleyway between two buildings. Hip-hop, salsa, soul, and techno drifted faintly from unseen speakers. But then they heard a slow blues played on a live saxophone. A guy leaned under a streetlight, his arms cradling his axe. He wore a black driver's cap, a black vest over a red shirt, skinny black jeans, and bright white sneakers.

Alfonso and Bingo stopped, sat quietly on a stoop in front of him. The brother didn't seem to mind the audience. He kept playing, telling stories. Staccato notes sounded like head-shaking chuckles, long notes like gut-wrenching laments. He purred sweet nothings and shouted obscenities. He played free improvisation, but borrowed riffs from familiar melodies, sanctifying his testimony with what had come before.

Alfonso wished he could be this musician and possess the ability to communicate without the clumsiness of words and syntax. What if he could play a blues like this for his father? Would he understand it? Could he relate to it, connect it to some deep blues he experienced in his life?

A long note trailed into silence. The player tipped his hat to his audience, then walked between two buildings and vanished.

"Damn, he was good," Bingo said.

"Amazing."

"I wanted to give him something, but he didn't have an open case or hat."

"Maybe he was warming up for a gig."

They got up from the steps, continued their walk.

"Are you hungry?" Bingo said. "We're almost at Delaware. We could go to Ox's Diner."

"Yeah, sure. Maybe a shake to settle my stomach. Bingo, how did you come out to your folks?"

"I didn't, really. They had me pegged early on, but we never had 'the talk.' My dad was really uptight. We never had any type of relationship. Mom was more hit-and-miss. My siblings? Eh. My older sister and I connect, but my younger siblings, not so much. When I reached 18, I was so out of there."

"Where'd you grow up?"

"Idaho."

The diner was a block away. They stopped so that Bingo could finish his cigarette. Even by his own standard, he had had too many. Normally he stuck to weekend cigars. Cigarettes reappeared recently, a symptom of the summer, Bingo confessed.

Alfonso began singing, spontaneously. He just felt it, and had to give voice to it.

"*Sometimes I feel like a motherless child...*"

Subtle, fluid movements from his hands and upper body embellished his voice. He sang the spiritual all the way to the end, a contribution to the blues of the neighborhood.

"Thanks, baby. That was always one of Eddie's favorites."

"Really? Which version did he usually play?"

"Odetta's."

Alfonso nodded. So did Carlton.

SEVEN

Asleepless night. Robert Glasper played softly next to the pillow, his funk-fusion exploration of "Afro Blue" featuring Erykah Badu. Hands and fingers danced in the air, turning and gliding in silhouette against the waning moonlight shining between the gaps in the blinds above his bed.

Did Granddad jitterbug? Do photos exist of him getting down to Count Basie or Chick Webb or Duke Ellington? Who was Granddad?

At 6'4", Al Berry would have been quite a sight on the dance floor, cutting the rug with high kicks and wide swings. Folks thought the big and tall young man would become an athlete. They saw basketball or track and field in his future, perhaps an athletics scholarship. Some talked Olympics, the second coming of Jesse Owens. World War II interrupted that vision. But young Al Berry didn't set his sights on athletics. He couldn't be bothered with "separate but equal" sports leagues. Such thinking went against his upbringing. His father, Rutherford Berry, was the first African American admitted to the bar in the state's history and fought the good fight for equality in the courts.

Thus, history and portent suffused the life stories Alfonso heard from his grandfather.

———◆———

Al Berry began working summers in his father's law office when he was 11. He dressed neatly, black pants and long-sleeve white shirts, but never wore a tie despite his father's gentle encouragements. Too hot and sticky, Al said. One day, the office hosted a special visitor. Everyone scurried to tidy up desks and empty waste bins in preparation. Al asked what he could do. His father placed him in a small office and told him to file papers. Make-work, but he did as his father instructed. The visitor came and went. Only later did he learn that it had been W.E.B. Du Bois. Shocked and hurt, Al asked his father why he could not meet him. Because, his father said, you did not look your best. From that day forward, Al wore a tie. He washed it nightly and set it out to dry so that it would be ready by morning. Impressed with this routine, Rutherford bought his son two additional ones.

Dr. Du Bois came back to the office a few weeks later. My father proudly introduced me to him as "the promise of a new generation." I have molded my whole life behind that comment and my father's lesson to always look my best.

Rutherford Berry had the means to own a 4-door Studebaker Commander. Young Al loved riding in the front seat to watch his father sit masterly behind the wheel. One Saturday, as they rode home down Lincoln Avenue, a group of white kids threw junk at the car, rotten vegetables, fruit rinds, dog shit. Al looked out the window in awe and anger while his father kept driving, never increasing his speed, never taking his eyes off the road. When they got home, they found nothing cracked or broken, but the car looked a mess and smelled foul.

My father did not express his true feelings after this affront to his dignity, but I could tell that he was a hurt man. That car symbolized his belief that anyone in America could get ahead through hard work and determination, even a black man. So to see this symbol defiled by dirty little white boys really took a toll on him. I knew at once what I had to do.

Al took a scrub brush, hose, and soap to the car and went over it from front to back until it glistened again and smelled brand-new. It took six hours, but he didn't care. *Dignity has no time limit and no price too high to pay.*

The Studebaker incident prepped him for college, where spit wads and crud in his locker became more or less routine. They are testing you, his father said, provoking you to act like the angry Negro they picture you as. Don't let them. Disarm with charm, his father instructed. Your words, not your volume, will ultimately win your arguments, so chose them wisely. By the time Al entered law school, he had already earned the moniker Gentleman Giant.

His advancement matched the changing times. He launched his long-shot bid for the state assembly in 1954, the same year the Supreme Court held a wake for Plessy v. Ferguson and banished "separate but equal" with all deliberate speed. Detractors continued to paint him as a Tall and Dangerous Negro, but he remained steadfast and rallied many to his campaign. When he won, Du Bois sent him a congratulatory telegram. It hung in his office, framed under glass, until the day he retired. His first legislative victory came quickly, a bill aimed at reducing the effects of redlining. Though modest in scope, it provided the framework for later legislation, like the 1967 Federal Fair Housing Act. And his law paved the way for blacks to purchase houses in the Beacon Hill neighborhood in his district, where his future son would reside.

Assemblyman Al Berry became known for his soaring rhetoric and pensive poses. His constituents called him the Duke Ellington of politics. He worked triple hard to maintain that image in the public eye.

But did he jitterbug? Alfonso didn't know.

Granddad spoke only of high mountains and vast horizons, of destiny and duty. Speaking about the personal, poetic sides of life, all its setbacks and little victories, eluded him.

———

The moon moved out of view. No stars peeked through the shades. Darkness. Still no sleep. Alfonso let the music go silent. His hands rested underneath his head.

"Sure sounds like Charlotte's gonna run again."

———

During the 2008 campaign, Alfonso's father began calling him his First Lieutenant, a recognition for his work running errands and organizing the volunteers for mailing parties and precinct walks. It felt so close between them.

Granddad Al became a fixture in the house. Advanced age had stooped his tall frame and he walked with a cane. But he engaged himself fully in his son's first political campaign. Indeed, at times he seemed more engaged than anyone else, including the candidate.

You have to win this, Al, Jr. You have to be serious. You have to give it everything you got. Once you're in, you're set. But you gotta get in the damn door.

He dissed Charlotte the way a coach disses a rival team before the Big Game. But his trash talk bore a menace that Alfonso alone seemed to hear. Charlotte became a nameless pronoun, *her*, spoken gutturally, like he was clearing his throat to spit. It sounded like a comical affectation, the type of thing a grandparent would do to elicit giggles from the grandkids. Indeed, Belinda and Lucy both laughed whenever they were within earshot of him saying it. Alfonso, not so much. Granddad also referred to Charlotte's "agenda" frequently, without defining what it entailed, but also without masking his contempt for it. At 13, Alfonso knew enough about the world and himself to recognize things not said outright.

Mostly, though, the campaign felt like one big party. The house throbbed nonstop. Pizza often fed the late-night organizing. The First Lieutenant got to sample beer for the first time, his father giving him knowing winks. Just be cool around your mother, he'd say. Senator Barack Obama's campaign for the presidency ran parallel, adding to the festive spirit. This is a new era of progress, Granddad Al declared.

On a quiet night while watching TV in the living room, a month before the election, Alfonso heard his grandfather's raised voice booming from his father's study. The two were discussing the latest development: retiring Councilman James Larkin endorsed his longtime aide over the heir to the Berry throne. Granddad didn't take it well.

He's a cock-sucking son-of-a-bitch! That's what he is! A dirty little cock-sucking punk! Heh! We know his agenda. And we'll show

*that pussy-whipped faggot how it's done. Mark my words. He will
rue the day!*

As much as Alfonso wanted to, he could not ignore those
words, wish them away, or pretend that his granddad had not
spoken them.

A couple of days later, the local black community paper, the
freebie delivered every Thursday, printed a letter. It published
letters in a section called "Kitchen Chat": *Folks always speak their
mind in the kitchen. Come speak your mind in ours.* After giving the
word limit and their email address, the blurb ended with the cutesy
tagline, *Remember! Be civil in the kitchen!*

Directly beneath those instructions appeared this:

*She says she's an expert on children and education. What
can a childless b***d*** teach me about child-rearing?*

Signed, A. Jones

Alfonso saw no civility. Asterisks failed to mask the breach of
etiquette mandated by the cutesy tagline, but succeeded at exposing
the tagline's provincialism. After its publication, "bulldyke" and
"faggot" flourished at school, none directed at him personally,
but often invoked in his father's name, the name they shared. He
became an unwitting accomplice.

But worst of all, his father cosigned their name calling by
never distancing himself from the letter. Worst of all, dog-whistle
language crept into his stump speeches; suddenly, the longtime
community organizer and City Hall aide knew nothing about the
community she ran to represent, words Alfonso heard as "She's
not one of us." Worst of all, his mother turned away when he tried
to talk to her about the letter; he could not articulate his thoughts
very well, but had hoped she would sense his pain. Worst of all, as
his parents argued over the letter in their bedroom behind a closed
door, his father declared loudly, *That letter might well help me win
this election. Did you think of that?*

In an instant, the election went from exciting to awful. He felt
dirty, helpless, and alone.

Ford Berry won, 52 percent to 48 percent. Champaign flowed
at the house. Alfonso got to share a toast of the bubbly with his
father and grandfather. The three Alfonsos. A framed photo of

the toast still hung in the entry hall of the house. Al Sr. turned to his grandson and said, Your turn will come soon enough, with an affirming pat on the shoulder. Alfonso smiled for his granddad.

Later that night, around 11:30 p.m., the networks called the presidential race for Barack Obama. The party moved into the streets. Neighbors danced together with music blasting out the windows. No one could believe it: a black man in the White House. It was the only time he could recall seeing his granddad cry.

Alfonso hung out as long as possible, outlasting his sisters and mother, finally drifting inside around 1:30. Neither fatigue nor parental orders prompted him to go up to his room. He had to find out about something he had been putting off. In his closed room, he turned on the TV and clicked around. The answer came quickly. In California, Prop. 8 passed, closing a door to same-sex marriage that had just opened five months earlier. The vote broke the same as his father's: 52 percent yes, 48 percent no. He buried his face in his pillow to muffle the sobbing.

———✦———

When Granddad Al retired in 2001 after some forty-seven years in office, unflattering stories emerged from political allies and opponents alike, shattering the Gentleman Giant image. The elder statesman dismissed the accounts as sour whine from sour grapes. The accusers, he stated further, were merely doing the bidding of the racists who had tried unsuccessfully to dog his career for decades. Alfonso promised his internet-illiterate granddad that he'd keep his Wikipedia page free from such stories, keep it 100.

The tirade against Councilman Larkin and the homophobic turn in the election challenged Alfonso's resolve. After the election, he began reading the "sour whine" books in the Central Library downtown.

Each memoir told a similar story, that behind closed doors the Gentleman Giant turned into a raging bear who threatened to ruin those who failed to obey his dictates. He similarly threatened to play the race card on anyone who told the press anything unflattering about him. One ex-colleague stated pointedly, *Duke*

Ellington of politics? Try Charles Mingus. Like the legendary master bassist, the ex-colleague explained, Al Berry was not averse to using his enormous physical stature to bully those who annoyed him. He cited the "gym conferences" as an example. A towel-clad Berry would appear out of nowhere and loom over a naked colleague heading to the shower, demanding political favors or dictating marching orders. Others also wrote about these encounters.

Alfonso didn't like it. He had already developed a dislike for school gyms for exactly this reason. The bully always waited until his victim was naked, his penis small and shriveled for all the world to see. He often wondered if the bully concealed a hard-on underneath his towel.

From one of the memoirs, he learned about an unauthorized biography on his grandfather by a journalist named Neil Verity. Since it had his granddad's name and photo on the cover, he didn't feel comfortable reading it in public, even in his hidden corner at the library. So he bought it and sneaked it home in his backpack, then read it at night in bed with one of those clip-on night lights. It contained a story he had never heard.

Ernest Little was a soft-spoken, prim and tidy little man who dressed impeccably. On the surface, he seemed a perfect match for the Gentleman Giant, a young black man who reflected his refined image, if not his physical stature. Al Berry kept Little close at hand during committee meetings and when on the floor of the legislature giving oration. He was being molded, insiders said, guided into a career in politics. He was his right arm. So it came as a great shock when Little's naked body was found hanging from a rope in Berry's office suite in the capitol one Sunday by the cleaning staff. The rope was suspended from a hook in the ceiling where a chandelier likely once hung. Little accessed it by placing a chair on the desk underneath it. His clothes sat primly and tidily folded on the floor next to the wastebasket by his desk. Why? What happened? A very pale Al Berry held a press conference that same day in the capitol rotunda, with his office upstairs and off the main gallery. Normally when he spoke to the press, he stood in such a way that his office door appeared just over his shoulder, high above. This time he angled himself differently, to avoid shots of the crime scene tape. He told the press that his dear friend, young Mr. Little, suffered an unfortunate and regrettable emotional breakdown due to a family issue. After the service, Ernest Little was never spoken of again.

Verity spoke with various people and learned a very different story. Little's former colleagues stated that Al Berry often berated his protégé, calling him "weak," "limp-wristed." Berry particularly lost his temper when a deal Little was responsible for negotiating with another legislator fell through. It was after this tirade that Little killed himself. While reading about this episode, Alfonso saw familiar words: "punk," "cocksucker," "faggot." He wanted to put the book down, but found he could not stop staring at those words. Nor could he stop hearing his granddad's voice when he read them.

Verity interviewed Little's life partner, who had remained silent for decades. He died just before the book came out.

Ernest was a sensitive man. And his employer was a master manipulator. He knew how to flatter and he knew how to hurt. He knew just what to say to get at Ernest the most. And like any abuser, he knew how to manipulate his victim so that he would always come back. You know, the flowers and candy after the name calling, the diamonds after the beating. He played that game with Ernest.

Alfonso noted how Little's partner never referred to his granddad by name.

And Ernest had no family. His work colleagues were his family. He was totally estranged from his blood relatives. I never met any of them, until after the suicide, when they fought to get his money. So no, there was no "family issue." If there had been one, Ernest would have been the last to know about it.

One Saturday, after he finished Verity's book, Alfonso took it with him on a commuter train out to a park in the suburbs. It was a beautiful late-fall day. A temperate sun shone brightly that afternoon. Naked trees cast elongated, angular shadows on the grassless soil. He sought out a picnic area. There were many to choose from. Apart from a few runners and bikers, the park was deserted.

He burned the book in a brick barbecue pit next to a picnic table. He watched as the cover he clung to under the sheets over several nights curled and blackened with the advancing flames, as each of the pages turned to ash. He wanted a more visceral disposal than taking it to the dump. In addition to destroying the evidence, he needed a ceremony to mark when his grandfather ceased being Superman. What other stories did Granddad keep hidden behind the high mountains and beyond the vast horizons? From that point on, he left his granddad's Wikipedia page alone.

—✦—

Alfonso shouted "SHAME!" at his father in absentia. He lay sleepless in bed, wondering where that act would ultimately lead him.

EIGHT

LFONSO ENDED UP GETTING OUT OF BED AROUND 4 A.M.
Sleep wasn't happening. He sat at his desk, opened his
laptop, and scanned the internet for pictures of the vigil
to confirm that no one captured a shot of him. He found nothing.
Eventually, he started playing video games.

He was still playing at 7:30, when Belinda pounded on the
door in her usual fashion, scaring the shit out of him.

"What?" he yelled.

"Dad wants to see you."

He froze, unable to even breath.

———

Without showering, he dressed and went downstairs. The house
seemed very still. Too still. It took all he had to walk from the
bottom of the stairs through the dining room and into the kitchen.
His parents sat at the small table, the newspaper spread between
them and their coffee mugs. He scanned for photos, but saw none.

His father looked up with a faint smile. "Hello, Son," he said.
The low kitchen chair hid his towering height. He wore a dress
shirt without a tie and dark pants.

"What's up, Dad?"

"We've got a problem. Sit down, Son, sit down."

He sat stiffly between his parents.

"I suppose you heard about last night's 'vigil.' It was more like a damn political rally. Way to stay classy after someone died, isn't it?" He gulped some coffee. "Do you know that some of them stayed there overnight? They're starting a damn encampment or something. Outrageous. Just outrageous."

Alfonso knew. It was all over the internet. He remained silent.

"Son, I don't know if you've been reading the news, but it's been a bloodbath for me out there. It seems almost every day someone is saying something is my fault. The needle exchange clinic burns down, it's my fault. Man gets killed in the park, it's my fault. Stores closing, it's my fault. It's all my fault, you see? So many things." He sighed and took another sip of coffee. "It's just gotten ridiculous. You see what I'm saying?"

Alfonso nodded but otherwise remained very still.

"Exactly. The election is next year and this isn't the publicity I need. So your mother and I started thinking and I'm going to call Reverend Johnson and see if he agrees. But we're thinking that now would be a good time to have a unity rally. You know, like in the old days, a revival."

"Like Grandad did?" How quaint.

"Exactly, Son. It's one of those feel-good things that brings the community together. We'll have some good food, some music, we'll invite all of the local preachers and let them do their thing. You see what I'm saying? We want to show the media that this is a thriving community, not 'The Huck.'"

Alfonso shifted in his seat a bit. Hills folks usually distanced themselves from the grit of the flatlands, even though the distance wasn't that great. The old rhyme went through his head. *9-1-1 don't mean a fuck, if you're living in The Huck.*

"The community has lost its center," his mother said. "That is why this rally is so important."

"Right, so that's the game plan. We'll set it up. It'll probably be in two or three weeks. Now, what I need from you is the ASA's support. You know how important it is when the young people come out in support of these things. I need them to endorse it. But more than that, I need help in setting it up. You guys put on a lot of events at school and you all have lots of connections. Cheap catered food. Maybe a good DJ to spin or something, as long as he doesn't cost a fortune. This isn't a lush budget production, you know. And of course I need the group's help to spread the word."

"I'm sure the group will help you out, Dad."

"Excellent. How soon can you get me that endorsement?"

"The group has its weekly meeting tonight."

"That's not soon enough, Alfonso," Ford snapped. "Didn't you hear me? They are in the park now, camping out. This is a public relations disaster for me. I have to counter this shit *now*. So many things," he sighed. "Sure wish you had become president of the damn thing. Woulda made shit like this so much easier."

Alfonso bowed his head, avoided eye contact.

"I want to make the midday news cycle and announce my supporters. I want to include ASA on the list. You understand?"

"Can't you call some of your friends, dear?" his mother said. "Maybe do a phone conference?"

He looked up at her. "Yeah. I can do that, Mom."

"Good," his father said. His demeanor calmed. "Let me know when you get it, alright? And then tonight, at your meeting, you can start talking about the logistics. Thanks, Son."

Alfonso got up and poured himself a mug of coffee. Even the bland house stuff was better than nothing. Then he marched straight to his room and closed the door, leaned heavy against it. After a moment, he took out his cell to make the first important call of the day.

"Bill, call me when you got a minute, alright? I might be on the phone, but call me as soon as you can, alright? Thanks, sistah."

He drank the bland coffee, waited to see if Bill would call back. Nothing. Finally, he started calling the ASA gestalt. Cynthia didn't answer. He left a message. Tamesha, no answer. Finally, he got through to Leon, who liked the idea of a unity rally. Just tell him it's cool, man, he said about the endorsement, promising to give Cynthia a heads-up.

Alfonso hung up, then checked voice mail. Nothing. Bill probably was in transit or in class. He grabbed his backpack, went downstairs to the kitchen, where he saw his father on the phone.

"Yeah, I'm sure Eunice can get one of her groups on board. And Thad, I talked to Alfonso. He said he was going to get ASA's endorsement." Alfonso nodded and gave a thumbs-up. His father responded in kind. "Yep, my First Lieutenant is standing here now, and he said he got the endorsement. That's great, Son," he said off the phone. "Yep, they're meeting tonight to start planning for it." He looked at Alfonso again. "Have a good day, Son." He went back to the phone. Alfonso kissed his mother on the cheek and left the kitchen.

"Yeah, that's fine," Ford continued. "No, no, I think that's right. We'll invite Tamera Woodson. She don't have to speak, but we'll invite her. … Right, exactly. That way, they can't say we left her out. If she don't show up, that's her problem."

Alfonso lingered in the entry hall when he heard Reverend Tamera's name. The old battle lines redrawn, religious Southside blacks versus hedonistic Northside homos. How fucking quaint.

Outside, walking down the hill, he lit the first of the day, but no amount of puffing brought relief.

Sammy looked up and saw Charlotte walk in with weighted footsteps. She went straight to the back room and soon emerged with a cup of coffee.

"You are the subject of many a rumor, lady," Sammy said.

For once, she did not shut him up with *Don't start with me, Samuel Turner*. She sat silently next to him, staring blankly.

"Liz and I had a fight last night," she said.

"What about?"

"Something stupid."

"Uh-huh. You two patch it up this morning?"

"No. I left the house before she woke up. I just came from Huckleberry Park. Can you believe that? I was walking around that damn park for about an hour."

Sammy turned and faced her.

"Saw Bill running for the bus. He waved hi." Sammy smiled. "And I saw Mrs. Parker sitting on her stoop, just staring into the park. She didn't even notice me looking at her. You know how you get when you're watching something good on TV? That's how she was staring into the park. You know, Sammy, until that moment, I didn't really understand. We've all heard her go on about how the park used to be or how the neighborhood used to be. And we remember, we just don't think about it."

"Mm-hmm."

"But until that moment, seeing her staring into the park, I never really understood just how lonely she was. And I don't mean that she don't have people who visit her or talk with her. I know she does. But she's lonely, Sammy. She's lonely for her used to be, you know what I'm saying? She ain't just lonely for herself, she's lonely for all of us. It was like I could see the world through her eyes. And it all just came together."

Sammy nodded his head, eyebrows low over his eyes.

"I went over to her and we said hi to each other. Then we both just sat on that stoop and stared at the park. And that's when I decided to start running."

"Great Dizzy," he sighed. He got up and shuffled behind Charlotte to get to the stereo. "Hang on, I got it here somewhere." He found the CD he wanted and put it on. Soon the Hallelujah Chorus from Handel's *Messiah* rang throughout the store at full volume. Charlotte nearly busted a gut.

"Miss Charlotte, I've been waiting to hear those words from you for too many damned years!" He bent over and gave her a hug as the Hallelujahs sang above them.

"You crazy, Samuel Turner!"

"Now," he said, standing upright again, "we'll figure out the particulars later. We got a whole lotta work ahead of our behinds. But right now, you march through this store and get what you need for dinner, then this evening make y'all's special dish and patch it up with Liz. 'Cause you two are in for a long haul, and you'll need each other."

Charlotte stood up, walked to the vegetable bin, and began picking over the onions.

"You're beautiful, Sammy."

He stood next to his stereo, arms folded, a grin on his face. But in the back of his mind, a thought lingered. What about Alfonso?

Bill suggested that they meet on one of the benches next to the creek leading up to the north side of campus. Besides its natural tranquility, it was tucked away enough to avoid unwanted peering eyes or listening ears.

Alfonso explained everything going on for him. No inhibitions, not with Bill. Their friendship hugged him like a security blanket. He even confessed to joining the chant at the vigil.

"So in case you were wondering why my voice sounds all deep and sexy like yours, that's why."

"I'm so sorry, babe."

"I love my father, Bill. That's why this is so hard. Four years ago I lucked out, 'cause he ran unopposed. I can't go through this again." His head dropped to the back of the bench. Bill took him and leaned him on his shoulder.

"I don't understand his thing against the clinic," Bill said. "Wouldn't think needle exchanges would still be an issue, at least not around here."

"You know, if the clinic had opened in another part of town, he'd probably be cool with it. Or at least neutral. I really think that. He just gets all NIMBY when it comes to anything queer, just like my granddad did. It's like he's channeling my granddad. It's so depressing."

Silence, apart from the creek gurgling behind them.

"ASA doesn't see me as Alfonso. They see me as Alfonso R. Berry III, my father's son. I'm his mouthpiece. And now I have to be him again and rally the troops for his campaign." His face fell. "I can't do this alone. I know I said you don't have to go to meetings if you don't want, but—"

"Alfonso, of course I'll go with you. You ain't gotta beg. I'm there."

"Thanks, sistah."

"Don't beat yourself up. We all gotta do what we gotta do to get by sometimes. And, you know, I gotta make a cameo sometimes while I'm still tutoring at Reverend Johnson's. Then maybe they'll stop tripping about me in the Cuddle Corner or some shit like that."

Alfonso snickered. Then he closed his eyes. Cushioned by the gurgling creek and Bill's muscled shoulder, he drifted into needed sleep, his worries put on hold for the time being.

ASA turned into a non-event. Before Alfonso could go into his spiel, Reverend Johnson called and spoke to the group on speaker phone. We must protect Councilman Berry from forces trying to take him down, he thundered with apocalyptic cadence. After riling everyone up, he handed off to Alfonso to talk logistics. The First Lieutenant did so efficiently. Then he and Bill departed, though not without some side eye from Jameel.

On the bus ride to Carver Street, they mocked the reverend's fire and brimstone cloudburst, a way to relieve the tension his dog whistling created in both of them. Silently, Alfonso wondered if the reverend's call meant his father didn't trust him.

Bill dropped Alfonso off at Sammy's, then reminded him that he lived in Mrs. Parker's building. "Call and I'll come running," he said.

Bingo arrived instantly. "No police, right?" Alfonso said with a nervous snicker as they exited the store. Bingo smiled. "We have awesome neighbors. They'd never call the cops on us."

Just as they reached the corner of Carver and 45th, Alfonso paused.

"Can we cut through the park?" he asked.

"Sure."

They crossed the street and went through the stone gateway.

"You heard about my dad's rally?"

Bingo nodded.

"He's circling the wagons. He's worried about everything that's been going on, and this is his way of dealing with it. It's bringing up a lot of old shit for me. I saw the backside of his first election, and it wasn't pretty. Like that letter."

"You mean the Anonymous Jones letter?"

"Is that what folks call it? Yeah, well, I don't know who wrote it, but it came out after my granddad had a fit 'cause Councilman Larkin endorsed Charlotte over my father. He went on a tear, man."

He described what he heard from the living room, the slurs again living in his head.

"Damn. Where'd all that come from?"

Alfonso shook his head. "That whole campaign, he kept on my dad until he made Charlotte's sexuality an issue."

"Which is ironic, because Charlotte made a point of not running as the 'lesbian candidate.' It was kind of a thing, really. Some of us thought it was a mistake for her to, in effect, run in the closet."

"Wow. I had no idea."

"Yeah, it was really unfortunate. A lot of hard feelings."

"Carlton and I didn't know each other that well during the first campaign. How did he deal with it?"

"Very subdued. He supported Charlotte, but kept it to himself."

"Huh. Interesting. He was no fan of my father's, I know that."

"He told me that he didn't want to get ostracized by your folks and make you off-limits."

"Ferreal, Bingo? He said that?"

Bingo nodded.

Alfonso stopped walking, took Bingo by the shoulders. They hugged in the middle of the darkened field. He sniffled a bit. They continued walking after a while.

"My dad's gonna play the queer card again, Bingo, just like Granddad taught him to. Only this time, he'll expect me to take part in it. I just can't with this shit."

"Honey, are you sure you wanna hang out with us? I'm not for a second saying that you aren't welcome. Of course you are. I just wanna make sure you're doing the right thing."

Alfonso pointed toward the trees and bushes that bordered the park along Lincoln.

"See over there? That's where I stood and hid during the clinic fire." He put his arm down. "I saw everything. You, Mrs. Parker. I didn't move from that spot 'cause I was afraid of what my dad would say if he found out that I had been there. I never went to the clinic when it was open because I didn't want him to find out. I can't keep being afraid of doing shit because of my father. I can't keep sitting on the sidelines, Bingo. I just can't."

They climbed the embankment and walked to the sidewalk. The van was just a few yards down. Harry and Lucinda huddled next to it under the canopy of trees that hung over the sidewalk. There was little vehicle traffic and few walked the sidewalk.

"Oh, lord!" Bingo said. "Is that Henny Penny standing there with them?"

"I think it is."

Henny wore tight black jeans and a loose-fit pullover sweater. They saw Lucinda listening to him go on while Harry gave him a fist full of condoms, which he stuffed into his pockets. He said hi to Bingo, who replied tepidly. Then he looked at the councilman's son, a shy grin on his face.

"Hi, Alfonso."

"Hi, Curtis." He didn't realize Henny knew his name. They looked at each other awkwardly for a bit.

"So," Alfonso said, "how did the date go?"

"Hmm?"

"The date with that guy? Sammy made some food for your dinner with him."

"Oh, yes. Well, that didn't go off quite as planned."

"Oh, I'm sorry to hear that."

"It happens. Well, y'all take care. Bye, Alfonso."

"Bye, Curtis."

He walked north on Lincoln toward 45th.

Harry waited until Henny Penny was out of earshot. "Uh-huh. He ain't fooling no one."

"What do you mean?" Alfonso asked.

"He's heading north now, but he'll curl around and head back that way," Harry said, pointing behind him, "and visit the black tearoom."

"Oh." Alfonso had heard about the cruisy restroom just off the basketball courts, but never visited it.

"That's why he bulked up on the condoms," Harry said.

"At least he uses them," Lucinda said.

"So I guess Mr. Wonderful didn't work out," Alfonso said.

"They never do," Harry said. "He was bugging Sammy the other day, telling him how the man never even showed up. Henny Penny is first, last, and always drama."

And sad, Alfonso thought, as Henny's eyes lingered in his.

NINE

Saturday Night
Sammy's Apartment, Carver Street

L AUGHTER. LOTS OF LAUGHTER. EVERYTHING SET OFF THE three young men at Sammy's table, and he embraced laughing at and with them. A 500-CD shuffler provided the evening's soundtrack and amusement. As it pumped out random tracks of jazz, the boys helped themselves to making fun of it. Get an iPod! Roy taunted. Sammy rolled his eyes while Miles and company played "In a Silent Way."

Roy presented his signature walnut-apple-feta salad. It quickly vanished, the bowl taking several trips around the table to refill plates. The conversation hopscotched from salad making to *RuPaul's Drag Race* to basketball. At Alfonso's suggestion, Bill joined him, Victor, and Jameel for their semiregular Friday game. Sammy nodded silently. He heard the undertone: reestablish Bill's creds as just another brother in ASA.

"We paired up against Victor and Jameel," Alfonso said, "the shrubs versus the redwoods. Yeah, I'm looking at you!" he said to Bill, who stuffed salad into his grinning teeth. "He hit us with this 'can't play no more' crap, but we saw through his bullshit real fast. He was darting across the court like a gnat. Buzzzzzzzzzz!"

Folks laughed. "Where's Bill? Under the net, connecting again! And again! And again! Shiiit! He was doing the work of both of us. I had to up my game real fast."

"Jameel was my main target," Bill said. "I wanted to 'thank' him for the bullshit he pulled at the Freshman Reception."

"Yeah. And he tried to give me some two-cent attitude afterward. I was like, son, you've sent me tumbling across the court more times than I know, so enjoy the payback!"

"Was that asshat Leon there?" Roy asked.

"No," Alfonso said.

"Too bad."

"That's alright," Bill said. "They better learn. We're Carlton's Posse and we don't take shit from nobody."

Alfonso was very moved. He raised his glass. Bill and Roy did the same.

"Carlton's Posse in da house!" Alfonso said.

"All up in da house!" Roy said.

Sammy raised he glass in salute to them, a warm smile on his face.

"So now," Bill said, "I got Reverend Johnson asking me if I'll join the church's basketball team. I smile and shit, but I'm like, naw. I'm there for my students, but otherwise don't get too close. I went through one falling-out with the church already. Don't need lightning to strike twice."

"Back home?" Alfonso asked. "What happened?"

"Yeah, well. Long story." He stabbed a chunk of apple, then played with the fork. "My hometown was pretty segregated back in the day. My mom told us stories. It's more diverse now. In fact, Gabriel's mother is Guatemalan."

"Wow," Roy said.

"Yeah. I never met her. He lived in town with his grandmother, on his father's side. Anyways, it used to be one of those towns where black folks literally lived on the wrong side of the tracks. And you couldn't go to the other side without catching shit. That doesn't happen so much anymore, but folk still act like it does."

"Die Mauer im Kopf," Alfonso said. "The wall in the head. Learned that in German class last year. It's the idea that some folks still act like the Berlin Wall still exists."

"Yeah, exactly. That shit lingers. So anyways, one of the beacons in the town was our preacher, Reverend Smith. He was like our own private Martin Luther King, Jr."

"Uh-huh," Sammy grunted.

"I looked up to him so much growing up. I wanted to be like him. But then a couple of years ago, around the time Gabriel and I got together, he dropped this sermon. Spooked the shit out of me. I thought it was God telling me, 'Don't wreck yourself.'"

> *Brothers and sisters! We all know that some men are addicted to a certain type of sin! And that they love their sin to the exclusion of all else! To the exclusion of their families! To the exclusion of their community! To the exclusion of their church! To the exclusion of their women! Yes, the women that they should love! The women who will bear them children! The children to keep our community alive! They can produce no children, brothers and sisters, if they love each other! If they love their sin! But we can't call it love, brothers and sisters! Their 'love' is lust and it is a sin! Their 'love' is lust and it is a sin!*

Sammy shook his head, having heard the story too many times. "Anthony and I had a falling-out over it."

"The choir director the church matrons used to set up on dates?" Alfonso asked.

"Yeah. I tried to talk to him about it, 'cause I could tell he didn't like it either. But he screamed at me. 'Don't ever criticize a preacher on the pulpit!' He never screamed at the rowdiest kid in choir, but he went off on me. That was it. I walked out. After that, I just spent time with Gabriel, up until he left for the army and we moved here."

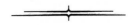

Sammy brought out the veggie chicken and dumplings. Roy followed with a bowl of steamed string beans and more dinner rolls.

"Eat up," Sammy said. "It's a carb fest, but y'all are young. You'll burn it off before the night's over."

Wayne Shorter swaggered through, matching the bravado with which they attacked the meal. Dizzy Gillespie kept the pace going, as did Mary Lou Williams.

Bill asked Roy if he went to church at all. Never touched the stuff, Roy said, with one exception. Growing up, they went to church for Christmas mass, the last ember of Catholicism that burned in his mother. "But after she died—" he said, his voice trailing off.

———

Dinah Washington entered their heads as the feasting mellowed. Sammy had long since pushed his plate away. Alfonso slowed down to occasional nibbling, as had Roy. But Bill went hard on yet another full slice of the veggie chicken. He couldn't get enough of it. Fake chicken never tasted so good. It's all in the seasoning, Sammy said.

"When this one went veggie, I had to learn a whole new bag."

"Not without a whole lot of drama," Roy said.

"Well, I learned!"

Alfonso experienced a spontaneous laugh attack. The other smiled and giggled as the fit continued.

"Oh, god!" Alfonso said. "I just remembered when you refused to dissect a fetal pig in Mr. Shale's class! He was so pissed, Bill! I was in Shale's class the period after Roy's and he spent almost the whole class going on about it. He. Was. Pissed."

"He. Was. Psycho," Roy said.

Bill laughed.

"It made the home page of the school's online paper," Alfonso said. "You became the most famous vegetarian on campus!"

Sammy shook his head. "And you still don't know when the stop! Go ahead! Tell them what your paper's about for Missy Quill."

"No!" Bill said. "You ain't going there!"

"Great Dizzy, yes, he's going there, Bill."

"I have to!" Roy said. "I found this book at The Other Bookstore about gays in ancient history. It has a whole chapter on Gilgamesh. Turns out there's some scholarship about King G and Enkidu getting it on. So I ain't just making this shit up. Missy will just have to deal with it."

Bill didn't know what say. He leaned over and gave Roy a kiss.

"Don't encourage him! Royboy, that uptight nelly's gonna flunk you!"

"I dare him to. Look, if I'm Miss Queer Revolution, you only have yourself to blame. I've been hanging out in his store since forever. With him and Harry and Bingo and Ms. Ashley and Charlotte and Auntie Vera. Get the picture? It was like being in Radical Queer 101."

"Busted!" Alfonso said.

Sammy feigned pearl-clutching innocence.

Roy took his vibrating cell out of his pocket. A text message appeared on the screen.

"To the surprise of no one," he said.

"What's up?" Alfonso asked.

"Jeremiah's not coming home tomorrow as scheduled. Said he'd be back later this week. Typical." He stuck his cell back in his pocket. "He's been hacking like a damn sailor for the past week. He shouldn't have gone out at all."

"Does your dad go on long runs in his truck?" Bill asked.

"Only as far as his girlfriend's. That's where you'll usually find him. Well, guess that means I don't need to cook dead meat for him tomorrow. Whatever."

"So you can rock the meat dishes?"

"When I gotta."

Sammy liked the progress he'd seen in Roy over the years since his mother died, but it still troubled him that he remained on a "first name basis" with his father, nomenclature indicative of distance, not warmth. It wasn't like that before his mother died. For how long would it last?

All three boys helped clear the table. Roy set out the dessert dishes and flatware. Sammy came in from the kitchen with the Main Event.

"Oh, it's getting mighty real in here!" Bill said.

"Are you a tiramisu fan, Bill?" Sammy asked.

"Oh, hell yeah!"

"Y'all eat up. And take some with you. Lord knows I don't need to eat too much of it."

They complied willingly with monster slices.

The next track caught Alfonso's attention. "Ozzie Bailey!"

"You have this one, Alfonso?" Sammy asked.

"Yes!"

Ozzie sang "Something to Live For" to composer Billy Strayhorn's piano accompaniment. The music filled the room with enchantment, like a warm evening under a starry sky where the well-dressed mingled with jazz and cocktails.

"This is one we listened to all the time," Alfonso said.

"It's nice," Bill said.

"I'll never forget when Carlton told me that both of them were gay. That rocked my world. I don't know how out Ozzie was, but Billy Strayhorn—"

"He was fierce, for real," Roy said.

The boys kept talking about music, shifting from Ellington and Strayhorn to Beyoncé and Jay-Z. No one noticed Sammy get up from the table and cross the living room to his bedroom. The old man snickered as they argued about which contemporary artists would endure like the jazz legends. He took out an old 4-track tape deck from his closet. Then he leaned over to dial in the combination to his safe. Dust caked the knob, got on his fingers. Has it really been that long? He wiped off the dust against his pants, then opened the safe. On the bottom shelf sat a black case with "J. Turner" inscribed on it. Per tradition, he opened the case, kissed two fingers, and touched the shiny golden trumpet within before closing the case again. He then took out a thin box from the upper shelf.

The boys had moved on to dissing the latest ins and outs on *American Idol*. Sammy turned off the stereo on his way through to the dining room. He quietly set up his tape deck.

Roy finally took notice, got real quiet. Alfonso and Bill also turned their attention to Sammy as he made final adjustments to the tape.

"You wanted to hear this, Alfonso," he said, as he pressed Play.

Brushes on the drums measured out a slow pulse. The bass played a muted line. Then came the piano and finally a trumpet and tenor sax, playing in unison. Delicate phrasing commanded attention instantly. Soulful lines rich in texture elevated the tinny speaker of the tape deck to beyond its limitations. The boys sat enraptured.

"What is this?" Bill asked softly.

"It's Sammy's tune," Roy whispered, "'The Lavender Veil Blues.' That's him on the drums."

Alfonso closed his eyes and slowly turned his head from side to side. Its mournful air made him think of Mingus's "Goodbye Porkpie Hat," the quintessential blues requiem. But he also heard traces of Strayhorn wistfulness from "A Flower Is a Lovesome Thing." As solemnly as the chords fell, the tune swung, even at its slow tempo. It lifted and glided him to the living room, like a breeze catching a silk tapestry. His arms stretched in wavelike patterns. His hands and fingers spoke in nimble gestures. Each leg arched one at a time high in the air. He lowered himself into a split, before rising back to his feet, all with incredible control.

Bill and Roy sat dumbfounded. They had no idea.

Sammy shed a tear, so moved was he that his old tune inspired such beauty.

TEN

S AMMY SAT AT THE KITCHEN TABLE WITH SOUTH AFRICAN
rooibos tea, hanging out with the boys as they scrubbed pots
and pans and loaded the dishwasher. He told them they
didn't have to, but they ignored him. About the food, though, he
was adamant.

"Pack it up and take it with."

He particularly wanted no trace of the tiramisu left in his
apartment. Bill and Roy obliged, but Alfonso said that he wasn't
going straight home. He mentioned a party while remaining vague
on the details. Uh-huh, who is he? the Posse demanded. I wish! he
said in his defense.

After a group hug, the boys bounded downstairs and hit
Carver Street Saturday night foot traffic. Across the street, the
Stud-Finder hummed and buzzed with activity. In the darkened
sky, storm clouds caucused over the fate of those below.

"Damn," Bill said, "I didn't hear any of this up in Sammy's
place."

"Double-paned windows and insulation around the sills," Roy
said.

"You guys, it's been real," Alfonso said. "Thanks for letting me
hitch a ride. This dinner was off the chain."

"Man, your dancing was so—I don't even know how to
describe it," Bill said.

"Thanks, Bill!"

"Seriously, you need to get your ass up to north campus with me and major in dance," Roy said. "And child! You must have said something real sweet to Sammy. He never goes there about his music. I mean Ne-ver."

"Roy, that tune is gorgeous," Alfonso said. "And his drumming is badass. Why?"

Roy shrugged. "I know. I know. He's never told me the whole story. All I know is that he never goes there. So you must be on his special list." He gave Alfonso a peck on the cheek.

"Have fun at your party, babe," Bill said, kissing him on the lips.

"Y'all have fun," Alfonso said with a teasing smirk. "Check you sistahs later."

He went north up Carver Street. Bill and Roy headed south toward 45th and Roy's apartment.

The apartment door opened to a flood of party funk created by the smell of drinks and body scents and by the din of loud music and voices. The space was filled four times its capacity. And the first person Alfonso ran into was Jameel, who shoved a plastic cup of beer in his face.

"You late!" he yelled into one ear.

"You early!" Alfonso yelled back.

Jameel made a face and moved on, sort of rocking to the music. Alfonso sliced through the crowd to get to the window, holding his beer high. The cool, stormy weather outside provided the funky space with needed air conditioning. Jerome, the host, approached him along with Cliff.

"Looks like you're already set, 'Fonso," Jerome yelled.

"Yeah. Jameel fixed me up."

"Let me know if you need something stronger! I got some good shit in the back."

"Thanks, brother."

Jerome moved on and Cliff moved in, pressing his hand into Alfonso's.

"How you been, brother?"

"I'm doing alright. How you been? How's Exec Board treating you?"

"I guess we're getting some shit done. I don't know. How about you and ASA? You didn't run for president, right?"

"Naw."

"See, man. They should have drafted your ass." Alfonso laughed. "I'm serious! You know how to get shit done. You got the passion and you got ideas."

"You should have been my campaign manager!"

"I should have." He moved closer to Alfonso's ear. "I mean, Cynthia Greenfield? Seriously?"

Alfonso smiled, tilted his head.

"Listen, Alfonso. If they ain't recognizing and treating you right in that group, then go do something else. Don't waste your talents where they ain't appreciated."

Cliff patted him firmly on the shoulder. "Keep it 100, bruh," he said, before moving into the crowd.

Just like that Cliff buoyed his spirits. He hadn't realized how much he missed hanging with him.

A breeze from the window kept him cool as he nursed his beer slowly. He wanted to adjust to the space before having to navigate its heavy zones to get a refill. Faces and bodies drifted by like riders on a psychedelic carousel. They dipped and switched one way, then the other in sync with the beats. He exchanged words with them as they passed. Then his eyes fell on Jameel in the distance. He was laughing and chatting with Cliff. Alfonso smirked. For real?

The night air kept inviting him out, and he couldn't resist. No one else braved the fire escape, so he dived out the window and took a spot on the landing. The room was like a sauna. It felt good to be outside with the caucusing clouds.

After a stretch of solitude, Jameel crawled out the window with another filled to the brim.

"Saw you sitting out here. Thought you might be on empty." He put the cup on the fire escape landing.

Alfonso smiled. "Thanks. Where you been?"

"Around."

He maneuvered to sit next to Alfonso. Both their legs dangled underneath the fire escape grating. Their faces looked between the bars. Their beers sat on the grating next to their butts.

"I was in the back room," Jameel said. "You been back there?"

"No, not tonight."

"Why not?"

"Just don't feel like it." He felt Jameel staring at him.

"He got some good pot tonight, man. You're missing it."

"Did I see you talking to Cliff?"

"Yeah, he's here. Taking a time-out, you know. Left his lady and the kid at home."

"I thought you hated his guts, man."

"What the hell made you think that?"

Alfonso laughed. "Well, maybe all that trash talk you did a few weeks back. Remember? At the first ASA meeting?"

Jameel closed his eyes and chuckled. Then he sucked his teeth. "Man, that's just, you know, whatever. I'm just keeping it real around folks, 'Fonso. You know I don't give a shit about what he do."

Alfonso took another swig of beer. "I can't figure you out sometimes."

"Maybe you just ain't paying attention. You ain't seen no one from ASA, have you?"

"Naw, they ain't here. You know they don't like coming to Jerome's parties."

"You right. They too uptight."

Jameel looked at him again.

"How come you never come over and play video games with me no more? I ain't seen you all summer and not since school started either."

Alfonso kept his look forward. "I don't know. I guess you don't invite me over."

"Since when I gotta invite you over? You used to just come over."

"Guess I figured you were sick of kicking my ass."

Jameel didn't say anything.

"Last summer was a hard one. I was visiting someone in the hospital when I wasn't at work."

"Uh-huh."

"He died."

"Uh-huh. Sorry to hear that. Anyone I know?"

Alfonso couldn't remember if he had ever talked to Jameel about Carlton. He picked up his near-empty cup, forced the trickles into his mouth, and licked the rim for the remains.

"No, you don't know him," he finally said.

Jameel drank the rest from his cup.

"How come you were so late?"

Alfonso turned and saw Jameel's eyes, but then turned away quickly. "I had to help Lucy with her homework." He spoke truthfully. He just didn't go there about Bill, Roy, and Sammy.

"Another paper?"

"Nah, math this time. She's having problems with pre-calc. Her last test score sucked, so the folks took away her TV and grounded her this weekend."

"Did you help her out?"

"Yeah. It took a minute, but I helped her through it."

"How are you dealing with the grief of losing your friend?"

"It's been a rough ride."

"Uh-huh."

"He left me his CDs, blues and jazz. I've been listening to it a lot."

"Uh-huh. Anyone in particular?"

Alfonso fidgeted. He didn't know why he brought up the music. He didn't mean to. He forgot where he was and it just came out.

"Mostly Billie Holliday, I guess. Yeah." No Strayhorn. He didn't want to go there about the other Billy.

"That's good."

A real heavy track throbbed inside. Some folks screamed. Alfonso turned around. Many ran to join the carousel. Jameel started sliding his head side to side. Alfonso turned his head forward again, tapped his foot in the air.

"You know," Jameel said, "hip-hop, good hip-hop, is just the blues with attitude."

Alfonso cracked a smile, turned and looked at Jameel. "Not the BHB shit."

"Naw, brother. Not the BHB shit."

BHB, Bitch-Ho-Bling, their term for lousy, commercial hip-hop. Jameel riffed it back in high school during a poetry slam.

Alfonso pulled his legs in suddenly, like he was about to get up and go.

"Where you going?"

"Thought I'd get a refill. You want one?"

"Yeah. But you stay here, alright? I'll go get it."

Jameel stood up too fast and was unsure of his footing. Alfonso caught him by the leg. Jameel put his hand on Alfonso's and held it there. Their eyes locked. For an instant, they both felt it. Then Jameel broke the spell by patting Alfonso's hand before taking it away. Alfonso released Jameel's calf.

"You got your momma's eyes, you know that?" Jameel said. "I'm OK. You stay here, alright? Promise?"

"Promise."

Their eyes met again.

"Your friend, did he live a good life?"

Alfonso nodded. "Just too short."

"Uh-huh. True grief is a blues never sung. I hope he sang as much as he could." Jameel slipped into the window, back to the din of the party.

Alfonso squeezed his eyes shut, tightened his lips. He lightly beat his head against the bars of the fire escape, creating a dull thud filled with many discordant notes as the metal vibrated. His hand reached into his back pocket for a stick to light up. Smoke flew into the unsettled air.

"Fuck."

He wondered if another beer was a good idea.

Bill stared at a photo of Roy's mother. How beautiful. Tamesha's Cliff-gate bullshit came to mind. Did they know, back in high school, that Roy's mother was white? He drifted to other photos and then stumbled on a few framed drawings. He recognized the penmanship.

"You could be an art major," Bill said. "These are just as tight as your Gilgamesh drawing."

"Thanks. For some reason, I couldn't stop drawing after my mother died. Oh, that reminds me, I have the Gilgamesh drawing for you. It's in my room. I meant to bring it to Sammy's but forgot."

"You're giving it to me? How sweet."

Bill walked to the dining room table. They sat next to each other with mugs of tea.

"What happened to your mother, if you don't mind my asking?"

"Cancer. She died when I was 13."

"I'm sorry. That's too young."

"For both of us."

Their fingers began to mingle and they looked at each other in playful snatches. The snatches soon lapsed into face nibbling. Roy stood, led them to the bedroom. Clothing quickly became optional. A heavy downpour against the bedroom window provided the perfect soundtrack for bodily explorations.

Jameel, looking drowsy and slurring his words, begged Alfonso to leave with him. Alfonso was getting tired of the party, too, so he agreed. They dodged the downpour by huddling close under Alfonso's tiny umbrella as they ran to a waiting bus. They slouched on seats across from each other.

Alfonso turned his face to stare out the front of the bus. Jameel sat with his eyes closed.

"There's something I've been wanting to tell you since the summer," Jameel said.

Alfonso blinked. The beer fueled too many possibilities.

"What?"

"There was a coup in the Party. I'm out."

"Ferreal?"

"New clique took over. They thought they were gonna criticize me."

"Criticize you about what?"

"They put you in the middle of a circle with them sitting all around you. And they criticize you, try and break you. Tell you what's wrong with you and why you ain't a good revolutionary."

"I know what the circle is, but why you?"

"Told you. It was a coup. Those punks thought they knew shit about me. Thought they were gonna break me. I wouldn't let 'em. I didn't go back. And I ain't going back. No one's gonna make me fucking cry, shit. Fuck them. I know what revolution looks like."

Alfonso wished he didn't have the urge to caress him. He wished he hadn't touched Jameel on the leg. He couldn't recall ever touching his leg, and now he didn't want to stop touching it. He cursed the beer.

"Why don't you come over, 'Fonso? We can play some games."

"You sure you're up for it?"

"'Course I am. Shit. I can still whup your ass, man. Walk me home, alright?"

"I gotta go to church with my family tomorrow."

"So. I'm going out to the fucking 'burbs to see my folks. If I wake up."

Alfonso said nothing.

Jameel pulled the cord for his stop. "Let me have your umbrella."

He handed it to him. "What am I supposed to use?"

"You got your hoodie on."

Jameel hopped up and pushed out the rear exit.

Alfonso leaned his head against the cold, rain-struck window. He took his cell out to play some blues in his ear. Whatever tune came up. He didn't care which.

.

ELEVEN

LFONSO STOOD ON THE BALCONY, SMOKING. HE HAD chatted a bit in the office when he first arrived, but did not linger. Nor did he help with anything. He couldn't be bothered.

After puffing through a couple of sticks, he reentered the office and scooped up his backpack. Everything cool? he asked Cynthia. Yes, all was well. Then he muttered some kind of goodbye and pushed out the door. It had barely closed when Jameel leapt to his feet to follow him.

"What's up with you?" he asked.

Alfonso was partly down the stairs and stopped. He turned around.

"What are you talking about?"

"You've been like this for weeks now. You get up and smoke your brains out during the discussions, then you bolt out before it's all over. What's up with that?"

Alfonso stared at him. Jameel looked upset in a way he never had seen before.

"I'm just working on a project, man."

"What, and your father's unity rally ain't important enough for you?"

"Don't start guilt-tripping me about what I should or shouldn't be doing, Jameel! It ain't your fucking business, alright? Just back off! You don't know what I'm doing and you don't know all my business, so just stay in your lane!"

"Hey, man, don't trip, alright? I'm just checking that's all. It ain't like you missing meetings and shit, 'Fonso. Just wanna make sure it's all good, man."

"Yeah, it's all good." Bitterness stayed in his voice.

"Alright, man," Jameel said.

Alfonso skipped down in a hurried clip.

Jeremiah had a long coughing fit. He picked up his beer, but another fit came on before he could douse the first. Yet he insisted on going out in the truck again tomorrow, just a short run, though, he said. He'd be back by Sunday. Roy didn't like it, but didn't say anything. Nagging never worked with his father, any more than it worked on him. But he really didn't like the hacking. It's been weeks now. So he got up and put his jacket on.

"Where you going?" Jeremiah asked.

"Just up to the store and get some cough syrup."

"Don't get the drowsy formula, alright?" Jeremiah reached into his pocket.

Roy nodded and waved him off. "I got it."

In the big window he saw Ms. Ashley on her usual perch, staring at nothing in particular. Through the door window he saw Alfonso sitting behind the counter next to Sammy, slurping on a Fudgsicle bar. He smiled as he walked in.

"Ellington?" Alfonso asked.

"Uh-uh," Sammy said.

"Mingus?"

"Nope! It's the Dave Holland Big Band. But the tune is called 'Blues for C.M.'"

"Ah! Love the way the reeds sashay. That's a sweet groove."

"I'll lend you the CD."

Roy looked over his shoulder and saw Alfonso get up and make wave motions with his arms and shoulders in time with the sashaying reeds.

"What you up to tonight?" Roy asked.

"Needle exchange."

"Better not get caught by no police," Ashley said.

"Yeah, that would be something, wouldn't it?"

"Juices flowing for your term paper?" Roy asked.

"Sorta, kinda. Talked with Reverend Tamera the other day. That was cool."

Roy brought cough syrup up to the counter. Sammy stood up to ring him out.

"Got a cold, Royboy?"

"No, Jeremiah does."

"Thought you had drama tonight, Thes," Alfonso said, still moving with the Big Band.

"Mr. Patrick cancelled tonight's class. We're meeting Saturday."

"We need to do something." Alfonso stopped moving and leaned against the counter. "Something besides dinner at the fake French joint up the street. Let's go dancing!"

"One of them clubs on Benjamin Street has an 18-and-over thing Friday nights, I think," Ashley said. "Forgot which one. Aaron might know, if he ever shows up."

"Hey, there you go," Sammy said. "Y'all should check it out."

"Think Bill will be down for it?" Alfonso asked.

"For sure."

Roy offered to walk Alfonso to the exchange site as they exited. Sammy sat down behind the counter again to finish reading a magazine.

"Better have your spare bedroom ready," Ashley said. "I'm just saying."

Sammy looked up at him, but didn't say a word.

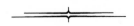

As Bill walked through the wood-paneled office area about to leave, Reverend Johnson appeared at the top of the stairs.

"William, have you finished for the evening?"

"Yes, Reverend."

"Do you have a few minutes? I want to ask you something."

"Sure."

Bill went up the stairs and followed the reverend's guiding hand into his office. The reverend went behind his large desk and sat in his leather chair.

"Have a seat, William. How's your game these days?"

"Not bad. Victor and I played a one-on-one the other day."

The reverend nodded. "William, I was talking to Reginald and he told me that you two were still reading Baldwin."

"Yes."

"He told me that you were reading *Giovanni's Room*."

"Yes. We've been reading it together."

The reverend made a half smile and blinked his eyes slowly.

"William, are you aware of the subject matter of that book?"

"Yes," he said, unfazed. "I did a book report on it for my English class."

"And that's fine for your English class at college. But William! We can't teach that sort of material here in the church, in the program."

Only then, as the pause seeped in, did Bill realize where the man of the cloth was coming from. For some reason, he never thought about it that way, especially since his student wasn't tripping on it at all.

"Baldwin left us a considerable legacy," Reverend Johnson continued, "more than enough to pick and choose from for your lessons with your students."

It had been a classic moment with Reginald, or as he preferred, Smooth. Bored with the history review they were doing, he shoved his hand into Bill's backpack and took out the book. With the power of teenage entitlement, he declared the history review over and insisted that they read *Giovanni*. Bill described this moment of impetuousness as diplomatically as possible. They had previously discussed *Go Tell It on the Mountain*, so Baldwin stuck in Smooth's head. He wanted more, Bill explained.

"And that's wonderful that you got him engaged with the literature, William, but I'm concerned about how others might perceive us, and this program, if they discover that we're using works like *Giovanni's Room* as educational material for our students. What sort of message does that send out? We have a dual mission here, which I know that you recall from your orientation. One is to educate, of course. But we also have to mold tomorrow's leaders. The students here are successors to you, as a freshman in a fine college, and eventually successors to me and to Councilman Berry and all the other fine black leaders of our community. That's what this program is about, William. We need strong black men. Or the community dies. Your mere presence here is an example to the kids you tutor. You are educated, poised, and thoughtful. You are giving back to the community that has nurtured you, generally speaking, William. I know you did not grow up around here, but generally speaking. You bring a lot of fine qualities to the program. You are by far one of our most dedicated tutors. All of your students have mentioned how you put in a lot of extra hours for them during crunch times. It's all very much appreciated."

"Thank you, Reverend."

"So think again about the materials you use with your students. Make sure that they thoroughly reflect the values of the program, OK? I have a copy of *Notes of a Native Son* around here somewhere. I'll find it and lend it to you so you can use that in your lessons."

"Thank you."

"So, Sunday's the big day. Are you ready to do your presentation on our tutoring program?"

"Yes, Reverend. I want to go over it with Alfonso one more time." He wanted to give props to Alfonso whenever he could. Carlton's Posse was tight like that.

"Excellent, William, excellent. This is an important event. And we have to stand behind Councilman Berry. I knew you were the right person to speak on behalf of the tutorial program. I'm glad you and Alfonso are developing such a good friendship."

The reverend stood, all wide smiles and teeth as he went to the door to lead Bill out of his office.

"Oh, and William, one more thing. I know he likes to be called Smooth, but use Reginald's real name when addressing him here, all right? We don't want them to grow up with any false images about themselves, right?"

Bill nodded.

"Thank you for your time tonight, William. Have a good evening. And oh," he added, grinning, "I'm still going to keep on you about joining the church basketball team!"

Bill saw Mrs. Parker on the stoop as usual, despite the darkness from the shortening days and the associated chill in the air. She smiled as he came up the steps.

"You just coming back from Reverend Johnson's?"

"Yeah, I had Smooth today."

"Oh, how's he doing?"

"He's doing real good," He sat down. "Real good. But I guess I can't call him Smooth no more."

"Why not?"

"The reverend doesn't want me to. He said it might give him a false impression of himself, or something like that."

Mrs. Parker rolled her eyes.

"He's such an elitist! Watch what'll happen if you start calling him Reggie, or worse, Reginald. He'll go off on you, he won't listen to what you're trying to teach him, and then you've lost your student."

"Right? I called him Reginald at our first meeting, and he was all 'It's Smooth, alright?' I'm like, fine, whatever you want."

"You do what you have to do, Bill. Johnson don't need to know nothing. Just watch yourself around him, and keep it real with your students."

"Mrs. Parker, has Reverend Johnson been there a long time?"

"Well, yes, I suppose it has been a while. Probably twenty years, at least. Or more like twenty-five. Now, I can remember when Reverend Hooper used to run that church. He was more in tune with the common folk. Johnson was his protégé. I went to that church back when Reverend Hooper ran it. Sometimes he'd let Johnson do the Sunday service. He tried real hard to sound like his boss, but I could tell he was just doing it for show. It wasn't the real him, in other words." Bill nodded. "And when Reverend Hooper retired and Johnson took over, the real him came out very quickly. He's all about the bling, sugar. He ain't folk."

Bill sat and processed for a moment, then stood up.

"Thanks, Mrs. Parker. Take it easy."

"Alright, now, Bill. You have a good evening."

He went upstairs and smelled that food had been prepared. The dining room looked used. Hip-hop didn't boom from Derek's room, so he must have chowed down, then split. Bill tossed his backpack into his room and returned to the kitchen to nuke something for himself. He opened the freezer to sort through the selection. His mother entered the kitchen to get a soda. She pecked him on the cheek.

"How was the day, Mom?"

"It was a day. I have to do a presentation tomorrow."

"That's why Derek's out of the house," Bill said, smirking.

"Yes!" she replied, rubbing his head. "I know you'll be quiet, but I can't count on that from your brother. And how was your day?"

"Alright."

"Uh-huh. Anything you're not telling me?"

"Naw, it ain't nothing. You know the event happening this Sunday? Did I tell you that Reverend Johnson asked me to give a presentation on the tutorial program?"

"No, you did not! Congratulations! See? You haven't been there two months and already you're running the thing!" She gave him a hug.

"I don't know about that."

"Well, it sounds good enough for me. This will be great, Bill, it really will. I hope they know how lucky they are up there at that church to have you."

She went back to her room where her PowerPoint slides awaited.

He took out a lasagna dinner and popped it in the microwave, then leaned against the counter and waited for it to cook.

Sammy put on his black jacket and beret, turned off the lights. He locked the store and headed south. The boys' brief visit had lifted his spirits somewhat, especially talking music with Alfonso. But the shitty morning still left a funk. Everything seemed askew, discordant. *That's what I get for playing* Bitches Brew *first thing in the morning*, he thought. A masterpiece he has worshipped since day one, it nonetheless continued to attract trouble.

The band shell rested silently on the far-left end of the playing field as he walked through. Back when he had a full head of thick black hair, summers meant gigs in the park for his trio. "Beanpole" Bob Rush on bass, Slack "The Jack" Jennings on piano, and "Sam-boom" Turner on drums. The audiences always turned out.

He crossed 48th and found Mrs. Parker on the stoop wearing her burgundy shawl and pink bunny slippers. Her face had a look of expectation. She'd probably heard. Charlotte likely visited earlier in the day. He took a seat one step below her.

"You just missed Bill," she said. "He was out here about thirty minutes ago."

"You remember the time my group played *Bitches Brew*?"

She started laughing. "I think I was the only old fart to get into it. All the rest of them, oh, my goodness!"

"We burned through three albums trying to learn how to play it. Goddamn if we didn't think we were hot shit."

"Admit it. You loved the chaos from the crowd."

Sammy did his slow chuckle. "Up until folks started throwing things."

For that gig, he augmented his trio with Funk It on trumpet, Logan X on tenor sax, and Beanpole's brother Big-L on guitar. They couldn't wait to bring Miles's revolution to Huckleberry Park.

They wanted a scene and got their wish. Folks around their age and younger quickly fell into the groove. Older folks, whose taste went no further than Art Blakey, hated it. *Stop playing that motherfucking shit! When you gonna stop tuning and play? Fuck Miles Davis!* It got crazy. The kids started dancing to the trippy, free-flowing music, while the old guard ratcheted up their indignation. They switched from yelling at the band to yelling at the kids for enjoying the music. The kids yelled back. Eventually it came to blows and when chairs started flying, that's when Sammy called for a time-out.

"By the time we stated playing again, I think most of the old folks had already left, 'cause Beanpole and Slack still played electric, and they weren't having it. But at least the crowd calmed down."

"Hmmm." Mrs. Parker leaned back and reminisced. "That was still a pretty funky version of 'Satin Doll' you all played."

"Yeah. We thought we were so subversive. So subversive."

———◆———

Charlotte strutted into the store with such confidence. Tamera had sparked her groove. Forget his dumb-ass rally, she told her—hell, we'll have our own. Charlotte riffed ideas to Sammy about how it would go down. Instead of talking unity, they'd show it, like the music playing behind them, the beauty of disparate voices. That's this bitch's brew, she said, raising her mug and taking a sip. Sammy wanted to catch her groove, but couldn't. Instead, he shuffled down a familiar path, youthful innovator turned crusty conservative. How can we pull it off so fast? How do we get press coverage? Non-issue questions that quickly exasperated Charlotte. Last time you said I was too passive, she complained. Harry came out of the storeroom and agreed. Steal Berry's thunder. Bingo walked in to buy cigarettes, asked what was up. Harry explained, then said that Sammy had issues. All eyes fell on the storekeeper, like spotlights. Time for his solo. Always speak your truth when you play, he often said. So he finally revealed his reservations. Alfonso—how will this affect him? *That's not fair, Sammy. You know how I feel about him.* Charlotte was hurt and angry. Harry sucked his teeth and wondered if Alfonso was really spying on the needle exchange for his father. Bingo exploded, sick of his conspiracy bullshit. He stormed out without his change, paying $20 for an $8 pack. Harry returned to the storeroom. Charlotte and Sammy stood alone. Nobody can control how Berry will react, she said, a point Sammy conceded. Then she sneered, You gonna come? He heard a loyalty test, copped a half-cent attitude, clammed up. She walked out, her mug nearly full.

——✠——

"I felt like shit all day," Sammy moaned. Faint music floated down from a cracked-open window. "Sounds like Frank Ocean."

"That's Bill's room," Mrs. Parker answered.

"Uh-huh. You know, other than the first time she ran, Charlotte ain't never failed at nothing she's started? She graduated top of her class for her BA and MSW. She owned her job with Larkin."

"I used to watch her practice double Dutch when she was little, right over there next to the community center. Some of the girls teased her, 'cause she kept getting tripped up. But a couple of friends helped her. She got it eventually, made it her own."

"She hates talking about herself. That's what tripped her up the first time. She's a great advocate for everyone except herself. We gotta help her win this time. I want her to win, you know."

"She knows, sugar."

He felt her hand pat him on the shoulder. He wiped his eyes a couple of times with his sleeve.

"Been thinking about setting my kit up. Shit, I haven't taken it out of storage since who knows when. I played my tune for the boys. Alfonso danced so beautifully to it. He just improvised it, on the spot, but it was like he had rehearsed it for years. He has the gift."

He began scat-singing "Lavender Veil Blues," tapping out the beats on his knees slow and easy. He could hear Mrs. Parker clapping softly behind him.

———✠———

The night had been an odd one at the van. Alfonso felt unspoken tensions. Few clients came by to disrupt that spell, so he kept the music going softly on his iPhone speaker, a mix of mostly mellow jazz and electronica.

He walked home alone after the van drove off. He figured he'd take 48th to Peel to Bentley. It didn't bother him walking around the park at night. He liked the solitude offered by the dark.

The basketball courts passed to his left. He walked onto the court with both hands in his pockets. Then he yanked them out to air-dribble across. He jumped and shot. "Swish!" he said, as he touched the chains of the net, causing them to jingle. He lifted his fists in the air, having scored the winning point.

Behind him sat the true object of his curiosity and the reason for his circuitous route home. The black tearoom. Time to check it out. Sirens sounded in the distant background, but for once Alfonso paid them no notice.

It was smaller than he imaged. A single bulb in the far corner provided the only light. Two porcelain sinks hung on the wall. Water dripped in one of them. Across from them was a urinal, and next to that, two stalls with the doors missing. He walked to the urinal and unzipped. As he released what little pee he had to offer, he glanced at the wall. The letters "BJ" appeared many times next to phone numbers and graphic cock drawings. In contrast, the consequences of blatant faggotry were spelled out in coarse language. His eyes lingered on the Got AIDS Yet? acronym.

He finished his business, but stood at the urinal. His dick got aroused. The room intoxicated him. The musk of past encounters smothered his body, a uniquely queer foreplay. He shoved the enlarged thing back in his pants, where it made an impressive display. He went to the sink and ran his hands under some water. There was no towel dispenser and the air dryer dangled on a single bolt, clearly inoperable. He started to dry his hand on his pants.

That's when the other appeared. A lanky body leaned out of the far stall. His hand rubbed a lump through his sweats. Alfonso stared at him, a mixture of emotions racking him.

"What's up, 'Fonso?"

TWELVE

I'M SORRY I SNAPPED AT YOU," ALFONSO SAID. "IT WASN'T right and you didn't deserve it." It seemed a strange place for confessions, but it jumped out of his mouth.

Jameel stopped rubbing the lump in his sweats and walked out of the stall. He came close to Alfonso, right into his personal space. Alfonso did not move or avoid his gaze.

"That was kinda harsh," Jameel said.

"I'm sorry."

"I feel like you've been avoiding me."

"I have."

Then it all flooded out. The body language. The lingering stares. The teasing lips. The sentences cut short before reaching their climax, leaving him hanging, wanting. He recalled when Jameel begged him to go to a school dance, only to abandon him for some girl he claimed to have broken up with. He found them in a dark corridor, face-sucking. He left alone, angry, defeated.

"I'm fragile right now, OK? I don't need this. I don't know who I am to you. One minute you're putting out the vibe, the next minute—"

"Don't cry."

"Dammit!" He didn't like the tears, but could not control them.

Jameel took Alfonso's head and held it under his chin.

"Don't cry, baby. I'm sorry. I'm so sorry."

Alfonso raised his arms to wrap around Jameel.

"I'm a coward," Jameel said. "I'm nowhere near the man you are. You looked so fierce out there tabling for what you believe in. I could never do that."

They cocooned each other for a very long stretch of time in total silence.

"Don't you think it'd be better if we went to my place?" Jameel asked.

Alfonso nodded in agreement. Having gone there, it seemed best to just keep on going.

Friday Night, 8:30ish
Sammy's Store

A cold snap gave the children of Carver Street an excuse to pull out showy outerwear: gaudy sweaters, full-length leather jackets, and multi-colored feather boas. Sammy kept it warm inside with the heater going and a pot of homemade hot cocoa in the back. Alfonso sashayed through the aisles with his warm mug. He eyed the marshmallows as he passed. Sammy told him to go ahead and open a package. He plopped some into his mug, then sashayed to the counter where he did the same for Sammy.

Ashley sat at his usual perch, bundled up against the chill of the window. Alfonso shimmied next to him to look at himself in the glass. He groused about his hair being tired. It looks too much like his dad's, he complained, which caused Ms. Ashley to chuckle. Then he recommended to the young man that he go to Bernard's up the street. Sammy called to see if he had time to do some quick and dirty cornrows. Bernard agreed. That sent Alfonso flying into the street to get his hair done.

"He must have had a good night last night," Ashley said after he left. "He ain't been that happy since forever."

They started ripping each other's clothes off seconds after entering Jameel's apartment. A trail of them led from the door to the living room sofa, where Alfonso tumbled on top of Jameel. Hands pawed over arms, calves, nipples, abs, face, hair. Faces mashed together as tongues explored each other's mouth.

Jameel pushed up on Alfonso to take a good look at him. Wild and untamed replaced neatly coiffed. Your hair looks so fucking hot like that, he told him, before lowering him to eat his face some more.

Underpants barely contained loaded balls and peering cocks. They would soon join the other clothing on the floor.

———

Bill came in with a shiver. Shit, it's cold out there, he announced. Ms. Ashley agreed, then fussed that his husband hadn't come to collect him yet. Bill leaned over the counter to give Sammy a kiss, just as Alfonso hot-strutted up to him with a mug of cocoa and marshmallows. Bill took the offering, though he was more interested in the moves Mr. Berry exhibited. He's been like that all evening, Sammy told Bill, wiggling like a bowl of Jell-O.

After friendly pecks, Continental style, on each cheek, Alfonso asked about their missing comrade. Still getting dressed, drawled Bill, adding that his man kept him waiting outside in the cold, after chiming, 'I'll be right dooooown' over the intercom. Sammy chuckled. Sounds like someone wants to make a star entrance, he said. But Alfonso beat him to it, ripping off his knitted cap to reveal freshly lined rows woven on his head. The days of tired hair are over, he declared.

Aaron finally arrived. Ashley gave him attitude and a kiss. The bouncy activity at the counter soon grabbed Aaron's attention. Alfonso, is that you? He received a hug from his longtime neighbor, who still wiggled to the beat. They're going dancing and he can't stop moving, Sammy said. Sound familiar? Aaron pursed his lips and shook his head. Carlton all over again. I miss him more than I can say, he said, but I'm still mad he never joined our company, always talking this 'I ain't good enough' shit. Alfonso readily agreed. Then Bill had to open his big fat mouth.

Well, what about you? You can dance your ass off! Did you study at Aaron's company?

Bill went into minute detail about Alfonso's improv to Sammy's "Lavender Veil Blues." Aaron raised an eyebrow. Suddenly, the dancing man grew stiff and stilted, his version of 'I ain't good enough.'

Wrong, wrong, wrong, and no, no, no, Aaron declared as he marched over to Sammy's CDs and thumbed through his collection to find something more up-tempo. He picked McCoy Tyner's "Salvadore De Samba." Its quick tempo proved irresistible. Alfonso started shuffling his feet again. Aaron stood next to him to show him the steps his company rehearsed. Alfonso studied the movements closely. Knees bent just so. Hips moving in a circle. Torso flowing like a river. Arms working it in and out in circles big and small. First Alfonso copied the foot movement. Aaron nodded. Loosen the hips, he instructed, a little more, a little more.

Then Ms. Ashley called out, "Come on, loosen those hips, baby! Toss them around!"

Alfonso loosened and he began waving his arms in the air in the same pattern as Aaron's.

"That's good!" Aaron said. "Now, just one more thing: Smile!"

As his face brightened, his body loosened even more. The flow owned him, granted him freedom.

—◇—

Once he established a rhythm, he continued it nonstop. Each thrust sent a kinetic wave through Jameel, who responded with satisfied moans and grunts. All his fantasies had not prepared Alfonso for this moment. He always imagined Jameel on top, his lanky body smothering him. But Jameel handed him the condom, then got into position. At first Alfonso felt intimidated. It was not the dance he had envisioned. Ultimately, Jameel's fine body dispelled all doubts. Inhibitions vanished.

—◇—

Giiiirl! Oooo! You go Miss Thing! Work it, honey! called out the assembled regulars in Sammy's store.

With a final twirl, Alfonso ended with a heavy breath and his arms stretched above his head. Everyone clapped. Aaron nearly ordered him to sign up for his company next week. We'll have you on stage in six months, I kid you not.

Alfonso was still taking his bows when the door opened with a pronounced billowing of cold air. A dark, slow-moving figure slid in. He wore black velvet pants, a black belt with a silver buckle, and a white long-sleeved shirt over which he wore his brand-new black leather vest. He finished the ensemble with a long black overcoat and a black porkpie. He posed for a second, before swishing to the counter.

Ms. Ashley complained that he left the door open too long. You lost your mind, child? But Sammy, hands on hips, chuckled and declared that Lester Young himself just walked into his store.

Just call me Pres, Roy said, sliding his thumb and forefingers along the brim of his hat.

With all three collected together, the fashion show began in earnest. They paraded down the middle of the store from back to front, switching and vogueing to the music. Aaron, Ashley, and Sammy, clapped on the offbeat. As Alfonso reached the end of the runway, he coyly looked around, then snatched off his knit cap again, so that Roy could see his cornrowed magnificence. Carlton's Posse whooped and hollered. Sammy rolled his eyes at the sight. Ain't this nothing! he said, though none paid attention. They twirled like dervishes. Each scream reached for E above top C. They carried on in their own little world cradled by a triangle of arm-crossed elders, each staring at them, each seeing their own past parade before them. The dingy clubs. The loud funk and house. Tight threads. Bodies locking, bumping, two-stepping. Home at sunrise, then up for brunch by 1.

"Look, you dizzy queens!" Sammy finally said. "Quit with the mutual admiration society and get out in the streets where you belong, 'fore I brush you outta here with my broom!"

"We're going, Mother," Roy said. "Don't stay up late waiting for us!"

"Give 'em hell in Boys' Town," Ashley said. "Don't take no mess."

"Show 'em how to dance, Alfonso!" Aaron called out.

Sammy said nothing further. He stood arms folded. "He-he-he-he-he."

Between passions, they talked, lights out, naked on top of the sheets, cuddled together, their legs intertwined. Further confessions came to light. We weren't that different in high school, you know, Alfonso said, I was pretty uptight. Jameel asked if he and Bill had been eyeing each other. Alfonso laughed. We're just tight, that's all. He helps me keep it together. Jameel smiled.

9:45 p.m.
Benjamin Street, Boy's Town,

They came as themselves, no fronts or pretenses, twirling, strutting, vogueing down the street, at home with each other in the space they created, blissfully ignoring side eye cast in the gray distance, forgetting that with them always traveled history.

Need for a caffeine infusion spun them into a café, where they ordered chai lattes. Roy got his dirty, claiming he needed the espresso boost to keep up with Alfonso. The dancer-in-chief responded with some fancy foot tapping and jazz hands. Then he made a declaration: to learn every damn move of every damn dance in that badass "Uptown Funk" mash-up video. "Oh, my god, that video's f-ing dope!" Bill said. He took out his cell and pulled it up. Huddled together, they marveled at Eleanor Powell's shuffles, Fred Astaire's slides, Ginger Rogers's twirls, Bill Robinson's jigs, and the Nicholas Brothers' acrobatics. All their feet jived under the table.

Their spark of color went unnoticed by two guys a couple of tables over, whose thin lips dully munched salads as they spoke in nasally monotone voices that carried throughout the largely empty joint. Only their hair color distinguished them.

A mutual friend went ethnic, Brunet reported. Ethnic? You mean Carver Street? Sandy asked. Oh, no, not *there*, Brunet assured him. So, what's he doing? Sandy asked. Asians, Latins, that's what he's into now, Brunet replied. Jaded eyes rolled whatevs.

Roy flung his arm grandly around Bill's chair, then spoke with full stage projection, "Did I tell y'all 'bout this number I did in the alley behind Ye Olde Leather Shoppe? Chiiiiile, that white boy just could *not* get enough of this fat nigga dick!" He spread his legs wide open in the direction of the salad munchers and pointed to his masked member with both middle fingers.

Alfonso and Bill lost it. Brunet and Sandy finished eating suddenly and hastily departed. Roy received the Ms. Ashley Award for bitchiness from his companions.

Spirits rekindled, they funked it down the street, eventually arriving at the fabled club where they segued into the long line. Chatter, giggles, primping and preening, a queue colored queer. It moved quickly. At the entrance stood a blond doorman wearing a name tag that read "Charles." Sharp-dressed Roy approached first. Charles glanced over his ID, took his money, and let him pass. As Alfonso and Bill fished for their wallets, Charles eyed them cautiously, scanning everything from their knitted ski caps to their oversized coats to their gleaming white sneakers.

"You know it's gay night tonight," Charles said.

"Yeah, I know," Alfonso said.

Charles stared at Alfonso's ID, then asked for a second one.

"Wha—Why?"

"Is something wrong?" Roy asked.

"He's asking me for another ID?"

"What the story?" Bill asked.

"We're getting the blues from Missy Charlie," Roy said. "He won't let you guys in. And me too, I guess, even though I paid already."

"You can go in," Charles said curtly.

Roy's face grew taut with anger. "Without my friends?"

The doorman ignored Roy, continued admitting others, scanning their IDs as cursorily as he had prior to the Posse's arrival. No one spoke up for the three young black men standing aside.

Alfonso so wanted to make a scene, to show Missy Charlie some old-school snap-diva attitude, to trash the club online. But for his and Bill's precarious relationship with the closet he would have. Instead, he could only watch the world ignore their existence.

Roy had no relationship with the closet. "You know something, Ms. Charlie, I ain't your fucking little 'Halfrican-American' whose light enough to pass. You treat us all the same! You ain't asking no one else for no two ID cards!"

Charles got agitated, called for security. After a brief conference with the harried doorman, two security guards with long, black flashlights stopped and frisked the Posse in full view of everyone. It took forever. Humiliation, like earthquakes, causes each second to last an eternity. After finally entering, they plopped into chairs and stayed there, feet and hands motionless.

"In elementary school," Roy said, "some fucker started hitting me and saying, 'You a Halfrican-American like Obama.' I kicked his ass. The school wanted to expel me. My mom told 'em she was proud of me."

"Carlton showed me some old personals ads from back in the day," Alfonso said. "'No fats, fems, or blacks; disease free.'" Bill smirked. "I showed him Grindr. He said, 'Jim Crow still wears pink.'" Alfonso stood up. "Sistahs, I came here to take my mind off the bullshit I have to face this weekend. And I'm not gonna let a bunch of racist pricks stop me. I'm going out there to show them what Carlton taught me. Who's down?"

Bill and Roy rose. They discarded their bulky outerwear at coat check, though Roy kept his porkpie hat and leather vest. On the edge of the main dance floor, Alfonso began moonwalking backward in an oval. Folks cleared out of his way. Then he started locking. Bill joined him. Then Roy. Some looked upon them warily, while others studied and copied their dope moves.

THIRTEEN

Sunday Morning, 10ish
Liberty Hall, The Huck—North Side

Roy ran into Reverend Tamera backstage. They exchanged a quick hug. He asked why the event was happening at Liberty Hall and not the church. Church and state, honey, she replied, stating that she understood the concept better than some preacher-folks. Roy laughed.

"Besides," she added, "this old rustic hall has hosted every radical movement from the Wobblies to Black Lives Matter. Let's add Charlotte to that list."

Roy emerged from behind the curtains. He saw Harry, Bingo, Liz, and other store familiars setting up chairs in the large space. He hopped down and started arranging chairs with Vera in the front row.

"Using the stage entrance?" she asked, then kissed him. "No sign of Sammy?"

"Naw."

"Hmmm." She looked disappointed, bordering on cross.

"Did I tell you about our night in Boy's Town?"

"What about it?"

"We got double-carded."

She stood upright and placed a hand firmly on her left hip. "You aren't joking with your Auntie Vera, are you? Are they still doing that crap?"

"I guess. We didn't let 'em get away with it, though. We stood there until they let us in."

She stood for a moment, shaking her head. "Outrageous. You know what I did when they pulled that crap? I had a special card made, about the size of a driver's license. It's a photo of me doing this." She cocked her head, crossed her eyes, stuck out her long tongue toward her nose, and flipped the bird right next to her cheek. "That was my second ID card."

"Love it!"

"I can take one of you and your friends for next time." She arranged chairs as she talked. "Only next time, I think you all should go to Club Copacetic."

"I didn't think they did 18-and-over anymore."

"Hmmm," she grunted.

10ish
Beacon Hill First Baptist Church,
The Huck—Southside

Alfonso had to stay close to his family, but when he noticed Bill entering, he held back. They greeted each other with a setting-appropriate manly hug. Both smirked at each other's suit. It seemed only a minute ago that Bill picked out the braids in Alfonso's hair on the bus ride home, returning Cinderella to her former self.

"You ready?" Bill asked.

"Just waiting for the end."

They left a lot unsaid.

"Well, take care, bruh," Bill said.

Alfonso broke protocol and grabbed Bill for a more-than-manly hug. He needed it, and Bill was happy to give it up.

Alfonso marched to the front row where his family sat. Bill found his mother and brother eight rows back.

The sanctuary looked fuller than on any previous Sunday. Even the balcony was loaded. That gave Alfonso pause. Did all of these people turn out because they felt their world threatened by the Carver Street people, by folks like me?

In time, he credited such thinking to paranoia. This was clearly a major social event, a see-and-be-seen do. The sanctuary screamed money. Suits came well pressed and in three-piece. Dresses looked fresh. Fly hats saw first light out of the milliner's. And a battalion of colognes and perfumes choked the air as they battled for supremacy.

Reverend Johnson strolled across the front to the pulpit, passing the row of reverends seated stage right, his whole face beaming at the throng that filled his capacious church.

"Bless you all this good morning!"

In Eddie's Grove, folks braced themselves as police vans appeared in the street.

"Amen!" the congregation responded.

The cops came in riot gear. Plastic handcuffs dangled from clips on their belts.

"I say again, bless you all this good morning!"

They wrenched the tents from the ground. Occupants began chanting, NO VIOLENCE! NO VIOLENCE!

"Amen!" the congregation repeated with greater volume.

Batons came out to push away onlookers.

"Yes, indeed! Before we start the program of this blessed day, I'd like to make an announcement. Just a short time ago, our police removed the so-called protest that for too long besmirched the northeast corner of the park."

Knees pressed into backs as plastic cuffs were put over wrists. They received one warning, but were not allowed time to pack up and go.

Applause erupted instantly and sustained itself as Reverend Johnson kept speaking.

"We have—My friends, we have Councilman Berry's tireless dedication to keeping our community whole and safe to thank for this action." He let loose his broadest, toothiest smile as an extended hand gestured toward Ford Berry in the front row. The councilman stood and nodded modestly.

Folks began to chant, THE WHOLE WORLD'S WATCHING!
THE WHOLE WORLD'S WATCHING!

Alfonso didn't clap. He wanted to grab his cell and start looking for tweets and live streams.

"We will start this blessed day," Reverend Johnson said, as the thunder died, "with the singing of the national anthems. All who can please rise."

The choir, composed of singers from all of the participating churches, stood stage left. The organist sat center stage under a huge banner that read UNITY. He led the choir and congregation through the "Star-Spangled Banner." Most sang with their hands over their hearts.

After they finished, the organist struck a familiar set of chords to introduce the next anthem.

On the bus ride home from Boy's Town, Alfonso had predicted that a heavy, solemn rendition of "Lift Every Voice and Sing" would be part of the ceremony. It was his grandfather's theme, making it an inevitability. We did a version with beats and rhymes at a Black Lives Matter demo, Bill said, then busted into the chant and rhythm—*LIFT Ev'ry VOICE and SING boom-BACK - boom-BACK-a-tack-a-boom-BACK*—causing Alfonso and Roy to start dancing.

That would be an improvement, Alfonso thought, as they lumbered through each verse. But it wasn't just the ancient paean's lifeless presentation that bothered him. How could they sing about ringing harmonies of liberty when just a moment ago the whole damn church applauded the breakup of a demonstration protesting the brutal murder of a black man? He knew the answer. Their harmony didn't include lavender notes. So he mouthed the words, gave them no voice, just as those who sang at full volume gave no thought to the song's meaning.

Everyone in the front row turned around during the third verse. Alfonso looked as well. He saw Bill and Derek raise their fists in a Black Power salute. So aggressive a take-back in so saditty a crowd made Alfonso break out in a broad smile. Bill winked back in response. How Alfonso loved his sistah.

The Huckleberry Women's Big Band led Liberty Hall through a rousing, up-tempo version of "Lift Every Voice and Sing," a soul sister of Linda Tillery's. No one sat still in the audience.

When the singing and dancing ended, and after several rounds of spontaneous applause, hoots, and hollers, Reverend Tamera took the stage. The curtain closed behind her. She, too, announced the arrests that took place at Eddie's Grove, but noted that not one new light fixture had been installed anywhere in the park. Boos sounded long and hard. Then she called those who had been arrested "freedom fighters" and the room erupted into applause again.

"I was going to talk about the other event happening this morning, how I was invited along with the other religious leaders in the Huck; about how they told me to come and bring my flock with me, but with the stipulation that there wasn't enough time for me to talk; about how I and some of my colleagues, who were also told there'd be no time for them to talk, saw the event as nothing more than a shield—a transparent shield—to cover the umm-hmm of the man who refused to even meet with the freedom fighters in Eddie's Grove; about how their so-called Unity Rally was really an attack against those who did not fall into their narrow definition of unity or community."

She paused.

"I was gonna talk about all that, and then I decided, nah." Everyone laughed. "Instead, I want to talk about my idea of unity and leadership."

Then she began listing qualities of leadership she admired: communicator, active listener, activist, organizer. Mrs. Parker, sitting front row center, cried "That's right!" after each point. Others in the audience made similar responses. Roy sat between Mrs. Parker and Vera, in anticipation.

"I think you know who I'm talking about," Tamera concluded. "And I have a feeling you'll agree that this person embodies unity."

She stepped aside and out came Charlotte, dressed in a fine suit and a bow tie. The crowd exploded. Mrs. Parker stared at her face and beamed, clapping hard despite her arthritic hands. Tamera stood by the podium a while before leaving the stage. Camera flashes flickered. TV lights turned on. Charlotte stood alone, smiling sweetly and nodding her head. Roy studied her expression closely, keeping a smile to himself.

Eventually the room settled down so she could speak.

"Hello, sisters and brothers. I guess I better just say it, before y'all explode."

The room buzzed with told-you-sos and uh-huhs whispered from the many who had predicted this moment.

"My name is Charlotte Hunter, and I would like to humbly announce my candidacy for the District 9 city council seat."

People rose to their feet. Mrs. Parker shed tears of joy. Harry whistled between his fingers. Bingo clapped above his head. Vera shouted, "You go, girl!" over and over as she snapped photos.

From behind the closed curtain came a loud drumroll, then cymbals, then a booming bass drum. A frenzied solo took place. As folks got into it, the curtain opened. Sam-boom reborn. His sticks and kicks exploded in a fury that rivaled Max Roach. He brought the house down.

"Gotcha!" Roy said.

"Remind me to slap you later," Vera said as she snapped photos.

Charlotte held her hands clutched under her trembling chin. She turned to the mic. "Now we got it going!"

The Huckleberry Women's Big Band joined Sam-boom on stage. He settled into a steady beat and on the count of three, they began playing "When the Saints Come Marching In," Liberty Hall's theme song. Everyone started dancing again.

Ford Berry spoke after all the reverends. The crowd remained respectful, but fidgeted. Alfonso wondered if his mother had been right, that too many had been scheduled to speak. He knew he felt relief that his father was the final speaker.

"We cannot let those outside this holy house rip us apart or tear us to pieces. We cannot let them dictate to us our agenda. We know our problems and we will solve them. We know our challenges and we will surmount them. We know what our community needs and we will seek it. We will nurture our community by nurturing each other."

He received polite applause that escalated to an ovation only after Reverend Johnson stood up and roused the crowd with his enthusiasm.

Alfonso only half-listened to his father's speech. Jameel filled his thoughts. He called a few times Saturday, but never got ahold of him. Texts and emails similarly went unanswered. Strange. The glow of their night together still warmed him, warding off doubts and anxieties fomenting in the background. But still he checked his cell constantly, wondering why nothing appeared.

To distract himself, he decided to act as the First Lieutenant and walked around to make sure all was in order. The food looked hot and ready. A line queued up quickly. He couldn't find Tamesha, but she was probably already eating somewhere. Then he turned around and ran into Leon.

"Oh, hey, sorry, man," Alfonso said, "Didn't see you."

The footballer looked at him queerly, like he had never seen him before.

"Looking good back here!" Alfonso said.

"Yeah, we got it tight for your father." Leon looked distracted, like he had something to do in a hurry.

"Hey, man, have you seen Jameel?" Alfonso asked quickly.

"Naw, I ain't seen him. Don't know if he here yet. Uh, excuse me, alright?"

Then he bolted. Alfonso thought nothing of the terse exchange. He continued scanning the crowd, wondering about Jameel.

His father approached.

"Everything together?"

"It's all good, Dad."

"Excellent, Lieutenant." Ford walked off to continue working the crowd.

Ms. Ashley slipped up to the piano on stage at Liberty Hall and began playing some old school gospel riffs, a coda for the day as folks mingled and departed. The Sammy Store Irregulars each stationed themselves at an exit with a donation bag. Charlotte worked the crowd. Many posed with her for selfies. Everyone wanted a piece of the day.

Eventually, the Irregulars gathered in the green room. A group hug filled the space with warmth and hope. Charlotte saved the biggest hug for her blues coffee partner. Folks cheered them on.

"Let's count all this loot!" Mrs. Parker said. With a laugh, they all dived into the bags and started sorting change, bills, and checks.

Roy called Bill.

"How's Alfonso holding up? Did you see him?"

"Just a couple of times. We couldn't talk much. Me and mine have been home for a while. I had to get out of my monkey suit."

"I heard that. How did your presentation go?"

"I had a packed room! I was freaked! But I guess I did OK. My mom thinks I did."

"Sho' you did, boy!"

"How's everything over there?"

"This was a beautiful day. We're in the green room counting out the donations. You got time to come over and count some loot?"

"I wish I could, babe. I have to finish a paper for my English class. Call me when you get home, alright?"

"I will."

Charlotte sat on the floor nearby.

"Everything OK, Roy?" she asked.

"Yeah, they're all good. Bill's at home already. Alfonso's still with his family."

"Let me know if you hear anything, alright?"

Alfonso sat in the car with his family, waiting for his father. His mom and sisters talked outfits and hairdos. Their banter made him grin, though his mind still resided in the world of two days ago, at Jameel's apartment, their night over and under the sheets.

———

It felt most real around four in the morning, high noon of halfway to dawn. They dozed lightly after their third go-round. Lazy thoughts passed their lips as they cuddled. That's when he asked Jameel the question: The black tearoom, did someone from The Party see you there?

———

He glanced out the window and saw his father emerge from the back door of the church. A TV camera and reporter intercepted. Good for Dad. More press coverage. He got what he wanted.

———

Yes, Jameel said. One day last summer, he entered and saw Brother Milton on his knees about to give service to someone hidden in one of the stalls. Jameel chuckled, recalling the moment, thought it ridiculous. Brother Milton rose to his feet, zipped up, then shuffled out of the room hurriedly. An email from The Party came the next day.

———

More cameras crowded around his father, more mics pushed into his face. It looked chaotic, a feeding frenzy. Dad knows how to handle them, Alfonso thought lazily.

———

Jameel got out of bed, walked to his laptop on his desk. Alfonso joined him. The screen cast their naked bodies in shades of grayish-white. Jameel pulled up the email from his former comrades. They read it together: YOU ARE HEREBY SUMMONED TO APPEAR BEFORE THE PARTY AT 1800 HRS ON TUESDAY IN THE PROSCRIBED LOCATION TO SIT IN THE CIRCLE. THERE, WE WILL DELINEATE YOUR FAILINGS AS A MEMBER AND AS A REVOLUTIONARY—

Alfonso shook his head. The all caps, the indignant language, the military time, all the clichés of sectarian claptrap appeared in the stupid missive. I'm sorry, baby, he said. I'm OK, Jameel assured him. I know who I am. They can't touch me no more.

The driver's door opened abruptly and slammed hard. Silence replaced the bitchy banter. The daydreaming ended. Ford started the car noisily and jerked out of the parking lot. He banked corners, tossing Alfonso into Lucy and Lucy into Belinda, only for the falling order to reverse on the next turn. They bounded up the hill on Beacon Street the way stunt cars do in Hollywood street chases. Another sharp turn screeched them into the driveway. What possessed him to drive like that? Alfonso wondered.

When he walked inside, his father loudly commanded him into the study. The night with Jameel now completely dissolved, he began thinking instead of the roller skate incident from seven years ago. Whatever could have triggered *that* type of anger?

His father slammed the door, then stood close in front of him.

"Alfonso," he said, his voice tense, "I want you to tell me something. And I want you to tell me the truth, alright?"

"Dad, what's wrong?"

Roy got home, then realized that he had totally forgotten about cleaning the apartment. It was past five o'clock. His father usually got home around six. He started to tidy up the living room. He didn't have time to vacuum because he needed to start dinner. As he fluffed the pillows, he heard a beep. At first, he thought nothing of it. Then he kept hearing it. He went into the kitchen and saw nothing had been left on. He still heard it. He muttered to himself when he realized what it was and went to the hallway. The light on the answering machine flashed. He pressed the red button to play back the message.

"Roy, I'm still in Packard. I'm at the hospital, Son. Jasmine's with me, and they're running some test. But it looks like pneumonia." His voice was faint and he sounded out of breath. "I'll give you a call when I know some more. The number here is—"

He stopped the message to grab some paper and a pencil. He tried to keep them next to the phone, but somehow they always managed to walk away. He started the recording again and wrote down the number, then the message ended and there was silence. He rubbed the top of his head, his hand rose and sat on his hip.

"Goddamn it!" he shouted, "I told him not to go out with no damn chest cold." He walked into the kitchen. "Now look at this shit, pneumonia!" He opened the refrigerator, then closed it. He saw nothing he wanted and went into the living room to turn on the television. He needed to space on his father's news for a bit and let his system absorb it before trying to call him back.

FOURTEEN

W HAT DO YOU KNOW ABOUT CHARLOTTE HUNTER running for my office?" Ford Berry asked.

"What?" Alfonso replied, genuinely confused.

"I said,"—Ford slowed his diction and softened his voice—"what do you know about Charlotte Hunter running for my office?" He started pacing about the study. "She announced today, Alfonso. That's what the press said. They said she announced her candidacy at an event hosted by Reverend Tamera Woodson that happened at the same time as our—my Unity Rally." He stopped directly in front of Alfonso. "So I'm asking you, what do you know? What do you know about Charlotte Hunter running for my office?"

Alfonso said nothing and his father offered nothing beyond his unending stare.

"Dad," he said, his mouth dry, "I don't know anything about what Charlotte Hunter is doing. Why would I?"

"Why, indeed." Ford turned his back on Alfonso and walked to the bookcases at the other end of his study. "So many things," he muttered.

"Dad, just what are you trying to say? You mean you didn't know that she was going to announce?"

"Stop lying, Alfonso!" He kept his back to him. "I already know about you working with the needle exchange and hanging out on Carver Street."

Alfonso shuddered, walked toward Ford slowly. "Who told you all that?"

"Do you deny it?"

"Who told you?"

"The whole fucking press corps, that's who, Alfonso! That's what they hit me with while I was trying to walk to the damn car. You know what this is, don't you? It's betrayal." Ford looked him in the eye, a piercing stare that lasted only a moment before he walked toward his desk.

Alfonso still faced the bookcases. Behind him, he heard his father shuffling papers, moving items, stacking books—a series of purposeless, random motions. During his father's noisy improvisation, Alfonso began to see. It really was all about betrayal.

"You know something," Ford said, "I figured it out. You still miss Carlton, don't you? You miss him so much that you wanted to become him. Isn't that right?" He loudly straightened papers on his desk, a pounding rhythm, a blues without resolution. "You go and work at his clinic and his friends take you in. You became him for them, didn't you?"

Alfonso experienced the sensation of all the guilt he ever held about himself flushing away. For the first time in his life, he felt as if he had nothing to hide.

"I defended you," he said softly.

"So now that you've become him, you've stabbed *me* in the back. Humiliated *me* in front of everyone, the whole press corps! That was your agenda from the start, wasn't it?"

"I said, I defended you."

"And why would I know anything about Charlotte Hunter announcing? She ain't got nothing to do with me."

Ford continued to shuffle things randomly. Alfonso whipped around and slammed his fist against the desk.

"I SAID I DEFENDED YOU!" he screamed.

Carlton had a temper. Rarely did he raise it toward Alfonso. But one time, on one of his darkest days, when he felt like shit, when nothing he took, drank, or chanted relieved the pain, he lashed out.

Your father ain't no better than mine, you'll see! You will see, young man!

"Even after you threw my skates away, I defended you!"

Uncle Ford ain't done shit for me, and he ain't doing shit for you, either!

"Even after you bullied me out of dance class, I defended you!"

You know as well as I that he don't give a damn about no faggots! Including you!

"Even after you bullied me into the Poli Sci major, bullied me into office in ASA, I still defended you!"

"What the hell are you talking about?"

"I don't know what anybody told you about me, but it ain't nothing that you shouldn't have already known. My whole damn life, you've been trying to bully me into being straight, and I've never said nothing. That's what I'm talking about. You brought this on yourself. I *am* Carver Street. Did they tell you that I'm hanging with the clinic? Yes, I am! Did they tell you that I'm doing a term paper on homophobia? Yes, I am! Did they tell you I'm a gay man? YES, FATHER! YOU'RE SON IS A FUCKING GAY MAN! AND GODDAMN IT, YOU WILL RESPECT ME!"

Ford folded his arms and glared at Alfonso. "You've ruined everything, you know that? Thanks to you, today's event was a complete disaster. Thanks to you, that bitch Charlotte Hunter will get all the press and I'll get shit. Thanks to you and your buddies at the needle exchange, what should have been my comeback has become just another setback."

"So am I Ernest Little now? You gonna do me like Granddad did Ernest Little?"

Ford raised his arm and backhanded his son across the face. Alfonso stumbled and grabbed hold of the desk. He stared up at his father. Neither of his parents had ever hit him.

"Get the fuck out of here," Ford ordered. "Just get out. Go join your needle exchange buddies in the park and go fuck yourselves!"

Alfonso tasted blood from his lower lip. He patted it with the back of his hand.

"Fuck you to hell," he said.

He stood up and flew around, slammed out of his father's office, then slammed out the front door to the street.

Roy called Bill, asked about Alfonso. No news. Might be out to dinner with his family, Bill said. Then they talked about Charlotte's event, the dancing, the singing, Sammy's drumming.

"Dang!" Bill said. "I was at the wrong party!"

"I'm still high from it. And we collected over $1,100 after it was over."

"Hey, aren't you having dinner with Dad right now?"

"No. Jeremiah ain't here. He's in a hospital somewhere."

"Say what?"

"Yeah. Pneumonia. That's what they think it is, anyway. I'm so pissed at him right now. I told him not to go out. You should have heard him before he left. Hacking like an old smoker. He'll be alright. He never stays sick for long. But I'm still pissed at him."

"Yeah, well, I hope he comes home soon."

"He will."

Alfonso sprinted the whole way to the man's apartment, still dressed in his Sunday best, his lip still bloody. He hopped across intersections, dodged cars, and maneuvered around the few pedestrians he encountered on his marathon course. Streetlights flickered on, signaling the beginning of nightfall.

When he reached his destination, he hit the apartment buzzer ten times. No answer. He twitched frantically, then hit it eight more times. He hopped off the steps and looked into the window. None of the lights were on.

"JAMEEL!" he screamed. "I KNOW YOU'RE IN THERE, MOTHERFUCKER! GET YO' ASS OUT HERE! JAMEEL! I know what you did, Jameel! You told Leon, didn't you? Didn't you! Jameel!"

No answers. No lights came on. No blinds shifted for spying eyes. Alfonso shuffled his feet against the dead leaves on the sidewalk.

"Goddamn motherfucker," he mumbled as he set off on a new course. Back to the scene of the crime. The asshole was probably looking for a new trick to fuck over.

"Jameel!" he shouted when he got to the black tearoom. "Why, Jameel? Why you do me like you did Cliff? Just to keep it '100'?" Silence. "Why you do me like The Party did you? Why? I trusted you Jameel!" He began sobbing. "I trusted you!"

He fell to the floor. No panting. No groping. No excitement from the musk of past encounters. There was only the blackness and dankness of a run-down restroom and Alfonso's crumpled body heaving and jerking as he sobbed uncontrollably under the sink.

Jameel spent the day at his parents' house out in the suburbs. Brunch. Chores around the house. He even helped a neighbor with a his Wi-Fi.

He learned about the fallout from the unity rally while he and his parents watched TV with their desserts. A chill disassociated from the sorbet shook his body and he nearly dropped the bowl on the floor. Quickly he got up and called it an early evening, under the pretext of having to study. I'll take the early train back tomorrow, he told them. They wished him a good night. While in the kitchen, he overheard his parents talking.

"Sounds like that fool finally got broadsided, by his own son, no less!" Jameel's father said. "Ruth, do you really think Alfonso's gay?"

"Oh, hell yeah. You kidding?"

"Well, Berry won't deal with that too well."

She agreed with her husband.

No, no, no, Jameel murmured to himself.

In his room, he jumped into bed with his old Huey Newton reader, the one his uncle had given him years ago. The book fell open to the exact page he wanted, a speech Brother Huey gave in 1970. It fortified him.

Homosexuals can be revolutionaries, Brother Huey wrote. Indeed, he posited, they could be the most revolutionary.

Jameel saw Brother Huey's prophecy for himself, upright and proud. He never knew Alfonso to look sexier.

He curled into a fetal position and pulled on the blankets for better coverage, to keep out the cold.

FIFTEEN

As soon as Ford and Alfonso slammed into the study, Eunice huddled her daughters into the kitchen to keep them distracted. Dinner had been prepared and just needed to be reheated. She had Belinda start a salad. Lucy emptied the dishwasher. After the first shouts reached their ears, Eunice turned to Belinda.

"Did you see what Mrs. Pert had on?" she said, rekindling their earlier banter. "Why does she think she can wear that color?"

Belinda rolled her eyes. "And did you see those shoes?"

Lucy giggled. They all giggled. The shoes killed them. But then they heard louder shouts and the giggles faded. They finished their chores in silence. When the front door slammed, they all looked at one another and read one another's faces.

"Lucy, go ahead and set the table, please. And Belinda, start taking the food out."

"Momma—," Belinda said.

"Go ahead, now."

Eunice went to Ford's study and found the door ajar. She knocked softly, then entered. He sat at his desk hunched over papers. She closed the door behind her.

"Ford, what happened?" He didn't say anything. She walked toward the desk. "What happened, Ford?"

"I don't know what happened," he said softly.

"Where's Alfonso?"

"I don't know. I threw him out of the house."

"You *what?*"

He looked up. "I threw him out. I told him—I just don't want to see him again." He stood. "He stabbed me in the back, Eu. He was reckless. He's gone, that's all there is to it. He's gone."

"Just like that? Ford, I deserve a better explanation than that. You can't just throw our son out of the house and not tell me why."

"He's not my son anymore, Eu. He's a fucking homo." He went to the door of his study. "Is dinner ready yet?" He walked out without waiting for an answer. Eunice froze, unable to move.

She heard Belinda ask, "Daddy, where's Alfonso?" but barely heard Ford's reply. Then she heard him walk toward the study, only to keep going out the front door. She heard it close behind him.

Henny Penny went into the black tearoom to cruise for sex when he saw someone in a suit under the sink, gently murmuring. Henny slowly approached and then covered his mouth upon recognizing him.

"Alfonso? What's up, honey?"

"It's all over, it's all over," he uttered, almost unintelligibly.

Eunice finally came out of Ford's study. Both daughters faced her. Any appearances she tried to keep up in front of them failed. Her whole presence drooped like a painting running off its canvas.

"Momma," Belinda said, "where's Alfonso?"

She looked at them and began shaking her head. "I don't know." She tried to add some strength to her voice. "He and your father had a big argument and your father told him to leave the house." Her chin began to quiver.

"Why, Momma?" Lucy asked.

Suddenly Alfonso's one and only dance recital went through her head. Only three other new students participated in the recital and Alfonso was the only one allowed a brief solo. How he leapt through the air! How strong his legs were! How powerful his presence! The dancing ended soon afterward, but she never forgot the image of her son, proud and tall.

How often he smiled—so hopeful, so eager to please. Despite everything, he always smiled. Until recently, he had always smiled.

"I can't talk about it now, children!" and she dashed past them and up the stairs, in tears.

Poor Henny felt like running out of the room and up the street, but something inside told him to hold firm. He crouched next to Alfonso and started to stroke him on the head.

"It's alright, baby."

Alfonso continued weeping quietly.

Henny stood up, took out his cell phone. He called Sammy at the store, but got no answer.

"Dammit!"

He didn't know Sammy's home number.

"I'm gonna be right back, OK? I'm gonna get some help, alright, honey? I'll be right back." He stepped outside. "I can't just leave him here."

Then he saw a familiar jeep coming down Lincoln. Henny dashed into the street right in front of it, waving his arms wildly.

"Hey! Help! Help!"

Bingo slammed on the brakes and stood up over the roll bar.

"What the hell is wrong with you?" he shouted.

"It's the councilman's boy, Alfonso! He's lying in the restroom crying!"

Bingo sat down and pulled to the curb. They both went into the men's room. Bingo fell to the floor and placed Alfonso's weeping face on his thighs. Henny stood by and watched.

"Alfonso, honey? It's me, Bingo. What's wrong? Did someone hurt you?"

Alfonso slowly pulled himself off the floor and onto Bingo, resting his head just under the leatherman's beard.

"I trusted him," he murmured. "It's all over now."

"Shhhhh," Bingo said, rocking as he held him.

"What should we do?" Henny asked. "Should we take him to the hospital?"

"No, we'll take him to my place. He doesn't look too hurt, but he's in shock. Come on. Help me get him up."

They stood on either side of Alfonso and helped him to Bingo's jeep. Henny went along and held the young man while Bingo drove the quiet streets.

Dinner sat on the table, untouched. Eunice did not return downstairs. Ford did not return to the house. The two girls went into the kitchen. Belinda stood at the sink while Lucy sat at the breakfast counter with a glass of milk.

"Lucy, I thought I heard Alfonso scream to Daddy that he was gay."

"Alfonso called Daddy gay?"

"No! Alfonso said that *he* was gay. Alfonso was telling Daddy that he's gay."

"Oh, wow. Is Alfonso gay?"

Belinda sucked her teeth. "Duh! Why you think he liked Cousin Carlton so much and got so upset when he died?"

"Oh." Lucy sat and thought for a moment, half sipping her milk. "Belinda, you don't think Alfonso has—"

"Don't. Don't even say it. No."

"I hope not."

Bingo's Condo, Northside

Bingo got ahold of Sandy Mellow, the head doctor from the clinic. She rushed right over. It looked like psychological shock to her, too. She gave Alfonso a sedative.

Henny Penny held his hand as the drug took effect. In Alfonso's face he saw his own—trembling, scared, rudderless, unable to see a tomorrow or even know if such a thing existed. When Henny's father tossed him out on his ass, his tailbone got bruised. It began bothering him again. It usually did whenever his past resurfaced. He ignored the sensation and concentrated on Alfonso.

"You're gonna be OK, alright baby? You're gonna be OK. Ain't nobody gonna hurt you no more, alright? You're gonna be OK."

He needed to believe that Alfonso would overcome and survive, better than he had.

Bingo put on some mellow Lady Day, the sweet ballads, to help soften the mood, make the space comfortable. Then he went upstairs to his room to call Sammy. He didn't want Alfonso to hear him get upset. Sammy took deep breaths and mostly listened while Bingo unfurled all his anger and hurt. I'm just glad you guys found him and that you got him taken care of, he said, telling Bingo to call back when he had more info. After hanging up, Bingo composed himself and returned downstairs to the living room.

Sandy prepared to leave, satisfied with Alfonso's condition. She offered Henny Penny a ride home. He asked Bingo if he needed any more help. Bingo smiled and gave him one of his tightest, warmest bear hugs. One day, Henny Penny would drive him crazy again. It was inevitable. But that moment lived in the future.

After they departed, he sat with Alfonso, who drifted in and out of consciousness. He did not want to leave his side and brought his comfy chair next to the sofa. Eventually, they both drifted to sleep as Billie crooned softly.

"Bingo? Is that you?" a groggy voice said.

Bingo sat up, startled. He saw Alfonso looking up at him from the sofa. It was 3:18 a.m., by the clock in the corner.

"I'm here, honey. Right here."

"I thought I heard a siren. Did I hear a siren?"

"No, baby."

"I thought I heard one. I remember when I heard sirens at the hospital from Carlton's room. Seemed like there were always sirens."

He stopped talking for a moment.

"Then, I remember sirens when Eddie got beat up. I always remember sirens. They drown out the music. I thought I heard sirens."

"We're at my place, honey. Do you remember anything else?"

"My father hates me."

The words weren't nearly as disquieting as their delivery. He spoke them in such a matter-of-fact tone.

"No, baby." Bingo had to force himself to say that, given how he felt about Ford Berry.

"I really think he hates me, Bingo." The sedative slowed his speech. "He blames me for everything. He thinks I work for Charlotte."

Bingo shook his head. "Try to get some sleep, honey."

"Bingo? Can I have some water?"

Bingo snapped to and went into the kitchen area of his great room. As he stood at the sink, filling a glass with filtered water, he kept glancing over the breakfast counter. The young man broke his heart, someone so strong shattered by cruelty. The sight of him brought back painful memories.

He helped Alfonso sit up so that he could take a few sips.

"Are you hungry, baby? You want a little something to eat?"

"No, thank you. Did Henny Penny bring me here?"

"Yes, we both did."

"I felt him looking at me. I think we were talking, trading war stories. He made me laugh."

Bingo nodded. He'll never be able to look at Henny Penny quite the same way again.

"Bingo? Did your father kick you out?"

"No. I left home."

"Oh, that's right, that's right. That was smart. I should have done the same thing. I really should have. Carlton tried to tell me. I guess I just hope—" Alfonso paused, lost in the memory. "I used to roller-skate. I didn't have a big boombox on my shoulder like they did back in the day." He giggled. "But I moved with the beats. I'd have my iPod and my earbuds on and I'd shimmy and squat and twirl. I did it all." He paused again. "I guess we had an unspoken rule: don't dance in front of the house. He didn't care if he couldn't see me. I can't remember how old I was, 12 or 13, something like that. I skated home from school and I had the latest Mocean Worker album playing 'Cinco de Mowo!' in my earbuds." He giggled. "Electronic jazz/funk stuff. Real cool. I turned Carlton on to him. Anyway, it gave me the boogie bug. So I just started twirling and dancing around, up and down our street. I didn't go down the hill. Oh, no! I did that once, and they told me don't do that no more, but they didn't have to. Our hill's too steep. Scared the shit out of me."

Bingo smiled.

"But anyway, my dad got home. He saw me swishing and shaking my ass while rolling backward. Man, if you coulda seen his face. What a face. I said, 'Hi, Dad.' He slammed his car door shut and went into the house. During dinner, he wouldn't say nothing to me. Finally, after dinner, he had me go out into the backyard with him. He had my roller skates. He dropped them on the ground. Then he walked over to the trash barrel and lifted up the lid and told me to pick up the skates and drop them in. I was like 'Why, Daddy, why? I didn't skate down the hill.' But he just told me to throw them away. So I threw them away. After he slammed down the lid, I asked him one more time: Why? He looked at me and said, 'I already got two daughters.'"

Bingo sat up, took Alfonso's hand and held it tightly. So often as a young boy, his own father had hurled similarly acidic words, his first education about his identity.

After a long pause, Alfonso continued.

"I stayed in my room, door closed, lights off. When I'm in a funk, I just wanna stay there for a while, you know what I mean? I listened to more Mowo, but not for dancing. He does some slow groove stuff, too. He did a remix of 'Blackbird' by Nina Simone. It's so raw. You know her 'Blackbird'?"

Bingo nodded.

"Mowo put on this layer of slow jam groove, man. It's so dark, like the darkest, loneliest, place on earth. Just pain. Pure pain."

"The lyrics are painful enough on their own."

"Yeah. Yeah. And he put Nina's voice through all this reverb. It sounded *ancient*, you know what I'm saying? An ancient pain talking to the present. She kept asking me why'd I think that I could fly, and I was like, yeah, who am I kidding? Never fly. Never love. Never know love. I just listened to it over and over, on a loop, nonstop." Tears streamed from his eyes. "Fuck being 13. I should've done what you did and left the house the next day."

SIXTEEN

FORD CLUTCHED THE STEERING WHEEL AS HE SAT PARKED in the church lot. He had snapped at his wife before leaving the house and now her expression caught up with him. She looked so much like his mother, belittled, diminished. He almost called, but she'd only start talking about Alfonso again, and he couldn't even. Send flowers? His father used to do that, send his mother a bouquet after blowing up at her, a perfunctory gesture that only memorialized her diminishment. No. He vowed to apologize properly later, just not now.

He dashed inside the church, wound his way upstairs to Reverend Johnson's office, entered without knocking, and promptly collapsed on the couch, burying his head in his hands. The reverend offered a glass. Ford reached for it like a man in a deep pit reaching up for a rope. He flinched when he realized it was only water.

"He didn't deny it, Thad. None of it. Said he was writing some paper about the needle exchange or something."

"I can't imagine for what class that would be relevant."

145

"Why now?" His hands bounced impatiently on his knees. "Why did he pick now to suddenly announce to the whole damn world 'Look! I'm gay!'"

"The power of sin can be overwhelming. Though it rarely acts in a vacuum."

Ford cast a sharp look. "What does that mean?"

Reverend Johnson smiled. "No, my friend. I know you keep a very righteous house." He patted Ford's knee. "Our children are often exposed to things outside our control."

Ford relaxed, took another sip of water.

"We'll root out the trouble and make things right again. I swear it. And I can counsel your family any time, morning, noon, or night."

"Thanks, Thad."

"Don't mention it. Hold tough and be strong. Shall we pray together?"

Ford put his glass down and sat up. The reverend took his hands.

"Heavenly Father. Please bring us the guidance we seek, that we may help to steer one of Your flock back toward righteousness. Grant us strength, Lord, that we may help our brother Alfonso, son of this very righteous man, find his true path and calling once again. We seek Your benevolence and forgiveness for any transgressions we have made and ask for Your eternal mercy. Amen."

"Amen!" Ford said. "Amen, amen!"

Bingo's Condo

Over the stereo, Billie Holliday chirped "I Hear Music," an homage to domestic bliss where sparrows sang and coffee perked, a hokey ditty that she made her own with her unique phrasing. Bingo flitted about the kitchen and made breakfast for the reassembled Posse, an apron over his tank top and jeans. Omelets, bacon, toast, coffee, orange juice. Don't worry, doll, he told Roy, the bacon's in a separate pan. He also made sure the thespian received his Earl Grey hot.

After getting food in his system, Alfonso talked. "Fine and Mellow" came on. There are happy blues and sad blues, Billie explained at the top of the track. Alfonso said that both often occurred in the same song, sometimes just a line or two apart.

"That's been my life with Jameel."

He stood up and sang with Lady Day about how his man treated him so mean. Bill, Roy, and Bingo kept him going, snapping the rhythm.

Bingo eventually went out, satisfied that his charge was in good hands. Bill and Roy skipped classes. They found Bingo's copy of *The Lord of the Rings* trilogy, extended edition, on Blu-ray. Marathon! Alfonso declared. Roy made microwave popcorn. They dimmed the lights.

"Let's be hobbits!" Bill exclaimed, then named himself Pip, the young innocent.

"Innocent, my ass," Roy said.

"Well, you're definitely Merry, the troublemaker!"

"Yeah, troublemaker, and the sexiest hobbit, bitch!"

Alfonso laughed, asked if that meant he was Samwise.

"No," Bill said, "you're Frodo."

Alfonso smirked a bit, but said nothing.

After *Fellowship of the Ring*, they paused for food. Roy made grilled cheese sandwiches. Bill heated up some boxed tomato soup.

During *The Two Towers*, Alfonso began thinking of home. Rohan's theme conjured images of family get-togethers, their large dining room table filled edge to edge with home-cooked evil. He tried shaking it off. But the feeling intensified during the scene where King Théoden, freed from Saruman's spell, learned that his son had died. Alfonso wiped his eyes as Éowyn chanted at the funeral, as Théoden lamented having to bury his child. Fear of further rejection had kept him from calling or texting his family. But now he couldn't stop thinking of them. Might they think that he has died? Are they looking? Do they care?

After the film ended, while Bill went to the kitchen and Roy to the bathroom, he finally fished out his cell from his dress jacket pocket. Out of juice. Damn. He found Bingo's landline on the breakfast counter. He dialed the first two numbers, then hung up. Midafternoon—his father should still be at work. But what if he wasn't?

"What's up, babe?" Bill asked.

"I wanna let my mother know that I'm OK. She may have tried of texting me, but my phone died. And I can't call the house. I just can't."

"I could take her a note."

"Could you? That'd be so fly of you, Bill."

"For sure. What's the address?"

Alfonso wrote a note, folded it, and wrote the address on the outside. They decided to postpone *Return of the King*. Alfonso and Roy channel-surfed.

———⊹———

Bill reached the top of the hill on Beacon and saw two girls approach from the other direction. All three paused and stared at one another.

"Hi, I'm looking for the Berry residence," he said.

"This is it," Belinda said. "Do you have news about Alfonso?"

"Yes. He's fine. He wanted me to let you know that he's fine."

"You know where he is?"

"Yes."

"Can you take me to him?"

Bill thought for a split second, but realized that it would be for the best to take her to Bingo's. "Yes, I can take you there."

Belinda took the note from Bill and handed it to Lucy.

"Go inside and take this to Momma. But don't give it to her right away, alright? Tell her that I met a friend of Alfonso's and that I'm going to see him. But give us a few minutes, alright?"

"Why?"

"'Cause, I don't want her calling me back or nothing. I want to go see him."

"I want to see him, too."

"You can go next time, but you have to take this to Momma so that she doesn't worry."

Lucy took the note. "Alright. But you'll tell Alfonso I'm thinking about him, won't you?"

"Of course I will." Belinda turned to Bill. "Is it far?"

"No, it's just off Lincoln."

She nodded.

Lucy stared at them as they descended the hill and didn't go inside until they fell from view.

"What's your name?"

"Bill. Are you Belinda?"

"Yes. Is he really alright? I texted him and called—"

"He's fine. He cell died, that's all. I'm sure he'll be happy to see you."

They crossed Peele and continued toward Carver Street.

"We've been with him all day, me and Roy. Do you know Roy?"

"No, I don't think so. Is that his boyfriend?"

Bill laughed. "No, he's *my* boyfriend."

"Oh, sorry!"

"No big deal."

"I've been so worried about him. I didn't do anything at school today. I couldn't concentrate. And I kept calling my mother to see if she'd heard anything, and she kept saying no. She doesn't always say what's on her mind. But I could tell that she was just as upset as I was."

"Probably more. Mothers are like that."

"Yes. How do you know Alfonso?"

"We're both in the African Students Association together, at State."

"Oh, I see."

"And my family goes to Reverend Johnson's church."

"Were you at the thing yesterday?"

"Yeah."

"Oh, my god, I thought those reverends would never shut up." Bill laughed. "And did you see so many made-up black folks in your life?"

"My kid brother called it a Negro bling-fest."

"He got that right."

Their chit-chat helped Belinda to steady herself. She hadn't slept all night and was livid that her parents hadn't contacted the police to file a missing person's report.

Arriving at their destination, they rode the elevator to Bingo's condo. Belinda took in the surroundings, satisfying herself that her brother was in good hands. She had already concluded that Bill was cool.

Roy answered the door.

"Is that Bill?" Alfonso called out. "Did he find my mother?"

"And someone else," Roy said.

"Hi, Alfonso."

Upon hearing Belinda, Alfonso hopped off the sofa and rushed to the door. He embraced her like she was about to fly away. Roy and Bill couldn't help but smile at the reunion.

"We'll be at Sammy's if you need anything," Bill said.

Alfonso nodded, tears running down his face. Roy grabbed their backpacks and they discretely exited.

"I was so worried!" she said.

"Belinda, I'm so sorry. I'm so, so sorry!"

They made their way to the sofa and sat down. The TV continued as background noise.

"You ain't got nothing to be sorry about. It's not like you threw yourself out of the house."

"Thanks." Her frankness, so refreshing. "I don't like making people worry. I wish I had talked to you sooner, that's all. I've been so fucked up in the head ever since Cousin Carlton died."

"That's what I was trying to tell Lucy. You know what she said? She asked me, 'Oh, is Alfonso gay?' I was like, girl, how clueless are you?"

Alfonso giggled. "Guess it's not a state secret."

"Please. But you're OK here?"

"I'm fine. Bingo said I can stay as long as I need to."

"Bingo?"

"Yeah. His name is Philip Cincinnati, but he goes by Bingo. He's a real sweetheart. He and Cousin Carlton were tight. You know Uncle Rand kicked him out, too."

She nodded.

"I don't want to become invisible like Carlton was."

She took his hand and gave him a long, solid stare. "That's not going to happen."

Her warmth touched him deeply.

"Can you stay for a bit? Want something to drink? I think there's Coke in the fridge."

"Sure. I can stay. Momma knows where I'm at."

He got up and went to the kitchen. "How do you like this place? Dope, ain't it?"

"So dope. Mind if I change the channel?"

"Go for it. The remote is right there."

He could hear her channel-surfing. It felt so good to have her nearby.

Belinda stayed long enough to meet Bingo when he returned home. By design, of course. He asked if she wanted to stay for dinner, but she thought it best if she went home. Her cell hadn't started ringing yet, but she sensed a call was inevitable. Bingo insisted on driving her. Alfonso appreciated that, but declined the invitation to accompany them. He wasn't ready to see Beacon Street. Instead, he asked Belinda to load some of his stuff into Bingo's jeep for the return trip.

Bingo had come home to a kitchen bustling with activity. He smelled fried chicken, saw vegetables steaming.

"And is that Carlton's lemon-cream sauce?"

"Yep!"

"Well, shit, girl, I was gonna cook something!"

"No, Uncle Butch. This time, I'm in charge. You just go set the table and get all comfy."

"Sir! Yes sir!"

Bingo pulled out a bottle of Sémillon. They feasted hard. Though a simple meal, it had the same tranquilizing effect of a Thanksgiving dinner. They eventually took their glasses and sat on the sofa, each sitting at opposite ends, their legs stretched adjacent. Bingo put a Kate Bush collection on the stereo. Both smoked cigars.

"How did you and Carlton meet?" Alfonso asked.

"Dance floor."

"That figures."

"You know it. That man loved the dance floor. He danced with others and he danced alone. But yeah, we met at the old Pendulum, Jesus, what, around 1988? He was there with a couple of friends, and I was there with some folks I knew. We're all on the floor, getting down. And you know what he did? He kept sashaying by and rubbing my head. Yeah! Like this." He leaned over and rubbed Alfonso's Afro. "Just like that. Every time he passed me."

"OK—"

"Yeah. So later I'm at the bar and I see him. I motioned him to come over and bought him a beer. Then I asked him, 'What's with the head rub? You trying to read my fortune or something?' He took the beer, guzzled about a third of it—he was sweating like a pig—and then he said, 'It's for luck. Don't you know it's good luck to rub a bald man on the head?' And I was like, 'Oh, really?' And he said, 'Yeah, it got me a free beer, didn't it?' That's when it all started. He was just like that. Fearless. If there's one word that describes Carlton, it's fearless."

"Seriously!"

"Uh-huh. If he wanted something, he got it. And heaven help you if you got in the way."

"But you two never dated, right?"

"No. Not that we didn't flirt a lot, mind you. He was a gorgeous man. And I think he liked vanilla as much as I like chocolate." Alfonso laughed. He thought as much. "We were tighter than lovers, in a lot of ways. I remember when he tested positive. He didn't mince any words. We were at a bar, a group of us, Harry, Aaron, and Ashley. He stormed in and announced, 'Well, I've joined the fucking club!' We all knew what he meant, 'cause we knew he was getting his test results that day. That was back in the days when it took two weeks to get your results."

"That's too damned long."

"No shit. Anyway, we all felt like a bomb hit us. I was really upset about it, 'cause Carlton didn't have health insurance at the time. I said to him, 'What are you going to do?' He just looked at me, rubbed my head, and said, 'Keep dancing, fool, what do you think?' Then he was off on the dance floor."

"Fierce!"

Bingo nodded. He reached for the bottle to fill his glass. Alfonso leaned his over for the same. Just as the last of it dripped into the glass, the doorbell rang. Bingo put the bottle down and hopped to the door. Alfonso stayed put. He heard Bingo let out a loud "Dahling!" so he knew it was a friend.

"Of course you can come in! Look who brought provisions!" He held up a new bottle of Pinot noir. Charlotte followed.

"Hey, Charlotte!" Alfonso said. He put down his stub of a stogie and stood, gave her a hug. "Come break up this old men's club we got going."

She sat next to him. Bingo brought over a third glass.

Alfonso saw nothing but worry and pain, not just in her face, but in the whole way she carried herself.

"Charlotte, before you say anything," Alfonso said, "I need to tell you something. I love my father, OK? But I don't like the way he won in '08. Between that and Prop. 8 passing in California, all when we got our first black president, I was pretty torn up that night. I cried a lot. The one thing I had to hold on to was your concession speech. You said your campaign wasn't just about winning office, but building a more inclusive community for everyone. Those words really kept me together that night. I've always wanted to tell you that."

She took both of his hands, her face radiating a warm glow. Then she took the glass Bingo just poured and raised it.

Alfonso raised his glass. A vision of his father came to him suddenly—in his gym shorts, in position with the ball close to his chest. He took a sip, then put his glass down.

Ford came out of his study in time to see Belinda going up the stairs.

"Belinda," he called out.

She stopped and turned around.

"I heard you saw your brother today."

"Yes."

"Well, how is he?"

She looked at him for a moment. "He's fine." Then she turned and continued up the stairs.

The silence and attitude were not lost on Ford, but he said nothing as he went back into his study.

SEVENTEEN

Thursday, 8 a.m.
Sammy's Store, Carver Street

A LITTLE TV SAT NEARBY PLAYING A LIVE INTERVIEW OF Charlotte on one of the local news programs. But Sammy was distracted by the alien contraption Alfonso plopped on his counter. He searched its sides and the back, and then finally looked at Alfonso, who sat patiently next to him.

"How do you turn this thing on?" Sammy asked.

"It's this button here."

"Oh. Now is it booting up?"

"Uh-huh."

"OK. Oh, OK, here we go," Sammy said, pointing to the television.

> "*—no secret that you are a longtime supporter of the clinic. Councilman Berry has been very opposed to its operations, in particular its needle exchange program.*"
>
> "*Yes,*" Charlotte said. "*And that's unfortunate. The Huckleberry Community Clinic has many service areas. The needle exchange is just one of them, though an important one, to be sure. It strives to be a total support center for those with*

HIV and AIDS, as well as a general health resource for the community."

"Councilman Berry's son, Alfonso Berry III, is involved with the clinic, at least according to a few press reports. Is he a supporter of yours?"

"I'm not commenting on that. To me, this is just another side issue that detracts from the main issues of this race. I'm not going to get into a discussion about the councilman's family or anything like that."

"Thanks, Charlotte," Alfonso said.

"So that's a spreadsheet program, huh?" Sammy said.

"Yeah. I'm setting it up for you."

Sammy shook his head. "I can't believe I let you talk me into this."

Alfonso smiled as he typed.

"All I know is I'm gonna do something wrong, push some button and then all of my information is gonna disappear forever."

"No, it won't. I'm setting it up to do timed backups so that it will automatically back up the spreadsheet every five minutes. That way, if something happens, you won't lose that much data."

Sammy craned to look at the screen through his glasses.

"Are you sure you don't need this thing for school?"

"Naw. I got a MacBook already. This is Carlton's. I was gonna donate it to a school or something, but I figure you need it more."

"This is Harry's fault. He talked you into this."

Alfonso laughed. He happened to visit the other day while Harry struggled with the ledgers. This would be a whole lot easier with a computer, he fussed. Sammy acted like he didn't hear.

"So this is where I enter the data?"

"Yeah, just type the numbers in this box. Right. Then press enter."

"Aha! See? It disappeared!"

"No!" Alfonso fingered the touchpad. "It's just that the column is too narrow. See? Now you can see it correctly."

"Huh. And it added the total at the bottom."

"That's right."

"What if I run out of spaces, then what happens?"

"You can add more rows, like this."

Sammy looked on as the tidy gridlines began dancing on the screen.

"Tell you what, you just set it up real big for me so that I don't have to worry about it for a while."

"Sure. And I'll enter the first set of data, so you can see how."

Sammy shook his head, but he kept looking as young fingers tap-danced on the keyboard.

"And just wait until I start loading your music collection on here."

"I got a big collection."

"That's alright. We'll be able to get most of it in here. So I got a big meeting tonight. Reverend Johnson has agreed to mediate between me and my parents."

"For real? Both your mom and dad with be there?"

"That's what he told me. He called last night. He said my father is anxious to make things right again."

"Good. Good."

He heard his own hesitations in Sammy's response.

"I don't know what to expect. I feel I should at least try. Maybe this will be the talk I wanted to have with him in the first place."

"Too soon?"

"Part of me feels that way."

Sammy turned off the TV, stood up. "You want some more coffee?"

"Thanks." He handed him his mug.

Sammy walked to the storeroom. On the way, he put on the stereo. The old tin pot filled the store with the usual scent of ancient blues. Alfonso lost himself in the odor as the ivories tickled over the stereo.

"Who is this playing?" Alfonso called out.

"Ahmad Jamal." Sammy walked back with the mugs. "This track's called 'But Not for Me.'"

"I like it." He took a sip of the straight black, then held the mug on the counter. "I asked Reverend Johnson if my sisters will be there. He said no. He seemed to think it's better if my parents and

I talk it out first. I should have insisted that they be there, though. I think the whole family should talk as a unit."

"Mm-hmm. I agree."

"I don't like feeling detached from them."

"There ain't no reason that the three of you couldn't just sit and talk. Take 'em out to lunch or something."

"Yeah, that's a good idea." He took another sip. "How did it go with your dad?"

Sammy wrinkled his eyebrows as he played some more with the computer.

"My dad was a jazz trumpeter. He taught me music. We were really, really close. And then we had a big falling-out." He paused for a second as the next track came on. "Now this is a classic here, 'Poinciana.'" Alfonso nodded with the pulse of the tune. "He used to play this so pretty."

"What happened? Was it the gay thing?"

"Naw. We lived on Carver Street for a while. Didn't bother him." He took another sip, scowled at the computer. "If I close this thing, will it explode on me?"

Alfonso smiled and shook his head. Sammy closed the laptop.

"We had a falling-out over Vietnam. My old man served during World War II. Hated it. My mom told me that, 'cause my dad never talked about it. But, you know, lots of black folks got messed up in the service during the war. A lot of jazz artists did. Lester Young, for instance. But anyway,"—he took another sip—"when Vietnam started up, I was fighting like mad to get a deferment. The antiwar radicals used to train the straight boys on how to act gay to get deferments. They called themselves 'hoaxosexuals.'"

"Seriously?"

"I'm serious! Look it up! So I was like, OK, how do I get this deferment? 'Cause if straight boys could do it, then my black fairy ass better get one."

Alfonso laughed.

"Am I right? Eventually, I got it. My dad didn't like it. He thought that if you're called, you should serve. And that was that. We had a big fight. He called me a coward. I called him a coward and a hypocrite. I was all big-headed, full of civil rights rhetoric. I thought I was such hotshit. But I didn't know shit. My father was a very complicated man. I had no right calling him a hypocrite. Anyway, we stopped speaking to each other, stopped playing together. Neither of us made a move to patch it up. We were both too stubborn for our own good."

Sammy stopped talking. "Poinciana" played to the end.

"You never reconciled?" Alfonso asked.

"You hear this piece?" He pointed up as "What's New" started. "I listened to this track a thousand times to learn how Vernel Fournier did the brush work. Finally, when I thought I had it down, I played it for my dad. He was so proud of me. He took his horn out and played along. He had such a beautiful tone, especially on ballads. When I was little, I used to imagine pure gold dripped from his horn." He touched Alfonso on the hand, a small smile on his face. "We came to terms at the end, just before he died. But by then, he was too sick to play. I sure wish we could have played together one more time. All those wasted years." He paused to absorb the memory. "I stopped playing after my dad died. It was just too painful. All the music we shared, I just couldn't." He paused again. "I even stopped listening to jazz, for years. Listened to classical."

"When did you, when could you start listening to jazz again?"

"Probably about four years after he died. Just gradually, you know. A piece here, a piece there. Some artists I still couldn't listen to, but eventually they all came back, like old friends returning from a long journey."

He turned to look at Alfonso. "Don't let pain get in the way of what you love. You work that shit out. I never should have stopped my music."

Alfonso smiled, trying to look upbeat. "I heard you put on quite a show last weekend."

Sammy did his staccato chuckle and squeezed Alfonso's hand. "If I get a combo together, will you dance for us?"

"Always, Sammy." He leaned over and gave him a kiss.

EIGHTEEN

A Quarter to 6 p.m.
Reverend Johnson's Church

BINGO HAD SUGGESTED TO ALFONSO THAT HE DO something special for himself, something simple, something fun. So he went to Bernard's and got his hair cornrowed again, this time in smaller, tighter braids. They tasseled against the back of his neck and behind his ears. When he showed Bingo, the leather queen screamed with delight, then gave him one of his old leather jackets. He left for his meeting feeling super fly.

His swagger-strut ended when he reached the shallow stone steps at Beacon Hill First Baptist, its high spires extinguishing all attitude. The heavy wooden doors resisted his opening them. The gray columns in the austerely lit sanctuary stared at him with judgment in their raised arches. The carpeted stairs seemed particularly long and steep during the ascent. Alfonso meekly pushed open the door to Reverend Johnson's office and entered.

Reverend Johnson sat in a chair placed directly in front of his large wooden desk. Alfonso's parents sat to the reverend's right. All faces looked up when Alfonso entered. His mother clutched her hands together, radiating elation. But this appeared to fade. The cornrows, the leather jacket—he came before them as his true self. And they reacted in kind: You have become one of *them*.

The reverend rose from his chair with an outstretched hand.

"Thank you for coming, Alfonso. Please, have a seat."

Alfonso took the vacant chair to the reverend's left. He sat facing his parents at a slight angle. He smiled nervously and nodded toward them. His mother responded, but his father did so only after a sharp glance from Reverend Johnson.

"It's so beautiful to have you all here together," the reverend said. "Let us join hands and bow our heads in prayer." They quickly joined hands. "Dear Lord, please bring us the wisdom and guidance we seek to heal this righteous family, that they may continue down their true path together. In Your name, Amen."

Alfonso found the language off-putting. His eyes opened to his unsmiling parents as he released the reverend's hand. He wondered if coming was a mistake.

"I know that some difficult words were exchanged last weekend," the reverend began, "the result of some unfortunate events. I want to assure you all that there will be no replay of that encounter here today. There will be no blame game. We will engage in mutual healing."

He played his voice like a Stradivarius, enunciating his words in the most soothing tones imaginable. Smiles flashed to accent his oration at just the right places. He evoked treasured memories, causing Alfonso to visualize a slideshow of his youth. Picnics. Bandstands. Summer festivals. Fudgsicle bars. Small, round, tightly wound fastballs. Alfonso looked across at his parents. His mother's gaze had softened to a glow he recognized. His father held her hand tenderly, his eyes no longer shooting daggers. Everything looked familiar and comfortable, normal and uncomplicated.

"We're all in the same place, I see," the reverend said. "Now we can continue forward together." He gestured to Ford.

"Reverend Johnson, I want to thank you for bringing us here, bringing us together." Ford cleared his throat frequently. "I believe I speak for Eu as well as myself when I say that this has been the most difficult week I have ever lived to see. However, your knowledge of our family history makes you the right person, the only person for this difficult task. So again, I thank you."

"Of course."

Alfonso sat with his hands folded on his lap. His father looked at him directly.

"Son, I have a few things I want to say, but I want to start, as Reverend Johnson did so beautifully, by setting the scene." More throat clearing. The reverend handed him a glass of water. Ford took a couple of quick sips. "My father created a legacy through his hard work and the sacrifices he endured during his life. And we are the caretakers of that legacy."

Alfonso didn't hear his father. He heard his grandfather. Destiny, duty, Du Bois. Ford even portentously placed the family in the Talented Tenth, a concept that Du Bois himself had long abandoned in later life, years before Ford was born.

"So, Son, if my obligations have meant that I haven't always been there for you, then please forgive me. Your mother and I want nothing more than for you to grow into the best person you can be."

"We love you, Alfonso," his mother said.

"I love you too, Mom. I love you both. I never wanted anything like this to happen."

The reverend leaned back in satisfaction.

"Of course not, Son," Ford said. "And that's why I want to work quickly to put all this behind us. We have an obligation to do right by the community. Sadly, our unfortunate situation has divided the community. We can't let that happen. So, first, your mother and I want you to come home with us, tonight."

The reverend smiled and nodded.

"We need you with us, Alfonso," his mother said.

"Yes, Son, we do."

"Alfonso," the reverend said, "your father is making a great gesture here. He is giving you a chance to return to your roots. The home is a healing place, Alfonso. We may stray from it, just as those who lose sight stray from the Word. But ultimately, those of clear mind and conscious always return."

"Amen, Reverend," Ford said.

No more slideshow. The fastballs evaporated. The park's pathways cracked. The band shell began to decay. Graffiti grew on the community center like ivy. And a bricklayer appeared, applying his trade one brick at a time. Others walked by casually as he built a wall in the middle of Huckleberry Park.

"Everything will return to what it had been," Ford continued. "Your sisters will greet you with open arms. Your friends in ASA will be happy to see you again. But the next thing we must do, to show a united front, is to make things right in the press."

On one side of the wall strolled well-dressed black folks in their Sunday best. Couples exchanged pleasantries. The men shook hands. The ladies kissed with polite hugs. They asked about each other's children, talked about the fine Sunday weather. Then words of parting trailed behind them as they continued on their way, with promises to have dinner together real soon.

"You and I can sit together and write a joint statement that will clear up any questions people might have about you and me and the needle exchange clinic. I'll have my office issue it generally. That way no one can say that we are not a united front anymore."

On the other side were the shadows of familiar faces. Sammy. Charlotte. Bingo. Harry. Henny Penny. Ashley. Aaron. Roy. Bill. Vera. Carlton. Next to Carlton, Alfonso thought he saw his own shadow, but before he could tell for certain, the bricklayer completed the wall and the shadows vanished. Simultaneously, the well-dressed black folks took notice of him, nodding hello as they walked by. But he could no longer see himself.

"Alfonso?" Reverend Johnson called to him.

He saw three sets of eyes looking at him. Without thinking, he looked down at himself. He saw his legs and hands. He hadn't vanished after all.

"So, Dad, so this statement, it would say that we're on the same page about everything, including the clinic?"

His father nodded.

"But we're not."

Three words obliterated all those spoken before them. They rendered the room cold.

"Dad." He took a deep breath, then sighed it out. "I wanted to have this conversation with you, but didn't know how so I didn't try. I should have. And for that, I apologize, because you and mom, and Belinda and Lucy, deserved better than to hear about me in the press. I never wanted that to happen. I'm hanging at the clinic and writing this paper to figure out who am I. I wanted to share the paper with you all so that you'd have a better idea of where I'm coming from. There's so much we've never talked about. When I first started noticing boys. When I felt my first heartache, after realizing that a boy I liked couldn't like me back the same way. How angry I used to feel, wishing that the feelings would just go away. My first kiss. You've shared moments like that with Belinda and you're starting to share them with Lucy. I'm older than both of them and you've never shared those moments with me. It's not because I've never had them. It's because I never felt like I could talk about them with you."

His father winced. But his mother allowed herself to see. Alfonso noticed, giving him hope.

"I want you to join me on this journey." His words reached out to them like an outstretched hand.

"I don't think you understand the situation, Alfonso," Ford said, the verbal equivalent of keeping his hands at his side.

Reverend Johnson cleared his throat. "What your father is saying, Alfonso, what he is trying to explain—" He paused. His face labored a smile. "This is a very delicate situation, Alfonso. I'm sure we all understand and respect the need for self-discovery. But there are larger issues at stake here. As your father explained, your family is a leading pillar of the community. As such, it cannot be seen to be in division or disarray. If it is, then this will affect the standing of the entire community."

Alfonso felt himself tense up, but he refused to get angry and utter words he'd regret later. He took several deep breaths, which centered him.

"Dad, you mentioned Du Bois. Recently I talked to friends about Du Bois's veil of invisibility and how one also surrounds LGBTQ folks. I'm living behind two veils. Really, it's like a veil within a veil."

"Alfonso!" Reverend Johnson said reproachfully. "You can't possibly use Du Bois's work to describe such things. He was talking about the historic position of African American people in this country, the souls of black folks. There's a lot of history there, you know."

"There's history for LGBTQ folks, too, Reverend Johnson. It's just that a lot of it has been invisible behind its own veil."

"Alfonso, listen," Ford said. "The bottom line is that I'm under attack, politically. Your friends have an agenda, Charlotte Hunter's agenda. Did it ever occur to you that they might be using you as a weapon against me, to discredit me?"

Alfonso's face went blank.

"Uh, now, Alfonso," Reverend Johnson said, "we realize that those people are friends of your cousin—"

"No, Reverend, it goes beyond that. Way beyond that." He looked to his left, away from everyone. "How do I even start? 'Those people.'" All he could see was Charlotte's face from the other night, how sorrowful she looked. He turned toward them again. "Let me tell you something about Sunday night. I lost my religion Sunday night. I wanted to kill someone Sunday night. I thought I was going to die Sunday night. I was lying on the floor in a filthy restroom crying my eyes out Sunday night. Sunday night was the darkest night I had ever seen in my life. I didn't think there would ever be light again. And then, you know what happened? A friend of mine comes in, Curtis." He smiled briefly. "We all call him Henny Penny, 'cause he acts real silly most of the time. He's a trip. But that Sunday night, he didn't trip. He didn't run from me. He embraced me. Curtis got thrown, literally *thrown* out of his house by his father. He barely finished high school, never went to college, works shit jobs. But he got by. This man, who's had nothing but shit thrown at him, had enough presence of mind to help me when I was down. Do you know why? Because he knows the road I'm on right now. Where I'm going, he's already been. And he remembers it like it was yesterday. That's why he helped me."

"Alfonso, watch your language."

"Reverend, let me finish. Curtis got violently thrown out by his father because he's gay. Carlton got thrown out by Uncle Rand because he was gay. And now, you've thrown me out because I'm gay. This has nothing to do with the campaign, Dad. It has to do with me, your son, being one of 'those people,' the ones you've trained yourself to loathe all these years."

"Now look, Alfonso," Ford said, "let's get something straight here, alright? Don't put words in my mouth. I do not loathe anyone."

"Then why didn't you say anything when that 'bulldyke' letter came out? Why didn't you denounce it?"

His father sat speechless. His mother squeezed her eyes shut.

"That's what I'm talking about. It doesn't have to be this way, 'us versus them.' The world is changing. I could have been your ambassador to the Northside all these years. Have you ever thought of that?"

"You can't serve two masters, Alfonso," Ford said.

"My soul is my master. I have to be true to myself."

"We all have responsibilities!" Ford stood up. "Do you think your grandfather liked being called a jigaboo? A coon? Do you think I like going to City Hall and have people snickering and plotting behind my back, calling me the ghetto councilman? It's hell, but it's my job! I'd rather be playing ball in the park, but I'm doing what my training has allowed me to do. To lead! To help make a difference!"

"Dad, you had a choice about your career. Frankly, I think you would have been happier playing baseball. I don't have a choice about being gay, any more than I have a choice about being black. And I can't be straight for you anymore. That's over."

Ford violently wiped his face with both hands, began pacing around. "I told you this would be a waste of time, Thad. He's not listening. He doesn't get it."

"Granddad kept on you until you started gay-baiting Charlotte. That was a reflection of his era. We're not in that era anymore."

"There you go again, badmouthing your grandfather! My god, what's happened to you?" He paused, sweat pouring off him. "I remember when you used to look up to him and—and defend him. I know he wasn't a perfect man. I know that. But he was a great man, an icon." Ford glanced at Reverend Johnson. "He accomplished great things."

"Yes, Alfonso," Reverend Johnson agreed. "Your grandfather is one of the legendary men of our people."

"You used to keep that crap off his Wikipedia page," Ford said. "Now you're quoting from it!"

"I love Granddad Al, OK, just like I love you. But I can't ignore his faults. Part of him was just full of anger and fear. I wish you could see that."

"SHUT UP!" Ford jabbed his finger toward Alfonso. "You are cut off from this day forward, Mister!"

"Ford, no!" Eunice said. "This is our son!"

"The hell he is."

Alfonso sat shaking his head. He thought he felt a tear cross his cheek.

"Everyone, please," Reverend Johnson said. "Let's not lose our center."

"It's long gone, Thad!"

Alfonso stood up. He walked over to his mother and gave her a kiss on the cheek. Then he looked at his father as he stood behind Reverend Johnson.

"You should have followed your heart and played baseball, Dad. You would have been a natural."

He walked to the door, paused. He turned and faced them one more time and gave a black power salute. Then he walked out. He skipped down the stairs with ease. He walked through the sanctuary, its tall columns and raised arches no longer bedeviling him. When he got to the front door, it no longer seemed big and heavy, but just a door, one of hundreds he's pushed and pulled in his short life. He no longer swaggered. The need to affect attitude had passed. He walked down the sidewalk in the crisp air, hands in his pockets.

Alfonso took the long way around to Bingo's condo, not wanting to run into any of the friends and relations, needing his own space for a while. He lingered on Lincoln in hopes of finding that sax player he and Bingo ran into. But the brother wasn't around. Rather than play his own music, he kept his earbuds off and melded with the living blues of the street. Car horns. Little feet skipping rope. Folks loud-talking on phones. Hearing their soundtrack of laughs, troubles, triumphs, and laments put his own situation into perspective. This time he contributed pensive silence to the mix, like Ahmad Jamal used silence to add texture to his music. He reached Ox's Diner at Delaware. Fries sounded pretty good. He got a bag to go.

When he opened the front door at Bingo's, the security panel began beeping. He typed in the code. No Bingo. He took off the leather jacket and hung it on one of the hooks near the door, then went into the kitchen. That's when he saw two gift-wrapped packages on the breakfast counter. One was small and neatly trimmed in staid colors. The other was very large, very fuchsia, and had a big pink bow on top.

He opened the smaller one first. It was from Auntie Vera—the photo of the clinic collective that he adored so much, beautifully matted and framed. He kissed the glass over his cousin's face, then looked at it longingly before putting it down.

An envelope was attached to the big, bright fuchsia box with the words 'Open and play me first!' written on it in squiggly letters.

He took the box and the envelope into the living room and turned on the entertainment system, plopping the CD-ROM from the envelope into the player. He laughed out loud. Melanie started singing "Brand New Key."

He ripped off the bow and wrapping paper and opened the box as the campy song continued. Inside he found a brand-new pair of slick, black roller blades with silver tracks and neon-blue wheels. A little metal key dangled from the lacing of the left skate.

He couldn't get his shoes off fast enough. In an instant, the resurrected skating queen took over the quiet street where Bingo lived, blasting Mocean Worker's latest electronic funk-swing in his earbuds, freely twisting, turning, twirling, and shaking his righteous ass.

NINETEEN

REVEREND JOHNSON MADE NO ATTEMPT TO HIDE HIS
anger. He snapped at his assistant when she called on
the intercom. He looked at the now-empty chairs in his
office and kicked one aside as he walked to the door. He stomped
downstairs to get some water from the kitchen. That was when he
noticed the tutorial schedule on the board. Bill was due to tutor
that evening, as usual for a Thursday. Back upstairs at his assistant's
office, he demanded pen and paper as she shut down her computer
for the day. He wrote a brief note and grabbed some tape. At the
classroom, he stopped himself before putting up the note.

"Reginald, you're here early."

"Yeah, well, I wanted to finish my reading before he got here."

"Let me see what you're reading." The reverend saw what he
expected, then handed the book back to him. "So you're finishing
Giovanni's Room. How did you like it?"

"It's good. I like it a lot."

"Well, I'm sorry to tell you"—his face all smiles—"but Bill is
not available for tutoring today. In fact, he said that he didn't have
time to tutor anymore. He sends his regrets."

"What? Just like that?"

"I'm afraid so, Reginald. Go home. I'll try to have a new tutor
here for you soon. We'll contact you."

Smooth packed his gear in total disbelief. But he left without incident, muttering whatevers under his breath. The reverend waited until Smooth left the area before posting his note to Bill. It requested him to go to the reverend's office as soon as he got in.

When Bill arrived and found the note instead of his student, he wrote on the chalkboard that he'd be back soon, so that Smooth would know that he was around. Then he went down the hall and up the stairs. He knocked on the reverend's door and opened it. Reverend Johnson sat behind his desk reading papers. A raised hand motioned Bill to enter. For a long while Reverend Johnson made no further acknowledgment of Bill's presence. He read a sheet of paper, then put it aside and read another. Then he went back to the first sheet. Bill sat patiently and silently, aside from an occasional throat-clearing cough.

"I see you did not heed my wishes, William," the reverend finally said, still looking at his papers, "and continued to read *Giovanni's Room* with Reginald."

Busted. Bill moved slightly in his chair, his mind racing for an answer.

"Yes, I know, sir. Reginald wanted to keep on reading it. He insisted, sir, and I didn't know how to say no."

The reverend looked up. Closed lips wore a tiny smile. "I thought you might say something like that, William." He rose from his chair and turned his back to Bill, hands clasped in the small of his back. "You mean that you were not man enough to take control of your lessons." Then he turned to his right and began walking. "Or, you mean that you didn't want to interrupt your grand agenda. It's one of those, is it not, William?"

"Sir?"

He began circling the desk. "You're a proud man, aren't you, William? Such a proud little man. I called the ASA office, to check in as I do from time to time. You see, I hold that group in very high esteem, William. But this time I called with the express interest of asking about you."

Bill felt his stomach hollow. The reverend continued walking, circling the desk and Bill.

"They told me some very interesting things. For instance, they said that you don't spend a lot of time in the office. Here I thought you missed a meeting here or there. But they said, and I quote, 'He's just not here.' But you do spend time with Alfonso. They also told me that you have been seen on campus in close company with some young man, holding hands, side by side in the café, quite close and intimate, so they said."

Bill cleared his dry throat. "Reverend, you said I was your most dedicated tutor."

"Did I, William? I can't recall."

Reverend Johnson walked directly behind Bill and stood over him. Bill refused to turn around and look at him.

"So, William, are you homosexual?"

No eye contact. Not a word spoken.

"I am waiting for a response, young man."

"I don't think it's any of your business."

"Really? How very interesting. You're obviously such a proud person, I thought that perhaps, given the opportunity, you might go tell it from the mountains. That is part of your agenda, isn't it? Just like using overtly homosexual-themed works with students in my church's tutorial program—works which I expressly forbade you from using. That's part of the agenda, too, isn't it?"

Bill felt he had heard enough. "Sir, if you don't want me working here anymore, then just, you know, fire me and get it over with." He bent over to pick up his backpack.

"Oh, no, you don't. You aren't going anywhere. Put that bag down."

Bill turned and looked up at him. The reverend pulled his leathered face taut. His eyes widened. His mouth sneered and wrinkled into a grotesque caricature of his trademark toothy smile. Without thinking, Bill dropped his bag.

"You have no idea what you've done, do you? Let me explain it to you, William." He glowered over him for a moment longer, then went behind his desk and took his seat.

"In this room not two hours ago, I hosted Councilman Berry, his wife Eunice, and Alfonso. I wanted to forge a reconciliation after Alfonso fucked up and got involved with that needle exchange group." He tilted his head. "I suppose you encouraged him in this work didn't you, William?" He paused for a moment. "The meeting was a complete and utter disaster. Alfonso not only disrespected his own father, he desecrated the memory of his revered grandfather and everything he stood for. Up until then, his father was willing to let bygones be bygones and allow him return home, so long as he renounced what he had done. But no. Alfonso wouldn't do it. You have him so pumped up with that gay pride shit that he stormed out of here, leaving his parents in the lurch. That is what your gay pride has done, William. It has destroyed our most important family. Three generations of prominence and dignity destroyed, just like that. But I suppose that doesn't matter to you, does it? The concerns of black folks are not your concern, since you're homosexual. You know what they say, don't you, William? They say that homosexuality is worse than crack, because with crack we lose only one brother. With homosexuality, we lose two. And here it is before us. We lost two. First you and now Alfonso."

"Alfonso was his own person long before he met me."

"I've known Alfonso since he was born! Who are you to tell me who he is and who he ain't. What do you know? Do you know Leviticus 18:22? 'Thou shalt not lie with mankind as with womankind; it is abomination.' Do you know Psalm 10:4? 'Through the pride of his countenance, the wicked will not seek after God: God is not in all his thoughts.' Describes you to a tee, doesn't it, you proud little man. You don't know shit, boy!"

"I know that you're a lying hypocrite. You're swearing like a sailor when you said never talk like that. And you *did* call me your best tutor!"

"Shut up! No one wants to hear from you. You're nothing but a little faggot, you hear? A dumb, stupid, little faggot. A pathetic faggot. A useless faggot. We have no use for you here, William."

Bill got up and picked up his bag without saying a word.

"Your mother's going to be so proud of you, isn't she?"

Bill paused, kept his back to Johnson. He wanted to keep walking, but couldn't.

"You might not recognize the damage you've done, but she will. All that networking she's done here, all for nothing. Folks around here protect their own, William. I'm just saying. She could lose clients, costing her company business. And all because of you and your stupid, stubborn pride."

Bill's eyes began to sting, his head quivered. He tried his best to hide it, but could feel Johnson behind him rejoicing. He slowly walked out of his office.

"Good luck to you, young man," Johnson called out. "Good luck and goodbye."

8:30ish
Carver Street

Sammy normally played John Coltrane when the Carver Street Business Guild convened at his store. The creative dissonance of the sax master's sheets of sound mirrored the dynamics of the group's loud, boisterous, high-snap diva, take-no-prisoner meetings. They were the Bid Whist game in the corner of the salon. Sometimes the music couldn't keep up. But this evening Sammy chose differently. He put on *Crescent*, Coltrane's somber album. Released in the spring of '64, it became part of his personal soundtrack for the Civil Rights Movement. "Wise One" in particular, with Coltrane's solemn invocation and McCoy Tyner's haunting, meditative chords, captured everything significant about the era: the enticement of freedom nearby, the acknowledgment of sacrifices made, the foretelling of challenges yet to come. Sammy sensed the same unsettledness again in the room and throughout the neighborhood.

Folding chairs squeezed into every nook and corner, between the aisles and behind the produce bins. Some people stood. Sammy sat behind the counter. Charlotte sat next to him. Roy, on loan from The Other Bookstore, stood at the register ready to check out any customers who braved the crowd.

Bernard the hairdresser had the floor, braids flipping from shoulder to shoulder as he turned his head while speaking. Normally he got teased as the one who doggedly wanted to stick to *proceeeedure* in the name of doing the right thing. So when he began, folks thought he would argue that they should offer Ford Berry one last chance to speak to the group before making their endorsement. But Bernard had no time for procedure. Ignore too many invitations, he concluded, and your ass stops getting invited. Folks cheered.

Roy felt a vibration, took out his cell, stared at the screen. "Tha fuck!"

Eyes turned toward him. A few looked on their own cellphones.

"What's up, Royboy?" Sammy asked.

"Bill said Johnson just fired him from the tutorial program. 'He called me a useless faggot and canned my ass.'"

"Aw, geez! Great fucking Diz— Has everybody lost their goddamn minds? Where is he?"

"I'm asking him now," replied Roy, his thumbs mad typing.

Otto from Ye Olde Leather Shop stood up. "People! I think we need to pay Reverend Johnson a visit!"

"By all means," said Angie from The Other Bookstore.

"Well, this meeting's adjourned," Bernard said. "Come on, everyone. Field trip!"

The store emptied. Sammy, Charlotte, and Roy stayed behind.

"He just keeps saying he can't go home. But he won't tell me where he's at. Fuck! I'm gonna text Alfonso."

"Roy," Charlotte said, "maybe we should go to the park and see if he's there somewhere."

They quickly exited. Sammy sat alone, Coltrane still playing. *This area's ready to explode,* he thought.

Bingo charged in wearing shit-kicker boots and leather chaps over his jeans.

"My phone's going crazy about Johnson firing a tutor. He fire Bill?"

"Roy and Charlotte just went to the park looking for him."

"What?"

"You got Bill's cell number?"

"Yeah."

Sammy called from his seldom-used, old school clamshell, hoping that caller ID would tell Bill who was calling, something he wasn't sure would happen with the store's landline.

"Bill? Honey, where are you? Are you safe?"

"Ain't no such thing as safe! It's over!"

He cried so hard. Sammy kept his voice calm, even-tempered. "No, Bill. Ain't nothing over. You are still Bill, beautiful Bill."

"I don't know who I am! He's gonna destroy me! I don't know what to do!"

A single vision tortured Bill: Johnson, his crinkled lips enraptured with schadenfreude, whispering poisoned words to Momma. How will she react? Angst permitted only one answer. After some sobbing, he told Sammy about the evening after Reverend Smith's homophobic sermon. One of his mother's girlfriends came over for dinner. While eating homemade vanilla ice cream on the porch, out of nowhere the visitor said, *Well, he's right. It's Adam and Eve, not Adam and Steve.*

"And Momma just said, 'Uh-huh' like she agreed with her! Momma's gonna hate me!"

The places an anguished mind can go, Sammy thought. "'Uh-huh' can mean many things, Bill. It can mean 'Yeah, you right' or 'Yeah, whatever.' Did your mother follow up her 'uh-huh' with anything?"

Sniffling and coughing, followed by, "No."

"And this girlfriend, was she one of those people who popped off a lot?"

"Yeah," he said, hesitantly.

"Tell me about her."

"Momma used to call her Ms. NBC, the Neighborhood Broadcasting Company."

Sammy chuckled. He thought so. "Honey, we all know a Ms. NBC. Folks 'uh-huh' them just to shut them up. Am I right?"

Silence, then a snicker.

"Yeah. Tell me something, what helped you to overcome Reverend Smith's sermon?"

"Well," Bill said, sniffling, "as penance I took my collection of underwear ads and burned them in the woods behind our house.

Sang hymns and everything. I was so serious about it. I avoided Gabriel at school, but that didn't last. He started sneaking up behind me and going 'Boo!' He liked getting me out of funks, saw it as a challenge."

"And then you two got together, right?"

"Yeah. I don't know. After a while I guess I was like, I'm one of seven billion people on Earth. Why would God care if I like man-ass?"

"Exactly, baby."

Bill could hear the water lapping under their homemade raft and sloshing against the mossy rocks along the banks as they punted to their private spot to suck face and skinny-dip. Gabriel usually wore a tight red bikini, the perfect accent to his deep complexion, darkened and mellowed further by the midday sun. Beaded sweat glistened like jewels on his shapely calves, thighs, shoulder blades, and biceps.

"You still with me, Bill?"

"Yeah, I'm here," his voice back to its normal resonance. "I just wish he hadn't brought my momma up. I don't want him erasing me from my family."

"He don't have that power. Whatever Johnson thinks of himself, he ain't God."

I always think they are, Bill thought to himself, and they always let me down.

"Bill, honey, Alfonso, Roy, and Charlotte are all out looking for you."

"They are? Damn." He felt embarrassed. "I'm on campus, by the creek." A safe space. Its waters took him back to the raft.

Sammy repeated the location for Bingo who texted Roy.

"They know where it is, Sammy. I'm going."

"Bill, Bingo just left. He's coming to get you. Stay with me, baby. Tell me something else about Gabriel, what y'all did together. But none of your filth!"

Bill snickered. "I'll tell you about our last hurrah, from just before my family moved here."

———◆———

After guiding Bill by the shoulder for what seemed like hours, Gabriel finally removed the blindfold. Turned out they hadn't walked far, just from Miller's field to the abandoned warehouse, a familiar path traversed many times. Anticipation had lengthened the journey. In the middle of the high-ceilinged expanse was a small folding table and two folding chairs. On the table sat a stereo, a candle, two covered plates, and a bottle of champagne on ice. What's this? Bill asked behind giggles. It's your prom, silly, Gabriel said. Don't you recognize this place? It's the grand ballroom at the Waldorf Astoria or the Château de Versailles. That's how it always went with Gabriel. A vision, a few props, and imagination. Itinerant fireflies flickered randomly like sprites, adding to the enchantment. Gabriel turned on the stereo. Luther Vandross. Bill choked up a bit, took Gabriel's hand, and allowed him to guide them to wherever imagination saw fit.

———✦———

"He made catfish for dinner. We danced till 2 in the morning. He picked Vandross 'cause he was my first musical crush. I was 8 when he died. Momma encouraged me to have a ceremony for him. I even wrote a little sermon. She was so there for me."

"Yes."

Bill saw Roy and Alfonso racing toward him. "The rescue team's here, Sammy. I better go. Thank you." He hung up, embraced Roy, then reached for Alfonso. "Sorry for all the drama."

"You should have seen girlfriend skating round the park," Roy said. "Like a fire engine!"

"Dancer's legs, child," Alfonso said, with a high snap. "I'm so pissed at Johnson. He's gonna get an education: Hands off my friends."

Bill kissed Alfonso, then asked Roy if he could stay at his place.

"It's required," Roy said.

TWENTY

ALFONSO ENTERED THE CLASSROOM AND TOOK HIS normal seat, stowing his backpack and roller blades under the desk. He made no effort to talk to Leon and Leon reciprocated. But the footballer looked skittish, his body contorting like he was trying to lean away from the infidel. Alfonso found it amusing.

Professor Euclid entered the classroom.

"Right, so I'd like to welcome back Brother Alfonso. I'm glad you're back with us. Alfonso spoke with me yesterday and asked if he could talk about his situation and how it relates to the issues of his term paper. I readily agreed. So I want to thank you, Alfonso, for your courage and willingness to speak to us today. Ready?"

"Thanks, Professor Euclid."

Alfonso went to the front of the room. Professor Euclid took Alfonso's desk. Various classmates said hey, welcome back, and the like. He sat on the front desk, legs dangling and crossed at the ankles.

"Nice braids, Alfonso," someone said.

"Thanks."

181

Silence, eyes on him. After a cleansing breath, he explained the motivations for his paper: Carlton, Eddie, the clinic fire.

"So, when I decided to write about all that, I didn't realize I would *become* the topic, at least not like this."

"You OK, Alfonso?"Todd said. He had spoken at the first class in favor of the Huckleberry Community Clinic.

"I'm cool, Todd. Thanks. And thanks to those of you who reached out to me. I do appreciate it. So, I told you briefly about Carlton and Eddie. What happened to me? I was outed and my father didn't take it very well. And he threw me out of the house." He scratched his right cheek. Hand fell back to his lap. "I'm staying with a good friend, so I'm OK."

The class gave him rapt attention.

"I'm not gonna lie. It's been painful, but I'm still a prisoner of hope." A slight smile came, then faded. "But this is what can happen when you out someone who isn't ready yet. I wanted to create a safe space with my family where I could talk about this comfortably and I was robbed of that opportunity. That's rude." His eyes lingered on Leon before shifting elsewhere. "Carlton got outed, too, when he wasn't ready. What happened was, he skipped out on his prom date to be with the boy voted most good-looking in class." Alfonso smiled. "He said he had a good time with him." Folks chuckled. "But then his prom date outed him to his parents. And that's when he got thrown out. A lot of bad can happen to queer youth who get thrown out by their families."

Continuing, he connected the dots between family rejection and depression. Without mentioning his name, he talked about Henny Penny and his life as a homeless teen. He also mentioned their common refuge without naming Sammy, but called him their Yoda. Then his voice got soft, somber.

"Folks don't usually die of AIDS anymore, like in the '80s and '90s, but it still happens. If you don't know your HIV status or if you stop your meds due to cost or other reasons, then you can get an opportunistic infection and die. This is what happened to Carlton."

He paused, covered his face. Sybil, who had spoken against the needle exchange during the first class, got up from her front-row desk, sat next to Alfonso, and put her arm around him. He took her hand. Words of support came from others. After a moment, Alfonso patted Sybil's hand and looked up. She nodded, got up, returned to her desk.

"Carlton developed Hodgkin's lymphoma a year ago, requiring more treatments and shit. His depression came back hard. He started missing his meds. I saw one of the strongest men I've ever known finally worn down by the cruelty of the disease he lived with for over twenty years. That cruelty included shade from his family, shade from society for being infected, gay, and black, and shade from insurance companies that didn't give a shit. He just couldn't deal anymore." He paused, sniffled. "So I'm telling his truth as well as mine so that his fucking death does not pass in vain." Folks snapped their fingers, including Professor Euclid.

He wiped his eyes and saw their faces, their humanity recognizing his.

"I've heard some people say, 'You can't serve two masters' or 'You're black or you're gay.' I've been thinking about that, and this is my response. If you slap me on the face and my cheek stings, it's not like my foot's gonna be all 'Hey, at least it wasn't me. I'm cool.' My whole body's gonna hurt. So if someone calls me a faggot, it's going to attack me just as if someone calls me a nigger. The pain's the same." He paused momentarily. "Things have changed for LGBTQ folks. And while there's definitely resistance and backlash to that change, the support for the community now is much greater than what Carlton and his generation experienced during the height of the AIDS crisis. And that gives me hope."

He got a standing ovation, making him choke up again, but with a smile.

"Thank you, Brother Alfonso," Professor Euclid said as everyone sat again. "Does anyone have any questions or anything to contribute to the discussion based on what Brother Alfonso just laid on us?"

Someone asked Alfonso if he had ever been bullied. He liked the question, though it brought up difficult memories. Without naming names, he recounted a time in high school when he rounded a corner and saw Roy at the other end of the hall. As he walked toward him, Leon suddenly appeared. Hey Roy Princess! he could hear Leon say in an affected falsetto. Then Leon started reciting jumbled Shakespearean lines. At the same time, he held up his hand and began wiggling it with his thumb and forefinger touching, as if ringing a bell.

"So, yeah, a 'Tinker Bell,'" Alfonso said. "Because I was too scared of outing myself, I didn't confront the person doing it nor did I go to my friend to offer support. I regret that to this day." He paused. "The true ugliness of the closet is its subtlety. It eats away at your soul bit by bit and you don't even realize it. If you never deal with it or come to terms with it, then ultimately the closet will destroy you. Being out can be hard, but it beats the alternative."

Someone asked about queer spaces of color versus white queer spaces. Alfonso talked about his recent Boys Town adventure.

"You know," Leon said loudly, interrupting the discussion, "some don't think that picketing an iconic church for the black community is such a good thing."

The room paused. Alfonso had forgotten Leon was even there.

"What are you referring to, Leon?" Professor Euclid asked, turning to look at him. "And how does this relate to the discussion?"

"Last night, some folks from Carver Street held a picket at Beacon Hill Baptist. It was all over Twitter. You should ask Alfonso about it. I'm sure he was there."

"Leon, you brought it up. Fill us in, brother."

Alfonso liked the way Professor Euclid put Leon on blast. He sat and stared at his ex-homie.

"Well, from my understanding, some people from Carver Street decided to picket Beacon Hill Baptist on account of a personnel action that Reverend Johnson took. I guess some people thought the action the reverend took was the result of some discrimination. I don't know the whole story. But my point is, neither did the protesters. They just jumped to a conclusion and then picketed a church that's been the center of the community for years. That's disrespectful."

"Well, I read some of the tweets last night, too," Sybil said. "The reverend fired someone for being gay after calling him the f-word. That's disgusting. They had a right to protest."

"But do we know that that's what really happened?" Leon asked.

"Why are you doubting their story?" Todd put in. "You know, man, in the last class you said that the mainstream media doesn't take us seriously when we talk about racist police violence. You said the victim's story is never believed. Aren't you doing the same thing now?"

"Todd, do we really know if he was fired for being gay or was he fired because he didn't follow the church's rules?"

"That's like saying 'was he beat up for being black or was he beat up for not following orders?' You're parsing words, man."

Others began to pile on Leon, taking apart his arguments. All Alfonso had to do was watch. He hadn't wanted to talk about Bill's business, even obliquely, and he didn't have to. The class has learned *his* blues and they sang them back to him beautifully.

7ish
Sammy's Store

Alfonso turned on the ball of his foot, leaned back, waved his arm behind him, then jerked as if to hiccup like a red-faced sot. Warbling notes and jagged rhythms from Mingus's "Fable of Faubus" inspired his mocking dance of a teetering, tongue-tied Leon in class that afternoon. Roy joined him, pulling up his pants and wagging his finger in exaggerated movements, his impersonation of a bloviating Benjamin Quill trying to chastise a student who got the better of him. Sammy loved the performances. Neither young men knew Governor Faubus, whom Sammy could recall standing guard at Little Rock High School to protect it from black kids. But Leon and Quill made suitable substitutes. All three were opportunists adopting untenable positions out of fear or to gain mass appeal and power, even though in their hearts they knew better.

That Quill would flunk Roy's homoerotic Gilgamesh paper felt particularly galling.

"So Little Miss Self-Hater changed your grade from a fail to a what, Royboy?"

"A C-plus. I'm taking the class pass/fail, so—" he said with a shrug, still dancing with Alfonso. "But don't be surprised if I take it to the department chair anyway. My TA said it deserves an A. Fuck Quill."

In walked Bill, big smile on his face as he looked at the weak-kneed dancing by his comrades. "What's up?" he asked.

Both rushed up and melted into him, all arms and kisses. Sammy stayed behind the counter, arms folded, a sweet grin on his face.

"All good?"

"All good, Sammy," Bill said, his face flushed. He walked behind the counter and sat down. "I'm such a drama queen."

———◇———

Alone in his bedroom, thoughts again bedeviled Bill, all the calming voices from his life squelched under the bedlam. He wondered what to do when he heard his mother enter the apartment. Without thinking, he stood up, walked to his bedroom door, and opened it. Whenever he had something bad hanging over him, like a shitty grade, he tended to tell on himself. Doing that seemed to smooth things over. His hand clung to the doorknob as if it were glued. Tears streamed down his face. "I'm not a bad person," Bill murmured, "I'm a good person. I don't know what Reverend Johnson said, Momma, but I'm a good person." Derek stuck his head out of his room, froze, stared at his brother. Marilene walked to Bill, took hold of him, held him close and tight, allowed her shoulder to absorb the dampness. Then she held him where she could look directly into is eyes and asked, "Why would Reverend Johnson think you're a bad person?" In his head screamed Reverend Smith's sermon juxtaposed with Johnson's taunts. With a weak voice he said, "Because I'm gay." Marilene hugged him again. "No, no, no, no, Bill. Momma don't hate you. Momma loves you." Derek stroked Bill's arm. "It's all good, bruh," he said. "Don't cry."

He stopped crying and felt an elation he had never known. Tears streamed against his soul.

———

"I feel like I lost a grip of weight," Bill said.

Sammy kissed him on the cheek.

"Celebration time, y'all! Let's go dancing!" Alfonso said.

"Damn shame we have to go to fucking Boy's Town," Roy said.

Sammy put on his horn-rims and pulled the computer closer. He entered numbers while the boys flinched and twitched about their final destination. "I hear Club Copacetic is doing 18-and-over on Friday nights now."

"Really?" Roy said.

"Mmm-hmmm."

"I thought they stopped doing that 'cause they were having security issues or something."

Sammy gazed over his glasses, his eyebrows wrinkling his forehead.

"Oh, I think that's all been cleared up now." His eyes slid around to look at all three boys before he relaxed his gaze and looked through his glasses at the laptop again.

"Oooooooo!" Alfonso said. "That was 'The Look,' wasn't it? Carlton told me about this look you had. That was it, wasn't it?"

"I don't know what you're talking about."

Roy walked over and stood behind him with his hands on his hips. But the attitude wasn't getting it done. Sammy refused to look up.

"Did Auntie Vera talk to you?"

Sammy didn't answer.

"Y'all went over there and talked to Estelle, didn't you?"

Again, nothing.

Roy bent over and gave him a kiss on the cheek. "Thanks, Big Guy," he whispered. He stood up. "Come on," he said to the posse. "You know where it's at, don't you, Alfonso?"

"Yeah, near downtown, right?"

"Let's dooze this!" Bill exclaimed. "Night, Sammy!"

"You boys have fun, now," he said, still engaged with his spreadsheet. Only after the door closed did he let out his staccato chuckle.

They crossed Carver Street, then continued down 44th to Stevens to catch the right bus. Roy started laughing.

"You were right, Alfonso. That was 'The Look.' Harry calls it the Godfather Look."

Bill laughed. "Did he whack someone?"

"I guess Auntie Vera told him about our little adventure in Boy's Town. So I'm thinking that the two of them went over to Copacetic to have a chat with Estelle, the owner." They stood at the bus stop. "Estelle's just a little thing, so just imagine Sammy on one side and Auntie Vera on the other."

"Shakedown!" Bill said.

The bus pulled up and they got on, flashed their student passes.

"Now, now. We don't call it that. We just call it a friendly chat. A friendly persuasive chat."

They took seats in the back, Bill and Alfonso sitting on one side and Roy sitting opposite.

"Sammy was probably all 'you know what those kids went through at that white boys' bar!'" Bill said in a husky voice.

"Yeah," Alfonso said, "and then Auntie Vera was like 'Do it! Just do it! Don't make excuses, just do it, Estelle! Do it!'" his speech clipped and fast.

Roy laughed at their imitations. "Yeah, it probably went down something like that."

The bus dropped them off nearby. They walked half a block until they got to a plush purple door held open by a small black counter. There was no line. The doorman, a muscled brother wearing a leather aviator jacket and tight black pants, with dreads that went down to his butt, greeted them with a rich, creamy voice.

"Alright, how are you brothers doing this evening? Y'all ready to get down?"

"I am!" Alfonso declared.

"Solid, brothers, solid. An ID and five are all I need, gentlemen. Alright, then. That's good, thank you." He passed Roy through. "And that's a five, thank you," he said to Bill. "Mr. Berry, thank you, sir. Alright, then, you gentlemen know, of course, no alcohol served unless you are wearing a bracelet. But soft drinks are available for the right amount of green. So just go on up the stairs and have yourselves a splendid time."

Pitch-black steps and purple walls carried them higher. The temperature increased gradually until they reached the top landing, when it blossomed all over. Folks of all colors vamped and vogued in lace, leather, and Levi's, in Vans, Air Jordans, and boots. It felt so natural to them. After making a few jabs at the Boy's Town club and its uptightness, they forgot all about it. Smaller, tighter, hotter, Copacetic was a homecoming. A slow grinding beat oozed from the room adjacent. Alfonso recognized it. He felt himself shifting and sliding. The Posse followed him. On the dance floor, bodies crunched together as one. The boys melted into the mass.

After a few more tracks, they took five next to a window overlooking the street on the bar side of the joint. Alfonso mentioned that he was giving an interview to the school newspaper, *The Clarion*. A friend of his worked for it and she approached him about doing a student profile. He saw it as a chance to clear the air, give his side of the story. It should run next week sometime, he said.

"That deserves a toast," Roy said. "I'll grab some waters on my way back from the boy's room."

"So, Bill. I broke my silence Thursday night and wrote to Jameel."

"For real?"

"Yeah. I had to, Bill."

—◦—

Jameel hid from everything. On campus, he avoided common areas like the Student Union and the gym. His classes met largely in the giant Engineering complex, so that's where he spent most of his time. Emails and texts from everyone except Computer Engineering classmates and professors went unanswered. But it surprised the hell out of him to see an email from Alfonso. The subject line read "The Profoundest."

I wanted to set this to a rhyme, but I couldn't. You were always the one with the mad skills. Remember how we used to ditch class and write shit back and forth to each other? You were the outrageous one. You didn't care, you just said it. Like the time you told our physics teacher that he was full of shit because he couldn't explain how vectors worked. I thought he was gonna kill you. Yeah, I remember all that shit from back in the day. That's why I have to write to you. We've known each other too long and our roots are too ancient for me to ignore. You might be able to do that. I envy you. I can't. I have to close it some kinda way.

———+———

Roy rejoined them with bottles of mineral water. They clinked a silent toast to each other before taking the first swigs.

"It rambles a lot," Alfonso said. "I don't know what the fuck I said. I just put it all out there. Lots of conflicted feelings. Lots of history. Lots of pain. Lots of laughs. Lots of self-pity. I blame him for shit. I blame myself for shit. I guess mostly I was just sad at how it ended for us. That was the space I was in after that meeting with Johnson and my folks."

———+———

We played one-upmanship to the hilt. Probably more than was healthy for either of us. If I got the high score, then you had to do better. If you got something, then I had to get it, too. Crowing cocks. When they finally crowed together, the one-upmanship ended. Along with, it would seem, everything else.

———+———

"I'm vibrating," Roy said, taking out his cell.

"Pervert," Bill said.

"Secret admirer?" Alfonso asked.

"Don't recognize the number." He stuck it back in his pocket. "And you called it 'The Profoundest'?"

"Yeah." He chuckled. "My sorry attempt at looking at the stars from the mud."

Tonight my dad used the word 'profound' a lot when he talked about our family history. I started thinking that maybe he's a profound-ologist. A profound-ist.

Profound-ist.
Profoundest.
Profound-dis
Profound-this
Profundis.

I'm not Oscar Wilde. You aren't Lord Alfred Douglas. I'm not languishing in jail—quite the contrary, I've escaped prison. Your father didn't invent Queensbury rules. I am, however, writing to you from the depths. My world continues to change in ways that I can't comprehend. I saw my father tonight and for the first time I did not recognize him. You were right, though. I do have my mother's eyes. I saw myself in them tonight, and that gave me hope.

The DJ played the Ellington Orchestra's version of Benny Goodman's signoff theme, "Goodbye," a melancholy coda to a night of booty shaking. Copacetic regulars recognized Johnny Hodges's heartrending solo as the call to depart, but Carlton's Posse put two and two together only when the lighting became garish. They moseyed down the stairs as part of the herd. Voices planned rendezvous at after-hours clubs or apartments or secret caverns where no one would find them. Those who lingered too long around the entrance were politely enticed to move along, so as not to disturb the neighbors. No incidents arose. The Posse walked to the bus stop. Alfonso pulled out a cigarette for the first time in a few days. Too many others around him were doing the same, and his resistance weakened. Bill played the good son and called his mother. Roy and Alfonso ribbed him, but he just smirked and waved his hand at them while trying to hear his mother at the other end.

"Yeah, I'm fine. We had a blast. We danced out tails off."

"He got down, Mrs. Hawk!" Alfonso yelled.

Bill kept talking. Alfonso smoked. Roy took out his cell, brought it up to his ear. He stopped walking while Bill and Alfonso continued.

"Everything cool, Bill?" Alfonso said.

"Oh, yeah, it's all good. My mother is watching a movie."

"She seeing anyone?"

"She was seeing someone, but I think that fizzled. I haven't heard much about him for a while. I feel kinda bad about it, 'cause I never got to know him that well. Derek liked him. They used to play soccer in the park."

"Uh-huh," he said, lingering on his last puffs. "Soccer, huh?"

"Yeah. He's really good at it."

"You guys ever hang out together?"

"Sometimes. Not as much since I've been in college, but I'm sure we can come up with something."

"Yeah. It's like that with my sisters. I'm actually taking them out to brunch tomorrow."

"Sweet. Where you going?"

Roy walked toward them very slowly.

"Well, I thought about the French place on Carver Street, but I don't wanna cause any more waves, you know what I'm saying?"

Bill chuckled.

"So we'll probably go to this place my family goes to after Sunday service. Lucy likes the pancakes there."

Roy stood next to them, no expression and no eye contact.

"I'm all over good pancakes. I'll have to make y'all some."

"Pneumocystis," Roy said.

"Huh?"

"Pneumocystis."

Alfonso got real still.

"Pneumocystis. My dad's got pneumocystis. That's why he called me on my cell phone in the middle of the fucking night, to tell me he's got goddamn pneumocystis."

"Oh, Roy!" Alfonso said.

Roy stood expressionless before rage entered his face.

"I don't even believe this shit!" he screamed.

He leaned the top of his head against the bus shelter, muttering 'pneumocystis' over and over. Bill put his arm around him. Roy did not respond.

"Is it some kind of cancer?" Bill asked.

"No," Alfonso said. "It's an opportunistic infection, Bill. It's something people usually get when their immune system is impaired."

Roy stood upright, his eyes red.

"It means he has AIDS, Bill! It means he got HIV probably a long fucking time ago and he didn't even fucking know it because he fucking thought ONLY HIS FUCKING FAGGOT SON COULD GET IT!"

"Roy, I'm so sorry," Alfonso said.

"Oh, it just figures, doesn't it? I'm the different one, but he gets fucking AIDS. 'You always gotta be so different!'" he said in a mocking voice. "If I had a dollar for every time he said that shit to me. I go veggie. 'You always gotta be so different!' I start acting. 'You always gotta be so different!' FUCK HIM! FUCK HIM!"

He kicked a bottle into the street. Then he kicked over a newspaper stand and kicked out its plastic window. He stood over his fallen prey, panting, before kicking it repeatedly. Bill and Alfonso went to him, took hold of him. He tried to wrench himself free.

"No, Roy!" Bill said.

"Roy, come on!" Alfonso said. "Come on, now!"

Roy stopped, still breathing hard. He started to move toward the street, but arms held him back. He turned and saw Bill's face. He slowed down. Alfonso guided him away from the curb. He slowed down. Bill told them the bus was coming. He slowed down. The bus stopped at the curb. They boarded. He slowed down. Alfonso flashed his pass and Bill did the same. He slowed down. They assured the driver that Roy was a student, too, and that he just needed to find his wallet. They sat in the front of the bus. He slowed down and in time took out his wallet, which

Alfonso grabbed and showed to the disinterested driver who barely nodded his approval. Alfonso gave the wallet back to Roy, who mechanically stuck it in his back pocket. He let Bill hold him, and he let himself touch Bill's hand.

"I'm so angry at him," he said, sounding as if he had been screaming for twelve straight hours. "I hate him!"

"Roy, do you want me to stay with you?" Bill asked.

He didn't answer, but held on to Bill's hand.

"Roy," Alfonso said, "we'll take you to Sammy's, alright?"

"Thanks," Roy said.

On Carver Street, they pressed through the sidewalk still crowded with those on the hunt after having been kicked out of the bars. Bill stared with big-eyed wonder. Alfonso remembered the meat market from when he lingered on Carver Street alone under his hoodie last summer after Carlton died. Roy didn't see anything at all as he defended himself from all thoughts. Stud-Finder had the thickest crowd in front of its doors. They bypassed it by jaywalking to Sammy's apartment building. Bill buzzed #8.

"You know, it's cool," Roy said. "I should just go home. I don't wanna wake Sammy."

Bill ignored him and buzzed again.

"If whoever it is don't stop, I'm gonna call the cops!" croaked the intercom speaker.

Alfonso grinned. Roy bit his lower lip.

"I'm sorry, Sammy. It's Bill."

"Bill? What's up, honey?"

"I'm here with Roy and Alfonso. Can we come up?" The door unlocked.

Sammy stood in his apartment door wearing a long nightshirt and boxers. He scanned them anxiously. Then Roy fell into his arms and buried his head in his shoulder. Sammy held him for a moment before pulling him inside. Alfonso and Bill followed. At once, Bill went to the kitchen to put the kettle on. Alfonso went with Sammy and Roy to the living room sofa.

Roy spoke in a tenuous voice. "Jeremiah called me tonight. He left a message to tell me he has pneumocystis. I'm so angry with him. I hate him, Sammy."

"No, no, baby," Sammy said, grabbing him again.

If you don't know your HIV status or if you stop your meds due to cost or other reasons, then you can get an opportunistic infection and die. Spoken just hours ago in class, the words came back and haunted Alfonso. This hit much too close to home.

Roy heard the kettle start to peal. He honestly didn't know if he could drink any Earl Gray, but was touched that Bill remembered.

TWENTY-ONE

Monday, 8 a.m., Seventh Week
Beacon Hill First Baptist Church

FORD SCHLEPPED UP THE STAIRS LIKE A CHILD SUMMONED by his irate father. He went through the open door and found Thad Johnson sitting, unsmiling. A motion from Johnson's eyes directed the councilman to a chair in front of the large desk. Silently, Ford sat as ordered, his large frame shrinking before Johnson's looming presence.

Squarely in the center front edge of the desk sat a copy of the *Clarion*. Ford picked it up. A photo of his smiling son sat in the left most column of the front page under the headline "STUDENT PROFILE: ALFONSO BERRY III." Ford sighed, slowly closed his eyes. When they reopened, he began reading the article.

"Alfonso, when did you know you were gay?"

He laughed. "6th grade. That's usually the age that girls stop seeming 'icky,' right? Well, for me it was boys."

Ford cleared his throat, read further.

"As a junior, I'm finally realizing that Poli Sci isn't where I need to be. I'm a dancer. Always have been." He got up to give a sample. Trust me. He has moves.

A graphic box printed a hyperlink to their online edition for viewing a brief video of Alfonso getting his dance on. Ford had a sudden urge to take out his cell and follow the link. But Johnson's office didn't seem the place for that.

More dance talk, influences, goals.

He animates so much while talking about dance, it's almost a form of dance itself. "I'm really getting into Robert Glasper. I love the collaborative stuff he does. Got me full of ideas."

Ford turned the page. A discussion of last week's protest at the church appeared. He glanced quickly at Johnson before reading further.

"Churches have a whole lot of power, all the more so in the black community because of their historic role as liberators and leaders. So it's real disturbing to see that power used to oppress their own for being LGBTQ. And, you know, queers of color still face racism, including in the LGBTQ community. So it's like getting it on both sides."

Ford kept his face down and read, though he felt Johnson's silent impatience.

Alfonso showed discomfort when I asked about his father. But his voice stayed focused, his words measured.

"I didn't like the way I was used as a weapon against my father. I didn't like seeing and hearing my name in the press like that. It shouldn't have happened."

Ford looked up, signaling that he had finished.
"You weren't at service yesterday, Ford."
"No, I had some business to take care of."
No pass. Ford got stink eye.

"I spoke about the protest that happened here last week. Were you aware of it?"

"Some."

"Did Alfonso lead it?"

"I wouldn't know, Thad. He's not at home and we're not in communication."

"Clearly. You've lost control of your son, Ford. He's attacking this church."

An exaggeration, Ford thought, but he sat silently.

"And he's trying to make you look bad. He must be stopped. You hear me?"

Ford nodded slowly.

"We will have our own press conference. We will talk about your accomplishments and service to the community. And we will also say that Alfonso is a naïve schoolboy who knows nothing and understands less. We will rip him apart, tear him down, and shut him up. Severe, I know, but we have to get serious about this, Ford." He paused, and then added, "I'm sure your father would agree."

Ford knew his father would, which scared him terribly. "I hear you," he said.

"Good. Set it up. I'll see you at City Hall."

As Ford walked to his car, he found himself in his father's office long ago, excitedly describing how interested the major league scouts were in him. He animated his story with several pitch poses. Ford bubbled so much that he failed to notice the long face his father wore.

A black pitcher? Al Junior, when are you going to get serious? What about law school? And public service? That's how we'll get ahead, not chasing no damn ball around on a field. They let a token in once in a while, and that's it. And trust me, it ain't you. Baseball got you through college, Al Junior, but that's all it will get you.

But, father remained unuttered. Ford could not see explaining to his father how the world had changed.

"Maybe Alfonso was right," Ford muttered to himself as he got into the car.

11:30 a.m.
Student Union Walkway

The Huckleberry Community Clinic decided to rent a medically equipped RV and hold a mini health fare Saturday on Lincoln across from their burned-out headquarters. Alfonso told Bingo he wanted to help, maybe spread the word on campus. He approached Bill, who was totally down with some tabling, but he hesitated calling Roy, not even sure if he was still in town. Then Roy called him.

"Checking in on you, Terp," Roy said. "Also wanted to say thanks for sitting up with me."

They had stayed at Sammy's apartment until daybreak. Sammy turned in around three, but told the boys to stay until whenever. He even offered to make breakfast in the morning. Alfonso wanted to keep his breakfast date with his sisters, so he returned to Bingo's to shower and change.

"Are you at the hospital?" Alfonso asked.

"No. It's five hours away and I have to figure out how to get there. I don't know. I just don't know what to do."

Tabling for the clinic on campus came up. Alfonso stressed that he didn't have to come, but Roy readily agreed. You'll need a third person to register the group so that you can table anyway, Roy reminded him.

Alfonso carted stuff he got from Bingo out to the walkway in front of the Student Union. It felt weird sitting across from where he had tabled for ASA for so many years. Cynthia sat there alone. The grotto behind her hosted the usual crowd. No one paid any attention to him. It went down as he thought it would: He had become invisible to them.

Roy arrived with a bag of french fries.

"Want some? It's my breakfast."

Alfonso gave him a kiss. "I'm good. Bill's bringing me something." He observed Roy's attire: an untucked T-shirt, no jewelry, a drab jacket. Nothing sparkled. Not Roylike at all.

"We talked this morning. He told me not to worry about going out to see him. I said of course I'll go, but part of me was relieved. Am I a piece of shit for not wanting to go?" He put his forehead against the edge of the table. "Maybe I should play Lady Bracknell." He affected a haughty voice. "'To lose one parent may be regarded as a misfortune...'" His chuckle turned to soft weeping. Alfonso rubbed the back of his neck. "Tell me he's gonna be OK, Terp. I can't go through this shit again."

"Go and hold him, Thes. Hold him for a long as you can, 'cause really, he ain't going nowhere. You gotta hold on to him."

Roy reached up and rubbed Alfonso on his back.

"You mind if I stay here, while you table? Don't know how useful I'll be."

"Don't be silly."

Bill brought Alfonso carne asada, as requested. Roy perked up enough to give Alfonso shit about eating so much dead cow.

"Well, *I'm* having a rice and bean burrito," Bill said. "But it does have cheese."

"Cheese works," Roy said, before taking a big bite out of Bill's thick burrito.

A few interested passersby stopped and glanced at their materials. Then a familiar face appeared.

"Hi, Victor," Alfonso said.

"Come here, Alfonso," Victor said. "I said, come here," he repeated, tilting his head.

Roy tensed up, as did Bill.

"What's up, brother?" Alfonso stood.

Victor reached for Alfonso and gave him a tight hug. Everyone relaxed. Zen Master V was in the house.

"I'm so proud of you," Victor said. "I loved your interview in the paper."

He asked about the tabling. Alfonso described the health fair. HIV and HPV screening. Prenatal care. Dental care. Basic exams. The works.

"Well, I think you guys need more publicity," Victor said. "This shit's important. Have you talked to any of the other groups here?"

"No."

"Would you like an emissary to help spread the word?"

"Sure!" Bill said.

"Alright, then." He grabbed a stack of flyers and walked down the hill to visit the other groups tabling along the walkway. Just like that.

The Posse's spirits jumped. Alfonso took out his cell and started playing some music. A swing entered their shoulders. Bill and Alfonso sat on the backrest, while Roy sat between them on the bench.

"Oh, my god," Bill said softly, "he's gonna go there!"

Victor had visited every table along the walk, down one side, then up the other until he reached the ASA table. His visit did not last long. He soon walked across to the Posse.

"Got a good response," he said. "Most of the groups down the way thanked me for the information."

"What about the group across the way?" Alfonso asked.

"I tried. But there is some bullshit going on in that group right now. Man—"

"What?"

Victor got circumspect, his eyes avoiding contact with anyone's.

"Come on, it's cool," Alfonso said. "What happened?"

Victor looked at Alfonso, sucked his teeth. He spoke in a lowered voice. "Last Thursday's meeting, I walk into 320 and it's Cliff-gate all over again."

"Alfonso-gate?" Alfonso asked.

"Uh-huh. A room full of folks ready to bury one of their own." Victor crossed his arms, shifted his body weight. "Cynthia started with her little bullshit thing—'I don't know what it all means'— then Leon went on the attack. By his estimation, you stayed DL until Bill arrived and fucked shit up."

"Leon, Johnson's muse," Bill interjected.

Victor nodded, then continued. "Tamesha cosigned Leon's bullshit and called you," he said to Alfonso, "a follower, claiming that to be your personality type. While she went on, I overheard some folks muttering and giggling with each other. I called them out. One said that Leon couldn't help it if he had a loud voice. So I asked Leon if he had loud-talked all the stuff he heard about you at the needle exchange so that the press heard. Eventually, he confessed, with attitude. You know, cocking his head and shit. Folks got hyped, expecting a rumble. But I had a different agenda. I just walked out the room."

Alfonso hugged him, as did Bill.

"Was Jameel there?" Alfonso asked.

"Nah, brother. He wasn't there."

Ford Berry's voice thundered from across the way. The Posse looked and saw a boombox on the ASA table.

> *In the pressroom at City Hall, Ford Berry and a group of his supporters all filed behind the podium and microphones silently, most looking down at their feet, their faces rock-solid tight.*
>
> *"I'm here today," Ford began, "to make clear my stance on various issues that have been talked about in the press of late."*

"You are fucking shitting me," Bill exclaimed. "I can't believe Leon's still pulling this shit."

"One-trick pony," Roy said.

Alfonso grabbed his cell, searched for the live stream of the press conference. He wanted to see his father's face saying these words.

> *"It is unfortunate that my son has aligned himself with this group. But that is his choice. I do not agree with it, and I certainly do not support it. My years of experience temper my judgment. And though it may be tempting to believe in the misplaced idealism of a few who claim to serve the community, as my son has chosen to do, my years of experience dictate that I not succumb to such dangerous naïveté."*

Charlotte and Sammy both watched on his small TV in the store. A mixture of disbelief and disgust colored their faces.

"Why the hell is he doing this?" Sammy wondered.

"He has lost his ever-loving mind," Charlotte said.

"I know he maintains that he has very personal reasons for working with this group, but let me be very clear. I do not support this. I do not support him. I do not have that luxury. I'm dealing with the real world, not the world of naïveté."

"Fucking Johnson!" Alfonso saw him next to and slightly behind his father, the puppet master pulling the strings. It looked all the creepier since his video didn't quite sync with Leon's audio. Still, it was his father's voice that he heard.

Ford took a few questions. A reporter asked about the free health clinic planned for Saturday.

"Well, my office will of course make sure that all the permits are in order," Ford said. "We want to make sure that they are in full compliance."

Belinda texted, <<Don't watch the news.>> Alfonso texted back, <<Too late.>> Another, from Lucy: <<Y U can't just keep quiet? Y U did interview? U said U loved Daddy. U lied!>> Alfonso sighed, went back to the video feed. Bingo called. "I'll call you back," Alfonso told him. "I'm watching it. Thanks." He switched it back on.

A question came up about Alfonso. Ford had ignored two previously, but in the absence of any other questions, he felt he had to take this one.

"I'm sure my son believes that what he's doing is correct. I don't. I can't, for the reasons that I've stated. Thank you."

Ford promptly left the stage, his supporters tailing close behind.

Leon cranked up Ludacris's "Move Bitch." The ASA homies grooved in triumph, strutting and posing, testosterone on parade.

Victor held his arms tight against his chest. "Y'all should be ashamed of yourselves!"

Leon gave him the finger, shifting it side to side with the beat, his tongue wagging out.

"That track's still tired," Roy said dryly.

Alfonso got up. He very calmly walked across toward the ASA table. He heard his Posse shouting at him. Don't do it. Don't go there. He ignored them. He walked straight up to Leon, who had five inches on him and way more girth. Leon's homies stopped posturing, stood rigid.

"You can't stop me," Alfonso said.

"Seems like your father just did," Leon replied.

"No, he can't stop me either."

Leon stepped closer, looked down at Alfonso, head cocked left. He softly hissed his words as the track blared on.

"You thought you were so smart talking about me in Euclid's class, didn't you?"

"I didn't say your name. And I only told the truth."

"You better watch yourself, Alfonso Berry."

Alfonso turned around and walked back toward the Posse. He took one of the flyers off the table and began waving it in the air.

"FREE HEALTH SCREENING! FREE HEALTH SCREENING THIS SATURDAY!"

Victor started shouting with Alfonso. And then Bill joined them. Roy got up and handed out flyers to passersby. Some stopped to ask questions. Can I bring my mother? Sure! Is this for students only? No, no! It's for everyone! Tell your family and friends! A growing rainbow surrounded the Posse's table. The ASA homies disappeared into their grotto.

TWENTY-TWO

Saturday, Early Morning
on the Road

OVER THE SUMMER, WHEN ROY WORKED AT HIS FATHER'S warehouse, he had met Carl, a big, burly guy with a long blond ponytail who wore Levi overalls and a grin under his bearded face. Roy picked him out at once: queen. They hung out frequently during lunch hour. In another life, Roy could see tricking with Carl in just the right cruising space. They flirted, but never went beyond that.

Carl came to mind as a possible answer to the how-to-get-there problem. So he called him Monday evening and explained the situation. He figured he could trust one of the tribe to help out and keep it on the down low. His trust had not been misplaced. Carl treated Roy to Thai food and agreed to take him to see his father on Saturday.

6 a.m. Roy tanked himself up with two cups of Earl Gray and prepared a thermos full for the road. He knew it would be a long ride.

They talked friendly as they wound their way out of the city and through the suburbs. He told Carl about his theater workshop. Carl promised to go to the performance.

"Meet any cutie-pies at school?"

"Yeah."

Roy stared out the window at the lanes of traffic, the mall just off the road, the vast flatness beyond, colored gray by the overcast skies. He so wanted Bill inside him last night, but they were afraid that if he had come over that he would have stayed the night, making getting up early that much harder. Their time together was too precious to be interrupted by scheduled obligations. So they went without. Instead, they chatted on the phone until the batteries nearly died.

———

"I hear music. What are you listening to?" Bill asked.

"Debussy."

"Classical?"

"Yeah. I played this a lot when my mother died."

"Oh."

"It's cool. Debussy is my blues."

"That's alright, then. Drinking tea?"

"Naw. Chilling with some brandy."

"How continental."

"I'm gonna miss you," Roy said.

"Yeah, me, too."

"Are you still going to the health clinic?"

"Oh, yeah, for sure. Then Derek and I are going to hang for a bit. Bonding time, you know."

"Sweet. You guys know what you're gonna do?"

"Not sure. Nothing but wack movies out right now. Might just get burgers or pizza somewhere and chill. He's been kinda worried about me. I can tell. You know, all this talk about bashings and AIDS. Derek's a good little kid. Need to spend some quality time with him."

"I like it, Bill. Nice."

"You gonna be alright?"

"I'm not even thinking about it. Just gonna take it as it comes. That's what I keep telling myself, so I hope that's what I actually do."

Roy described their adventure in Boy's Town. Carl smirked, but was proud of their activism. Figures those youth temples would be racist, too, he commented, adding that they also would have ignored his 40-something, blue-collar ass. Roy agreed, then asked if he was seeing someone.

"No, not right now."

Their banter had gradually diminished by the time they got into more rural territory. The tea was wearing off and Roy didn't feel like guzzling more. He stared at the empty rows of plowed fields as they whizzed by—dusty furrows of bone-dry, hardened soil colored grayish brown under the cloudy skies, an alien landscape devoid of any living thing, flora or fauna. He lost himself in their geometry.

Carl put on *Madame Butterfly*. Roy raised no objections.

9:45 a.m.
Huckleberry Park

Bill started the day with pancakes and bacon for his mother and brother. They brunched hard.

Afterward, he played a quickie pickup game across the street in the park before walking with Mrs. Parker to the health fair. She asked who he was playing with.

"Oh, that was Smooth. I saw him over there, so I ran across and snatched the ball from him. It turned real as we talked. You know what Johnson told him? He said I had quit, that I didn't have time to tutor no more."

"What an evil little coward that man is."

"Yeah. When I told Smooth that I got shit-canned, he gave me a look and said, 'Ain't that illegal?' He said he has a gay uncle on the West Coast."

"Uh-huh. That's right," Mrs. Parker replied. "See, Johnson and them, including Alfonso's father, unfortunately, they are living in the past. They spend a lot of time talking about helping the youth and building them up, but really, they just want the young people to be carbon copies of themselves. They don't listen to them, they just talk at them. If you want to stay young, you listen to the young, listen to what they have to teach you. Then you'll both learn."

Heavy cables snaked on the ground. Cameramen were training their equipment on reporters. Just beyond all that was the medical RV, puffed up and humming with its own generator. Bingo was in the distance talking to someone. Harry came up to greet them.

"Hey, Mrs. Parker! Good to see you. You can go right inside."

"Thank you, Harry."

"Bill, can you help me carry some stuff in?"

"Sure."

They went up the block to Harry's van to unload grocery bags, bagels and orange juice donated by the Carver Street Business Guild.

Bill's eyes popped upon walking into the pimped-out RV. It really did look like a medical office. Dave Brubeck played in the background, tracks from *Time Out*. As he put the jugs of juice in the refrigerator, Alfonso bounced up from behind. They fell into an instant and deep embrace.

"Have you heard from Roy?" Alfonso asked.

"No, not yet."

"I've been thinking about him all morning."

"Alfonso, will his father really be OK?"

"It's way better than it used to be. He'll make it. If they treat his PCP aggressively, and get him on the regimen, then he'll be OK."

"What regimen?"

Alfonso handed him a brochure. "Here."

Bill read the brochure as he walked outside, vaguely following Alfonso.

Young Mr. Berry was in his element—every bit as frenetic as he was during his ASA years, but with a drive that he never displayed in that setting. Wherever he was needed, he was there, in your face with a smile, a strong hand, and a quick mind.

Everyone landed in their places. Harry and Bingo did HIV counseling. Lucinda monitored intake and triage. Mrs. Parker worked with Dr. Sandy Mellow on the physicals. Other members of the Huckleberry Clinic collective provided child care for those who brought their kids along. A pediatrician stood by to give them exams, too. A line queued up instantly. Alfonso and Bill sat together at the information table on the sidewalk.

The bright lights and big cameras also got busy. They gravitated to the councilman's son living large, sitting front and center.

"Why is the group here today?" a reporter asked.

"We are continuing our mission to provide quality health care services to the community, including comprehensive STD and HIV services."

"The clinic has been operating at All Huckleberry Community Church since the fire. Why is the group out here today?"

"We want to make sure that the community knows that we are still here and that we are not going anywhere. We want folks to know that we haven't forgotten about them."

A group of a dozen men arrived, some in suits and bow ties, some in street clothes. They carried large placards: "Our Neighborhood" "What's Your Agenda?" "The Party United". Alfonso ignored them, kept talking to the press. Then he saw Leon in the pack. Their eyes met from a distance, a brief, tense exchange. Silently, the group approached the info table, Leon hanging in the back.

"How is this a help to the community?" one of the Party brothers asked. "Are you even of this community?"

Alfonso looked at him, maintained his calm demeanor. "I grew up here, brother. Lived here all my life. My father and I used to play baseball in the field behind you."

"What you are doing is a disgrace to your father."

"Is it? Brother, do you know what the HIV infection rate is in this area? It's three times the city's average. And guess what? This area also has the highest rate of medically uninsured citizens in the entire city. That spells a crisis to me."

Bingo stood at the door to the RV and Harry stood behind him. They watched as the cameras caught the exchange.

"You are pushing drugs on our community," the Party brother continued. "You are trying to keep us chained, confused, and dependent on what the white man inflicts upon us. Can't you see? The curse of homosexuality with its AIDS and its decadence is killing off black men, one by one."

Harry wanted to make a move, but Bingo shook his head and held him back. "It's OK," he said.

"Your father, who you have totally disrespected, is a wise man for not wanting to keep this clinic around here."

"You know what my agenda is?" Alfonso said. "Get folks the health care they need by getting them checked out and helping them enroll in Obamacare. If that's your agenda, then let's get it done. If not, then we have nothing further to discuss."

Folks in the line started to clap. So did Bill, as did Harry and Bingo. And the cameras rolled on.

"You know something?" Harry said to Bingo. "He's every bit as fierce as Carlton."

Bingo nodded. "But without the drama."

"Uh-huh."

Disarmed by the response from the crowd, the Party began a chant. "WHOSE HUCK? OUR HUCK!" They started to march around on the sidewalk and hand out flyers again. But folks couldn't be bothered.

"You all are just here grandstanding," a woman in line said. "You need to do what he said and either help out or go away!" More clapping. And the TV cameras rolled on.

The Party brothers remained stoic, but received no support. They turned and walked away as disciplined as they had arrived. They barely lasted five minutes. Leon gave one last hard look before turning and going with the others.

"Since when did Leon start hanging with The Party?" Bill asked.

"Since it turned into the We Hate Alfonso Club."

"You doing OK, babe?"

Alfonso flashed a quick smile. "Yeah, I'm alright. I'm not thinking about those punks. I'm thinking about home. It's been kinda rough lately." He sighed. "Lucy thinks I'm out to make our dad look bad. I thought I was giving him a break. I said, I don't like how I'm being used as a weapon against him. How more direct could I be than that? But Lucy doesn't see it that way. She thinks I should just keep quiet. Now she's mad and not talking to me. Belinda's mad at Lucy and my father. And my mother's stuck in the middle."

"It's gonna get better, babe. Just know that it will get better."

"I'm beginning to wonder, Bill. I really am."

11:07 a.m., 5 Hours out of the City
Jeremiah's Hospital

An unseasonal cold snap held the temperature in the upper twenties. Dirty ice patches hid in shadowed corners. Carl and Roy emerged from the car and walked into the hospital building, a one-story affair that sprawled in various directions like a resting spider. Roy thought it looked more like a convalescent home, which added to his general state of unease. The receptionist directed them to the proper wing. Just follow the gray line on the floor, she said. It curved around a lot, but they managed after a fashion. Some of Roy's discomfort melted away—his city snobbery feared the worst about the hick-town hospital his father had been in for the past week. But it looked all right, as far as he could tell.

The gray stripe deposited them at nursing station #6.

"We're here for Jeremiah Prince."

"You must be Roy," said a friendly voice. "I'm Stan, we talked the other day."

"Right." Roy offered his hand. "Good to meet you."

"Likewise."

"This is Carl, one of my dad's coworkers."

They shook hands.

"Your father is in number two, the green door on the end and to the right. Go on in."

"Thanks, Stan."

They walked down the corridor.

"He's a cutie," Carl said.

Roy nodded.

The door sat open. The TV was on full blast with a football game going. Jeremiah's girlfriend Jasmine sat in a chair next to the bed and her daughter Lola sat in a chair under the TV, playing a video game on her cell. Jeremiah glared at the TV, then flung his arms in the air as much as they would go. One arm bore an IV drip and wires were connected to his chest.

"Try catching the ball next time!" he said, coughing.

"You got visitors," Jasmine said.

He turned and saw the two as they entered.

"Hey, Jer," Carl said. "You look pretty good to me."

"Hey, Carl, thanks for coming. Thanks for bringing Roy with you. Pull up a chair. Is there another chair over there?"

The room had two beds, but the other sat unused. Jasmine got up and brought over one of the chairs. Carl pulled over the other. Everyone crowded around Jeremiah's bed except for Roy, who stayed near the door. Seeing his father with tubes and wires attached to him brought back the worst of his childhood memories and took him to a place he sought to avoid. All the noise in the room did not mask the slow pump of the oxygen machine, the steady ticks of the IV drip, and his father's labored breathing.

"Another fumble! This is your school losing, Roy."

"I never watch the games."

Jeremiah turned and looked at Roy by the door. Their eyes locked. For an instant, it felt real for both men. But Jeremiah quickly looked back at the TV. Roy resumed his blank stare.

"Don't you want to sit here, Roy? Next to your *father*?" Jasmine said.

He glared at her—a look that said *Floozy! Charlatan! Third rate wretch! You ain't qualify to lick the dirt off my mother's shoes, much less speak to me with some two-cent attitude, like you have any authority to speak to me at all*—then turned and left the room in a hurry.

Carl felt awkward, out of place. Jasmine lacked that level of awareness and got up to go after Roy, but Jeremiah reached up for her.

"No. Leave him be."

Twenty-Three

J EREMIAH WOKE UP AND SAW ROY SITTING IN THE CHAIR
next to the bed. They were alone, the TV switched off.
"You came back," he said with a slight chuckle.
No reaction. Roy kept his head down.
"Whatchu working on, Son?"
"Nothing. Just a drawing."
Jeremiah closed his eyes.

The therapist encouraged Roy to draw after his mother died,
since it seemed to calm and center him. Jeremiah never wanted to
look at the pictures, despite his son's willingness to share them. He
just didn't want to go there. After coming home from a long haul,
he found over twenty of them taped on the walls in the apartment.
He studied them closely when Roy wasn't home. They weren't what
he had expected. Instead of imagines of his late wife, he saw scenes
of dramatic vistas and bleak landscapes all devoid of life. His son
had captured his own state of mind in ways no words ever could.
For that reason, they were even more disturbing, but still he could
not stop looking at them.

"Can I see it?" Jeremiah asked.

Roy handed it to him, then got up and walked to the window,
his hands in his back pockets.

The dusty furrows off the highway became even more alien in
Roy's hand. The rows stretched into the distance, and at the far end

sat a tiny figure on a cross. On the left was a wall of tall, sharp cliffs. And beyond the horizon, through a hazy sky that bore flashes of lightening, rose a ringed world.

"Is that Saturn in the background?"

"Yeah. It's a view from Titan."

Remote. Distant. Lifeless.

Jeremiah looked again at the figure on the cross. "That's not Jesus, is it?"

"No. It's a scarecrow."

Tattered. Frozen. Weatherworn. Protecting nothing from nothing.

Jeremiah put the notebook on his nightstand.

"Roy. Come here, Roy."

Roy hesitated.

"Come here, Roy. Please. Please, Son."

He turned around slowly and shuffled to his father's bedside and fell into the chair.

"No, up here. Come up next to me."

The request startled him. He looked and saw his father move over, patting a spot on the bed.

"Come on."

Without hesitation Roy climbed onto his father's bed. He buried his face deep into his father's shoulder as he began to sob freely. Jeremiah tugged the IV line in his arm to reach over and caress his son on the head.

"It's OK, Son. It's OK. It's alright. I'm so sorry, Son. I'm so sorry. I'm sorry."

A few tears found their way to Jeremiah's eyes, too.

By midafternoon, the media trucks had departed, even as the line to go into the RV remained active. Mrs. Parker sat with Alfonso for a while to get some air. She was enjoying herself to the fullest. Then Bingo came out to light a smoke. Alfonso broke down and got up to join him. They gave each other enablers' guilt glances and then puffed in peace.

Alfonso's phone chirped.

"Roy! How are you doing? … Naw, we're all good here … No, you just missed him. He left about fifteen minutes ago to go hang with Derek."

"Damn. Well, I'll catch him later."

"So how are you doing? We've all been thinking about you." Bingo nodded.

"My father's OK." He sighed. "It's just intense. It's been real."

———————

Roy touched his father's face and felt the moisture on his cheek. He couldn't recall ever seeing his father cry, even during his mother's service. He thought him incapable of it. Now he wondered if his father went on long drives to get out in the middle of nowhere, perhaps playing a favorite tune or looking at a photo, just so he could be alone and cry in the back cabin of his truck.

I'm sorry, too, Roy whispered.

———————

"I can't put it into words. But I'm glad I came."

"Beautiful. Beautiful."

"Yeah. I wanted to ask you something, if you're not too busy."

"Of course, girl! What is it?"

"I'm trying to learn more about the therapies and treatment he'll have to start. I read up on a little of it."

Alfonso broke out in song. "'You've gotta have HAART!'"

Then Bingo joined in. "'All you really need is HAART!'"

Roy heard laughter and applause over the phone and recognized Bingo's voice. He began to giggle himself. "All right, now, girls. What's with the show tunes?"

"It's—" Alfonso said, trying to catch his breath. "It's HAART. H-A-A-R-T. Highly active antiretroviral therapy. That's what they'll put your father on to keep the viral load down. It's the cocktail, basically."

Nothing Roy hadn't heard before during his years hanging at Sammy's. But it felt better coming from Alfonso. The camp put him at ease.

"I'm not gonna lie and say it's a picnic," Alfonso said. "Some of that shit has some nasty side effects. Carlton always kept his eyes out for trials of new therapies. I can tell you where we used to look." They made plans to get together when Roy got back into town Sunday.

"Call me, OK?" Alfonso said. "Don't worry about how late it is."

"Love you, Terp!"

"Does your father like show tunes?"

"No!" Roy laughed. "But he likes baseball so maybe I can get him to watch *Damn Yankees*."

Alfonso hung up and paused. He looked at the burning stick in his hand and let it fall to the ground, where he stamped it out. He hung his head.

"You OK, doll?" Bingo asked.

"Yeah, I'm cool." He dialed up Sammy. "Hey, Sammy … Naw, we're good here. It's all good. I just spoke with Roy. He and his father really bonded. They really did." Alfonso's voice squeaked. "It's so beautiful!"

Saturday Night, 7:30ish

Bill and Derek took up Smooth's offer to check out his middle school's basketball game that afternoon. Smooth's team won. Requisite boasting ensued from the home crowd, but both sides kept it together under the watchful eyes of guardians. Smooth went off with his teammates to celebrate. Bill and Derek went somewhere else and had pepperoni pizza. They walked home animated. The game was fun, but somehow it felt like more. The day had been good for them both.

"So when you inviting your boyfriend to dinner?"

"Dang! Why y'all wanna meet him so much?"

"Bruh, you've been giving me shit about every girl I've ever looked at since forever. Now it's payback time."

Bill rolled his eyes and blushed.

"We'll see. I'll have to prepare Momma for it. He's a vegetarian."

"Ferreal?"

"Uh-huh. Since he was 13."

"No shit?"

"Uh-huh." Bill smiled.

When they reached Lincoln and 48th, flashing colors interrupted the pale glow of the streetlights. They turned their heads to see what was up.

"Drug bust in da Park!" Derek said.

"Uh-uh. I think that's the needle exchange van up there." He stared, looked for Alfonso. "Go home, alright? I'll be there in a minute."

"You ain't going down there."

"Look, just go, alright? And tell Mrs. Parker what's going on."

Derek didn't like it. But he thought he saw Mrs. Parker sitting on the stoop, so he dashed off in her direction. Bill walked toward the flashing lights.

———✦———

Four police cars sat parked around the van. An officer approached Harry, a young dude with short-cropped hair. Bingo stood nearby. Lucinda had already called Sammy, part of their contingency plan. Sammy would then call their attorney and Vera.

"Hello, Officer," Harry said calmly.

"Good evening," he replied politely, but stiffly. "What are you all doing here?"

"We're from the Huckleberry Community Clinic and we are engaging in needle exchange activity."

"Sir, is your group aware that such activity is against the law?" And he went on to quote chapter and verse of their offenses against the neighborhood, the state, and humanity at large.

Harry glanced briefly at Bingo, Lucinda, and Alfonso.

"Officer, the County Board of Supervisors has acknowledged the need for needle exchange programs to help stop the spread of HIV disease. They also sanctioned our particular program and they have asked that this work not be interrupted."

"I am not aware of that."

Harry tried to show him a copy of the Board of Supervisors' years-old proclamation, but he refused to look at it. "We've received complaints," he said.

"Complaints from who?"

"That's all I can say, sir, is that we've received complaints. You need to stop what you're doing now and leave the area. If you don't, I'll have to call this an illegal assembly and make arrests."

"I'm just surprised, Officer, because we always talk with our neighbors. It's part of our practice to dialog with them. In fact, we just talked with them yesterday. So I'm concerned about who may have lodged a complaint, because we thought we were cool with everyone."

"Sir, that's all I know. There have been complaints." He raised his voice. "Like I said, if you don't leave the area, this will become an illegal assembly and your group will be arrested."

"Let me talk to them."

The officer nodded but stood his ground. Harry walked over to the others huddled on the sidewalk.

"We got a Young Turk here just dying to make arrests. He says they've received complaints."

"Bullshit!" Bingo said. "And they waited until everyone was gone, all the cameras—"

"Convenient, isn't it?" Alfonso said, standing at the table. He had been talking with a client about addiction treatment programs.

More flashing lights rolled up. More cops appeared in the street.

Vera walked up in a leather jacket, her camera draped around her neck.

"What's going down?"

"Well," Bingo said, "looks like we got a firecracker just gunning to arrest us if we don't split."

"Hmm." She looked askance at the officers. "Will you guys do civil disobedience?"

Harry looked at the cops and sighed. "We might just pack up and go."

"I don't think so," Alfonso said.

"We don't have enough media here, Alfonso," Bingo said.

"Auntie Vera's got her camera. Shit, if 'Councilman's Son Arrested at Needle Exchange' is the headline he wants, then hell, let's give it to him."

Bingo, Harry, and Lucinda looked at one another. The police talked into their walkie-talkies as they shuffled their feet.

"I'll be back there in the bushes, then," Vera said.

"You sure got here fast, lady," Harry said.

Vera made a half-smile. "Would have gotten here sooner. I was looking for my damn flash, until I remembered I left it in the car. Take care, kids." She walked discreetly in the direction of her car, then dodged into the bushes to film out of sight.

The client kept asking Alfonso for information on addiction treatment programs. There had been leaflets on the table, but none were left. "Just a second," Alfonso told him. "Let me check the van." He walked to the back of the van and climbed inside.

"Hey!" a voice behind him called out.

He felt a tug on his leg. Then another. He heard shouting and began crawling backward until his foot hit something. Before he could do anything else, hands grabbed each ankle and yanked him out. His head smashed against the rear bumper.

Alfonso reached for his sore head as he lay on the ground. He felt hands trying to stop him, but he persisted. He wanted to touch his head. It really hurt. The hands grew stronger, more controlling. Everything became fuzzier. Did someone yell, Stop resisting?

Then he felt violence.

His mind released itself, granting him a double vision even Du Bois never imagined. As he felt clubs strike his arms and legs and boots kick his stomach and ass, he saw his father, face snarled beyond recognition, repeatedly pummel him with mean fastballs. He suddenly realized, as his body began trembling the way bodies did before shutting down, that he no longer needed to defend his father. This gave him a great source of relief.

Then he blacked out. His head sat in a pool of his own blood.

———

Sammy stood in the bushes next to Vera when the beating began.

"Great fucking Dizzy! What the hell are they doing?"

He ran out onto the sidewalk. "Hey! That's the councilman's son!"

Others followed his lead.

"THAT'S THE COUNCILMAN'S SON!"

"THAT'S THE COUNCILMAN'S SON!"

Everyone chanted except for Vera, who poured all of her emotions into the documentary she filmed. Their voices echoed against the buildings across the street. Faces came to the apartment windows. Bill tried to get to Alfonso, but a female officer stopped him before he could get much closer.

"That's my friend!" he cried.

The beating ceased. The officers looked at the ground and saw the motionless, crumpled body and the blood. A lieutenant, a towering black man with a linebacker's build, walked over. He looked at the body and recognized the face from the news.

"Holy shit. What happened?" he asked sharply. "Was he armed?"

"He resisted us, Sir," the Young Turk said sheepishly.

"What have you done to him?" Bingo shrieked. "Let me go! Let me see him!"

"Move back, please," an officer said. "We have an ambulance coming."

"I'm a nurse! Let me see him!"

Bingo kept pushing forward toward the street. He saw the blood and put his hand over his mouth.

"Oh, my god!"

TWENTY-FOUR

TWITTER POPPED WITH THE HASHTAGS #TheHuck, #Police, and #BlackLivesMatter. Even before more details emerged, a disturbing air developed over the neighborhood. Like after the time an unarmed young black man, subdued on the floor of a subway platform, was shot point-blank by an arresting officer. Or like after the time the assassin got off lightly, courtesy of his Twinkie defense. Or like after the time when the four were acquitted a year after they and many more waylaid an unarmed black motorist who drove into the wrong part of town for his kind. Or like after the time when the police raided the bars just once too often and the sissies threw bottles at them and said enough was enough.

When paramedics loaded Alfonso into the ambulance, Sammy marched to the street, went straight to the lieutenant, and squared his own large frame against the officer's.

"I'm going with him."

"Sir, please step back," the lieutenant said.

"I'm going with him in that ambulance."

"Are you a relative, sir?"

"I am the mother of everyone in this goddamn neighborhood! Let me on that ambulance!"

The crowd began chanting:

LET HIM IN! LET HIM IN! LET HIM IN!

The lieutenant wanted no more confrontations. He let Sammy into the ambulance. Harry told Bingo that Sammy got in, but he was too distraught to care. Vera came to the curb and took video of the ambulance driving off. Then she panned down and recorded video of the blood in the street. Only her sense of purpose helped her hold it together.

The crowd swelled to 100, at least. It grew more restless now that nothing remained of the scene except the police. Two dozen officers suddenly felt outnumbered. Their calls for peace and calm were instantly rebuffed.

FUCK YOU!

WHAT ABOUT ALFONSO?

GET THE FUCK OUT OF OUR NEIGHBORHOOD!

Harry saw the look of fear in the lieutenant's face. Part of him enjoyed it. Yeah, motherfucker, you should be scared. But he knew better. He went to his van and climbed up its ladder to the roof. He whistled between his fingers. The swelling crowd gave him unsettled attention.

"We're all upset about what happened here. We're all worried about our brother, Alfonso. Sammy Turner went with him to the hospital." He ignored the crowd's call for vengeance and questions asking if Alfonso had died. He pressed on. "There's nothing more we can do here, alright? But we can let City Hall … Hey! … We can let City Hall know that we ain't gonna put up with this bullshit in our neighborhood! We were trying to save lives! That's what we were doing here all day! That's what Alfonso was doing! So let's tell City Hall we want justice for Alfonso! Justice for Alfonso!"

The crowd picked up the chant. They began moving toward 45th Street. Harry climbed down. He shot a glance at the lieutenant, who looked thankful that Harry got the crowd directed elsewhere.

Bingo came up and patted Harry on the back. Then they followed the swelling mass as it turned on 45th and headed for Carver Street.

Bill's Brownstone, 48th Street

Marilene rushed downstairs to the stoop.

"Where's Bill?"

"He went to see what was going on at the park," Derek said. "There were police—"

"I know that! It's on the news! Where is he?"

"He hasn't come back, Mrs. Hawk," Mrs. Parker said. "What's going on?"

"There's a riot starting! People are marching and banging on things!"

They could hear helicopters and sirens in the distance.

Mrs. Parker got up and went into her apartment. Marilene and Derek followed her.

"I tried to stop him, Momma!" Derek said.

They stared at Mrs. Parker's small color TV. A very large crowd slowly working its way up Carver Street, a close-up from 1,000 feet above.

"We don't know what state he's in. We have a team heading to the hospital now. But eyewitnesses say that he lost a lot of blood."

They played the tape from earlier in the day when Alfonso jousted with the Party brothers. In the corner of the screen they saw Bill look on as Alfonso laid down the fierce and the cool. Just as the applause started from those in line, the anchor cut in again.

"I'm now told that there was a witness to the beating who caught it on video."

———◇———

Vera went straight home after filming the blood-soaked pavement. She got on her computer and uploaded her photos and video. Then she called her media contacts and gave them a heads-up of what was coming. "I can't talk now," she said. "I have to catch up with the march."

———◇———

The news aired the video, unedited.

"Sweet Jesus!" Mrs. Parker cried.

Derek bolted for the door. "Fuck that shit!"

"Get back here! Right now!" Marilene grabbed Derek by the arm. "I got one son out there, I'm not sending another!"

Derek glared at her, red-faced.

"Mrs. Parker, is it alright if I use you phone?"

"Of course, sugar!"

———

WHOSE FUCKING STREET?

OUR FUCKING STREET!

SHOW ME WHAT A PISSED FAGGOT LOOKS LIKE…

THIS IS WHAT A PISSED FAGGOT LOOKS LIKE!

SHOW ME WHAT A PISSED BULLDYKE LOOKS LIKE…

THIS IS WHAT A PISSED BULLDYKE LOOKS LIKE!

They continued up Carver Street until it merged into Delaware and Lincoln. Traffic came to a standstill. Their mouths became their placards. Slogan after slogan. But the refrain remained the same: Justice for Alfonso. All the Sammy Store Irregulars came out, even Henny Penny. Even Ms. Ashley. Hundreds who never met Alfonso came out. They read about him in blogs and tweets. They saw video of him holding his own that afternoon. They talked about what a brave young brother he was and that his own father had done him wrong. Some talked about Eddie and Carlton. Some talked about the clinic fire. Conspiracy theories flourished. Many organized as they marched and chanted. The police stayed out of the way, only loosely flanking them as they made their way downtown.

Bill caught up with Harry and Bingo. Both stood and traded long hugs with him as the multitudes filed past. They told him all they knew. Charlotte was at the hospital with Sammy. What about his damn family, Bill asked. They didn't know.

"That's fucking bullshit! He's his motherfucking son! You mean they beat his son and he ain't doing shit?"

He felt his cell vibrate in his pocket. He took it out and saw E PARKER and a number.

"What!" he yelled into the phone.

"Bill! Where are you?"

"Momma! They beat Alfonso! They fucking beat him on the ground!"

Hysterics. Bingo and Harry held on to him as more and more marched by.

"I know, angel. They showed it on TV. Look, are you OK? Bill? Bill? Are you OK?"

"I'm safe, Momma. I'm with Bingo and Harry. They're cool, Momma. I'm OK."

"Oh, good, OK. Stay with them, alright?"

"Momma, why they have to beat him? They didn't have to beat him!"

"I don't know, angel. Listen, you shout for all of us now, you hear?"

"I will, Momma. I love you."

"I love you, too, baby."

"Peace, man! Kick their asses!" Derek yelled.

"Tell Derek that's a promise!" He hung up.

Berry Residence

Sammy pulled Alfonso's cell out of his pocket and called his family's home number. He shouted above the screaming siren.

Eunice answered the telephone. She asked the caller to speak up because she couldn't hear him for the noise.

They're taking him where? Who is this? Oh, no. Oh, no!

He cut to the chase. Your son was badly hurt and he's lost a lot of blood. He's in critical condition. Come to the hospital, *now*.

Eunice had no time for reactions and clicked into gear.

She knocked twice, then opened Lucy's door. "Come on. Hurry!" She went to Belinda's room and did the same. "Belinda, come on. Get your sister. You're both going to Aunt Emmy's. Come on, now."

"What's up, Momma?" Belinda asked.

"Listen, both you. Your brother was in some sort of accident. He's being taken to the hospital."

"What?" Lucy said.

"I want to go with you," Belinda said.

"No!" She walked to her bedroom and entered. "Ford, we have to go."

"Go where?"

———

The Hospital Emergency Room

Charlotte went to the hospital mainly for Sammy. She went straight to his side and gave him a big embrace.

"I held his hand the whole way, Charlotte, the whole way."

"Honey, what happened?"

"Those creatures fucked him up!" he bellowed, then began to weep. Charlotte guided him to a couch and held him as he let himself go.

"He called me," Sammy said after a while, "to tell me how Roy was doing. Just this afternoon. He was so happy. Oh, god, Charlotte!"

Eunice entered the waiting room and overheard their quiet conversation. She rushed straight to them.

"Are you Mr. Turner? Where's Alfonso? How is he? What happened?"

Sammy dried his face and began describing the scene. The police presence. Alfonso getting yanked out of the van. His head cracking against the bumper. The blood.

"Who did this? Who was the supervising officer?"

"Some lieutenant. I didn't get his name. Harry might know, Charlotte."

"I'll try to call him."

"What about Alfonso? How is he?"

"We don't know yet, Mrs. Berry," Sammy said.

Ford appeared suddenly, hovering over his wife as she talked to Charlotte and Sammy.

"Thad is here." He motioned for Johnson to come over. "He can help you."

Eunice looked up at Johnson, then back at Charlotte again. "Did you get the lieutenant's name yet? Ford, she's trying to find out who did this."

He pulled her up. "Come on, dear. Let's go inside."

"It's Lieutenant Irving!" Charlotte called out. But Ford escorted Eunice away. Now they had Thad Johnson in their faces, his leathery brow furrowed earnestly.

"The family needs privacy now. I'm sure you understand. Thank you for your concern, but they need privacy now."

"Ford! Those people came in with Alfonso!" Eunice said.

"That's Charlotte Hunter—"

They went through double doors to another room. Johnson walked away to join them.

Sammy scowled severely.

"Great Dizzy."

———◇———

Jameel's Apartment

Jameel sat in his T-shit and boxers, watching the NBA with a bowl of chips on his lap and salsa on the coffee table. A news crawl appeared at the bottom of the screen. His eyes caught it and he grabbed the remote to switch channels. He saw the helicopter feed. Over a thousand strong, the anchor said, it just keeps growing and growing. They neared City Hall. Then they ran Vera's video again. The bowl of chips was flung from Jameel's lap as he stood up. He gasped and covered his mouth.

As the images held him transfixed, the last paragraph of Alfonso's *Profoundest* email went through his head.

Jameel, you said you are a coward. You live in fear. Don't. There's no reason for that. Your father is not my father. I know your parents and they are way cool. Believe me when I say to you that they'll have your back no matter what. They'll love you no matter what. Don't live in fear.

He threw on some clothes and flew out the door, only to end up waiting and fidgeting at the bus stop. They never came on time. His mind went several places. He took out his cell. What hospital was he at? The tweets didn't say. No, he thought, he couldn't go there. No, not there. City Hall. Join the march at City Hall. #Justice4Alfonso. He cursed the slow bus.

"Yo, taxi!"

He told the driver to take him to City Hall.

"You know there's a big rally there. Big rally."

"Yeah, I know! It's for my friend! The police beat my friend!"

"Oh! I'll take you, then."

The driver talked about the police beatings in his native Egypt. "Quite frequent," he said. "They brag about how many people they beat. They even videotape it, to show off. On YouTube," he said, "you can find them on YouTube." Jameel listened to the radio in the taxi. The crowd was at City Hall. The driver kept talking about the police in his homeland and how they abused people. "It shouldn't happen here, not in America."

He didn't charge Jameel. "Go. Shout for justice for your friend."

Jameel gave him a tip anyway, five bucks. Then he sped into the crowd, his chest pumped and his fist raised. Though he didn't kid himself—he was just one face among the many. He didn't stand out by himself looking fierce, the way Alfonso had at that isolated table on the west side of Huckleberry Park.

TWENTY-FIVE

Sunday, 9 a.m.
Sammy's Store

SAMMY BENT OVER TO PICK UP THE SUNDAY PAPERS AS HE entered the store. He threw the stacks on their racks still bound by their tight plastic straps. Then he stopped. The front page showed the world what had happened the night before. The photo credit read Vera Hurston.

He carried the papers to the counter, Alfonso's first visit on his mind.

That coffee sure smells good.

"Happy Reunion" was playing. Paul Gonsalves's sax echoed in his mind as he took some scissors and cut the plastic straps. Then he took eight papers and cut out Vera's photo. After rummaging a bit, he found the tape dispenser. He walked to the front window and gently removed Charlotte's campaign poster. He put up the photos, a montage that echoed Warhol with its repetition and Soweto with its brutality.

From the sidewalk, he viewed his installation. He wished he had more, enough to cover the whole window.

Someone walking by stopped. "That looks awful!" she said.

"It looked worse in person," Sammy said.

She made some comment about how sad the whole thing was and walked on.

Sammy lumbered back into the store and flopped behind the counter. For a while, he sat motionless, dead to the world. Then he saw the laptop Alfonso had given him.

And just wait until I start loading your music collection on here.

He went over to his bookcase and took a stack of CDs. He booted up his MacBook. The screen went through its gyrations. Then the desktop appeared. He clicked on iTunes.

I got a big collection.

That's alright. We'll be able to get most of it in here.

One by one, he began ripping his vast jazz library.

Charlotte found him behind the counter in the darkened store working on the computer. She almost flicked on the lights, but stopped herself.

"I'm loading up my CDs the way Alfonso showed me." Tears stung his eyes.

"You want some coffee?"

"No."

She walked to the back room and started up the pot. After a while she returned to the counter and sat beside him. They had stayed at the hospital until 2 a.m. Alfonso remained in critical condition.

She glanced at one of the photo-less papers on the counter. "Harry said they ended up going to police headquarters. They started calling for that lieutenant."

"Irving?"

"Yeah, Irving. They called his name and demanded that the Chief launch an investigation."

"Alfonso wanted to borrow this one." He held up the Dave Holland Big Band CD. "He said he liked the sassy reed section." Charlotte took his hand. "There ain't nothing to investigate. Vera caught it all. He bumped his head when that fool dragged him out of the van. Then they started kicking him. He was already hurt when they were beating on him. Does that make any kind of sense to you? He loves his father so much, Charlotte. This is the worst, the absolute worst. I ain't never seen nothing this ugly in all my life."

Sammy kept ripping CDs. Charlotte moved the mug to her lips mechanically and took small sips.

Ashley crept through the door, carrying a large pot with a lid on it. The aroma of Cajun spices accompanied him.

"Is that jambalaya?" Charlotte asked.

"Yes. It's my jambalaya. I did nothing but toss and turn after I got back from the march."

"*You* were in the march last night?" Sammy asked.

"Of course. Anyway, as I was saying. I wasn't doing nothing in bed but tossing and turning, so I figured I may as well go to the kitchen. You know how black folks are when they get upset. They head straight to the kitchen and start cooking something. You hungry?"

Sammy sat stone-faced. "You know where the bowls and silverware are," he said.

Ashley left the warm pot on the counter and went to the back room to get the bowls and the silverware. As soon as Sammy got a bowl in his hand and some food ladled into it, he started to scoop it up. Damn if it didn't just hit the spot. He filled another bowl and passed it to Charlotte.

"It's a keeper."

A moment later, Aaron came in with a cake pan. He put it on the counter next to the jambalaya and took the plastic film off of it.

"7-Up cake?" Sammy asked.

"Uh-huh. I heard this one in the kitchen chopping things, so I go downstairs to see. Next thing I know, I'm baking a damn cake."

"You know where the knives are."

Aaron walked to the back room to get a knife.

Then Liz walked in. "Oh, I'm too late. I thought you two might be hungry so I made huevos rancheros." With the eggs scrambled, just as Charlotte liked them.

"Aw, sweetie!" she said.

"You ain't late," Ashley said. "I'm hungry and I made this for Sammy."

"Go get some tortillas off the shelf, Liz," Sammy said. "You can heat them in the toaster oven in the back."

Liz gave Charlotte a kiss on the check as she left her plate on the counter and went for the tortillas.

More folks drifted in—from the clinic, from the Business Guild, from campus, from all the worlds Alfonso touched. Dan Euclid brought homemade zucchini bread. He arrived with Reverend Tamera, who brought a salad. Dan gave Sammy a warm greeting, mentioning that Tamera had spoken of him often. "Alfonso didn't use your name during his presentation," he said, "but I knew who he was talking about. He called you his Yoda."

Henny Penny arrived, deflated. He fell to the floor behind the register and cried. Folks comforted him, even Ms. Ashley, who brought him a bowl of jambalaya.

Sammy turned on the lights so that the growing crowd didn't stumble in the dark. Then he told folks to help themselves to whatever to drink, but not to clean him out, sparking a few chuckles. He played music from his computer as he continued ripping, a soft canvass of blues, music more felt than heard.

No one inside noticed a tall, skinny brother in a black hoodie and blue jeans standing outside the store, staring at the multiple pictures of Alfonso crumpled on the ground. No one noticed as the man touched each copy and traced Alfonso's figure with his fingertips. No one noticed the water crawling on both of his cheeks.

Jameel didn't go inside. Going inside seemed too giant a step to take on his first visit to Carver Street, requiring credentials he felt he did not possess. He soon walked away.

A half-hour later, Mrs. Parker arrived. She walked up to Sammy ahead of two worried neighbors.

"Sammy, this is Bill's mother, Marilene, and his brother, Derek."

"Oh, it's so good to meet you," Sammy said.

"Thank you, Sammy. Bill texted me last night and said he was staying with Vera. Are they here?"

"I haven't heard from Vera yet, but let me call over there."

Just as Sammy picked up the phone, the door opened. Bill walked in carrying a plate of drop biscuits. Derek ran to him, took his plate and put it next to the register. He held him on the shoulder.

"You OK?"

Bill just shook his head. Marilene joined them, took Bill and held him close.

Bingo entered, then slumped behind the counter onto the floor next to Henny Penny. They held hands.

Vera carried in a pot of chili. Folks helped her find space on the counter for it. She went to Sammy.

"My refugees. I took them in as the rally wound down. None of us wanted to be alone. Bingo was terrified of going to an empty condo and seeing Alfonso's skates in the corner. And poor Bill couldn't stop crying." She shook her head. "Bingo and I were drinking bourbon. Eventually I offered some to Bill." She shrugged. "But he declined, said that bourbon scared him. He said he and Gabriel tried it once. All he could remember was waking up the next morning to a half-empty bottle, said he still wondered what happened that night. Don't tell his mother this." She snickered. Sammy smiled, nodded. "That little story did us both good. We started cooking around four in the morning. He turned to me and said, 'Auntie Vera, is this halfway to dawn? Is that what time it is?' You know I'm not a weeper, Sammy, but that just hit me."

Sammy gave her a hug as a few tears entered her steely eyes.

"I've never been so angry in all my life," she whispered into his ear.

"Me neither," Sammy whispered back.

Marilene joined Vera and Sammy. "Ms. Hurston—"

"Oh, Vera, darling—Vera." She wiped her eyes.

"Vera, thank you for taking care of Bill."

She took Marilene's hands. "He took care of me."

Derek and Bill sat behind the counter next to Bingo and Henny Penny. Ashley sat on his usual stool by the window. Aaron stood next to him, as did Bernard.

"I haven't told Roy anything," Bill said. "He's got enough on his docket with his dad."

"What's wrong with his dad?" Derek asked.

"He has HIV."

"Whoa!"

"They got him on the cocktail?" Aaron asked.

Bingo nodded.

"God! Remember when we had to fight for them to release anything, even AZT, back in the old ACT UP days?"

"Oh, honey!"

"Were you in ACT UP?" Bill asked.

"We all were," Bingo said.

Ashley spoke up. "Bingo, you remember when Carlton dragged us to one of their meetings." Bingo laughed. "Carlton wanted us to go. 'We gotta represent,' he kept saying. So me and Aaron and Harry went with him, four black queens in this sea of lily white. Child, you'd think we had landed from Mars when we got there." Derek laughed. "And honey, those queens didn't know the meaning of the words 'Act Up.' They sat around and talked, talked, talked, talked, talked—the world's biggest gabfest. Carlton tried to get in his two cents, but this blond thing moderating the meeting kept looking the other way whenever he raised his hand. Just looked the other way!" He paused as Bill and Derek stared at him, wide-eyed. Aaron smiled and looked in the other direction. Bernard nibbled on corn on the cob.

"Every damn time he did this—pretended not to see Carlton's hand in the air. We knew her number. We've all been around that type too many times. And Miss Carlton, she had a temper on her, OK? So, finally, she stood up and did her loudest <<**SNAP!**>>—as loud and round and mean as she could, till all them white boys was staring at her. Then she said, 'I am an African American living with AIDS and you all need to do something that is relevant to *me*, you hear?'"

Derek busted up.

"That's right, shoot, 'cause we were sitting there listening to them go on about procedures this and rules that and process, process, and Carlton said, 'I ain't got no time for no damn process. I gotta take these goddamn pills all day and I get tired too easy to have deal with process.'"

"What they say after all that?" Bill asked.

"I laughed my ass off," Bingo said.

"Oh, they gave us the look, honey," Ashley continued. "You know that 'Who let this pickaninny in the room' look. But honey, we didn't care, least of all Carlton. I mean, if you're gonna ACT UP, then do it! Don't sit around and talk it to death. Carlton and them went to meetings after that, but I didn't. It was a waste of my time."

"They started processing about race," Bingo said. "Nothing they'd ever thought much about, but they pretended for a while. Carlton gave them a rude education."

"Sounds like Alfonso," Bill said.

"Yeah. He's a lot like Carlton that way. A lot like him."

Bill stood. "Hey! Hey, everyone! Y'all, I just have a few things I want to say, if that's alright."

Testify! folks called out. John Lee Hooker and Carlos Santana played faintly in the background.

"I wanted to say something last night, at City Hall." Bill paused. "I haven't known Alfonso long. I guess just since August. It seems longer, our connection is that deep. I've never met anyone like him. He's the most woke person I've ever known. He might not think so, but he is. He says that I help hold him up. But he's—" Derek stood up and held his brother as his deep voice began to crack. "He gives so much. Courage. Warmth. And have y'all seen him dance? He should be with Alvin Ailey." Aaron began snapping his fingers. "Right? Everything he does is dance. When he walks, he dances. When he talks, and gets the hands going, he dances. He's so special. I love him."

Bill reflected on his image of Alfonso, vital, strong, alive.

He continued, "It's good we're here helping each other get through this. But let me clarify something. This is not a fucking wake for my best friend! OK?" Clapping, snapping, cheering. "He's coming back! He's gonna dance again! If I have to fucking sit by his bedside 24/7, I will, because I want him back! I want him back!" The cheering lasted for a minute. Derek held tight to his brother's hand. "This is Carlton's Posse, OK?"

"That's right!" Vera said.

"We hang tight! So we're gonna help Alfonso through this."

Bill was about to sit on the floor again when Ashley got up and gave him his stool. His mother came and hugged him, as did Sammy.

"Momma," Bill said, "did you meet Sammy? He's the mother of Carver Street."

"Yes, I sure did." She kissed Sammy and then her son.

Berry Residence

Alfonso's room had become something of a tomb. Apart from a couple of visits by Belinda to get stuff to take to him, it sat undisturbed. When Eunice opened the door, she paused for a moment. Turbulence stirred the slumbering air, liberating Alfonso's presence. He was lying on the bed. Then he was sitting at his computer, looking up at her. His smile faded along with his scent as the air began to settle. She soon returned to her purpose and began looking around for anything she could take with her to the hospital. Pictures, toys, anything. She wanted to put them around his bed, build a comfort zone for him, a safe space, so that he would open his eyes again. She packed them all in a bag and when she thought she had enough, she left the room, resealing it to slumber again.

Belinda met her at the top of the stairs.

"Are you ready?" Eunice asked.

She nodded, then handed her mother a note. "Give that to him, OK? Put it in his hand. Tell him I love him, Momma."

"I will, sweetheart." She caressed her face. "Where's Lucy?"

"I'm here."

They went downstairs, walked to the front door. As they passed Ford's study, Eunice caught a glimpse of him. It looked like he was on the phone.

"You two go on outside, alright? I'll be right there."

"Momma?" Lucy said.

"Yes, angel?"

"I love Alfonso. Please tell him that I love him, too!"

"I know, angel." She hugged her youngest. Belinda stroked Lucy on the head. "Go on, now." She released Lucy. "I'll be right there."

They went outside, both carrying overnight bags and backpacks. Eunice turned and entered her husband's study. He had just hung up the phone.

"Well?" she said.

"That was Thad." His voice sounded dry, hollow. "He said someone graffitied the church." Eunice didn't react. "Anyway, he's helping me to set up a press conference for later on. We just have to put together—"

"You weren't on the phone with the hospital? I thought you were talking to the hospital."

"No, no. There's no news from the hospital. I was talking to Thad. He said if we need him to counsel the children, that he'd be happy to."

"I don't want my daughters going anywhere near that man."

"What?" He finally noticed the bags in her hands. "What's that, Eu? Where are you going?"

"To the hospital, where do you think?"

He looked out the window and saw his daughters on the sidewalk with bags.

"Where are the girls going?"

"I'm taking them to my sister's."

"Why?"

"Ford, I'm not going to be here. Someone needs to look after them, so I'm taking them back to Imogene's."

"Where are you going to be?"

"I told you, the hospital. I'm not leaving that hospital until our son opens his eyes again."

Ford looked startled, confused. "Eu, there's nothing we can do."

"Nothing we can do! Ford, what the hell is the matter with you?"

He stared at her.

"I thought you were on the phone with someone important just now, like the doctors or the police department, not Thad Johnson. Our son is lying in a hospital fighting for his life and you're asking me where am I going and telling me there's nothing we can do? Are you serious? For Christ's sake, you saw that video. Where is your outrage, Ford? Why aren't you on the phone calling your friend, the mayor? Why isn't the chief of police himself in here, in this very room, explaining himself to you? Why did two thousand people, two thousand perfect strangers, rally in front of City Hall demanding to know why our son was beaten by the police, while you sit there talking to Thad Johnson about some damn graffiti and more spin strategies for the press? And you're asking me where am I going? *Are you fucking crazy?*"

He had no words for her. He could only stare at a face he has never seen wrenched into an anger he has never known.

"I don't know who you are anymore, Ford Berry. I really don't." She picked up her bags.

"Eunice!"

"You know where to find me. The taxi's waiting. I've got to go."

She turned and went to the front door. He could hear it open and shut behind her.

He didn't have a license to, but Roy drove his father's big rig part of the way home, just to prove he could. Carl was suitably impressed. But the breakdown came while he was driving Carl's car. Over the radio, he heard a news bulletin give an update on Alfonso. He pulled onto the shoulder and started banging on the horn. Carl stopped the big rig and ran back to check on him. Inconsolable. Roy grabbed his cell and made angry phone calls. "Why didn't you fucking tell me?" he barked at Bill. "Where is he?" he yelled at Sammy. "What the fuck is wrong with everyone!"

For a long stretch, all he could do was curl up in the seat and cry. Carl held him as the cars whizzed by on the highway, as the mid-autumn sky turned quickly to dusk.

Roy didn't see his neighborhood again until almost 9 that evening. Carver Street was subdued. He told Carl not to worry, that he would go stay with a friend, he hoped. He arrived at Sammy's and buzzed #8.

"Hi. You're not pissed at me, are you?"

"Of course not, boy!" Sammy buzzed him in.

When he got upstairs, the apartment door was ajar. He went inside and shut it, joined Sammy at the kitchen table. A cup of Earl Gray was waiting for him. Sammy drank a cup of rooibos.

"How is he?" Roy asked.

"Nothing new."

They sat and sipped.

"Were you in the march?"

"No, I was at the hospital. I rode with him in the ambulance."

"Oh, god, Sammy. I can't handle this. I really can't handle this."

"I know, baby."

"How the hell did this happen?"

"One of the cops just freaked out, lost his head. And then the others did, too."

"Did they fire them and throw their butts in jail?"

"I don't know. Don't think so. Charlotte's been looking into it."

"*Charlotte?* And his father is where?"

"Hello!" Sammy exclaimed.

Roy took out his cell. "Hi, bae ... Yeah, I'm back ... No, no, I'm sorry, Bill. I shouldn't have yelled at you like that, not after all you've been through. I'm sorry ... No, I'm at Sammy's right now ... Uh-huh ... Yeah? Hang on." He looked at Sammy who was already nodding his head. "Yeah, he said you can come over. Take Uber, alright? Please be careful. Bye."

"How's Jeremiah doing?" Sammy asked.

"Dad's doing OK. He was really happy to see me." He giggled. "We watched Turner Classic Movies last night. They were showing a bunch of old Bob Hope and Bing Crosby road movies."

"Oh, lord!"

"Yeah, right? But it was fun. Just stupid fun. I didn't know my dad was into them. But he said he always had a thing for Dorothy Lamour."

"He-he-he-he."

"We had a good time. I told him about my fight with Quill over the paper. He said he was proud of me."

Sammy nodded, slowly sipping his tea.

TWENTY-SIX

ALFONSO'S EYES REMAINED CLOSED. CHEMICALS PARADED through him to dull the pain. They had the effect of unhinging his mind so that it wandered. The faces of his life came and went like images in a kaleidoscope. Sammy sat in the store. Charlotte sat with him. Henny Penny clucked through the streets. Bingo sat in the clinic. Harry sat in his van. Mrs. Parker sat on her stoop, staring into the park. Professor Euclid sat on the desk at the front of the classroom glaring at Leon, unable to let professional detachment mask his contempt for him. Bill and Roy sat in the Cuddle Corner. Belinda sat in the kitchen. Lucy sat in her room. His father sat in Thad Johnson's office. His mother sat nearby.

Eunice welcomed all of Alfonso's close friends to visit whenever they wanted. Their presence fit her agenda that her son be surrounded by warmth to promote healing. She met Bill and Roy together. After exchanging hugs, she prepped them for how Alfonso looked, the swelling of the face, the bandages around his head. Bill broke down.

"I was there, Mrs. Berry!" he cried.

She took hold of him. "I'm so sorry you had to experience that," she said. They held each other for a long time. After a while, they went into Alfonso's room. Bandaged and bruised, he looked at peace, calm, tranquil. Both kissed him on the forehead.

"He needs music," Roy said.

He suggested that they set up a Pandora station on Alfonso's iPhone. Eunice loved the idea. Jazz soon began streaming in his private room 24/7. They seeded the station with Lady Day—"I Hear Music," "Fine and Mellow," "Speak Low," and "Some Other Spring."

Other friends and relations brought cards, flowers, stuffed animals, other trinkets. Bingo brought the clinic founders' photo that Vera reproduced and framed for him. Mrs. Parker suggested to Eunice that she set up a rotation to allow herself time to take a breather from her vigil. "We will help you carry this burden, sugar," she said. Eunice welcomed the friendship and the breaks. She put the time away from her son's bedside to good use.

Thursday Morning, Eighth Week
The Hospital

As the machines hummed quietly, as Billie Holiday sang softly, Eunice made a phone call.

"Hello. Is this Charlotte Hunter?"

"Yes?"

"This is Eunice Berry, we met at the hospital last Saturday."

"Mrs. Berry!" Charlotte sat up. "Is there news on Alfonso?"

"Nothing's changed, dear. Listen, I hope it's OK that I call you. Mr. Turner gave me your number. I hope you don't mind."

"No, not at all, Mrs. Berry."

"Charlotte, I am trying to find out what happened Saturday night and who's responsible for beating my son, and I'm getting nowhere. The police department is stonewalling me and I'm not getting any traction at City Hall. I need to know who did this and why. Why would anyone beat an unarmed person senseless?"

"I understand completely, Mrs. Berry. How can I help you, though?"

"You were Councilman Larkin's top aide. Are you still in touch with him? Because I believe that there are people who will still listen to him. He held a lot of sway in City Hall. Do you think he can help me? I am at my wit's end."

"I certainly am in touch with him, Mrs. Berry. I talk to him regularly." She paused for a second, then added, "He's advising me on my campaign."

"Good, good," Eunice said. "Would it be possible for him to try and find out what is going on in terms of an investigation? Because I'll tell you something, my biggest fear is that they try and do something behind closed doors just for the sake of not embarrassing my husband. And that is not going to get it done. Not as far as I'm concerned." She paused, sighed. "This has not been a great time for my family. We haven't...I haven't dealt with his coming out as well as I could have. And now all this happened." She paused again, collected herself. "You knew Carlton, right?"

"Yes."

"About a month ago, my sister Imogene, Carlton's mother, just burst into tears while we were having breakfast together. She kept mentioning Carlton indirectly as we talked and then she just fell apart. I could hear the guilt in her voice. She kept trying to blame Carlton for separating himself from the family, when in reality she knew that none of us made it easy for him. Charlotte, I keep seeing myself in my sister's place, crying over a dead son that I did not allow myself to know. I swear to God that I will never forgive myself if I let that happen. One way or another, I will know my son and I will help him."

Charlotte took a deep breath. "Mrs. Berry, I can meet you this morning. Let me make some arrangements and call you back. But I will help you with this."

"Thank you, Charlotte. Thank you so very much."

Eunice hung up and put her cell phone down. She stared at Alfonso's face, then closed her eyes.

Friday, Noon Hour
The Cuddle Corner

Their hands mingled freely. Multicolor hues from the stained glass dappled their faces. Food and drinks waited while their lips met over the table.

Roy received a text. He took out his cell.

"Uh-oh!"

"What's up, babe?"

"Sammy said, 'Watch the noon news, NOW.'"

"Shit!"

Bill fumbled over his own iPhone to launch the TV station's app. Roy walked to the counter. He told the student barista that news about Alfonso was about to come on and she immediately changed the channel on the café's TV and shot up the volume.

On the screen appeared a familiar podium. Then up walked retired Councilman James Larkin. He looked over his glasses at the cameras. To his right stood Eunice Berry.

> *"Mrs. Berry asked for my assistance yesterday in finding some answers to the terrible tragedy that happened to her son, Alfonso. I am here to announce that the mayor has appointed me chair of a blue-ribbon panel that will begin investigating what happened that night. The panel will consist of retired members of the police force, the police review board, and community leaders."*

The café's normal lunchtime bustle subsided. Bill and Roy held on to each other.

> *"Finally," Larkin continued, "I can announce that the officers involved in the beating of Alfonso Berry have been suspended and put on immediate administrative leave pending the investigation."*

Cheers erupted. Many began the chant that shook the city last Saturday.

JUSTICE FOR ALFONSO!

JUSTICE FOR ALFONSO!

Bill stood up on a chair and whistled loudly.

"Hey! This is all good, and maybe someone will have to pay for what happened." The chanting quieted. The barista turned down the TV. "But this doesn't change the fact that my best friend is lying in a coma over something that never should have happened! I saw it, OK? I was there when they beat the crap out of him! I'm praying like I've never prayed before that he'll recover. But I don't know what's gonna happen. I do know that his life is changed forever behind something that never should have fucking happened! OK? So, just remember that, OK?"

Adrenaline still pumped him up, but he couldn't think of anything else to say. He climbed down from the chair. Folks clapped. Some nearby patted him on the shoulder and offered condolences as he sat down and leaned over the table, his forehead touching Roy's.

Leon had entered the café when the chanting started. He heard all of Bill's rant and did nothing but stare blankly. He soon departed.

1 p.m.
Beacon Hill Baptist Church

Ford arrived a half-hour later than he said he would. Thad Johnson greeted him with the usual firm hand and toothy smile. Something must have kept you in the office, he said jovially. Ford made a weak smile and mumbled unintelligibly. They sat next to each other in front of the big desk. Johnson asked if Eunice would be joining them after all. Ford said no. Johnson asked if she was still spending most of her time at the hospital. Ford said yes. Johnson nodded.

"Motherhood is a powerful force, Ford. Just give Eunice some time, and she'll—"

"She was at City Hall just now."

"What was she doing there?"

"You didn't watch the noon news?"

Johnson shook his head. Ford filled him in, his voice distant, ghostly, as if it did not originate from his own body.

"Did you get appointed to this blue-ribbon panel?" Johnson asked.

Ford shook his head no. "She wouldn't even look at me, Thad. My own wife would not acknowledge my presence. She looked right through me, like I wasn't even there."

"Ford, this is incredible. I can't believe Eunice would act this way. She's acting as if what happened to Alfonso is—your fault!"

Ford sat hunched forward, his knees spread wide apart, his elbows heavy upon them, his hands clasped. Then he looked up.

"Isn't it?"

Johnson reared his head back. "What are you saying, Ford?"

Ford stood up and began pacing around the desk.

"The night Alfonso and I fought, when he told me that he's gay, he said to me, 'You're doing me like Granddad did Ernest Little.' And I slapped him. I slapped him. I wanted to do worse than that." Recalling that moment made him lose his train of thought. He closed his eyes briefly to refocus. "You know about Ernest Little, don't you?" Johnson remained silent. Ford kept pacing. "Ernest looked up to my father so much, and my father trashed him relentlessly. He bragged about it, like it was his greatest accomplishment. But he took no responsibility for driving him to suicide." He stopped pacing and stood behind Johnson. "My father destroyed Ernest Little. And as God is my witness, I've nearly—" He paused and looked up, saw bandages, tubes, wires, stillness in a bed. Nothing like the young man he knew. A tear came to his eye. He quickly wiped it away. "'Rip him apart, tear him down, shut him up.' Isn't that what you said we had to do, Thad?" He shook his head. "My wife told me that she didn't know me anymore! That was the day after Alfonso got—" His voice trailed off.

"Ford, sit down. Sit down. Listen. Eunice is worked up, and I know how upsetting that must be."

"No, you don't." He loomed over Johnson. Power returned to his voice. "You aren't married. Never have been. You don't have any children. How do you know how I feel, Reverend?" He described the rush of memories that filled his mind. Birthdays, holidays, trips abroad, moments as a group, moments with just him and his son, their moments in the park.

Johnson pinched his lips.

"A man's supposed to protect his family. Isn't that what you preach? I'm on the city council. I'm on the goddamn, motherfucking city council, but my wife had to go to my predecessor to find someone with some balls to investigate what happened to my son. You wanna know something, Thad? I wouldn't vote for myself!"

Ford walked toward the door. "Alfonso was right. I should have played baseball."

"Where are you going, Councilman?"

Ford stopped and turned around, saw bitter sarcasm curl Johnson's lips. He couldn't give a shit.

"Don't call me that, Thad. I'm not on the council anymore. I'm resigning, effective immediately."

He left Thad Johnson sitting alone in front of his desk, his teeth clenched and hidden.

Roy met the Hawks. Marilene made a vegetarian enchilada casserole and brown rice. They feasted hard on seconds, thirds, and fourths. Even Derek didn't miss the dead flesh. Save room for dessert, Marilene called out, and then presented a chocolate mousse cake. She received a round of applause from the boys.

Later, as he and Bill were taking Lyft to Club Copacetic, Roy raved about the dinner. He asked Bill where his mother got the recipe for the sauce.

"She doesn't cook with recipes. She just sort of throws it all together."

"Yeah!" Roy said, laughing. "Just like Sammy."

At the club, the same doorman greeted them with the same smooth, chill voice.

"Thank you, gentlemen, but I don't need your ID cards. Just five will get it done." They gave him the cash. "Thank you, gentlemen." He stamped their hands. "And I just want to let you know that we're all thinking about and praying for your friend Alfonso. I know he'll be joining us here again real soon."

"Thanks, man," Bill said.

"Thank you," Roy said.

"Peace, brothers."

They walked up the purple walled stairwell. Mellow phat beats greeted them at the top.

"I wonder if he was in the march," Bill said.

"Sounds like everyone was in the march."

They went to the bar, got three mineral waters, took them to the front window. They held hands, a smiling, animated face and ever-moving body on both of their minds. Each toasted the third bottle as it sat on the counter.

For a while, they kept silent and let the club's spirit get into their being. That's when Bill noticed an animated butterfly flitting about the bar. He had just come in from the dance room, all sweaty in his opened long-sleeved shirt and baggy jeans. He got two beers, then flitted over to a muscled stud in black slacks and a tight-fitting blue dress shirt. He gave him a beer and a sensual kiss that involved much tongue action.

"Oh, my fucking god," Bill said.

"What?"

"I'll be back."

Bill put down his water and hurried to follow the flitting butterfly into the restroom. He slammed through door, rushed the dude, and shoved him violently against the wall. The man fell backward, slumped onto the floor. Others in the space quickly departed. The dude looked up at his attacker.

"Bill? What's up?"

"Fuck you, Jameel! Fuck you!"

"It's not my fault, Bill! I swear!"

"You tell the truth, alright? Did you tell the press about Alfonso?"

"No, Bill! God, no! I didn't! I swear, I didn't."

"Then did you tell Leon or Tamesha?"

"I didn't mean to. Oh, god! I shoulda just stayed home!" He sobbed.

Bill relaxed his stance. "What happened?"

Jameel sniffled. "The Friday before the Unity Rally. I barely remember how I ended up going out with Leon and them. I spent the night at the bar. Got lit. I babble when I get like that. Guess I said something. 'Cause then Leon and Tamesha are all in my face getting all—" He waved his arms in the air. "I tried walking it back, but it was too late. Bill, Alfonso means so much to me."

He talked about wanting to slow-dance with Alfonso at all their high school dances, about wanting to ravish him when they played Xbox. He talked about seeing the beating on TV, how he couldn't stop seeing it.

Roy entered the restroom. He saw Jameel on the floor and Bill standing over him.

"He's not worth it, Bill, OK? Just leave him."

Bill bent over, helped Jameel to his feet.

"I came out to my folks," Jameel said. "I just told them, straight out. And they gave me a hug!" He started sobbing again.

"I'm glad to hear that, Jameel," Bill said. "I really am. But if you want to get right by Alfonso, then this is what you need to do. You go to the ASA office, on a Thursday when everybody's there. Tell them that you're a gay man. Tell them how you really feel about Alfonso. Tell them everything you just told me."

"Come on, Bill," Roy said. "Let's go."

"And Jameel, I know how hard it was seeing Alfonso get fucked up like that. But I didn't see it on a TV screen. I saw it from six feet away."

"I'm sorry, Bill."

"I'm sorry, too."

He and Roy walked out of the restroom and back to the corner with their drinks.

Roy gave his boy a sensual kiss that involved much tongue action.

"You're a class act, bae," Roy said.

"I don't know about *that*. I wanted to kick his fucking face in, but I didn't want Sexy Voice to get pissed at me."

"Sexy Voice?"

"Oh." Bill snickered. "That's my nickname for the doorman."

Roy laughed. "When you wanna dance?"

"In a bit. Hold me, alright?"

Roy complied.

TWENTY-SEVEN

Two Months Later
The Hospital,

ALFONSO'S EYES REMAINED CLOSED. CHEMICALS PARADED *through him to dull the pain. They had the effect of unhinging his mind so that it wandered. The faces of his life came and went like images in a kaleidoscope. Sammy sat in his apartment listening to jazz. Bill and Roy sat on barstools at Club Copacetic. Bingo sat in his fly condo working on another grant proposal, puffing hard on a stogie, looking butch. Jameel sat at the ASA office. Victor sat with him. His sisters sat at their respective friends' places talking boys and hanging out. His father sat alone in their large house, pouring over legal briefs, hoping to make things right again. His mother sat nearby.*

He thought he could smell his mother. Mother? Mother?

"Mom?" a voice croaked.

Eunice turned her head quickly and saw his eyes open.

TWENTY-EIGHT

Early January 2016
The Adrian Jefferson Room, City Hall

BILL PUT OFF HIS APPEARANCE BEFORE THE BLUE-RIBBON panel until after the end of the semester. Finals. Papers. But he wanted to go and testify, despite having to relive the trauma of that night in October.

Chairman James Larkin conducted the hearings with his trademark gentleness. A quiet man with a strong presence, he started each testimony session in a similar fashion.

"This is not a judicial hearing, but you are under oath. We are not empowered to make indictments, but we can make recommendations to the district attorney. We are seeking as much information as we can about this incident to get as full a picture as possible. Please feel free, Mr. Hawk, to tell us anything that might help us in our search for the truth."

Roy sat next to Bill, holding his hand. His mother and brother sat behind him in the front row of the audience. Eunice Berry sat next to Derek. Bill testified that he was not with the needle exchange group before the beating happened, that the police presence caught his attention as he was walking home with his brother.

"I got up to the police line, and a woman officer kept me from getting closer." He paused, sniffled. "I saw my best friend get beat down like a dog. It seemed the more he tried to protect himself, the harder they hit him."

Roy put his arm around him, passed him water. After a short sip, he cleared his throat.

"Alfonso was all about hope. I first met him when he was in deep mourning over the loss of his cousin, Carlton. And even during that time and all that he went through last semester, he still was about hope. After I got fired from the church tutorial program, and I thought my family would reject me, he helped me through it, because he was all about hope. I'm not seeing hope right now. It's like they beat hope out of him."

He paused and took another sip of water.

"Within a couple of days after waking from the coma, the nightmares began. He wakes up screaming. It's horrible," he said, his voice cracking. "It's the most horrible thing I've ever heard in my life."

———

Bill was asleep on a reclining chair in Alfonso's hospital room. Night noises no longer kept him awake, not the equipment at the bedside, not the visits by the nursing staff. All that had become white noise. The recliner was comfortable. The jazz was always playing, smooth and mellow. He could sleep. And then came the scream. Wailing. Unnerving, unearthly wailing. It scared the living shit out of him. Bill dashed to the bedside. Alfonso thrashed about madly. The IV yanked from his arm. Bill tried to steady him and took one across the jaw. *Alfonso! Alfonso! Wake up!* Could he not hear for the screaming? *Nurse! Help!* Bill had a fright. What if Alfonso hit his head? Could he knock himself back into a coma? Eventually the nurses arrived and assisted. It took three of them. Alfonso stilled, opened his eyes. Sweat poured off his forehead.

———

The hearing room sat in silence. Derek rubbed his brother on the shoulder from behind. Bill patted Derek's hand.

Chairman Larkin adjusted his glasses subtly.

"Mr. Hawk, part of what this panel wants to document is how events such as the beating of your friend by the police affect the community at large. It's obvious that are you very distressed. Can you tell us further how this event has affected you personally, Mr. Hawk?"

"I'm angry. A lot. At school. At the club we go to. At home. At first I didn't realize how angry I am all the time."

———

One random night, Derek was listening to some of the usual beats he always played, when Bill slammed into his room without knocking and told him *shut that shit off now, goddamn it!* Derek responded with a raised middle finger and hard stare. Bill lost it. *Why I always gotta hear this shit in the house? I don't wanna hear nothin' about niggas getting fucked up! It's not a game! It's not fucking cool! Getting the shit kicked out of you isn't fucking cool! Don't you get it? Why can't y'all fucking understand!* Bill didn't realize right away that he was screaming. Derek's face switched from annoyed to worried. And his mother appeared behind him, equally disturbed. He started to apologize, then fell apart. Soon afterward, he finally began seeing a therapist at the campus health center. Derek began listening to his music over headphones, as his mother had begged him to since forever.

———

"I don't watch half the shows I used to. No more 'Game of Thrones.'" The audience laughed. "I try and stay away from anything too violent. It just sets me off. This never should have happened. Never."

"Thank you, Mr. Hawk," Chairman Larkin said.

TWENTY-NINE

Friday Evening, 7ish, First Week,
Spring Semester, Mid-January
Club Copacetic

BILL SAT ALONE AT THE BAR. SEXY VOICE THE DOORMAN walked up to him.

"Mind if I sit here?"

Bill smiled. "Yo, SV."

He sat to Bill's left. The bartender brought him a mineral water.

"Hope you ain't going soft on my account," Bill said.

"My own policy: no drinking on duty." He took a couple of swigs. "You here alone? Where's your bae?"

"He's with Alfonso tonight."

"I'll sure be glad to see him here again."

Bill raised his bottle. Sexy did the same. They toasted.

"He can stand now," Bill said. "He's doing physical therapy, uses a walker. It's so hard seeing him like that. The doctors say he's doing real good. But he's still in a lot of pain."

"It takes time, brother. Please give him my love."

"Thanks, bruh."

"But I'm sure you came here for a time-out. You plan to get you freak on tonight?"

"I might. Actually, I'm here to meet Jameel."

"Solid. Now, y'all ain't gonna take up from where you left off, right?" He smiled teasingly, but his eyes held a fixed gaze.

Bill cocked his head back slightly. "How'd you find out about that?"

"That's why I don't drink on the job. Very little gets by me."

"Sorry. I was pretty hot that night."

"I saw your testimony, Bill. Believe me, I understand. Just keep it together, alright? I got the club to think about."

"I promise, SV."

"In a different city, in another life, I was on the force. I knew guys like the ones who went off on Alfonso. We were expected to defend them, or at the very least look the other way. In those days, videos were rare. So these eyes," he said, pointing toward his own, "were the only ones of record. Rookies learned real early to keep quiet. But I guess I skipped that lesson. I saw something, so I said something. Internal affairs was like, You sure you want to say anything? And I said, Yeah. They asked again, Are you really sure? I said, Yeah, I'm sure. They went off on this dude for no reason. Wasn't armed, wasn't resisting. I felt like I needed to say something. But internal affairs didn't want to hear it. They said, Tell you what, you think about it and come back when you're sure. You can guess what happened next."

"They fucked you up?" Bill asked.

"Not physically. But word got around. I got dirty glares, even a death threat. Whatever whistleblower protection laws existed back then clearly did not apply to me."

"Were there any other blacks on the force?"

"A few. They gave it to me the worst of all, said I was fucking it up for the rest of them. And also, you know, I wasn't out, but I wasn't exactly in, either. They made it real uncomfortable for me. So, despite my otherwise spotless record and commendations, I left."

"And left town, it sounds like."

"Hurried up and left town, brother. I'm not trying to make excuses, but if you wanna know why 'good' cops don't talk? This is why. If you're a lone voice, ain't nothing you can do. So I understand your anger, Bill. I really do."

He got up, gave Bill a kiss on the cheek. "Keep it strong, now."

Jameel came up the stairs as Sexy walked toward them. "Good evening, Mr. Wilkerson," Sexy said, as they passed.

"Hey, bruh," Jameel said. He walked to the bar, sat next to Bill.

"I didn't even know you had my number," Bill said.

"I saw it once, got a photographic memory for numbers. How you been? Can I get you something?"

"Another water with lime, I guess."

He ordered it and a beer with lime for himself.

"I got something for Alfonso." He took a small, gift-wrapped package out of his bag. "Keep it on the DL, alright? Till you get it home," he whispered

Bill had a feeling he knew what it was. Alfonso mentioned the time Jameel scored some Maui Wowie. He slipped the package in his pocket.

"Thanks. Was that why you wanted to meet?"

"Not just that. I want to do what you said and come out to the group. Victor said he'll come and some others will, too. Can you come?"

Bill stared at him.

"I'm doing this for Alfonso and I'd really like you to be there. Please, Bill."

9ish

It hovered around forty degrees with a threat to go lower. Alfonso didn't care. Outdoors became a thing for him. He called it one of the basic food groups. The doctors told him to stick to the basics, so he called everything he liked doing one of the basic food groups. That included pot. He and Roy indulged while lying on their backs on the wooden deck atop Bingo's condo complex. Each wore comfortable outerwear. Bright stars appeared fleetingly between wisps of passing clouds. It had rained the other day, so the air was crisp. Alfonso wished it would snow on top of them. He'd love to feel a snowflake land on his nose.

"Fathers, man," Alfonso said.

He took another drag, then passed it to Roy, who did the same, then held the joint at his side.

"Fucking fathers," Roy said.

"How's your dad's viral load?"

"Low. Very low. Almost undetectable."

"Nice. You know what I really wanna do, Roy?"

"What?"

"I wanna take my walker and fucking throw it in the harbor and watch one of those big ships fucking crunch it up." He laughed. "I'd pay real money to see that shit."

"I saw you try going without it."

"Got to, Roy. Gotta keep it 100. Give it to me." Roy passed him the joint. He sucked on it, then gave it back. "They tell me not to fall. I'm gonna fall one day. I just wanna fucking get it over with, you know what I'm saying? Just do it, then move on."

Roy stayed quiet.

"Just go doooooooown, splat!" Alfonso giggled. He glanced at Roy. "Am I freaking you?"

"Don't Humpty on me, Fro. That's all I'm saying."

"You gonna start calling me 'Fro,' too? Shit. Bill's contaminated you."

"You *are* the Fro, girlfriend. You've been to Mt. Doom and back."

Alfonso sucked his teeth. "I ain't gonna Humpty on you, Merry Mary Sexy Hobbit." He giggled. "Promise. I'll fall, then I'll get up. That's what I'm saying. This Humpty's been scrambled already, sistah. But you all are putting me back together again. All Humpty had were kings and horses and shit. I got you guys."

"I'll bring my duct tape." Roy took another hit.

"That's what I'm talking about." He giggled. "Little Pipp'n ain't got no father to worry about, right?"

"Naw. His father left the family when he was little. A couple of years after Derek was born."

"And how old is Derek?"

"14, 15, something like that."

"So Bill ain't seen his daddy since he was, what, fucking five or something?"

"Something like that. He said his dad came and went a few times, but then he left for good."

"Like maybe Mother Hawk told him not to come back?"

"Probably."

"She's fierce like that. You getting hungry?"

"Born hungry. I forgot the fucking chips downstairs, though." Roy sat up. "Shit, it's cold up here. Feels colder sitting up. Wind hitting my face."

"Leave mary with me, alright, Merry Mary? Promise to leave you some." He flashed a lopsided grin.

"Yeah, fuck you." Roy handed him the joint, then stood up, walked inside.

Alfonso toked some more, looked at the clouds as they went by. He started making shapes out of them, wanting to see horses or birds like when he was a kid. Instead, grimaces snarled at him. Anxiety kicked in. He shut his eyes. When he opened them again, he was looking toward his left at the furniture on the deck. He avoided the sky for a while.

Roy returned with a huge bag of potato chips. He lay down next to Alfonso, the bag of chips between them. Both tore into it with large handfuls.

"So you two getting on alright?" Alfonso asked.

"What, me and Bill? We're fine."

"No. You and your dad."

"We're cool. Is there any left?"

"Fuck you. I told you I'd save some." He gave Roy the joint.

"Just barely." He smoked the last of it, grabbed a bunch of chips and put them on his chest, ate them slowly. "Yeah, Dad and I are good. We do a lot more real talk now. Sucks that it took, you know, Armageddon for us to get there. After Mom, we both shut down. Hurt's such a motherfucker. So, anyway, on Christmas Eve we went out for Chinese, like we always do. Then he blew my world up."

I was a bully in school. I'm not proud of that, but that's who I was. I picked on the nerds. They was all scared of me. Except for one. He'd just look at me and I'd be like, 'Tha fuck you looking at, nigga?' but he wouldn't flinch or nothing. He was fearless, like you. And I guess he saw something in me I didn't see in myself. We started talking, eating lunch together. He started helping me with my math. I tried to teach him how to fight, 'cause he was so little anybody coulda run over him. Next thing I know, we was kissing and shit. I was sweet on him before I was sweet on any girl.

"That must have nuked your world," Alfonso said.

"Gurrrl. My mouth hung open, couldn't say shit. But he kept on."

I didn't have a name for what we had. I just knew how it made me feel. Then his family moved away. I started dating girls. Never gave another thought to being with a boy again. Never did, until after your mother died. I fought it real hard. But then some dude picked me up at a rest area. Why me? I don't know. Maybe he saw something, or I projected something. He wanted to suck me off, and I let him. Next thing I know, I'm 13 years old again and with my boy. It felt so natural. So I kept doing stuff like that, here and there. Even after I met Jasmine, I kept seeing guys on the side. I'd tell myself I'm just doing it 'cause I don't want to make another commitment, to Jasmine or anyone. Your mother meant the world to me, Son. Losing her was the worst thing to happen in my life.

And you don't wanna hurt like that again.

Yeah.

Roy munched on potato chips. Alfonso had scooted closer so that their heads touched. "I asked him," Roy said, "what he meant by that kid was fearless like me."

He accepted himself for who he was, like you accept yourself for who you are. I couldn't accept myself as being nothing but straight, even though I'm not. It's taken me this long to finally come to terms with that. If I was fearless and faced who I am sooner, then maybe I wouldn't have—

"I jumped in and was like, 'No, no, no, Dad. Don't go there. Ain't no guilt, OK? Don't do that to yourself.' I got up and went to his side of the table and we just held each other." Alfonso took his hand. "Finally, I said, 'I love you, Daddy.' And he said, 'I love you, too, Son' and kissed me on the forehead." Roy wiped his eyes. "We're both a couple of queer atheists, but damn if that wasn't the best fucking Christmas we've ever had."

"That's so beautiful, Roy." Alfonso turned and kissed him, then took some potato chips off of Roy's chest and ate them. "My father and I used to be close like that. Now I don't know who he is. Did I tell you he hit me when he threw me out of the house?"

"No. You never told me that."

"Backhanded me so hard, I fell against his desk. And he was fucking staring down at me like he wanted to do it again. I'm scared of him, Roy. I really am. I think I've always been scared of him, but I just hid from it, denied it. The night he kicked me out, I told Bingo that my father hated me. At the time, I really believed it. Then I backed off. Then the meeting happened, and I thought it again. Then I backed off. Then the press conference happened, and I was like, whoa. But I kinda backed off again. But now? I'm convinced. He hates me, wishes I was dead."

"Don't say that."

Alfonso gave him side eye. Then he looked up and saw the stars, most of the clouds having parted.

"Carlton used to talk about halfway to dawn, never said it had a doppelgänger. And she's a bitch. I'm in this halfway state all the time, awake and asleep, where I can't tell what is and what ain't. So the shit that happened, I remember it one way but then I dream about it another way, and I can't tell which is which. They're both real."

———⟡———

December 16, his 21st birthday. Eunice arranged for cupcakes. His sisters decorated the hospital room with balloons and party favors. They gave their brother a dark-green, pointed birthday hat to wear over the bandages. Everyone came. Bingo brought a plastic tiara that read "Queen Bee." Alfonso wore it around the birthday hat. Sammy brought a little bongo to play. Ms. Ashley brought a mix CD. You said you wanted to go dancing on your 21st, he said.

Alfonso encouraged everyone to boogie, even did a little shimmying himself while sitting up. Folks cheered him on. Everyone indulged on carrot, red velvet, and vanilla cupcakes. It was a great day.

Sammy, Bill, and Roy were the last to go. Alfonso hated saying goodbye to them, even though he was getting tired.

Twenty minutes after they departed, Ford arrived. He entered the room with a big grin. Eunice, Belinda, and Lucy greeted him. Alfonso, still wearing his birthday swag, tried to smile, but his breath became shallow, his eyes larger.

After that, a blur. A childhood nickname. A baseball. Then bats, clubs, boots, and projectiles pummeled his body. And a long, loud siren drowned out everything. And then oblivion.

Long after the day had ended, his mother alone with him in the room, he looked up and asked her if his father had visited.

<hr />

"For months after my mom died, I dreamed about her so much that I thought she was still alive," Roy said. "I'd wake up crying, 'cause I'd worried that she was gonna die all over again. My head was so fucked up. So yeah, I hear you."

He held Alfonso's hand and they lay quietly as stars shined upon them in the icy air.

"Can you roll another one?" Alfonso asked.

Roy reached into his pocket and pulled out a fresh joint.

"Merry Mary's way ahead of you, 'Fonso Fro."

Alfonso took it and lit up. After a toke, he passed it back to Roy.

9ish
Bill's Brownstone, 48th Street

No dancing after all. After meeting with Jameel, Bill felt like going home and spacing out on pretty much everything. He rounded the corner from Stevens to 48ᵗʰ and walked the empty street to his brownstone. Mrs. Parker only came into view once he got within a couple of doors.

"Mrs. P!" he said, a wide grin on his face, "it's colder than cold out here!"

"I know. Don't you love it? Love this weather! So long as it's dry, I'm alright." She wore a scarf, a heavy overcoat, thick socks, and her pink booties.

Bill snickered, shook his head. He wore multiple layers topped off with a puffy parka and TARDIS ski cap and still felt it when the wind kicked in. But he sat on the steps with her anyway.

"How's the new semester going, sugar?"

"Fine so far. I don't know. Despite everything last semester, I still managed to pull straight A's. Got on the Dean's List."

"See there!" She gave him a brisk rub on his head. He smiled, readjusted his ski cap.

"Now I get to take an honors seminar. I'm in a class about the city's history in the 20ᵗʰ century."

"We got a whole lotta history around here."

———✦———

Ford wore a driver's cap, a long gray trench coat, and a beige woolen scarf. He stood across the street from Sammy's store and looked through its big window. Sammy sat at the counter. How large the man loomed in his family's life, Ford thought. Only recently did he recall that they had in fact met very briefly many years ago. That first interaction had also involved his son.

It was late 1994. A very pregnant Eunice craved ice cream. Ford asked what kind. She didn't care, but then said that peach would be nice. He scurried out of their new home on Beacon Hill in search of a place to get it. He had no car, not yet. Everything had gone into the house. All the nearby stores were closed already, since it was past five on a Sunday. Taking the bus to a supermarket seemed like not a thing to do. She wasn't due for another couple of weeks, but first-time-father jitters kept him from straying too far. He decided to go down the hill and walk to Carver Street. Not a place he would normally visit, but he thought he remembered seeing a little corner store at 44th Street.

He wished he could remember more about that first trip to Sammy's. He knew so little about Carver Street, by design. Now he actively studied its street life to learn more about his son. Even this cold night offered many faces alive with flash and color to observe. Did any of them know Alfonso? Did they hang together? What stories about him could they tell?

Ford remembered speaking to the baby bump while Eunice devoured his little present. *Hey, Little Dude. You like the ice cream I got you?*

———✦———

"What's Carver Street's story?" Bill asked.

"Carver Street has always had a queer history," Mrs. Parker replied. Bill giggled. "It's been a home to folks on the fringes since the Jazz Age. Before my time," she added with a wink. "During Prohibition, there were speakeasies full of bohemians. Poets, painters, musicians. You know the building where Sammy lives? The old-timers used to say that a madam operated a brothel there. The sailors would come to this area, fresh off the boat, all wide-eyed, looking for liquor and ladies.

"But they also looking for boys to play with. Mmm-hmm. They'd be in the bushes just off 45th, like they do now."

"Where Eddie got attacked."

"Yes, that's right. The beatings are a long tradition. So heartbreaking, Bill, that stuff still happens. Today we got the street patrols. And back when AIDS first started, they used to go out there and hand out condoms and little business cards to tell 'em how not to get infected."

"Nice."

"Uh-huh. Harry and them used to do that. But I can remember back to the '50s and '60s. When guys got beat up or killed, you didn't hear nothing about it, not in the papers. Only by word of mouth. When the papers did run the story, they did it not because of the crime, but to out whoever it was who got beat up, to shame him. If they survived the beating, then they'd go and kill themselves anyway because of that."

———◆———

Ford walked into the store. Jazz played. He stood directly in front of Sammy, nervous, but smiling. Always start with a smile, his father had taught him.

Sammy looked up at him. "Good evening, Mr. Berry."

"Hello, Mr. Turner," he said, sticking out his hand. Sammy shook it. "That's a pretty tight track you're playing."

Sammy turned his laptop around and opened up iTunes. Anton Schwartz and his quintet. Their "Alleybird" swung slow and easy over the speakers.

"Young man from out west I've been getting into," Sammy said, turning the computer back toward him. "I like his composing chops."

Ford stood and listened a bit. "Nice. It's got attitude."

It made him think of his days as a young man, when he thought his swagger owned the streets. Good times. Then he realized that his son was about that same age, his swagger now a dream deferred. For how long? He refocused his thoughts.

"I hear you used to play drums."

"I still do."

Ford nodded his head, felt awkward.

"So, is, uh, Alfonso staying at your place tonight, Mr. Turner?"

"He's at Bingo's. Roy is with him. Do you want to call over there?"

"No, that's OK. I just wasn't sure where he was tonight."

"Uh-huh." Sammy returned his attention to the crossword on his screen.

"Looks like quite a setup you got. How is the computer playing over the speakers?"

"Those are Bluetooth speakers." Sammy pointed to the corners of the store. "Got 'em last Christmas. I retired the boombox." He pointed to a low bookcase against the wall near the freezers, where the old device sat in dusty repose. "I got my music collection on here now."

"Did you get that for Christmas, too?"

"No. Alfonso gave it to me."

"I see." Another awkward pause. "You have Wi-Fi here, too?"

"Mmm-hmmm."

"Sweet. Alfonso set up our Wi-Fi at the house. He's good at that." Sammy finished typing an answer to his crossword.

"I, uh—," Ford started. Sammy looked up at him. "I wonder if you—" A small grin came to his face. "I'm having a sudden craving. Do you carry Fudgsicle bars?"

Sammy nodded. "They're in the freezer on the right, second section."

"Thanks."

Ford went to the freezer and found a box full of them. He took one out, but before closing the freezer door, he scanned the ice cream cartons for peach. None appeared. He walked back to the counter, reaching into his pocket for his wallet. Sammy waved him away.

"No charge, Mr. Berry."

"You sure?"

"I never charge Alfonso for them, either."

Ford tore open the wrapper, started licking.

"Thanks. I used to buy them for him in the park, from one of those vendors with the pushcarts. God, he loved them. That was in the summer, after we played—"

Baseball wouldn't come out. He dropped his head, covered his face with his hand.

"I want to be there for him, Sammy! I want him to know that I'm there for him!"

"He knows. It's just gonna take time."

Ford uncovered his face, looked up. He saw the photo of Charlotte and his late nephew on the wall. They looked so happy. Above that he saw a membership certificate for the Carver Street Business Guild. So many regrets.

"He gave me the courage to finally resign. I almost didn't. I mean to say, I almost didn't go through with it." Sammy closed his laptop and looked up at Ford. "My wife's press conference with James Larkin was my wake-up call." He looked at Sammy. "After telling Johnson I was resigning, I went to my office at City Hall. I started writing some long-ass letter, explaining myself so that people would understand. And I couldn't. I kept hearing voices in my head telling me not to do it.

"I was about to go home, but went to the hospital instead. I got there, looked at him still unconscious. There was my explanation." Sammy nodded. "I sat next to him and I said, 'Hey Little Dude, I'm gonna make it right.' I took out my cell and typed out a simple message to the mayor. 'I resign, effective immediately.' Hit Send. Done. I've always had the freedom to resign. Alfonso gave me the strength to do it. That boy has given me so much!"

"He's given us all so much, Ford. Each of us. Every person he's ever met. He's a very special young man, and you clearly had a lot to do with that."

"That's very kind." Ford smiled faintly, an attempt to contain his emotions. "Thank you, for everything, Mr. Turner." He wanted to say more, but couldn't. Instead, he bowed his head slightly. "You have a good evening, now." And then walked toward the door.

"Take care, Mr. Berry."

———◆———

"Everything south of Huckleberry Park was black," Mrs. Parker continued. "And everything north of it was white. And you can still see reflections of that today by the churches. Carver Street has always been neutral territory, more or less."

"Did people mix in the park?" Bill asked.

"No. Black folks could play on the south side of the park, but everything from the big field north was considered off-limits. Now, most of your black-owned businesses were below 48th, but a few lined the park, particularly on Lincoln Avenue. Where the clinic is now, that used to be a grocery store, sorta like Sammy's, but bigger."

———◆———

Ford sucked on the last of his Fudgsicle bar as he stood in front of the burned-out Huckleberry Community Clinic, still boarded up, mired in the red tape he had created to keep it from rebuilding. He hoped Charlotte would be able to untangle his bullshit.

Old Mr. Green's store. Fresh donuts every Monday, a baker's dozen still warm in the bag. Mr. Green treated his mother like royalty, with the folksy chivalry of a suitor in a Tennessee Williams play. *And how are you this fine morning, Miss Dorothea?* Her married life to Al, Sr. largely existed as a showpiece for the society pages, gaudy displays of fine dining and trips to the theater. But Ford saw his mother truly sparkle during those Monday-morning visits, from her giddy voice to her crinkled-nose smile. Mr. Green completed his mother in a way his father never did.

She wore all black for a week after Mr. Green passed away. Maybe they had a fling, Ford thought. He hoped so. His father treated her as an accessory to his legacy, like cufflinks on a tux. Lord knows, she deserved something special.

—◆—

"Now a real ugly thing happened when Alfonso's grandfather was still in office," Mrs. Parker continued. "The area had been changing. Black folks moved into Beacon Hill, where Alfonso's family live. And the area around Carver Street got more gay and more diverse. So one summer, these skinheads came from out of the suburbs and did a cross burning in the middle of the park."

"Holy shit!"

"Uh-huh. This would have been mid-to-late '70s. They called it the 'Take It Back' rally. Some stores got smashed up on Carver Street, including Sammy's. Real ugly."

"They haven't come back, have they?"

"No, not like that."

—◆—

Ford walked north on Lincoln Avenue for several blocks.

Avoid that area, his father advised during his first run for the city council. The area has changed a lot, Ford countered. The familiar creases emerged on his father's brow, but he continued. It's so diverse now, nothing like when those kids threw things at your dad's car. Finally, Al Berry told his son pointedly, *Al Junior, they have an agenda up there. And it ain't YOUR agenda. You'll remember that if you know what's good for you.*

At Chestnut Street he paused, saw Bingo's condo building on the right several doors down. He hoped Alfonso was OK. That track Sammy played stayed with him, made him lament missing his son's teenage years behind working on the damn city council. They could have been alley birds together, dressing sharp, slow-strutting down the block, catching the eyes of all the ladies and lads they passed. A blues never played. And now his son was scared to death of him.

Ford had pledged to himself on Alfonso's 21st birthday to make a new start. Wipe the slate clean, begin again. Politics was history. No more worries about keeping up appearances or maintaining superficial community standards or whatever other bullshit he said at that lame-ass meeting with Johnson. Now they could just be Ford and Alfonso, father and son. They could play ball in the park again, to help bring back his strength. Alfonso'll love that, Ford thought as he bought a brand-new baseball, small, round, tightly wound, regulation down to the last stitch, just like in the old days.

He excitedly took the ball to his son in the hospital. When he entered the hospital room, he called out, *Hey, Little Dude! Happy Birthday! Here, catch!* and tossed it underhand, gently. Alfonso responded quickly. He curled up, covered his head, trembled, and then shrieked louder than anything Ford had ever heard before. His mother and sisters tried to calm him. Finally, nurses and doctors arrived with sedatives. He calmed only after the drugs took effect. The baseball ended up under the bed somewhere.

The doctors had said that certain situations—images, sounds, actions—could trigger flashbacks to the beating. Ford wasn't prepared to *be* one of those triggers, to see his son shrink away from him in terror, the way he always had from his own father.

Just as a tear started to crawl down his cheek, he heard a saxophone. He looked up Lincoln and saw a well-dressed brother in a black driver's cap, similar to his own, leaning against a lamppost, wailing the blues. He crossed the street and walked toward him. The brother kept playing as Ford took a heavy seat on the stoop. He felt more water cross his cheek, but these blues were just what he needed.

He took out his cell and again browsed to the video of his son dancing, the one that the college paper had posted back in October. It played on a loop as the sax man blew long, lamenting phrases, each fading into the chilled air before the next one began.

THIRTY

HE PICKED A TIME WHEN HE KNEW BILL AND ROY WOULD be in school. Of the familiars, only Charlotte and Mrs. Berry attended.

"Mr. Turner, please feel free to tell us anything that might help us in our search for the truth."

Sammy spoke in a slow tempo, like the slowest blues he had ever accompanied.

"By the time I arrived, Alfonso was already in the van. I saw when the officer yanked him out. I heard his head crack against the bumper, just like you can hear on the video. My heart stopped. And then they started beating on him."

"Is that your voice on the video saying, quote, 'Great fucking Dizzy! What the hell are they doing?'"

The panel sat patiently.

"Yes."

"Did you hear any of the officers say anything prior to Mr. Berry being pulled out of the van?"

Another pause before he answered, "No."

"Thank you, Mr. Turner. Is there anything else you would care to add?"

Sammy sat very still. Scattered coughs and fidgets punctured the silence.

"It was 1959. I was about 12. We lived on Carver Street next to one of the bars, The Owl. It was a two-story joint. I could see into the upstairs room from my bedroom window. I liked watching them dancing." Remembrance of their tender faces touching while slow-dancing brought a glow briefly to his face. "It got raided one day, like so many bars did. Police started hassling people, hitting them. Some of the guys upstairs jumped out the window to get away. It was a good drop, but they risked it, 'cause if you got arrested, they printed your name in the paper.

"One guy didn't make it. He impaled himself on a cast-iron fence post. I'll never forget the way his face looked, tongue stuck out, eyes bulging. His arms and legs flailed for a bit before he went limp. They had to saw off the post to get him down. The newspapers reported the raid, printed names, but glossed over the man on the fence, calling it 'a minor incident.' Someone posted flyers telling the truth. I still have one. His name was Stevie Sampson. He loved to dance. Stevie survived four days with that pole stuck inside him before he died.

"I went into shock. Didn't speak for a month, just played my drums. Finally, my dad come up to me and ask if I'd seen the police raid. I nodded my head and started crying. I couldn't stop. I don't think I've ever cried so much in my life. My dad took hold of me and said real soft, almost whispering, 'Shhhh. That ain't gonna happen to you. When you grown, they won't be chasing folks out the bars no more. Know why? 'Cause you gonna see a better world, Son. A better world is waiting for you.'"

Mrs. Berry handed Charlotte a tissue behind Sammy's back and used one herself.

"I'd had nightmares where I was the man on the fence with my eyes bulging and my tongue stuck out. I thought that was how my life would end. I don't know how my dad knew, but he knew.

"For thirty-eight years, my store on Carver Street has been a safe space for young folks coming out into the life. That's my contribution to make it better."

Sammy felt his throat tighten. He squeezed shut his eyes and bowed his head slightly.

"But I couldn't do nothing for Alfonso!" he shouted.

Mrs. Berry put her arm around him.

"This can't happen again," he said softly. "We can't go backward. Not now. Not now. Not now. Not now." His voice faded like the last track on an LP.

"Thank you, Mr. Turner," Larkin said.

Sammy rose slowly. Chairman Larkin stood, as did the rest of the panel and the audience. All remained standing as Sammy and Charlotte left the room.

THIRTY-ONE

AUNTIE VERA HUNG PROMINENTLY ON HER LIVING ROOM
wall a photo of Isherwood holding a camera. In October,
Bill barely took notice of it or the other photos that
stretched up to the high vaulted ceiling. So many faces. His inner
historian must have recorded the gallery subconsciously, because
now, months later, no longer in tears and despair, he could recall
the faces and the stories they evoked, the history they told—now
that he was about to become the camera.

Bill came around to the dumpster area behind the Student
Union. He saw Victor and two other brothers. One was as tall as
Victor, square-jawed, intense, but had large eyes that softened his
features. The other was shorter, around Bill's height, dressed in
black. Victor introduced them as Michael and Fred, respectively.
Jameel soon joined them. He asked if Cliff was coming. If he can,
Victor said.

"Alright." Jameel blew out a deep breath. "Thanks for coming,
y'all. This means a lot to me. I got some truth I need to lay on them.
They won't wanna hear it, but it's gotta be said, OK? So it might
get a little real up there, is what I'm saying. So—"

"We got your back, bruh," Victor said.

Jameel gave him a tight, back-patting hug. They held it for a while. Michael and Fred rubbed Jameel on the shoulders. Bill looked on, his lingering issues about Jameel lessened by the sight of these brothers supporting each other.

"Thanks," Jameel said. He and Victor released. "OK. So I think we should go in staggered. You three go on. Enter maybe one at a time, alright? I don't know how crowed it will be, but try to spread yourselves around as best you can. Victor, you should go last. When you're in, text me, then Bill and I will come up. OK?"

They moved out. Jameel turned to face Bill.

"Will this shirt work?" Bill asked.

"Let's check." He stuck his iPhone in the front pocket. "Yeah. Just right."

"I'm your camera."

Jameel nodded like he caught the reference. He took his cell back and started fiddling with it.

"Try to keep it trained on me, alright?"

"Were Fred and Michael in ASA before the split?"

"Uh-huh. They're good guys. Glad they could make it."

"You said it was gonna get real. How real is real?"

Jameel smiled briefly. "We'll find out. How's Alfonso doing?"

"About the same. He liked the Maui Wowie."

Jameel looked up from his cell. "Thanks for doing this, Bill." His eyes lingered, just the way Alfonso described. Bill could see how easy it was to fall into them. "You take care of 'Fonso for me, alright?"

Jameel's phone buzzed. <<In>>

"Come on. It's show time."

They waited until they got outside the room before turning on the video recorder and positioning the phone in Bill's pocket. Jameel entered first, then Bill. A packed house of unfamiliar faces. The room felt very still, like their sudden appearance stopped everyone in midsentence. Victor made space in front of the patio door. Bill walked through hurriedly, awkwardly. He risked a quick peek in his shirt pocket to make sure that the phone was still recording and saw enough of the screen to see that it was.

Cynthia sat at the desk. Leon and Tamesha sat on the sofa. Jameel stood in the middle of the room.

"Excuse the interruption, Madam President."

"You're always welcomed, Jameel," Cynthia said. "All brothers and sisters are. But we were in the middle of a discussion—"

"That can wait, Madam President. I've come to testify. I got some things I need to get off my chest."

No one spoke. Folks adjusted in their seats a bit. Tamesha put her book down on her lap.

"I've been doing some heavy soul-searching and I need to come clean about some things. Some of you remember that back in high school I had a lot of girlfriends. That was a lie. In the process, I hurt a lot of fine sisters, some of whom held deep affection for me. That was wrong. And I'm sorry. I fronted on a lot of things, to stay popular, to keep it 100." He glanced at Leon and Tamesha, blinked slowly. "In reality, I was the definition of weak. In the process, I hurt a lot of people. For instance, I have nothing against Cliff. He's more together than most of us put together. I'm sorry for the things I said about him, behind his back. I'm sorry." He chewed his lower lip for a moment. "But there is one person I've hurt more than any other." Tears came to his face. "The one person I never had no business hurting because he's everything to me. He means more to me than anyone alive." He clenched his fists. "I hurt him in high school by playing him, leading him on. And then, when we finally got together, I hurt him again by outing him when he wasn't ready. His name is Alfonso Rutherford Berry III. And I'm here to tell you that I love him."

As Tamesha shifted in her seat, as Cynthia went deer-in-headlights, as Leon folded his arms in front of his chest, some in the room began to clap. A few hands at first, but it grew from its own momentum, taking Jameel totally by surprise. The unexpected support added strength to his voice.

"So yeah, I'm a same-gender-loving African American. When you hurt someone you really care about, you take something away from yourself. I didn't realize how damaged I was until someone literally knocked some sense into me." Bill smiled to himself, but stayed in character. "So that's why I'm here, to make it right." He took out a wad of paper from the pouch of his hoodie. "I also found out some interesting things about Alfonso's attack that I want to share. He didn't fall, he was pushed. The main pusher is in this room.

"The Party got humiliated after Alfonso shut down their bogus demonstration. So they decided to get back at him. *They* called the police that night from a payphone, pretending to be upset neighbors." Some audibly gasped. "They bragged about it on their message board afterward. Let's hear what they had to say."

He held out the sheets in front of him.

"'You see that video? Guess he's sorry now, yo.' Signed, Brother Bart X. 'Now he knows how it feels to be a real nigga. LOL. Bet he wished he stayed in the damn closet.' Signed, Brother Milton. 'Let's hope he daddy'—sic—'take up where the police left off. I'm sure his whole body hurts now! Told y'all it was a good call to make!' Signed, Brother Leon."

"That's fucked up, Leon!" someone said very loudly.

Victor shook his head. Cynthia gave her beau major side eye. Even Tamesha leaned away from him on the sofa. Bill remained very still, present in his duty, but inside he was popping.

"I got a whole lot more, but you see my point. This mighty fine gentleman right here"—he pointed at Leon—"instigated The Party into calling the police on a fellow black man, something strictly against Party policy, last I recall. And then, even after that heinous beating, even after that horrific video came out, even after Alfonso suffered a major concussion and was in a coma for two months, even after Alfonso nearly *died*, he pats himself on the back. Job well done, job well done. Yeah, you did it Brother Leon. You are now the World's Biggest Homophobe!"

Leon said nothing, but the muscles in his neck grew taut.

"So the question for the rest of y'all is simple. Do you want to be known as the world's biggest haters of queer people? Or do you want to change that by banning the hate and those who practice it?"

Sybil spoke up from a back corner of the room.

"A few of us here were with Alfonso in Professor Euclid's class last semester. We came to find out what the group was doing *for*

Alfonso. Now it sounds like it did things *to* Alfonso. Leon, you had problems with Alfonso all last semester. But this is going way beyond too far. Now you owe him some major restitution." Some folks snapped their fingers.

Cynthia cleared hear throat very slightly. She sat up, hands folded on her lap.

"Leon, is any of this true?"

He ignored her, rose very slowly, squared up in front of Jameel.

"You want something, brother?" Jameel asked.

Leon crunched his face into a foul expression, hocked, then spat in Jameel's face. With Jameel's eyes stung closed, Leon grabbed his shoulders and head butted him quick and hard. Jameel stumbled and fell backward. The footballer fell on top of him and started pounding him repeatedly in the face.

Everyone jumped to their feet. Cynthia covered her mouth. Victor, Fred, and Michael went to pry Leon off of Jameel. A few others joined them. Bill wanted to get into it, too, but to beat the shit out of Leon. Instead, he thought of Auntie Vera, remembered his role. He stood on a chair to get a better view.

Cliff walked into the room and saw the pileup. He joined the masses trying to pry Leon loose. After some struggle they managed, throwing him onto the sofa. Two sat on him while a third pressed hard against his legs. Jameel remained motionless on the floor, face up, nose bleeding, right eye swollen nearly shut.

Bill finally broke character. He rushed to Jameel, got on his knees beside him.

"What the fuck is wrong with you people?" he yelled. "Call 9-1-1, now!"

Jameel touched him on the thigh.

"You get it all?" he asked softly.

"Everything, sistah."

"Thank you, my camera."

THIRTY-TWO

Ms. Hurston," Chairman Larkin said, "your video has provided the most informative testimony available to us. Thank you for sharing it."

Vera bowed her head at an angle. Restraint marked her demeanor.

"And thank you for coming. We just have a few questions to help us contextualize your work. Were you at the needle exchange from the beginning?"

"No. I had been there earlier in the day during the health fair."

"When did you arrive that evening?"

"Nearly a quarter to 8, just minutes before the time stamp seen on the video."

"And what specifically brought you back out to the site of the needle exchange?"

"Samuel Turner called me."

"He called you because there was an anticipation that something might happen?" Chairman Larkin asked.

"Yes."

"Now, there has been some confusion over something on the recording. Some have testified that Officer Fitz, prior to pulling Mr. Berry out of the van, said, and I'm quoting, 'Don't you kick me, boy.' Officer Fitz denies saying this and the audio isn't clear."

"I heard him say it."

"Are you certain, Ms. Hurston?"

"Quite certain. If you look at the recording, you'll see he says it after Alfonso taps him on the knee as he's backing out of the van."

"Thank you, Ms. Hurston. How has this event affected you, personally?"

"Profoundly. As an African American transgender woman, my whole life has been a fight against cruelty. I was subjected to much cruelty growing up. I'm part of a network that helps homeless trans youth escape cruelty and find safe shelter. My work as a photographer and documentarian has largely focused on how cruelty can disrupt at-risk communities. Events such as this vile beating can terrorize whole communities for years to come. What happened to Alfonso Berry was one of the cruelest things I have ever seen."

"Thank you. Thank you very much, Ms. Hurston."

THIRTY-THREE

AMEEL SUFFERED A MILD CONCUSSION AND NEEDED stitches around his right eye. Miraculously, he did not lose any teeth. After an overnight stay in the hospital, he went to his parents' place in the suburbs.

Roy, Bill, and Alfonso took the commuter train out to see him on Saturday. Jameel's father came to the station to pick them up. He greeted them warmly, but saved his biggest hug for Alfonso, happy to see him getting around, even if by cane. He did not, however, hide his anger toward Leon.

"My wife never did like that boy," he said as they drove to the house. "He'll pay. That motherfucker will pay."

Jameel, sitting up in bed, put his Huey Newton reader down when Carlton's Posse walked into his room. An eyepatch covered his right eye. The other looked bruised, but not swollen. When Alfonso's stare became too intense, he looked away.

"'Fonso, Roy, you mind if you give Bill and me a moment, please?" he said softly.

"Sure," Roy said. They left the room.

Jameel smiled as he looked directly at Bill.

"Shoulda recognized who you were after you spanked my ass on the court first time." Bill chuckled. "I deserved every tumble." He scooted over. "Sit down, sit."

Bill sat on the edge of the bed.

"I wasn't expecting him to go HAM on my ass. With that head of his, he don't need no helmet." He giggled until he started to cough. "I'm so sorry you had to see that."

"I'm just glad you're healing." He took Jameel's hand. "That was one of the bravest fucking things I've ever seen."

"When the blue-ribbon panel said that the police call was a 9-1-1 from a payphone, I was like, huh. I went to their message board on a hunch, figuring they'd brag about it. Sho'nuff." Bill nodded. "Those assholes thought they had purged my access. Idiots. I hacked their site my eyes closed. I wanted to destroy Leon."

"But he fucked you up, babe."

"I fucked him up worse. His ugly ass is off the football team now. They got a zero-tolerance rule for fights. And he missed a game behind his bullshit. He wasn't on the roster, but they still want you to go. I exposed his ass so now he can kiss his scholarship and his 'great' NFL career goodbye."

"Cliff thinks Leon might get expelled. And he's talking about sensitivity training for ASA."

"Good. We did it, my camera. I can't thank you enough."

"You sure you'll be alright?"

"Promise." He kissed Bill's hand. "You're fierce, Bill Hawk. I'm gonna miss you."

Bill went into the dining room. Everyone sat around the table.

"He wants to see you, Fro."

Alfonso stood up and walked slowly to Jameel's room. It was only after he shut the door behind him that they realized he walked without his cane.

He sat on the bed like Bill had. For a while they said nothing, each lost in his own thoughts.

"I feel like I'm seeing my double," Alfonso said.

"Is this what you looked like?"

"That's what they said."

"How do you look?"

"Like shit."

Both laughed, breaking the spell. They lay down together.

"You didn't have to do that. You could have just told me."

"The hell I didn't. You taught me the importance of not living a lie. I had to face up, regardless of the consequence." He snapped a slow, swinging beat. "*Chivalrous ain't frivolous, if your knight keep it tight, it'll be alright.*"

"Nice." They cuddled, the sides of their faces touching. "Your dad said you moved out of your apartment."

"Yep. In December. Dropped out of school, too. Cut all my ties. Had to. I knew once I did this, they'd come after me."

"Seriously?"

"I am very serious. The Party's gettin' tore up online. #ThePartyIsOver. They blame me. Shit's already happened. One of my old neighbors told me that someone threw a rock through the window in my old apartment."

"Damn."

"Uh-huh. We tend to cut folks a lot of slack when we think they're on the 'good side,' know what I mean? A whole lotta folks in that group got passes they don't deserve. To be honest, some of them brothers just ain't too stable in the head."

He looked at Alfonso, began stroking his face.

"I sure am gonna miss my old place. It's where we finally did it. That was a magical evening. I'll never forget it."

"Are you gonna stay here? What are you gonna do?"

"Moving to the Bay Area. They can't touch me on the West Coast. I got half a dozen start-up ideas in my head. And if they don't pan out, I can transfer to Cal or whatever, and then get a tech job. I feel freer than I've ever felt in my life."

"You gonna change your name? Go by Wallace?"

"Hell, naw. I still ain't no Wallace. I was thinking maybe Dub-J. That's pretty dope."

"Wallace Jameel Wilkerson. Alright, then, Dub-J." He kissed Jameel on the lips.

Hands soon slipped beneath shirts, jeans, and underpants.

THIRTY-FOUR

Wednesday, 10 a.m., Third Week

BILL SAT ON ONE SIDE OF ROY, JEREMIAH ON THE OTHER, and next to Jeremiah sat Vera. Sammy wanted to attend, but couldn't. The whole hearing process depressed the hell out of him. Showing up for his own appointment was hard enough. I'll be alright, Big Guy, Roy told him.

"Mr. Prince, I understand that you were not a witness to the events that happened that evening," Chairman Larkin said.

"That is correct, sir."

"But you have a sworn statement you wish to read from Mr. Alfonso Berry III?"

"Yes, that's correct, if that's OK."

"We've received several sworn statements and normally we just add them to the record. However, seeing as this is from Mr. Berry himself, it is entirely appropriate for it to be read aloud for the record. Please proceed, Mr. Prince."

———————

Previous Saturday, Late Afternoon

The boys improvised a ceremony. With Sylvester playing and a wooden spoon posing as a sword, they officially dubbed a kneeling Jameel

293

a member of Carlton's Posse. He proudly accepted. Jameel's parents bought them Chinese takeout for dinner. Later, Alfonso asked Jameel's parents if he could spend the night. Of course you can, they said. They drove Bill and Roy back to the Huck, then stayed in town with Mr. Wilkerson's brother. Alfonso and Jameel had the place to themselves the whole weekend.

———

"Forgive me if this rambles a bit or if I seem to go off topic," Roy began. "I don't know where to start or where to end this." Roy paused, took a sip of water. He had read it over a few times, preparing his reading like he would a performance. Parts still affected him, though. "This past weekend was the best I've had since getting out of the hospital. I spent it with a man I care about very deeply and who cares for me. His name is Jameel. He has provided you with evidence proving that a group with animus against me called the police that night, not neighbors of the clinic. I leave it to the Panel to decide if this evidence is relevant or usable. I can say that it has provided me with some closure, knowing how I got to where I am. But now my pain goes beyond the physical and psychological. Now I feel intense emotional heartache. Jameel got this evidence at the risk of his own safety and he must now leave the area. After he's gone, it may be a long time before I ever see him again. But despite this additional hardship, Jameel has given me something that lately I have been sorely missing: hope."

———

They sat on a park bench and ate gelato from a nearby shop. Burnt-caramel for Jameel. Cookie-dough for Alfonso. Their canes rested on either side of them. We must look like some old couple, Jameel joked, hobbling around with our walking sticks. He took a selfie, making sure to include the canes, tagging it "lovers for 50 years." Are you getting around much? he asked. A little, Alfonso replied.

———

"My doctors keep remarking on what good progress I've made. I suppose. It's hard for me to see sometimes, knowing where I was versus where I am currently. I'm used to going and coming when I please. Now, I'm sheltered inside most of the time, usually not going any farther than the deck on Bingo's building. But on the day Jameel revealed what he had learned, that morning I went to Sammy's store on Carver Street for the first time in months. It felt like a homecoming. In fact, Sammy put on our special track, 'Happy Reunion' by Duke Ellington. That's what was playing the very first time I visited his store last fall. Like before, I lost myself in Paul Gonsalves's sax solo. I drank the strong black coffee from Sammy's old tin drip pot. I laughed with some of the store regulars. Henny Penny and Ms. Ashley were going at it again. It felt good to be there, and also sad to be there. The tune 'Happy Reunion' has a melancholy edge to it, in contrast to its title. The first time I heard it, I envisioned two old friends meeting up after a long absence, perhaps for the last time. At the time, I was thinking of the past, and the many times my late cousin Carlton visited the store. Was I the ghost of my cousin, coming to say a final goodbye? But now I wonder if I had been projecting into the future. Was this our final reunion? What lies ahead for me now?"

——◦——

They discussed black Twitter and the debate in some circles about whether Alfonso's beating fit into the #BlackLivesMatter narrative. Some of the responses were disturbing, saying that he didn't qualify because he was still alive. Some felt that since Alfonso didn't get beat up at a black event, that it really didn't count, suggesting that it was more a case of #QueerLivesMatter. Others found such lack of intersectionality ludicrous. And so on. Alfonso said he even heard a podcast debate the issue for over thirty minutes. Jameel rolled his eyes, sucked his teeth. People are idiots, he said.

——◦——

"I've become a meme. Pictures of my beaten body, accompanied by various words, can be found all over social media. They are shared by thousands I've never met. The support I've received has been and continues to be overwhelming, and I am deeply touched by it. At the same time, being a meme has taken away part of my personhood. 'By any means necessary,' 'I have a dream,' 'The Talented Tenth,' are all memes. Malcolm, Martin, and Du Bois evolved beyond these memes, yet folks focus on the meme and not the full person. A meme is a moment in time. I am trying to get past that moment and on with the rest of my life."

In bed, lying under the sheets and blankets, Alfonso told Jameel about his double vision during the beating and the dreamscape it created, how he doesn't know whether the police or his father beat him near to death. After he finished, Jameel turned to lie on his back and stare at the ceiling.

"What's he been doing lately," Jameel asked.

"Working on a case against the city," Alfonso said.

"I went into the van because a client asked for information on drug abuse treatment programs and that's where the brochures were located. After I crawled in, I felt someone tugging on my leg. I started to crawl out and that's when I got yanked. From that moment, my memory becomes fluid. I could feel the boots and clubs as the police beat me. But what I experienced and envisioned was the weight of all the homophobia and all the racism I've ever known raining down on me in one big effort to kill me. I thought I was going to die. I think if I didn't have such a beautiful network of friends and family—" Roy stopped. His voice cracked. He cleared it. "I probably would have."

"The last time I saw my father face to face, I blacked out. Apparently I started screaming. I don't know how to get past that."

Jameel lay silently.

"What are you thinking?" Alfonso asked.

"Have you told your father?"

"No. How can I?"

"Just like you told me how you really felt. I printed and laminated 'The Profoundest.' I'm never letting that go. It's beautiful."

Alfonso smirked a little. "I don't even remember what I wrote."

"Yes, you do. Just be straight with him. If he really loves you—and I think he does—then he'll get it."

Alfonso reached over and held on to Jameel as he faced the ceiling. "Sure wish you weren't leaving."

"I'm not going right away. Gotta heal up first."

Alfonso kissed Jameel's cheek, then held on tightly.

"I used to dance and was about to start studying it again. That's on hold. I don't know when I'll be able to go back to school. My life has come to a stop. I'm trying to find the switch to turn it back on again."

THIRTY-FIVE

BLACK HISTORY MONTH. THE SHORTEST MONTH. THEIR month. A ballad sung sweet and low. The threat of its ending caused only minor discord, a melancholy chorus between otherwise pleasant verses.

The Party brothers kept up their slander and threats against Jameel in cyberspace. Another minor discord that largely kept them out of the city. So they spent most of the month in the suburbs with Jameel's parents. However, one week they stayed at Bingo's. The leatherman went out of town to a conference, so they had his condo to themselves. The Party won't find you here, Alfonso assured him. Jameel agreed. Carver Street's not their beat. On Sunday, they hosted Eunice, Belinda, and Lucy for brunch. Jameel made French toast. Alfonso made a fruit salad. Bill and Roy visited one night. Roy made vegetarian lasagna, with some sausage on the side for the carnivores. Sammy also made dinner for the couple another night. The rest of the time they binge-watched TV shows, movies, they talked and cuddled, they chilled.

All too soon came the last weekend. Alfonso dreaded it, but Jameel's parents had a surprise for them. They booked a grand suite for the boys at a hotel near the airport. They spared no expense: champagne and caviar, a lobster dinner for the first night, and a box of condoms. Alfonso and Jameel put the suite to good use by never leaving it. Over their lobster, Jameel played Mary Stallings,

"Watching You Watching Me." Hope this ain't too corny, he said. Alfonso stopped eating and listened. Stallings's voice glided over piano, bass, and drums. The sparse arrangement felt more bittersweet than Bill Withers's original, more vulnerable. No, it's not corny, Alfonso said, it's our history: Our secret language; Our fun and (video) games; And your eyes always gave you away. He got up from the table. May I have this dance? Jameel stood and held him securely as they swayed very slowly to the sultry melody, cheek to cheek. They ended up in the bedroom, where clothes quickly fell off. Jameel made a bet that they would have sex in each room before the end. Alfonso said, *you're on!*

That night, while lying in bed together, Alfonso finally heard the question he felt lingering over them.

"Will you come with me?"

Last Saturday of February
Berry Residence, Beacon Hill

Ford stared at his laptop screen. Eunice entered with two glasses of wine. She sat on the edge of his desk. He took a glass.

"Thanks, Eu."

"Is it ready?"

"Yeah." He sighed. "Yeah, I'm ready to file." He closed the laptop, sipped some wine. "I'm going to announce after the Panel presents its report Monday morning."

Her bare foot stroked his thigh through his slacks. Ford savored the sensation.

"Have you heard from Alfonso?" she asked.

"He emailed back and gave his OK, but said that he wasn't going to be there. Jameel flies out that morning." He took another sip. "I hope they're having a good time this weekend." He wrapped his hand around her ankle. "I hope he'll be happy. I want him to be happy, Eu."

He wished he could have gone to the brunch last weekend, but thought it best if he kept his distance. The birthday episode still tortured him. The last thing he wanted was to cause more pain.

"That was a beautiful dinner," he said. "Thank you."

Eunice got off the desk and kissed him, then walked out of the study. Baby steps, Ford thought, but a start.

"I can't," Alfonso said after a long pause.

"Why?"

"I'm not whole. What would I do with myself?" He sighed. "I can't dance anymore." Tears filled his eyes. "You saw what happened when I tried."

It happened during their dinner with Sammy. "Lavender Veil Blues" came on and Alfonso got up and started his routine. The slow hand and arm movements came off effortless, but all went to shit when he tried to lift up one leg. It felt like a chasm opened beneath his feet. He fell over. Jameel rushed to him. An angry fist pounded on the floor. *Dammit! Dammit! Dammit! Dammit! Dammit!*

"I've tried my tai chi. I can't even do that. And forget whipping my head around or moving fast, 'cause the room won't stop spinning when I stop. The doctors say that I might never be fully OK again."

"They also said you'd never walk again. And you're doing it."

"Baby steps. I can't even carry a fucking five-pound bag of sugar without worrying about falling. I'm dependent on people to do so much now."

"There's gotta be treatment programs that can help you."

"The thing Carlton feared the most was losing his independence. Until the very end, he never did."

Jameel kissed Alfonso, then he got out of bed. He walked naked across the room to the desk that sat in front of the floor-to-ceiling window of their suite. At thirty-two stories up, no one could see the floor show Jameel put on, apart from Alfonso looking at him from the bed. Jameel sat down and opened his laptop.

"What are you doing?" Alfonso asked.

"Finding you a program to help you get your balance back."

Alfonso got up to join him. Jameel typed with one hand and fondled his boy's ass with the other.

Monday Morning
Sammy's Store

Charlotte entered, the usual bag of croissants in her hand. She walked to the back room and poured herself a mug of Monday blues. Sammy already had his. He sat at the counter with the TV going, a live report from City Hall. She sat next to him. Henny Penny walked in and joined them, sitting on the counter. They saw Vera in the hearing room, camera in hand. Harry and Bingo sat together. Then they saw the Berry family enter—Ford, Eunice, Belinda, and Lucy. Bill and Roy entered behind them. Lots of camera flashes accompanied their arrival.

"Bill and Roy look good in those suits," Charlotte said.

"Uh-huh," Sammy grunted.

Members of the blue-ribbon panel entered the hearing room and took their seats. The audience stilled. Chairman James Larkin gaveled the session to order.

"We have completed our work and are ready to present the results of our investigation on the beating of Alfonso R. Berry III."

"I don't like being in this room," Bill said softy to Roy.

"I heard that."

"Copies of the entire report have been provided to the mayor, the city council, the city administrator, the chief of police, the officers involved in the beating and their representatives, and to the family of Mr. Alfonso Berry III. Copies will be provided to the media after this briefing. I will summarize our main findings. Number one, the responding officers escalated the situation.

Number two, responding officers did not observe the county's policy to allow a county-certified needle exchange program to continue uninterrupted, so long as no criminal activity took place. We found no evidence that criminal activity took place that evening warranting a response. Number three, no official announcement was made advising citizens that arrests were imminent when officers descended upon Mr. Berry. Number four, excessive force was used on Mr. Berry, in particular by Officer Watt, Officer Lee, Officer Sanders, and Officer Fitz."

—✦—

Other Carver Street Irregulars gathered around the little TV, arms folded and lips pinched. Bernard looked ready to hit the streets again in protest.

"So nothing's being done to the cops that beat him," Otto said.

"Didn't Fitz resign?" Henny Penny asked.

"Uh-huh," Sammy said. "Coward."

Larkin continued to describe what reforms the police department needed to undertake. Sensitivity training. Community-based policing programs. Regular community meetings.

"Baby steps," Angela said.

"Not even," Charlotte said. "We did a report with these same conclusions ten years ago, when James was in office."

"I remember," Sammy said.

The hearing concluded. Coverage turned to talking heads analyzing the report. Folks in the store grumbled. You should be up there talking, someone told Charlotte. She said she had an interview that afternoon.

Henny Penny sat frozen in front of the TV. "Hey! Hey!" he called out. "Mr. Berry is suing the city for $10 million!"

Everyone crowded around the TV again.

—✦—

Ford stood on the steps of City Hall, his family, Bill, and Roy standing behind him.

"My son's life has been forever altered by this event. He will have need for continued medical care. His career as a dancer barely got off the ground when this attack happened. He must now undergo advanced and expensive treatment if he is to have any hope of restarting this career. We hold the city liable for the injuries inflicted and therefore we are seeking immediate and full redress."

"Now they're shitting bricks," Otto said.

"You think Alfonso has a case?" Henny Penny asked.

"Oh, hell yeah, he's got a case. But better than that, he's got Ford Berry going against them. Don't forget what his career was like before he got on the city council. After a while, folks didn't wanna see him coming, 'cause they knew they were gonna lose."

Monday Morning
The Hotel

Breakfast in bed, one last time. Orange juice, eggs, bacon, sausage, toast. No TV. However, Alfonso couldn't resist checking his cell. The mayor pledged that the city would adhere to the Panel's recommendations. At the same time, the grand jury announced it would not file charges against the officers. The case against Fitz hinged on whether he said, *Don't you kick me, boy!* The Panel recommended that he had, but the grand jury could not reach consensus. Thus, they could not establish animus. Videos ain't never enough, Jameel grumbled. I call him Der Teppichschlepper, Alfonso told Jameel, invoking both the Yiddish and German meanings of "Schlepper." Teppichschlepper! Ich bin kein Teppich, Schlepper! Carpet mover! I'm not a carpet, jerk! Lots of chatter about his suit against the city also filled cyberspace. He had emailed his father links to facilities with programs for head trauma victims.

The best one we found is in Berlin, he wrote. Ford upped the damages amount by $2 million based on that information.

"Your father's gonna kick their butts," Jameel said.

"Yeah."

"I'm thinking of that suit he did against the garment factory, when they forced their workers into overtime and wouldn't pay them for it. Man, he went gangsta on their asses."

Alfonso nodded, staring at his cell.

"You OK, 'Fonso? Should I not talk about your dad?"

"No, it's cool." Then he realized that during their whole time together he never woke up screaming. "I'm gonna miss you."

Jameel took their breakfast tray and put it on the tray holder beside the bed. Then he gave Alfonso a deep kiss.

"Let me show you how much I'll miss you," he said.

He got out of bed and guided Alfonso to do the same. Then he took hold of him and pushed him against the floor-to-ceiling window. Their lips mingled and sloshed, until Jameel went down Alfonso's naked body. He took his boy's cock and sucked it good and hard. Alfonso moaned. Jameel started licking his balls and the inside of his thighs, staring at his reflection in the glass. He stood up again.

"Don't stop," Alfonso said.

"Fuck me against the window."

Alfonso smirked. "Get a rubber, boy."

Jameel took one from the nightstand and ripped it open while holding it in his teeth. He took the condom and spat out the wrapper. Then he worked it onto Alfonso's hard cock, pressing him into the window, his tongue inside his boy's mouth. They flipped around so that Jameel was against the window. His own hard-on pressed flat against the glass as Alfonso began pumping from behind. Both got turned on by their exhibitionism, the city sprawled out before them, the cool winter sun striking their bodies.

Jameel's folks drove Alfonso to Bingo's from the airport. He held it together until they got to the Huck and drove up Lincoln. They passed the park and Alfonso began to cry. Mr. Wilkerson immediately apologized for driving past the beating location. No, Alfonso said, that wasn't it. That hadn't even occurred to him. His eyes focused instead on the black tearoom, where they first kissed.

He stayed in his room all day, crying and sleeping. The Mary Stallings song played constantly. Instead of denying his blues, he went all-in. He ate next to nothing. Cell phone stayed on Do Not Disturb. At close to 11 p.m., he finally came out. He walked down the stairs with his cane, its first use in over a week. In the fridge, he found some leftover Cambodian food, lemongrass chicken and veggies. Perfect. He popped it in the microwave, then ate it out of the container while sitting at the breakfast counter. Bingo came down in his bikini briefs. Alfonso reached out his arms and Bingo obliged with a bear hug. Afterward, Bingo went to the fridge for a beer, offered one to Alfonso.

"Your dad did an interview this afternoon. I recorded it if you want to see it."

"Thanks."

Alfonso flopped onto the couch, went to his cell. The Posse had sent texts. He read them and sent both Roy and Bill a reply. <<Hanging. Crying. Eating something at last. Let's get together soon. Love you madly.>>

He turned on the TV. The president of the police union was on. He called the blue-ribbon panel's report a piece of anti-cop propaganda.

"Teppichschlepper," he said, switching off the news and starting the interview.

The reporter sat in a comfy chair and Ford on a sofa. He felt no distress watching his father on screen. He had, in fact, started watching old videos of him on YouTube, just to see if he could. He still didn't know what a face-to-face would feel like.

He zapped through the commercials while sipping his beer.

———◇———

"Welcome back. Former city councilman Ford Berry is here with me. Councilman, I'm sorry, Mr. Berry, that's what you prefer, isn't it?"

Ford smiled and nodded.

"Mr. Berry, before the break, we discussed the blue-ribbon panel report and your lawsuit against the city. But now I want to talk about your relationship with your son Alfonso. Previously, you went on record denouncing your son for his involvement with the Huckleberry Community Clinic."

"Yes."

"You called him naïve for supporting their work."

"Yes."

"How has your perception changed? Has your view of the clinic changed, or just your view of your son?"

"Alicia, I made a lot of mistakes during my career in politics, clouded by a lot of outmoded thinking. I first want to say that there is absolutely nothing wrong with the work done by the Huckleberry Community Clinic. The same people who run that clinic are the same ones who have been taking care of my son. The community needs dedicated healthcare professionals like that, so I hope that they reopen soon so that their work can continue and thrive."

"What about the needle exchange program, which was the main basis of your objections to the group?"

Ford shook his head. "My thinking was outmoded. And I used excuses, like the federal government's failure to fund such programs, to maintain an untenable position. Well, the government just quietly approved funding in January. I hope the HCC will be able to take advantage of that.

"I was not a collaborative person in office. Charlotte Hunter is a collaborative person. She will make an excellent councilmember."

"Are you endorsing Charlotte Hunter for your old seat?"

"Wholeheartedly. I think she will be terrific and will do wonders for the Huck. Alicia, I want to clear the air on some things, and one of them is my past relationship with Charlotte Hunter. Eight years ago, when I first ran for office, a newspaper published a letter that basically called her a highly derogatory name, an antigay slur. I said nothing about that attack and I did not distance my campaign from it. And I should have. It's too late to undo the damage that letter did to her campaign back then. But I do want to apologize to Ms. Hunter for the hurt and pain that letter caused her and her family. I should have done so sooner, and I didn't. And I'm very sorry."

He paused.

"And regarding my son. Regarding my son," his voice softening. "The testimonies his friends gave were gripping. Bill described the nightmares. Everything he said was true. My son's testimony, that Roy read, devastated me."

"He wrote that himself?"

"He wrote it himself, without any input from me." He paused, cleared his throat. "My son is not naïve. He's the bravest man I know, that I've ever known in my entire life. And he has taught me what it truly means to be a man, more than anyone else in my life."

"More than even your father, Assemblyman Berry?"

"Yes."

———◆———

Alfonso turned off the TV, leaned back, eyes closed. He thought of Roy and his father, their openness with each other, and couldn't imagine such a thing with his own father.

He picked up his cell.

"Yo, Thes. Am I waking you?"

"Not at all. Just finished making notes on this dog of a script I'm stuck with."

"That bad?"

"Girlfriend, please. They tell you that you can't start rejecting scripts until you get creds. So I guess that's what I'm doing. How are you?"

"I feel like shit. But damn, did we go out in style. I'll save the details for later. Maybe," he smirked.

Roy laughed.

"Did you see my dad's interview?"

"No."

"He apologized to Charlotte for the 'bulldyke' letter. Then he called me the bravest man he's ever known."

"Wow."

"Yeah. It kinda threw me for a loop. He didn't tell me that he was doing it. He just told me about the press conference."

"He never said anything about it. After the press conference, Bill and I went up to campus, in our suits."

"Hope you guys took selfies in the Cuddle Corner."

"Yeah, we did. I'll send it to you. But yeah no, I didn't know about your dad's interview."

"I feel like I should call him."

"Yeah?"

"I don't know. I feel like shit. My head's just—I'm not in the space to deal with anything, really."

"Send him a text. Or an email."

"Yeah—yeah."

Ford was in his study when the phone rang. Normally he let Eunice answer it, but when he saw Alfonso's name come up, he picked up the receiver.

"Hello? Son? It's your father."

"Hi, Dad."

"How are you? Are you at Bingo's?"

"I'm OK. We took Jameel to the airport this morning. He's gone. I'm having a hard time dealing with it."

"I'm sorry, son."

A long pause.

"I was just watching your interview."

"Yes."

"I just wanted to say thanks. Thank you."

"Son, I love you. I love you."

Another pause. Ford held the receiver anxiously against his face.

"Thanks. Bye, Dad." Alfonso hung up quickly.

Ford held the receiver for a while, before slowly putting it down.

Baby steps.

THIRTY-SIX

THE UNITY BANNER HUNG ABOVE THE CHOIR AND organist again. Early tulips decorated the pulpit and entrance to the sanctuary. Black folks donning Sunday threads saved for special occasions again filled the space with anticipatory chatter and socializing. Another community happening at Beacon Hill First Baptist Church. Johnson had called some of the other Southside reverends to see if they would participate. One said maybe, but turned into a no-show. The others shied away with mouths full of alibis and excuses. Community groups were similarly circumspect. The African Students Association was no longer at Johnson's beck and call. At Cliff's urging, Victor took over as interim president after Cynthia's abrupt resignation. And Zen Master V wasn't thinking about Johnson. Leon was under indictment and the threat of expulsion. Tamesha and other hangers-on that had supported Johnson in the past evaporated. No matter. Johnson knew how to run events and declared that he would fill every pew. Damn the haters. Indeed, a group of young folks came out of nowhere and promoted the event with the hashtag #NegroBlingFest, much to Johnson's glee. He felt vindicated when he stepped out to a full house, with spillover cramming the balcony.

"Friends," Johnson started, "we have been through a lot these past few months. Unrest has torn our community asunder. Our values have come under attack. Protests have desecrated this house of worship. But I come to you today with a renewed sense of hope. Yes, brothers and sisters, a new day is dawning. And with that new day comes rebirth and rejuvenation. Before discussing this new day, my friends, we must first assess our current situation to understand how we got to where we are so that we may chart the appropriate course going forward."

Mmm-hmmm. Yes. Yes. Amen.

"The crisis we face has, most disturbingly and alarmingly, robbed us of leadership, a voice within our city. How are our interests to be promoted without this vital voice? Perhaps we're spoiled, brothers and sisters. Perhaps we've counted on the historic Berry family for too much over the long decades that their men have represented this area."

Amen. Yes. Yes.

"We had Rutherford Berry, one of the first black attorneys in the state, who defended our community during the age of lynchings. We had Al Berry, Sr., longtime representative of this area in the state legislature. And we had his son, A. Rutherford Berry, II, Ford Berry, also an attorney, represent this area on the city council for just under eight years, until his abrupt resignation late last year. Ford Berry was a righteous man who bore witness to our struggles, our determination, and our unquenchable spirit for those many years. And we thank him for that."

Yes. Amen. Yes.

"But now, the former councilman has chosen a different path, a path he declares was necessitated by his family's recent tragedy. And while we certainly wish him and his family well as they continue to heal, we should note well that tragedy can often show the true colors of a man. This instance is no exception."

Amen. Amen.

"The tragedy involving Ford Berry's son was indeed a sorrowful affair, even if it was one of his son's own making. The ex-councilman himself once proclaimed that the clinic his son worked with did not represent the needs of this community. Just as those who suffer abuse in the park do so because they place themselves in danger, his son willingly participated with a group that engaged in illegal acts that required police intervention. Acts, I should remind you, that the ex-councilman spent most of his career fighting. Now, apparently, he supports them. True colors begin to emerge."

Amen.

"The legacy of Assemblyman Al Berry, Sr. is under threat. The man once charged with maintaining it has turned away from his path and calling. Temptation has led him astray. What are his sins? First, he abruptly quits his position, just like that. Second, he is turning around and biting the hands that once fed him, filing suit against the city on behalf of his son. He was a defender of righteousness, in the mold of his father. Now, he is using his God-given gifts to take from the community that has nurtured him, seeking monetary gain for a tragedy that was of his son's own making."

Crickets.

"We now must look elsewhere for a new champion. It is therefore my pleasure to present to you Mr. Walker Wright."

Wright stood from the front row and waved. He was a slender man with triangular sideburns whose limited stature was augmented by platform shoes and accentuated by an oversized suit.

"Mr. Wright will provide the guidance we seek as we approach the election of a new city councilman." Applause began. "A longtime member of this church, Mr. Wright will bring us the victory we deserve. He will challenge Charlotte Hunter and he will win. A new day is dawning!" Wright joined Johnson at the pulpit, waving at the congregation.

Derek, Lucy, and Belinda sat together in the very back of the church surrounded by their peers. They all had kept very quiet during Johnson's sermon.

"Come on," Belinda said.

They rose from the pews and made their way for the aisle. The rest of the church continued cheering, the loudest coming from the back half of the sanctuary and the balcony. Those in other sections continued their hand clapping just to keep up.

When the three came within six pews of the front, Johnson caught sight of them. His smile vanished. His leathered face wrinkled with confusion.

"How dare you!" Belinda shouted. "Our brother nearly lost his life in a racist, homophobic attack and now you're trying to say he deserved what happened? How dare you!"

"You're not a man of God! Liar! Liar!" Lucy screamed.

"Yo, you call yourself righteous?" Derek yelled. "Since when do the righteous call people 'faggot' like you did my big bruh, huh? Since when do the righteous fire someone for being gay, humiliate 'em, and then make 'em so full of shame and self-hate, that they're too scared to face their family again? Huh, bruh? What kinda— righteousness is that?"

"Now, now," Johnson said, flustered.

"You're not a man of God! You're not a man of God!" Lucy was nearly screeching.

"Belinda, Lucy," Johnson said, "this is not the time or place for this discussion."

"The hell is ain't!" Belinda said. "You ain't nothing but a hypocrite and a bigot!"

"Bigot! Bigot!" Lucy and Derek shouted in unison.

Just as three men in the front pew got up and approached the threesome with determined steps, a banner unfurled from the balcony. Thick black letters on white canvass read *#JUSTICE4ALFONSO*. The three brothers stopped and turned around as the whole back half of the main floor and the entire balcony erupted, standing, shaking their fists, and chanting.

Johnson jerked his head in shock. Nearly two-thirds of his congregants were really well-dressed protesters lying in wait, a Negro bling fest in revolt.

"Please! Please! This is not right!" Johnson pleaded.

"Was it right to say Alfonso got what he deserved?" Derek yelled. "Was it right to send my brother to the brink of *suicide?*"

"How dare you insult our father!" Lucy shouted.

"Black Lives Matter, Reverend!" someone shouted from the pews. "Get in line or get out of our way!"

Mrs. Parker stood in the front row of the balcony next to Smooth, Bill's tutorial pupil, shaking her fist along with all the young folks that surrounded her. When they started shouting PALPATINE! PALPATINE! at Johnson, she asked Smooth what that meant. He explained the reference to *Star Wars*'s wizened evildoer and she gleefully joined in.

Walker Wright looked visibly annoyed.

"Do something, Johnson!" he barked. "Call the damn cops! Get these bitches out of here! Do it!"

The mic picked him up. His words went all over the sanctuary. Now everybody clutched their pearls.

"You don't use that sort of language in here!" someone shouted.

"Since when are our young ladies 'bitches'?" shouted another.

The brothers who were approaching Belinda, Lucy, and Derek turned their attention to Mr. Wright. Some of the church matrons got up and joined them. They surrounded the pulpit and shouted at Wright, who tried in vain to backpedal.

"Of course I support the Berry family," he said, "and those girls have every right to their anger. It was terrible what happened to their brother." With astonishing speed, Wright threw his benefactor under the bus.

But the worse sight of all for Thad Johnson, the stuff of anxiety dreams for any preacher, was seeing his congregants rise, turn their backs on him, and walk out of his church. They left en masse. Soon only the protesters remained. They cheered their success before also departing. Belinda, Lucy, and Derek gave one another's high fives and hugs. They turned to leave, but then Derek hung back and ran toward the pulpit. The church matrons and brothers still surrounded it, but he pushed his way through. He wanted to get in Johnson's face. His mother loved and fully supported the takeover and protest, but not without a certain amount of internal conflict. It was, after all, the church. She had compromised with her misgivings by making Derek promise not to shout any profanity during the confrontation. And he didn't.

"Your ass got owned, didn't it, motherfucker!" he said softly to Johnson, inches from his face. Then he ran to catch up with the Berry sisters as they exited, all of them laughing and hanging off each other.

The bling fest trio joined Carlton's Posse on Bingo's deck. Other Carver Street Irregulars arrived at scattered intervals. The Leather Queen, clad in his apron, barbecued burgers—including some veggie ones for Roy—and had sodas, veggies, and chips on hand.

Everyone gathered around Alfonso and his Laptop to look at the various videos made during the takedown at the church. Bill nearly laughed himself hoarse. Derek stood next to him.

"I hope you're not upset about my mentioning suicide," Derek said. "It just came out."

Bill responded by kissing his baby bro on his forehead. They held each other for a spell.

"I promised Mom I would write a paper about this," Lucy said.

"I look forward to reading it," Alfonso said, all smiles.

"So, what did that fool have to say for himself?" Ms. Ashley said in his usual drawl.

"Not much," Belinda said. "He was all 'abada-abada-abada' like he forgot how to form words or something."

"Mmm-hmm. Turned into a motormouth, did he?" Aaron said. "Figures."

Harry couldn't stop laughing at the jerk Johnson picked to run against Charlotte.

Alfonso Googled Walker Wright. He was not a longtime member of the church, as Johnson claimed, having moved to town recently from DC. Black Twitter pulverized him.

Palpatine's Imperial Walker got a flat before he got out the gate.
Imperial Walker needs to give his daddy his suit back.
Imperial Walker meets Bitches Brew.

The last one sent Alfonso into hysterical laughter. Everyone asked what was up. He read the tweet aloud.

"That was from Sammy! When the hell did he get on Twitter?"

"Oh, I've been on for about a month, child. Where have you been?" he said, walking out onto the deck.

They all gave him a big hand. Charlotte followed, along with Mrs. Parker.

"That smells mighty fine, Bingo," Mrs. Parker said.

"You'll get the first one in just a minute, hon! You doing OK? You look tired."

"I haven't had that much fun in nearly fifty years, sugar!"

Lucy went up to Sammy as he sat down on one of the lounge chairs. Someone storified his tweet. He chuckled.

"But check this out," he said. "It's on the mainstream media already."

Lucy smiled as she read the headline aloud. "Walker Wright All Wrong—Steps in It During Debut!"

More shouting and cheering. The Berry sisters high-fived again.

Charlotte sat next to her old friend. They clasped hands for a bit. Sammy furiously read more from his iPhone.

"Samuel Turner, I never thought I'd see the day. Soon you'll be making music on your damn phone."

"Too late. I already started. I got the app the other day. Can't stop playing with it. Sure wish I knew what the hell I was doing." He looked up. "Royboy! When you gonna show me how to work this thing?"

"Eh!" he shouted back. "You'll figure it out before I can show you."

"Ugh," Sammy grunted. "That boy is useless. He-he-he."

"You know Johnson is toast now," Charlotte said.

"Just waiting for the headlines."

Alfonso ate his burger quietly, smiling and laughing with friends and relations as they passed nearby. Johnson's speech ran on his laptop. It felt surreal. He called Belinda over.

"Roy let me taste his veggie burger. It's good," she said.

"Oh, no! Don't be contaminating my sister with your veggie shit!"

Roy smiled and gave him the finger.

Alfonso turned back to the computer. "I can't believe this shit he said about Dad."

"Child, I was sitting there just getting more and more angry. If you had put a kettle to my forehead, the water would have boiled in a nanosecond."

"Dad worked with him for so long. For him to just turn like that."

"He's a coward and a fool, Alfonso. And let me tell you something, the people that were there for the service? Not all of them were getting mad at us. Some of them were clearly turned off by what he had said."

"Uh-huh."

"I think when we started up, that just gave them an excuse to leave."

Alfonso smiled. "You need to run for office, after Charlotte moves on up."

"Please. Let me finish school first."

She got up from kneeling next to him to get another burger. Alfonso took out his cell.

"Hey Mom. Yeah, we're all here at Bingo's having barbecue… Where you at? … Oh, nice!" They went to one of their favorite restaurants downtown.

"I just knew that man's true colors would show eventually," Eunice said. "It was inevitable."

Alfonso laughed. He paused a moment. "Can I talk to dad?" he said, softly.

"Of course, sweetheart."

Alfonso heard his father's voice over the phone.

"Hi, Dad … Yeah, it was great. I'm so proud of them. Derek, too. Have you seen any of the videos? They're all over the internet. … Yeah. Yeah. … That was all their friends from school, some from State. Belinda organized the hell out of it. … When you think you can stomach it, check out Johnson's speech. What a dick, excuse my language."

"All you kids got your language from me. At least that's what your mother tells me constantly," he said, chuckling. She nodded her head.

Alfonso laughed. He felt warmth from him for the first time in ages. "Well, I'll let you get back to your lunch. I just had to call. We're having fun here."

"Let's talk soon, Son. OK?"

"OK, Dad. Bye."

Alfonso saw Sammy looking at him. He smiled, then gave the old storekeeper a thumbs-up. Sammy responded in kind.

THIRTY-SEVEN

Sunday, Mid-March
Vera's Condo
How did I end up here?

DINNER, TUESDAY NIGHT AT SAMMY'S. JUST THE TWO OF
them. Jerk chicken, rice, and veggies. They listened to some
tracks Sammy created with his new music app and portable
keyboard. Reluctantly, Alfonso resisted the urge to dance, but he
liked what he heard. For dessert, he brought gingerbread and port,
which they took over to the sofa. Sammy switched on the stereo,
Gerry Mulligan and Ben Webster playing Strayhorn's "Chelsea
Bridge." Alfonso closed his eyes, soaked in the music and the port.

I have to watch the beating video, he told Sammy, I have to
see what really happened.

The brief chat with his father made him think that he was
moving beyond his double vision of beaning fastballs. But he
needed to be sure.

Then you should watch it, Sammy said, and you should watch
it alone.

Alfonso agreed, but he wanted to have someone nearby. He
knew it couldn't be Sammy. Auntie Vera?

Yes, Sammy said, she would do it.

That's how I came to be here. Waiting.

With his mother he spoke openly. They've chatted about Carlton, the clinic, dancing. Some of her oldest friends don't talk to her anymore. Seems these society ladies don't believe in accepting a gay child. She doesn't miss them. She always gives me hope, Alfonso said.

Sammy mentioned Ford's visit to the store last January. He admitted acting coolly toward him. After I dropped the attitude, Sammy said, that's when I saw that he was the most guilt-ridden, lost, and scared a man I had ever seen and that he'd do *anything* to regain your trust.

I am here. Waiting.

Alfonso sat in a big, futuristic, black chair, wide at the bottom, narrow at the top. A Niels Diffrient design, Vera said. He felt like a starship captain sitting in it, all the more since he sat in front of a ginormous computer screen with a photo of blue Neptune as its wallpaper. Vera called her office the Ready Room. All it lacked was a fish tank. She offered him a drink. Bourbon, but later, he said. She kissed him, then went to the living room.

He thought about seeing the Rodney King beating in Mrs. Turnbull's American History class in 11th grade, how silent everyone became. Trayvon's murder happened during his senior year. Other atrocities soon followed. But the King beating always stayed with him, a grainy documentary of evil from a time just before his birth.

He bit his lower lip, stared at his hand on the mouse.

Waiting.

Roscoe.

When he was 12, he took a swimming class at the local Y from some brother named Roscoe. He had a swimmer's build, that distinctive distribution of muscles and body fat that came from spending thousands of hours in the pool. He wore loose trunks during class, but Alfonso remembered seeing him in his Speedos during a meet. Forbidden fruit for a closeted youth. The image of that man in Speedos fueled many a jack-off session, even as he tried to convince himself at the time that it didn't. Roscoe came to mind because of one particular lesson, the one he never forgot. After having the class fart around on floating devices for a couple of weeks, Roscoe threw them into the deep end. Literally. One by one, he held each student tight and jumped into the deep end of the pool. Alfonso was so petrified that whatever lust he held for Roscoe vanished, even as the man's muscled arms pulled him close to his tight body. Before Alfonso could stall by asking questions, they were in the water. Instead of drowning, he marveled at the beauty of the pool from beneath, the glistening light bending gently under the waves. How cool is this? Roscoe never let go, and after a short period he brought them back to the surface. Alfonso never stopped smiling. He wanted to do it again.

"OK, Roscoe. Let's do this."

He clicked the mouse.

When he came out, Vera was still watching TV. He joined her on the sofa.

"Ready for your bourbon?"

"Oh, yeah. Thanks." He had forgotten. She poured herself some, too. He took a healthy gulp before putting it down.

"I wasn't expecting to feel like this," Alfonso said. "I'm so sorry."

"Sorry for what?"

"That you all had to see that. I can't imagine what that was like."

"Sweetie, it wasn't your fault." She turned to face him. "It wasn't your fault at all."

"I didn't have to go into the van like I did. It wasn't worth it, having you all there seeing me like that. All that blood. I should have stayed fucking put."

"Don't do that." Her clipped diction made her words sound severe. "You're taking the blame for something that happened to you that wasn't your fault. Don't. Don't." She took his head and cradled it on her shoulder. "You're like your cousin, a thoughtful, sensitive person. Quick to please, quick to take the blame when things go wrong. I know. Because I'm that person, too. I had to develop a thick callus. We have to, sweetie. Sometimes you have to give the world the finger just to keep your own damn self from going crazy, or getting fucked."

Alfonso reached out for his glass. She passed it to him. After a few sips, she put it back on the coffee table for him. A sitcom played in the background, indignant voices and a laugh track. Both ignored it.

"I'm sure you had to develop a callus in the fashion industry," Alfonso said.

"By then, I was already 'rough.' No, my training started in high school, in the girl's room."

"Please tell me about it."

She took another swig.

"When I started high school, a group of girls let it be known that they did not want me using the girl's room or the girl's locker room in the gym. Fortunately, we had a prince of a principal. After my first confrontation with these girls, we got called in to explain what the drama was about. He met with them first, then with me. Before I said one word, he said to me, 'So, you want to use the faculty restroom here in the main office?'"

"Sweet."

"Mr. Peña. Very sweet man. No discussions, no explanations. That was it. Problem solved. Until my junior year. Mr. Peña left. And in came the bitch."

"Oh, no."

"Not only did she tell me that the faculty restroom was for faculty only, she called me 'Vernon.' Always 'Vernon.' Never once did she call me by my name."

Alfonso shook his head as he rested on her shoulder.

"I knew from junior high that the boy's room was out of the question."

"When I was in middle school, if you used the stalls too much, they called you a fag, 'cause only fags didn't use urinals. Don't ask me where that came from."

"Mmm-hmmm."

"But then if it looked like you didn't keep your eyes to yourself, they called you a fag anyway."

Vera took another sip of bourbon. "School restrooms. Gotta love 'em. I tried a charm offensive with the mean girls. Got me nowhere. I blamed myself for not being able to win them over. I tried to time my trips to the restroom during class times, when they were empty. But that didn't work for long. You can't get out of class like that day in and day out. And for gym class, I tried getting there as early as possible to change, or even just to use the damn toilet. For a while, I got away with it. But this one time, the mean girls found me. They went under the stall walls, opened the door to the stall, and dragged me out."

"Oh, fuck! That's horrible!"

"I was barely dressed. Awful, Alfonso, positively awful. I was devastated."

"Well, what did the school do? Did the principal go after the girls that did that to you?"

"Oh, dear me no! She didn't even talk to them. But she said to me, 'Use the boy's room from now on, Vernon.'"

"Evil."

"I was faced with the choice of getting beat up every day in gym or not taking gym. So I stopped going to gym. Flunked it. I hung out in this hidden area on campus and read. Of course, my parents punished me and I just took it. And I 'solved' my peeing problem by going without water or food during the day. I fasted, in effect, daily, until I got home. Lost a lot of weight."

"And nobody noticed?"

"They just called me sullen, my parents, the school counsellor. And I believed them. All my own fault. Finally, one day, a really hot day, in the middle of my math class, I just passed out. An ambulance came. They examined me. Dehydration. The EMT was like, 'Well, why don't you just drink some water? It's your own fault.'"

"Fuck!" he whispered.

"And I believed him, Alfonso. I believed it was all my fault. My folks at home told me the same thing. It was all my fault."

They sat still for a moment. A commercial for toilet paper played in the background.

"I was getting to that point where suicide seemed the only answer. I thought about it daily. Never made any specific plans, but that's where my head was at. I had one friend I could talk to. He kept me from going totally over the edge. He had his own challenges. We helped each other. But you know who finally turned my thinking around? My dad. I was in my room when I overheard him and my mother talking. I heard him say 'Well, maybe he'll stop pretending and to go back to wearing pants.'" She paused. "Somehow, Alfonso, hearing him make that crude, crass comment behind my back broke the spell. I decided right then and there, Fuck you, I'm getting out of here. I started putting my things together and day by day I took my shit to school and stuffed it into my locker. My one friend helped me. He let me put some of my stuff in his locker."

Alfonso sat up.

"Carlton?"

"Carlton."

Water came to his eyes.

"Finally, when I had all the stuff I wanted to take with me, I brought a big hiking backpack and transferred everything to that. I left school, left home, never went back. That was it. I was gone."

"Where did you go?"

"All over. Eventually, I became an emancipated minor. I worked two jobs, finished high school, a little late, but I finished it. I got into photography, modeling. And so on. But by the time all that happened, you better believe I had developed my callus. Carlton and I stayed in touch, of course. Eventually, he got his callus, too."

"All blues players need one."

"Yes, sweetie. That's exactly right. Cruelty is the worst violence we inflict on each other. And the worst thing that can happen is to believe that the cruelty of others is somehow your fault. It isn't. It never is. The bastard that yanked you out the back of Harry's van was a firecracker ready to go off. You had nothing to do with that.

"Alfonso, I know what you told the panel about why you went into the van. I want you to ask yourself, was that the only reason? Don't answer that now. Think about it. And don't be afraid or ashamed of the answer. Whatever it is, it's legitimate.

"And remember, sweetie, the strong too often blame themselves for the faults of the weak."

He went back onto her shoulder and she cradled him. The TV still played in the background.

"I'm just sorry you all had to see it," he said. "It shouldn't have happened."

"No, my dear. It sure the hell shouldn't have."

THIRTY-EIGHT

Tuesday
Berry Residence, Beacon Hill

ALFONSO LEANED AGAINST THE FRONT DOOR, SWEATY, panting, having just walked up the hill by himself with only his cane for support. He had received an email from his father that morning saying that he needed to talk to him about the lawsuit, that it would be better to talk on the phone to go over the details. Alfonso instead agreed to a face-to-face meeting and said he would come by the house that afternoon. He looked back at the sidewalk, the way it descended out of view from the steep incline. Something so familiar had become a terror ride.

Key turned the lock. Quiet. Still. He tapped on the door to his father's study to the left. It was ajar. He entered.

"Son!" Ford said, standing up. "I didn't hear you come in."

No response.

"Sit down, please."

"I don't wanna meet in here."

Ford lowered his outstretched hand. His eyes averted Alfonso's. "Should we go in the kitchen?"

Alfonso processed for a moment. Triggers all over the place. Kitchen: Unity Rally. Living Room: Bulldyke Letter.

"Let's go to the dining room table." He turned and walked away.

Ford followed, papers in hand.

They took opposite sides of the large, formal, dark wood table. Alfonso sat with his hands at his side, upright, stiff. Ford hunched over the papers he fingered. The grandfather's clock conspicuously meted out the seconds.

"Are we the only ones here?" Alfonso asked.

"Yes."

More paper shuffling. Finally, Ford looked up.

"The city came back with a settlement offer. Six and a quarter million."

Alfonso raised his eyebrows for a second. "For real?"

"Yes. We don't have to accept. We can go to trial if you want. It's up to you." He started shuffling his papers again.

Alfonso impatiently ran his hand through his hair.

"Dad, just stop it with the papers, alright?" He stopped. "This ain't just another client meeting." Silence. "You know how hard it was for me to get up that hill just now?"

"Son, you should have called. I would have picked you up."

"That's not the damn point! I used to could sprint up that hill!" He slowed, tried to contain his pulse. "When we talked a week ago, I thought maybe I was getting over being scared of you. So last Sunday I watched the beating video just to confirm in my head that you weren't there."

Ford sucked his lower lip.

"But you *were* there. *You* did this to me. You were Johnson telling me I got what I deserved. You were Leon telling me I'm not keeping it 'real.' You were the cops punishing me for defying you." He slowed again. "I went into that van to give you the middle finger. And now I'm broken. I can't dance. I can't skate. I can't run. Coming up that hill just now? Like walking a fucking tightrope."

"I'm sorry, Son." Ford kept his head down.

"Look how broken I am!" He stood up forcefully, flinging the chair to the floor. He grabbed his head. "See? Move fast, get dizzy."

"I'm sorry," his voice an anguished whisper.

"Remember how you accused my friends of using me as a weapon against you? Uh-uh. This is how it really went down. That fucking sociopath Leon used *you* as a weapon against *me*! Again and again!" slamming his open hand against the table. "You heard what he said! 'I hope he daddy finishes the job!' You did this to me! All to save your stupid, fucking, bullshit career! FUCK YOU!"

"I'm so sorry!"

"FUCK YOU!" He threw his cane, striking Ford on the forehead. "Fuck you!" He sobbed. "You hurt me! You hurt me so bad!" He leaned heavily on the table. "It hurts so much!"

Ford went around the table, picked up the fallen chair, tried to help Alfonso back into it. Alfonso refused him, pushed him away. Ford choked up, left the dining room abruptly. Crashing noises soon came from the study. Alfonso wiped his eyes, slowly limped toward the noise. He stopped at the doorway and observed his father rip everything from his bookcases. Books, binders, plaques, his clawed hands spared nothing. Then he came to a plaster bust of Al Berry, Sr. Alfonso watched in shock as his father smashed it on the hardwood floor and began stomping on it.

"YOU RUINED EVERYTHING, DIDN'T YOU? YOU SICK MOTHERFUCKER!"

Larger chunks splintered.

"ALL FOR THE SAKE OF YOUR FUCKING LEGACY!"

Pieces shot across the floor like hockey pucks.

"COULDN'T LEAVE ME THE FUCK ALONE!"

They ricocheted against the baseboards.

"NOW, LOOK WHERE I'M AT! I HATE YOU!"

Remnants reduced to powder.

"I HATE YOU! I HATE YOU! I HATE YOU! I HATE YOU!"

Ford stomped repeatedly on his father's bust, like he couldn't destroy it enough to satisfy himself. He finally collapsed to his knees, howling and sobbing.

Alfonso hobbled over to him, slowly lowered himself to the floor. His father took him, held him tight.

<<I'm at the house. Dad and I are meeting. It's been real, but we're OK. If you can, please don't come home right away. Please? I apologize for the inconvenience. We're OK. I love you all very much.>>

His mother texted back instantly.

<<Thank you, Son. We'll go to my sister's and stay the night if we have to. Don't worry. XOXO>>

Lucy texted back kisses as well. Belinda texted back privately.

<< >>

They ended up on the living room sofa. A bottle of Irish whiskey and two shot glasses sat on the coffee table. Alfonso flipped on the TV. SportsCenter. He poured the shots.

"When did you develop a taste for my favorite drink?" Ford asked.

"You used to let me sip some of your Irish coffee when Mom wasn't looking, remember?"

"I did?"

"Uh-huh."

"Damn. I made those things pretty strong, too."

"Yeah, I know. Cheers."

"Cheers."

They both took healthy gulps, then stared at the TV, a soothing, hypnotic distraction.

"I never knew you felt that way about Granddad."

"I buried it so deep."

Alfonso nodded, took another sip.

College colors and hoops came on.

"Here comes the madness," Ford said. "You done your bracket yet?"

"Naw. You?"

"Uh-uh." Hopeful players filled the screen. "I've lived my whole life in that man's shadow. I got used to the dark, lost myself."

Next came highlights from Mesa, Arizona. Ford finished his glass, refilled it, topped off Alfonso's. On the screen, someone hit it out of the park. Bodies flew around the bases.

"Nobody ever got a grand slam off of me. When the bases were loaded, that's when I got real serious." Ford took a sip. "I told him about the scouts and he crushed it. Straight out. Wouldn't even entertain the thought of it. Law school. That's all he wanted to hear." He sipped a bit more. "He wanted me in politics. Period."

"How well did you know your father? Growing up I thought of him as high mountains and vast horizons, someone who inspires but could never get close to."

"That's your grandfather in a nutshell. You hit the nail on the fucking head," he said, emphatically bobbing his glass against his knee. "I never knew the man. He kept himself very tightly wrapped. What I learned, I learned by accident. The racism he grew up under scarred him for life, made him bitter, insecure, and mean. His sole accomplishment was being the first, Alfonso. Everything else was bluster that he maintained by bullying people. And he was hell to live with. He bullied my mother so bad, she just evaporated." He closed his eyes briefly. "And nothing I ever did satisfied him. Order of the Coif in law school. Good law firm. Partner. Didn't mean shit. I had to get elected to something, to keep his legacy going."

"I get the feeling he wasn't happy that you didn't run for his seat."

"He wasn't. When Larkin announced his retirement, I counted down the minutes. And damn if he didn't call right on cue. 'You file your papers yet?' He was chuckling, but he wasn't joking. The only answer he'd accept was 'on it.' So I gave up my practice, became a shitty councilman, to satisfy him."

He reached for his glass, hesitated, then finished the contents. It went back on the table. Alfonso filled it up again. Ford took it and held it against his knee.

"Alfonso, I shoulda talked to you about him a long time ago. So many things." Ford downed a full gulp.

A hot, sticky summer night sent Ford, topless, in his underwear, leaning out his second-floor bedroom window in search of relief. But nothing moved. The outside air was just as still. A taxi pulled up. Father. Nanny said he'd be late. Ford tucked himself out of view and peeped over the edge of the windowsill. His father exited the car, went to the driver's side and stood. For a while, nothing happened. Then the driver emerged, a tall white man with wispy red hair. Very skinny. They walked into the house together. Odd. Father was usually very particular about who he let into the house. Maybe he needed to get money to pay the fare and the driver came inside to save him the trouble of walking back to the car with it. Ford waited, but no one exited. After fidgeting for a bit, he quietly got out of bed and gently lifted the rug so that his ear sat directly on the hardwood floor, a habit he had developed to eavesdrop on his parents' dinner parties. Unlike at those events, though, he heard no community gossip or details about his father's latest political dealings. He heard no words at all, only noises. Slurping. Sucking. Grunting. Moaning. Uncomfortable images entered Ford's mind, footage from the news a month ago, in late June. People marched down the middle of the street, women with women, men with men. The men walked arm in arm. Topless. Their privates bulged in their pants. One man clutched another man's booty. Just as two men began kissing each other, his father snapped off the TV and ordered Ford to his room. At summer school, the kids couldn't stop talking about it. *Did you see those men KISSING? You'll never see me walking with no boy like that! I ain't no FAG!* A new rule took over the schoolyard: If a boy stood close to you, and you didn't move away fast enough, you got punched in the arm and called a *FAG*. Ford learned to move quickly. He punched a few arms himself that summer, to prove the point. He was no *FAG*. The slurping and moaning wouldn't cease. Maybe they were eating spaghetti. Spaghetti can make you eat loud sometimes. He didn't want to believe that his father would bring a man into the house, while Mother was out of town, and eat his face, or worse, touch his privates. He didn't want to believe that his father was a *FAG*. Finally, it stopped. The front door opened and closed abruptly. Ford hurried back to the window, reaching it just in time to see the cab door close. The man sped off. Footsteps on the stairs. He dived under his covers, panicked. Then he quickly sat up again and looked down. The rug. He reached out and flipped it back, got under the covers again and stayed there. His father entered without knocking. He flung the covers up. *You asleep, boy?* Ford remained very still. *You asleep?* Silence. His father lingered, hard breathing through his mouth. For his part, Ford barely breathed at all.

"I thought he was gonna beat the crap out of me. Instead, he just told me that I had better stay sleep, if I knew what was good for me. Then he flung the covers back over me and walked out."

Alfonso sat and stared, reflected. As a kid, he imagined that if he angled his windbreaker just right, like the Flying Nun did with her habit, he, too, could catch the wind and take flight. Over the ocean he traveled until he reached a remote island, dotted with palm trees, surrounded by sandy white beaches lapped by gentle waters. The latest boy who caught his eye would always be there, waiting. Now he wondered if he had flown differently, beyond the mountains and horizons his grandfather sculpted with vacuous rhetoric, would he have found someone Granddad kept hidden, waiting?

"The next day he called me into his study. He kept asking me what did I see, what did I hear, and I kept saying 'Nothing, Father.' He snapped, 'You're lying!' Then he said if I told anybody about that night, including my mother, that he'd make sure that the whole world hated me. I'd have no friends. I'd get kicked out of school. He said to me, 'When I get through with you, all the black folks will despise you forever because you told a lie about the savior of the race.' He said, 'I *am* the savior. Sin against me, boy, and you sin against the race!'

"This was 1972. I was eleven. I didn't know shit what he was talking about, but he scared me to death. What I came to know, eventually, was that my father hated himself and that hatred slowly poisoned him."

Alfonso told Carlton about his island and the boys he met there, during one of their mellow times, when the music played softly and they sat on the floor eating sweet and sour shrimp from takeout cartons with chopsticks. His cousin sat thoughtfully and let time pass before saying something. *I want you to vote yourself off that island one day.*

"The true ugliness of the closet is its subtlety. It eats away at your soul bit by bit and you don't even realize it. If you never deal with it or come to terms with it, then ultimately the closet will destroy you."

"Who said that, Son?"

"I did during my presentation on black homophobia for Dan Euclid's class."

Ford sat and rocked, his hands clasped near his face, his eyes squeezed shut.

Alfonso took the remote and turned off the TV. He scooted closer to his father.

Ford took his son and embraced him, gently stroking the back of his hand against his cheek.

Alfonso opened his eyes, grabbed his cell. 7:13 p.m.

Ford woke up, yawning. "Too much whiskey, I guess."

"You wanna go for a walk?" Alfonso asked.

"Where to?"

"I don't know. Wherever."

"Fudgsicle bars?"

"Yeah, why not?"

"OK," Ford said. He insisted on driving them down the hill.

Alfonso asked him to wear a hat, not wanting folks to ask about the hickey on his left temple.

Sammy looked up from his Laptop when Alfonso walked in with his father.

"Well, well. If it isn't the Berry boys."

"Hey Sammy," Alfonso said, hobbling around the counter. He slipped into his usual space.

"Hi, Mr. Turner," Ford said. "We had a hankering for—"

"You know where they are. Help yourself."

As Ford got the goodies, Sammy gave Alfonso a quick hug.

"All good?" he whispered.

"Ask me later."

A story on Sammy's computer caught Alfonso's eye. He pulled it closer. His laughter overtook Andy Bey's piano playing on the stereo. Ford came back to the counter, his money again waved off by Sammy.

"Dad, did you hear about this?" He flipped the computer around.

Reverend Thaddeus Johnson Retiring From Beacon Hill Baptist

Ford chuckled. "So he decided to take the honorable way out. First smart thing he's done in a minute."

"Was he getting pushed?"

"Big time."

"From what I've heard," Sammy said, "he pissed off the wrong people with that Walker Wright stunt he pulled."

"You got it, Mr. Turner. My wife told me that the major donors were pressuring the board so the board made an ultimatum: resign or get fired."

"Don't fuck with the green," Alfonso said.

"Don't fuck with the green," Ford repeated. "Cheers, Son."

"Cheers."

They toasted their fudge bars, then tore into them.

"That man lived by the bling, and now he died by it," Ford said.

"He-he-he-he," Sammy chuckled. "Gonna tweet that out."

Ford gave Sammy a surprised look. Alfonso smirked.

"Yeah. Give a queen a computer, and she thinks she's all that all of a sudden."

"I have always been All That, Missy Berry," Sammy shot back.

Ford laughed.

A customer came to the counter. Sammy stood to ring her up. She looked at Alfonso and smiled, asked how he was doing. OK, he said, then introduced his father. They shook hands. She left the store with her artisanal bread. Alfonso asked Sammy something as he sat down. Ford stood next to the counter. Mr. Bey played a delicate tune.

"Hey, what is this?" Ford asked.

"'Something to Live For,'" Alfonso and Sammy said simultaneously.

"I know this."

Alfonso started singing along, sweetly conveying Strayhorn's ode to love and belonging with easy control and sincere phrasing. The whole store took notice. A young couple in the back stopped as they were looking at the ice cream. Someone at the fruit counter paused. Sammy leaned his head on his hand, eyes closed. Ford stood against the counter, transfixed. Alfonso concluded with a long, sustained note. The whole store applauded. Sammy whistled through his fingers. Ford walked around the counter and kissed Alfonso on top of his head. Alfonso wrapped his arms around his father's legs.

Before leaving the store, Ford asked if Ella Fitzgerald ever recorded it. Sammy confirmed that she had, with the Ellington Orchestra. They took turns hugging Sammy, then departed. Alfonso felt a hankering for chili dogs and fries at Ox's Diner. So they headed north on Carver Street. As they passed The Other Bookstore, Roy whistled teasingly at them while standing in the doorway. Alfonso laughed. Roy sprinted out and gave his sistah a hug.

"Bingo's deck?" Alfonso whispered.

"In-doobie-tably," Roy whispered back.

"Hey, don't I get one, too?" Ford asked.

First Roy put his hands on his hips, looked him up and down. But he smiled and embraced him.

"Where y'all going?" Roy asked.

"Ox's Diner. For some meat, boy!" Alfonso said.

"I'll pray for you. Enjoy!"

They cut through the Leather Strip to get to Lincoln. Folks embraced the warmer weather by eating dinner on their stoops or just chilling in the temperate evening air. Both paused at the spot where the sax man usually played. They gave each other knowing looks, then sat on the stoop, hoping he might show up.

"When you were talking about Granddad, I realized that it was at his funeral that Carlton and I first connected. We were standing near each other when the music took a real left turn. We looked at each other and started giggling. Then we started talking about music we liked. I told him how I was getting into Chicago house, so he invited me to his place to listen to his old mixtapes. That shit blew me away."

He told Carlton that they should be in a club somewhere. That's right, honey, Carlton said, with the lights barely lit, the bass pulsating in our chests, the sweat flowing, and all the beautiful bodies working it together. Carlton bolted off the love seat and started moving.

"Damn, he could dance his ass off. So Granddad helped to introduce us to each other."

"That's so perfect."

"You've never told anyone about Granddad, have you?"

"You're the first."

"Even after he died, you felt you couldn't talk about him?"

"No. I felt him reaching for me from beyond the grave through folks like Johnson. They're his ghosts. I answered to them just like I answered to him." His gaze drifted upward. "He always called me Al, Jr. It wasn't a term of endearment, just another form of control. He hated that I called myself 'Ford,' the one bit of rebellion I can claim." He paused, looked at Alfonso. "But the truth is, I did become him, the worst part of him. A coward. And you paid the price.

"Alfonso, I'll never forgive myself for what happened to you. To the end of my days, I'll never forgive myself."

He stared at his father's face, startled by how aged it had become, hairs wiry and gray, skin mottled and pitted.

"Guess we ain't hearing no bluesman tonight," Ford said. "Still want some food?"

You are the bluesman, Alfonso thought, always have been. Finally learning of his heartache brought some solace.

———

My father was a tyrant, who lived his life a lie
My father was a mean man, who lived his life a lie,
By maintaining his fiction, I nearly caused my son die.

My son dances and swings and lives freely in the life,
My son, he dances and swings and lives freely in the life.
But I saw him as a danger and gave him nothing but strife.

I took my daddy's poison and my soul became bereft,
Yeah, I sipped my daddy's bad brew, and my soul became bereft.
With the poison of my words, haters nearly beat my son to death.

My son is living, but I can't give myself a save
(Naw, I didn't win no game)
Yes, my son survived, but I can't give myself a save
It's a heavy burden that I'll carry straight to my grave

———

Alfonso patted his father on the knee, then leaned on his shoulder to stand. They walked up the block and across the street to Ox's Diner. They took a booth next to the window, looking out at the busy intersection where Lincoln, Carver, and Delaware met.

"What do you think about the settlement, Son?"

Alfonso laughed. He had totally forgotten about it.

"How much was it again?"

"Six and a quarter."

"Yeah, let's just do it. Maybe we could get more if we went to trial, but you know what?"

"Yeah, I hear you." Ford raised his water. "To moving on. Cheers."

"Cheers," Alfonso said, raising his root beer float.

"How's your German these days?"

"Rusty. I'll find an app and start working on it."

"When do you think you'll go?"

"Not for a while."

Ford nodded.

Alfonso could tell that his father liked that answer.

THIRTY-NINE

June
Flight to Europe

FIRST CLASS LIVING. SEATS THAT RECLINE INTO BEDS. STAFF at beck and call. An embarrassment of riches.

———

Belinda put up the most fuss. Typical. She explained to her brother in great detail why he needed to keep his money and not give it away, at least not to her. Too late! he said gleefully. He gave her and Lucy $250,000 trusts.

Now, at least, you can afford college, he told them.

———

They offered so much food that after a while it became a situation. The urge grew to take it, just because it was there. So that's how the love of bling starts. They tempt you until you just can't say no. Alfonso indulged, but with outsider's eyes. He spent most of his time staring into the dark. Faces from his life reflected back in the window.

———

Carlton's Posse spent their last few months hanging, jiving, going out. Alfonso became a hit at Club Copacetic. Everyone was excited to see him again. He developed a type of Irish step dancing that he could do with his cane and while sitting down. Even Sexy Voice gave it a try. The DJ played all of Carlton's old favorites, lots of the electronica that Alfonso liked, and even added a few Billie Holiday tunes creatively to the mix. It was a party every time they came.

Alfonso proposed giving the Posse some money and each time they laughed it off. Until the end, they laughed it off. Finally, just two days before the flight, while meeting at Bingo's, Alfonso got serious.

"Look, I'm giving you some fucking money, alright? I don't need it all. Trust me. I'm cool. Don't fight me on this, alright? If it weren't for you two, I'd be dead! I mean that!" He twitched, shifting his weight from one foot to the other. "You helped me get this money anyway, so you're entitled to some of it."

"That's bullshit," Roy said. "It's yours. Keep it."

"Shut up!" Alfonso barked. "Sammy won't let me give him some, OK? He refused. Bingo said just give whatever to the clinic, and I did. I can't give him any. I have to give you something. YOU SAVED MY FUCKING LIFE, ALRIGHT?"

"Babe, it's OK," Bill said. "It's OK. We'll take it." Roy looked askance, but stopped rolling his eyes when Bill gave him a sharp stare. "We just don't want you to screw yourself over, that's all. You'll need it to survive. But if you want to give us some, it's all good, babe."

"Good." Alfonso took out two envelopes. They opened them. He made out trusts, $100,000 each.

"What the—" Bill said. "Naw, man, come on!"

"You said you'll take it, Bill! You promised!"

"Fro! I thought you meant like a couple hundred or something, not some shit like this!"

"Take it, GODDAMMIT!"

"I DON'T WANT YOUR FUCKING MONEY! I WANT YOU!" Bill broke down. Roy started crying too. Then Alfonso.

"Told you you're the Fro, man," Bill said, still weeping. "You made life better for everyone. And now you're going over the sea. I hope you find what you're looking for over there."

They held each other, unable, unwilling to let go, eventually rubbing the tears on each other's face, giggling.

———✦———

He stared at the selfie they took, their faces still wet. It was his favorite photo.

Sammy opened his eyes, yawned, looked around.

"We there yet?"

"Not yet."

Sammy agreed to help Alfonso get set up in Berlin—Sammy's first vacation in years and his first time to Europe. He was going to pay his own way, but Ford and Eunice wouldn't hear of it. They paid for everything.

He squinted at Alfonso's cell.

"They're visiting next month. Jameel said he'd come in August. Said he had a surprise." Alfonso smiled at the possibilities.

Sammy nodded. "You get any sleep?"

"Naw. I was playing with this new app before I started daydreaming." He put his phone in his pocket. "I told those assholes not to get me anything. Look." He reached in the side pocket of his seat and took out his new MacBook Pro. "They got me this thousand-dollar app called TerpSick. It's a professional choreography program."

"No kidding?"

"Yeah. Check this shit out."

Three figures slinked onto the screen. They went around each other, then hooked arms. As they circled, each took a turn leaping into the air while bracing against the other two.

"And see." Alfonso paused the playback. "There's a window for the footwork. And you can get them in 3-D and do a 360 pan. This shit is tight." He closed the program and opened email. "'Dear Fro, I know you told us not to get you anything, but we did anyway because fuck you. Love, Little Pipp'n and Merry Mary.'"

Sammy chuckled. "I hate those motherfuckers." Alfonso closed his computer. "Beethoven and I share a birthday, you know. Maybe I'll create dances I'll never dance, like he wrote music he never heard."

"Hey," Sammy said with a queeny lilt. "But never say never."

A flight attendant came by.

"Would you like something, sir?" he asked Sammy.

"Nothing for me, thanks."

"Und wünschen Sie noch etwas, mein Herr?" he asked Alfonso. He promised to speak to him in German. "Noch ein Whisky?"

"Bitte, danke," Alfonso said.

He smiled and walked back to the galley.

"I got an email from my dad. He sent a draft of the first chapter of his memoir. You wanna read it?"

"Sure, if it's OK."

"Yeah, totally."

The flight attendant came back with a new little bottle of whiskey. He opened it and poured it into Alfonso's glass.

"Danke!" Alfonso said.

After a sip, he opened his laptop again. He downloaded the chapter and forwarded it to Sammy. Then he reread his father's email.

Here you go. First chapter. BOOM! I thought if I told the truth about that man, the community would ostracize me. Now I'm like, 'bring it.'

———◆———

Alfonso and his father walked daily in various parts of the city—different parks, downtown, along the docks. Their talks ranged from romantic crushes to family history to regrets. You all gave my life meaning, Ford said once. My career goals I kept sidetracking onto cul-de-sacs posing as boulevards. During one walk, Alfonso casually mentioned burning his copy of the Verity book, and why. Ford stopped suddenly and took Alfonso's arm.

"I fucking want to do that. Can you remember where you did it? We have to do this."

"What do you wanna burn?"

"His portrait."

Done in oil, by commission, it had hung in Ford's City Hall office. Now sat in the basement squeezed between boxes of Christmas decorations.

They were going to drive to the park in the suburbs, but Alfonso suggested that they take the commuter train instead, the way he had all those years ago. It seemed more like a pilgrimage that way. Ford agreed. For him, it was all about ritual, so he followed his son's lead.

"I told your mother what we're doing," Ford said, breaking the silence as they rode the train.

"How'd she take it?"

"She understood."

It was a beautiful late spring day. The trees were green, the last of their spring buds adding other colors. Kids played on the grass. Only one picnic table was occupied. It was Tuesday and the park was largely vacant. They went to the same barbecue pit where Alfonso burned the book. The elements had long ago absorbed those ashes, but the symbolism was important to Ford.

They lit the portrait and held hands as the flames consumed the image of Al Berry, Sr.

———

Alfonso remembered the blues effect. Bruise the coffee, but not enough to make it bitter.

"I still get angry about what happened," he told Sammy, "but I don't want anger to define me. I don't wanna carry bitterness for a third generation."

"Yes."

Alfonso stared out the window for a moment. Still no hint of light. He turned and looked at Sammy.

"He said he's already getting feelers from agents and publishers. They're talking a possible seven-figure advance. He said he wants to assign the rights to me." He choked up, bit his lips. "He doesn't have to do that!" Alfonso leaned onto Sammy, who rubbed him on the back of the neck. "I'm gonna miss your shoulder."

"You got it for another month, baby. And it'll be back home waiting for when you visit us."

"You never told me how you knew who I was when I first came to your store."

"Child! You're the spitting image of your cousin when he was your age."

Alfonso giggled. After a bit, he sat up. Sammy put on his horn rims and took out his iPad to open email and start reading the draft chapter. Alfonso typed a reply to his father.

Dear Dad,

Thank you for the chapter. I haven't read it yet, but I'm looking forward. I was thinking about what you said, about Granddad listening to "Something to Live For" over and over as he was dying. I think it was a final cry from that part of himself he kept sealed up. When I was in the closet, I thought of myself as living inside a bubble made of one-way glass. I could see out, but others could only see their own projections of who they thought I was. I don't know. Just something to think about, put his story in context. You may want to hit up Bill and talk with him about Giovanni's Room."

As for the royalty thing. I don't know what to say, except that I love you, Dad. I'll never stop telling you that. Please be kind to yourself. I'm gonna be OK.

Love, Fro
P.S.: Here's a title suggestion: So Many Things.

Alfonso stared out the window, the night sky finally yielding to light breaching the now-visible horizon. Morning. He sighed. Another dawn. Two weeks before his flight, he met privately with his doctors one last time. Tests confirmed what they had warned him about. He had a time bomb lodged deep in his brain, a tiny aneurism. It hadn't ruptured and thus escaped immediate detection. No one could say if it resulted from the beating or if it had been there all along. Increased attention on his head because of the beating brought it out of the shadows. In other words, the ordeal that nearly killed him may have saved him by showing him how he might die. His doctors advised him not to go to Germany, to stay and take more tests to determine if treatment was possible, or even necessary. Maybe it wasn't. They prescribed a whole life of ifs and maybes, of living each day shifting from worry to worry. A life trapped in rooms, fed by tubes, tested week in and week out. A life with no drinking, no smoking, no moving, no doing, no being.

Didn't Carlton live with a time bomb in his body for over two decades? And what did he declare he'd do after it had been discovered?

Keep dancing, fool.

Alfonso took another sip of whiskey, put on his earbuds, and played Nina Simone's "Feeling Good" while watching the sunrise. He chose to ignore the doctors.

Instead, he pledged to give thanks for each new dawn he saw, and to live fierce.

CPSIA information can be obtained
at www.ICGtesting.com
Printed in the USA
LVOW11s1421291017
554203LV00001B/149/P